No Pat Hands

Other books by J. J. Lamb

Zach Rolfe PI Series
A Nickel Jackpot
The Chinese Straight
Losers Take All

With Bette Golden Lamb
Bone Dry
Heir Today…
Sisters in Silence
Sin & Bone
Bone Pit

No Pat Hands

by

J. J. Lamb

TWO BLACKSHEEP PRODUCTIONS
NOVATO, CALIFORNIA

J. J. Lamb

No Pat Hands
Copyright © 2012 by James J. Lamb

First print and e-book publication, August 2013

ISBN-13: 978-0-9851986-4-0

Print Edition produced by CreateSpace.com
Book Cover by RitaWoodCreative.com

E-book produced by Wolfpack Publishing LLC
E-book cover design: L. C. Martin

www.jjlamb.com

For Bette, who is my muse, now and forever.

My deep appreciation to those who made significant contributions to the creation of this book – Frank Ross, Miwok extraordinaire; members of the Federated Indians of Graton Rancheria; The Miwok Museum, Novato, CA; and the ever-helpful Tuesday Critique Group of Bette Lamb, Peggy Lucke, Shelley Singer, Nicola Trwst, and Judith Yamamoto.

CHAPTER 1

Northern California — 1776

The one-man tule canoe bobbed and floated lazily on the bay waters, never more than a few canoe-lengths from the shoreline. Móloku came to fish, but it was much more enjoyable to lie on his back and feel the rays of the early spring sun on his nude body. Now and then he would rise up, cast a small fishing net onto the water, then slowly pull it back toward him. He was pleased when he caught a fish, but not unhappy when the net returned empty.

Móloku, like his ancestors—whom he seldom thought about and, by custom, never mentioned—felt no pressure to hunt or gather food. There was always something to eat within easy walking distance of his village, no matter what the season.

When he awoke this day, he had a craving for fish. But it wasn't important to him whether he actually caught any fish. He was quite comfortable floating in his şáka with the sun and a warm breeze caressing his body. If a fish did get caught in his net that would be good and one of his wives would fix it for the evening meal.

A few weeks earlier, perhaps sooner than was wise, Móloku had cracked away the coating of dried mud on his body and tossed aside the scratchy deerskin he had used for winter protection. Some men in the small village said it was too early to make the year's first visit to the lámma, but Móloku had insisted on a sweathouse gathering. No one had objected strongly enough to threaten his reign as headman.

All of the adult males from the coastal village had gathered around fire-heated rocks in the lámma and scraped away sweat with bone knives. When the heat became so intense they could no longer stand it, they cried out wildly, ran from the buried sweathouse to the bay, and jumped into the frigid water.

Móloku, who was approaching his twenty-third year, knew the moment he splashed into the cold bay that he had been wrong. But he was still proving himself, having inherited the

1

position of headman only two seasons earlier. He could not allow himself to show surprise at the numbing effect of the water.

Becoming headman was a simple matter of inheritance—his father, an elder of the tribe and former headman, had been mauled to death by a bear during a ritual hunt in the nearby hills.

Móloku had not gone on the hunt. He'd said it was foolish since the acorn harvest had been more bountiful than in any recent year. Why expend the energy and face possible harm, or death, only for a bearskin and some meat? Besides, most years the tribe didn't even see a bear during the late fall hunt.

But his father and several others had decided to go after a bear anyway, armed with their seldom-used bows and arrows. They knew that should they find a bear, it would be slow and sluggish from gorging itself in preparation for hibernation. After brewing and drinking a batch of towalache, the drunken hunters left the village, boasting in advance of their hunting prowess.

When the sobered hunters returned from the hills, there was no bear skin and no meat, only the lifeless body of the village's headman.

Móloku, together with his younger brother and his father's three wives—all sisters—dug a pit to hold the corpse, which they curled into the posture of an unborn child. The remains were cremated, along with the meager possessions the headman had accumulated in his thirty-nine summers.

Soon after the cremation, the husband of both of Móloku's sisters also married the father's wife, who was Móloku's mother.

Now, watching the passage of scattered clouds, Móloku thought of his second wife, who was beautifully large and ready to burst with child. Wife number one had borne him two sons, and this would be the second child from wife number two. Yet, he was without heirs—none of his children had lived more than a few months. He was cheerful, though, and looked to the future and the coming of the new child. He'd also gathered almost enough abalone shells to carve the shell beads he would use to purchase another wife.

Móloku tugged at his net and felt resistance. When he pulled it up across the tightly woven tule reeds, he found several fish caught in the strands. He picked two large salmon for his evening meal, then heard his named called from the path that led down to the shoreline. He waved in response, returned the unwanted fish to the water, and watched for a moment as they flicked their tails and swam away. He hand-paddled the canoe toward the shore until the water was shallow enough to pole his way in with a trimmed sapling.

Kay-luk, husband of his sisters and, now, his mother, was waiting for him.

"Why do you call me from the home of the fish?" Móloku said.

"Another has come to our village."

"Do we know him?"

"No," said Kay-luk. "We do not speak the same tongue. I think he is of the Rumsen."

Móloku nodded thoughtfully as he tied his şáka to a deeply driven stake. He did not want Kay-luk to know that he had little knowledge of the Rumsen. He tried to remember what his father had told him about these people who lived many days' journey to the south. He knew of no elders in the village who had ever visited the Rumsen.

"Why has this Rumsen come to the village of the Wirok?" Móloku said.

Kay-luk shook his head. "He made sign that he must speak only with our headman."

"That was proper," Móloku said. "Go tell him I am returning to the village." He dismissed Kay-luk with a wave of his hand and watched the unhurried departure of his sister's husband.

Móloku walked slowly away from the water until he came to a huge live oak. He stood beneath the tree's ancient, gnarled branches and looked upward.

He prayed: "Hummingbird, my knowledge will be unworthy unless you come to transport me to that place where I can see the past."

He closed his eyes and waited silently, visualizing the tiny iridescent bird with its flutter of blurred wings. Soon, he felt his

3

inner self lifting, floating through the limbs of the oak. His mind's eye opened to see the huge expanse of the bay, his village, and other Wirok tribelets close by the water's edge.

Móloku's thoughts drifted away and sped to another time when he had eaten outside the family wikiup with his father. He strained to hear their conversation once again. It became clear what it was he needed to know in order to meet with the waiting Rumsen.

"Thank you, Hummingbird," Móloku said. He opened his eyes and started for the village.

Later, he sat in his wikiup with the Rumsen, who called himself Num-soo. Through sign and the small amount of language they had in common, Móloku heard a story he found difficult to accept. At the same time, the story frightened him. He had Num-soo repeat the story twice while they waited for Móloku's wives to prepare the fresh-caught salmon for their meal.

Num-soo told how many, many moons past, strange men had come to the Rumsen village. These men wore coverings over their entire bodies, from head to ankles, through all of the seasons. They had forced the Rumsen to help them build strange wikiups of trees and mud, then kill all the plants in an area that was so large it would have held many villages. The Rumsen were made to dig long furrows and many holes for strange plants they had not seen before.

If the Rumsen refused to work, their backs were beaten. If they tried to run away, hard things the strangers called "irons" were wrapped around their ankles. And if one of The People did manage to run away, other strangers who wore iron on their bodies would chase them and take the spirit from them with long sticks that roared like thunder.

Num-soo said he escaped after four attempts, but he was afraid the strangers might still be following him all the way to Móloku's village.

He told how the strangers wanted the Rumsen to forsake the Eagle and the Hummingbird and all the other gods of the plants and fish and water and birds and trees and animals and speak only to a god no one could see called "dios".

"I do not want to live like the strangers," Num-soo signed. "They spend long days working and talking to their 'dios.'"

Móloku invited Num-soo to remain in his village and become a Wirok, but the visitor would not stay.

"I think these iron men will come to all of our villages," Num-soo said.

"We will not allow them in our *village," Móloku declared. "We will tell them they are not welcome and send them away."*

"They will come anyway, and they will stay," Num-soo said.

"No! You will see."

"They will come," Num-soo insisted. "But I will not be here. I will take myself on a journey of many moons to the north where the white-skinned strangers cannot find me."

"You will see," said Móloku. "We will send them away." He began eating the salmon and acorn meal his wives had brought into the wikiup.

"These strangers are not of The People," Num-soo said. "They do not honor the ways of The People."

"That may be so, but they cannot have the land of The People."

When they finished eating, Móloku invited Num-soo to join him and the village elders in a gambling game played with salmon bones.

"I have stayed too long here," Num-soo said. "I must continue north and find a place safe from these men who want to kill The People."

As Num-soo pushed aside the deerskin flap of the wikiup, a long shaft penetrated his chest. Móloku rushed to the side of the Rumsen, but it was too late.

Frightened, Móloku turned to look out the wikiup opening and heard loud cries and screams coming from every part of his village.

CHAPTER 2

"I'm not licensed as a PI in California," I told Hayes Moreno. "The Temkut Rancheria wouldn't be getting its money's worth."

"The Rancheria isn't hiring you, Zach, I am."

I hadn't heard from Moreno since he left Vegas, where he'd been one of the star reporters for the *Las Vegas Sun.* Our paths had crossed a few times as a result of my activities in catching card mechanics, chip cup artists, and crossroaders on both sides of the gaming tables, but we were really more acquaintances than friends. From my perspective, though, he was a fair and honest newsman.

That Native American blood flowed through Hayes's veins had never entered my mind. In fact, it wasn't until now that I became aware that he had gone to California a little more than a year ago to become the Temkut tribe's vice chairman.

I listened while he told a confusing story about how the Temkuts were running into obstacles in attempting to open up their own casino. It sounded like they were having trouble with the syndicates that provide the upfront money and financing to build and operate Indian casinos.

"Not my thing," I interrupted. "The California Gaming Commission handles all of that … I do gaming fraud … in Nevada."

"I still want you to come out here, Zach."

I stared down into the engine bay of my 1963 Porsche Le Mans coupe, shook my head, and walked across the garage to put Moreno's call on the speakerphone. I'd bought this very sleek, compact cordless phone not too long ago, then discovered there was absolutely no way to clamp it between shoulder and ear so I could have both hands free.

"So if the Rancheria isn't involved in hiring me, why are you picking up the tab?" I adjusted the idle on the rare, vintage Porsche while I awaited an answer.

After a couple of beats, he said, "It's something I need to do."

"Hayes, I don't do cheap."

"I'm well aware of that."

"I know damn little about Indian tribal gaming in California, or in any other state, for that matter. What I do know comes from the newspapers and the grumblings of unhappy Nevada casino owners."

The small two-liter flat eight engine was now evenly ingesting the right mixture of air and gasoline through its four twin-throat Weber carburetors.

"Maybe so, but I can't think of anyone legitimate who has a better handle on the dark side of gaming than Zachariah Tobias Rolfe III," he said.

"Thanks, but you need to give me some specifics, Hayes. Could be you just need some good legal advice … from a California lawyer."

"Look, all you'll have to do is read through some documents and background material I've gathered since coming to the coast," he said. "I need to know if you see any discrepancies between what's going on here and what happens in Nevada when someone sets up a legal casino gaming operation."

"In general, it's not much different than any other corporate operation. The bottom line is always first and foremost."

"But getting there?"

"Are you worried about organized crime?" I asked.

"Yeah, and any other kind of bad-asses that might try to grab a piece of the action."

"Hell, Hayes, if all you want is to download what I know about casino gambling, we could do that over the telephone, or by e-mail."

"Don't think so."

"Worried about electronic surveillance?" I switched off the car's ignition and sat down on my castered mechanic's stool.

He barked a short laugh. "Isn't everyone?"

"So what about the local law, or the state gaming commission?"

"Haven't tried," Moreno said.

"Why in hell not? That's where you should have gone first."

"Don't know who I can trust around here."

"And the tribal council is in agreement with your concerns?"

"Zach, as far as I know, I'm the only one on the council who thinks there may be something wrong."

"So what's the local jurisdiction, city or county?"

"It's the Appa Bay city council, which voted unanimously to sell the land to the Temkuts. Most everyone around here thinks the casino and resort will put the town back on its feet, financially."

"Sounds like a good start."

"Maybe, maybe not. One of the councilmen, Benny Perucci, has been running off at the mouth lately, suggesting to anyone who will listen that the town could have gotten a better deal. Then at last week's meeting he tried to get the town to delay the permit process, make it conditional. Wanted more input before the city council signed a memorandum of understanding with the Rancheria."

"And if the town doesn't sign the MOU?"

"Gives the opponents more time to make their case," Moreno said. "At least two of the naysayer groups are headed up by some pretty influential people."

"How influential can they be if they don't have a majority of the city council in their pocket?"

"Perhaps I should have said *wealthy* instead of influential."

"Often the same thing," I said. "Anyway, I take it you think some of this wealth may have influenced Councilman Petrucci to take another look at having a casino in Appa Bay."

"Never said that."

"Mmm-hmm. Just the vagaries of small town politics, I take it."

"Didn't say that, either."

"You're not giving me a whole lot to go on, Hayes."

"I'm willing to give you a roundtrip airplane ticket, pick up your expenses while you're here, and, of course, pay your going daily rate. That seems a lot to me."

"I won't argue that. But if all you want to do is talk, it would cost you a lot less if you flew to Vegas."

I didn't tell him that my minimum retainer when working for a major casino was usually $10,000. I'm not sure why I didn't, other than I've been getting more than just a little satisfaction out of reading about the Indians having found a way to get even with us round-eyes after all these centuries.

"This is sort of show-and-tell," he said. "Will you come?"

"Let me take a look at my calendar." I carried the cordless into the house and sat down at the computer. I was still irritated with Hayes for interrupting my day, for asking me to get involved in something I had no business going near. When I saw there was nothing important posted on the calendar for the next couple of weeks or so, I decided this would be good opportunity to get a first-hand look at an Indian gaming operation. It was something I'd been meaning to do ever since Native Americans became a major force in the gaming industry.

"How soon do you need me there?" I said.

"I'm patient; I'm an Indian."

"Good, because I'd prefer to drive, if it's all the same to you ... and I won't charge for the extra time it takes."

"Don't sweat it. But speaking of charges, I'll have a retainer for you when you arrive."

"That'll work." I wondered what he thought would be a suitable retainer, but again didn't say anything. "I can probably get away early tomorrow, if that's okay."

"Great," Hayes said. "But before you leave, maybe you could do me a favor?"

"If I can."

"The Rancheria's partner in the project is a Lake Tahoe-based venture capital group called Twin Arrows Investments Inc. We—the Tribal Council, that is—are convinced these are money people who have no organized crime affiliations, but I would really appreciate it if you could look into their *bona fides* before heading west."

"That shouldn't be too difficult."

"Thanks, Zach. I'll be waiting ... patiently."

* * *

It took only one phone call to my old employer, Mike Rollins at the Nevada Gaming Commission Control Board, to get the lowdown on Twin Arrows.

"I'm not all that familiar with them," Mike said. "Give me a moment to bring them up on the screen." After a few seconds, he said, "Ah, ha!"

"What does 'Ah, ha' mean?"

"They've had a few problems here and there, but nothing really serious."

"Explain 'nothing really serious.'"

"Well, let's see: Twin Arrows' operations in Nevada have collected a few fines for such things as allowing minors to gamble, sloppy bookkeeping, and unfair business practices."

"That's about par for *any* gaming corporation," I said. "Anything really big?"

"Cost them almost $30 million last year to settle with a competitor who claimed Twin Arrows obtained its New Mexico gaming license through improper channels and some questionable lobbying shenanigans."

"Was that an Indian casino deal?"

"Yep! But I can't tell you any more than that. The tribes are the primary regulators of gambling on their own land. Individual states and the Feds are secondary regulators of tribal gaming facilities."

"Do you have anything else on Twin Arrows' Indian dealings?"

"Only that they signed agreements with tribal governments to develop and manage two casino resorts in California—Putah Creek, which is up and running, and another not too far away on the coast near Appa Bay that's still in the planning stages."

"Hmm. Curious."

I thanked Mike and filed away what he'd told me in the back of my brain, but not too far back.

Getting the Twin Arrows info from Mike was much easier than trying to map out a route to Appa Bay that would keep me off the freeways for most, if not all, of the trip. Despite my original reluctance to go to California, the more I thought about it, the more inviting the prospect became. There's a sense of freedom in traveling through the brooding Sierra and across vast stretches of open land.

As I laid out a route, my enthusiasm grew and I started looking forward to driving a series of back roads and lightly traveled highways that would put me in Appa Bay within a couple of days.

Besides, I can't stand what metropolitan airports have become, and I've never liked the helpless feeling of being jam-packed into an airliner. When I fly commercially, it's usually under protest.

It would have been nice to take the little '63 Porsche, which I used as a daily driver for several years. It was still an excellent over-the-road car, but the 50-year-old classic had become far too valuable to leave unattended in unknown territory. The more practical decision was to take my screaming yellow Porsche Cayman.

I logged onto the Internet and used Google to help bring me up to speed on what's happening with Indian gaming casinos in California and around the country, along with the federal laws that have made them legitimate.

I already knew what the Nevada-based gaming industry thought of its Native American competition, but I still called a couple of casino generals managers I trusted to find out if they'd heard any rumors of strong-arm countermeasures.

Both said no, but I got the distinct impression they wouldn't have been unhappy if someone or some group would have successfully engaged in those tactics much earlier on. Now, the industry seemed to be more interested in working with Indian casino groups rather than becoming their enemies. It had become both wiser and more profitable to partner-up than to do battle.

* * *

Some people say Porsche's little Cayman coupe was never meant for extended trips—simply not enough trunk space. I say a selection of quality Cordura nylon soft luggage in a variety of sizes and shapes, along with a well-thought-out wardrobe of near wrinkle-proof clothes from TravelSmith, will take you anywhere, for any length of time.

By 9:00 a.m. Friday morning, the Porsche and I were on State Route 160, headed northwest for its junction with US 95. The plan was to cross into California west of Hawthorne and then use as many secondary state highways as possible until I reached Appa Bay and the Pacific Ocean.

Taking the most direct route, it was about a 600-mile trip. I figured my meanderings would add close to an extra 100 miles.

It would have been nice to have a traveling companion, but I don't know too many people who enjoy the challenge of spending a couple of days driving two-lane roads, or wondering whether or not there'll be a nice bed to stretch out on at the end of the day. You also have to have a healthy trust that there'll be a gas station or two when the gauge gets close to the empty mark.

I stuck with US 95 until Hawthorne, crossed into California near Mono Lake, turned south on US 395, and decided to spend the night at Tioga Lodge, a couple of miles north of the High Sierra town of Lee Vining. The lodge offered private cabins without the intrusion of either television or telephone. Perfect.

An over-the-top breakfast the next morning in the lodge's rustic restaurant set me up for the nearly 10,000-foot altitude of Tioga Pass and the snake-like drive through Yosemite National Park on State Highway 120.

Everything went as smoothly as if I'd used AAA or an on-board navigational system. In fact, it was close to noon on the second day when I called Hayes from Calistoga, hoping he could recommend a place to stay in or near Appa Bay, preferably a bed-and-breakfast.

The editor of the *Appa Bay Sentinel* took my call and, with a resigned sigh, said Hayes had taken off for parts unknown.

"When?"

"This morning."

"So he'll be back later today?"

"Haven't the slightest. Hayes has a tendency to wander off like that now and then." He was silent for a moment and I could hear the tap-tap-tap of computer keyboard keys. "He's a damn good journalist, though, and never misses a deadline. But I've given up trying to keep track of his comings and goings."

When I asked about a place to stay, he grumpily touted me onto a couple of "respectable" B&Bs and then hung up on me.

CHAPTER 3

Hayes Moreno was neither the first nor the last to arrive at the home of City Councilman Benito Petrucci. More correctly, dead City Councilman Petrucci. The body of the elderly barber and perennial officeholder was sprawled face down on the steps leading up from the flower-lined front walkway to the wrap-around porch of the Petrucci home.

Several people were standing in the yard and out into the street, trying to catch a glimpse of the bloodied, lifeless body from behind two EMTs squatted down beside the body.

The last light of the summer sun was fading away on the horizon. Sitting in his six-year-old Ford Explorer, Hayes noted that most of the onlookers appeared to be neighbors, including Mayor Joey Tobin, who lived next door.

Hayes assumed someone in the crowd had made a 9-1-1 call, which in turn had resulted in a coded radio call for Police Chief Lance Chubb to go immediately to 312 Sequoia Lane. Hayes, on his way home from the newspaper, had caught the call on his scanner, recognized the address, and immediately altered course. Now, he saw that he was more prompt than the chief to respond to the call.

Hayes grabbed a notepad, a tape recorder, and his iPhone from the passenger seat, unwound his lanky frame from behind the steering wheel of the dirty, dark blue SUV, and ambled over to the gathering.

Mayor Tobin and a few others nodded to acknowledge his arrival, but no one offered a verbal greeting. Some actually glared at him. It had been that way since his arrival more than a year earlier to double the editorial staff of the weekly *Appa Bay Sentinel* to two, and become vice chairman of the Tribal Council of the Coast Temkuts. He wasn't sure which it was, his job or that he was an Indian that created the schism between him and the locals.

Today, though, Petrucci's corpse was possibly more than enough to explain everyone's stunned silence. Two small holes, surrounded by bloodstains, dominated the back of the barber's white short-sleeved dress shirt; his suit jacket was clutched in one outstretched hand.

"Any witnesses?" Hayes asked the mayor, who was still wearing his signature bow tie.

Tobin, who owned the only hardware-general store in the coastal town, shrugged. "Don't think so, at least no one's come forward." He pulled the palms of his hands down the sides of his face and shivered. "God, I drove Bennie home after the council meeting and offered him a cold beer, like I usually do. He thanked me, but said he needed to water his flowers before it got too dark. Last I saw of him, he was crossin' his lawn from my driveway."

"What time was that?" Hayes asked.

"Time? Hell, I don't know." Tobin dry-washed his face again, unclipped his bow tie, and loosened the collar button of his blue chambray shirt. "Must have been around eight, eight-thirty. It was a short meetin' ... for a change."

"Yeah, I know," Hayes said, making notes. "I was there, remember?"

Tobin nodded curtly. "Seems you're just about everywhere lately."

"That's my job," Hayes said. He shook a lock of black hair off his forehead, raised his iPhone, and took a couple of photos. "Who called the chief?"

"I did," Tobin said. "Suppose I'll also have to be the one who calls his two kids." He turned and nodded toward the crowd. "Sara Bethune, there, just happened to be lookin' out her front window, of course, and saw Bennie lyin' on the steps. She called me and I ran over here to see what the hell happened. Figured he'd had an attack or somethin' like that. Saw the gunshot wounds, checked his pulse. Too late. I thought he was already dead but I wasn't sure, so I called 9-1-1." He raised a hand that still clutched a cell phone.

"No one actually saw the shooting, or heard the shots, though, right?"

"I told you before, I don't know. I sure didn't hear anything, and Sara says she didn't either." Tobin looked down the street.

"Seems strange, you and Sara not hearing anything," Hayes said.

"Look, all that's for Chief Chubb to figure out."

"If he ever gets here," Hayes muttered.

"You're not gonna take off on Lance Chubb again, are you?" Tobin said.

"Hey?" Hayes crossed his arms in front of his chest in a mock display of self-protection. "I only report what happens; I don't make it happen."

"Maybe. Seems a lot of strange things been happenin' since you came up here from Vegas."

"What's that supposed to mean?"

Tobin stared at the top button of Hayes's brightly colored print sport shirt, shook his head. "Don't mean nothin' other than I get a feelin' sometimes your reportin' isn't as straightforward and serious as it oughta be."

"*That's* plenty serious," Moreno said, pointing toward Petrucci's body. He started pressing buttons on the smart phone.

"Who you callin'?" Tobin demanded.

"Harkins. He may want to extend the deadline for this week's edition."

Tobin nodded unenthusiastically. "Suppose you'll be calling the *San Francisco Chronicle,* too."

Hayes held up a finger to indicate he couldn't speak right then. When he finished talking to Ed Harkins, he did call the *Chronicle,* and the Associated Press. Unless he missed his guess, Bennie Petrucci's death would be on the front page of every Bay Area newspaper the next day, and maybe for a few days after that.

There'd been a lot of outside interest in Appa Bay since the town decided it would grant a permit for a huge Indian gaming casino complex. Environmentalists and county boards of supervisors had chased the project out of two other locations, in one instance after the Federated Indians of Temkut Rancheria had already purchased the site.

Anything remotely connected to Indian casinos in California, and across the nation, continued to attract broad media coverage. People liked to gamble, and they enjoyed the live entertainment that casinos featured, but there was an underlying negativity toward the relatively tax-free status of the Native American gaming operations.

Now, the spotlight was on the Appa Bay city council and Wirok County supervisors, which were at odds over the proposal by the Temkuts, a tribe once thought to be extinct.

In addition to the political infighting, there was very little support from county residents outside of Appa Bay. Hayes wasn't pleased about it, but it gave him great satisfaction to see the coastal tribes finally garnering recognition after more than 200 years of social and legal neglect.

As a journalist, he had to be fair and not augment accounts of every anti-casino demonstration with reminders of how for centuries the coastal tribes had been run off the land, enslaved, hunted down and killed, and almost totally eliminated by Russians, Spaniards, Mexicans, Californios and Americans.

Chief Chubb finally arrived, siren at full blast. He delayed braking his blue and white cruiser until the last second, allowing it to slide past the EMT ambulance and come to a halt partway onto the Petrucci lawn. The coroner, in his converted minivan, arrived a few seconds later in a more sedate manner.

Once the chief and coroner had performed their individual investigations, and the body had been dispatched to the Appa Bay Urgent Care Center, which served as a temporary morgue, Hayes tried to question Chubb.

"Got nothin' for you or your newspaper at this time," the chief said.

"Any idea who might have a reason to shoot Petrucci?" Moreno insisted.

"When I got somethin' to say, I'll say it." Chubb got into his cruiser and drove away.

Hayes smiled and returned to his grungy SUV. He quickly read through his notes, added a couple of comments, and called in the details of the shooting to Harkins. The *Sentinel* would get put to bed on time and be out to the subscribers and newsstands the next day, just like every other Thursday. Only this week, the front page lead story would be more sensational than what readers of the small weekly were accustomed to seeing.

That taken care of, he reported the shooting to the *Chronicle* and the AP. While he was suspicious that Petrucci's death was related in some way to the Appa Bay-Temkut casino negotiations, he was hoping Zach Rolfe would straighten that out for him.

He really needed Rolfe's expertise on the gaming industry to help steer him in the right direction, and maybe he would be able to sweet-talk him into helping investigate all the parties involved.

The problem was, he could still hear Rolfe saying, "Hayes, I don't do murder."

Hayes decided it might be best to wait until Rolfe arrived to tell him about Petrucci.

CHAPTER 4

I didn't put much stock in being able to find a room in a coastal town on a summer weekend.

I used my cell to phone ahead and was surprised when both B&Bs recommended by the *Appa Bay Sentinel* editor said they had vacancies. I opted for the one that had a private entrance to a first-floor room. It was a surprisingly low $90 a day, which included taxes and a sit-down breakfast.

A little more than an hour and a half later I pulled into Appa Bay and followed the simple instructions I'd been given to find The Pomo House.

"Just for tonight, or longer?" asked the owner, who introduced herself as Vanessa Jimenez. She was in her late thirties or early forties, attractive, without trying to be. Her black hair and *café au lait* skin contrasted nicely with a long multi-colored fiesta skirt and off-white peasant blouse. She wore an intricate abalone-shell necklace that barely touched the neckline of her off-the-shoulders blouse. The necklace was obviously an antique.

"Not sure how long I'll be here," I said as I filled in the registration card. "Can we leave it open for now, or do you have reservations you need to honor?"

She gave me a humorless laugh. "I only wish. Appa Bay's never been much of a tourist destination. Up until fifteen-twenty years ago it was all fishing and forestry."

"Suppose that will change once the casino gets built."

"*If* it gets built." She turned the registration card around, stared at it for a moment, scowled, and fixed me with dark, intense eyes.

"Las Vegas?"

"Yes, ma'am."

"You part of the bunch that's trying to get the casino approved and built?"

"Nope. Not my thing." I suppose that was hedging my status a bit, but I wasn't sure the truth would have been appreciated, and I didn't want to lose the room. "Just here to visit a friend."

"Oh!" She glanced again at the card. "Was it your friend who recommended The Pomo House?"

"Nope again. Couldn't reach him. It was the editor of the local newspaper, the *Sentinel?*"

"Ah, the *Appa Bay Sentinel.* Probably Ed Harkins."

"Sounds about right."

"How'd you happen to call him, if you don't mind my asking?"

"Thought he might know where my friend was, since he works for the newspaper also."

"Hayes Moreno?"

"That's the one."

"Hmmpf!" She made a note on my registration card. "How do you know *that one?*"

"Hayes? Well, our paths crossed a few times when he worked for the *Las Vegas Sun.*"

"Cash or credit card?" she asked.

I reached for my wallet. "Take a debit card?"

"Sure, if it's backed by Visa or MasterCard."

I glanced at the card to make sure it qualified, then handed it to her and waited while she ran it through an electronic reader.

"You a reporter, too, Mr. Rolfe?" She returned my card and gave me a receipt to sign.

I was about to come up with a little personal history when it occurred to me that she was almost as good at getting information out of people as I was ... and I'm supposed to be a professional. I settled for, "Haven't worked in journalism for a long time."

"Well, breakfast is served from seven to nine in the dining room." She used her head to indicate a large room behind her.

I could see four small knotty pine tables arranged to take advantage of a huge bay window that provided a view of the bay waters in between the trunks of bay laurels, live oaks, and second-growth redwoods.

"Sounds good to me," I said.

She made a couple more notes on the registration card, filed it in a box with two or three others, and then pulled a key from a drawer and handed it to me.

"This opens both doors in your room—the one to the outside and the one that opens into the hallway. Turn left for the bathroom, it's right next door; turn right to reach the dining and family rooms. If you need to watch television, there's a small set available in the sitting room, but it has a 10 p.m.-to-10 a.m. curfew. Other house rules are posted in your room."

"I can live without TV and if I need to catch up on the news, I'll use the radio in my car."

"No need ... there's a combination radio-alarm in your room, but—"

"—but a ten-to-ten curfew, right?"

"Well, more like ten to seven for the radio. A lot of people prefer to be awakened by music or the news. Not too loud, though."

"Okay." I started to leave. "And I'll be sure to let you know as soon as I can about how long I'll be staying."

"No problem."

* * *

Mine was a corner room—spacious, with large picture windows on two sides and plenty of closet space. One window looked out onto the shrub-lined, curved driveway that led up to the house; the other nearly duplicated the view from The Pomo House dining room.

The room's décor was a pleasant surprise—sort of a combination of California ranch and Mexican rancho rather than the chintz or lace themes too many B&Bs seem to think is *de rigueur* for this type of hostelry. I flopped onto the queen-size bed, which had a welcome firmness, and tried to reach Hayes Moreno again. When I got no answer, I left a message that I was staying at The Pomo House, and again gave him my cell number.

I also tried the newspaper, where I got a recorded message: "The *Appa Bay Sentinel* offices are closed until Monday. The off-hours news line is 555-1718."

I drove back down into town, cruised up and down the main street, and then explored a few of the side streets, most of which extended outward for no more than a block or two in either direction. The longest of the streets dead-ended at a trio of old piers, one of which supported a large ramshackle structure, now apparently used only by sea gulls.

The streets were clean and most of the properties well kept, both residential and commercial. There were several empty storefronts and my guess was that no new structure had been built in Appa Bay for 25, maybe even 50 years.

A hardware-general store dominated the center of town and appeared to be doing a brisk business. It was flanked on one side by a drug store/gift shop and on the other side by an auto repair garage, fronted by a row of three in-use fuel pumps.

On the other side of the street, people moved in and out of a grocery store that also displayed a "U.S. Post Office" sign. A couple of doors down was a small one-story store, much in need of paint; a hand-carved sign said: Temkut Trading Post.

A feed store that doubled as an antique shop stood sentinel at the north end of the main street, while the Wirok Café protected the south end and appeared to be the only place to eat in the main part of town. Nestled in between was a pair of rustic saloons, on opposite sides of the street, with the usual assortment of neon beer signs in the windows.

I suspected there were other places to eat a little farther out, but I decided to try the Wirok Café rather than the saloon to see if I could gain some insight into the inner workings of Appa Bay.

There were only three booths, half-dozen counter stools, and one other patron in the cafe, which almost made me reconsider my choice. But the "fresh-caught salmon" was exactly that; the bread was hot sourdough; and the side vegetables were crisp and nicely seasoned.

"See you've come over from Nevada," the waitress said as she cleared away my dishes. I must have frowned because she nodded her close-cropped head of steel-gray hair toward the front window, where you could see my Porsche angled-parked, the front license plate displaying its blue and silver state colors.

"Guess I'll have to plead guilty," I said.

"Most you fellas bypass this place and go back down to one of those chi-chi touristy restaurants in Fort Bragg or Mendocino."

"Well, whoever those other fellows are, I'd say they've been missing out on some excellent food."

"Thanks." She smiled. "Dessert?"

"Think I'll pass ... that was a big meal."

"See you finished it, though."

"Every bite."

She gave me another smile. "You connected some way with our casino?"

"Didn't know you had a casino in Appa Bay." There I was, hedging again.

"We don't. Least not yet." She wiped the table with a clean, damp towel. "Looks like we're gonna get one before long, though ... unfortunately."

"You don't think a casino would benefit the town?"

"Oh, I reckon it'll have its good points—provide jobs for some people who really need them." She shrugged. "Bunch of broken stuff around town will get fixed; school buildings probably get new roofs and some long-needed air conditioning; a few more teachers will get hired. You know, that sort of thing."

"Doesn't seem like there's anything bad in any of that."

"No, sir, but the town will change. Probably get bigger, busier, less friendly." She closed her eyes and shook her head.

"Tough choices to make," I said.

"Yup." She squinted at me, then swiped the table again with the towel. "Probably be the end of the café, though."

"Why do you think that?" I looked around: The other diner had left and we were alone. "Seems to me it would be a boon to business."

"Hah! I mean, look at this place, mister—can only get a handful of people in here at any one time." She sighed. "And of course the casino will have food." She sighed again, cocked one hip out and planted a palm on it. "And after that, the chain restaurants will move in. Competition's gonna be somethin' fierce."

"Place like this could easily have the upper hand, though."

"How do you figure?"

"Already an established name, knowledge of the best locations, able to capitalize on a good reputation,"

She snorted. "The big word in that is *capital,* which I ain't got. Even if I did, got no desire to see even this dinky place filled from sunup to sunset ... or later. Done did that in San Francisco for more years than I care to count. Don't intend to do it again."

"So I take it this is your place?"

"Yup!"

"A casino might double its value."

"Hell, maybe triple or quadruple it for all I know ... least that's what some folks claim," she said. "But I ain't ready to sell out. Like my business the way it is ... like the town the way it is. Don't see no reason for any change."

She looked down at me for a moment, took a deep breath, and added, "And you can tell your people I said so."

"As I told you, ma'am, whoever you're talking about, they're not *my* people."

"Whatever." She put the check on the edge of the table. "Pay me when you're ready, bub."

I watched her retreat behind the counter and carry my dishes through a swinging door into the kitchen, her almost-plump frame ramrod straight. This was a woman who would be a good source, if I were in town long enough to need one ... or more. And the Wirok Café was probably a gathering place for locals during the breakfast and lunch hours; a place to eavesdrop on the gossip surrounding the portent of an Indian casino within the city limits.

But that was getting ahead of myself. While I figured out what would be a generous tip without making me look like a suspicious high-roller, I decided that if Hayes Moreno didn't call or make an appearance by noon the next day, the Porsche I were on the road again, headed back to Vegas.

* * *

When I returned to The Pomo House, I found an envelope that had been shoved under my room door. It contained a check for

$5,000, drawn on Moreno's personal bank account. On the "For" line, he'd written, "On account." There also was a note:

Mr. Rolfe:
Hayes Moreno asked me to give this to you.
Said he had to go out of town for a day or
two. Asked you to please wait.
V. Jimenez

"What the hell's going on with him?" I muttered.

It was still an hour before curfew and much too early to go to bed. I wandered out to the sitting room, which was furnished essentially in the same style as my bedroom. The television was off and I couldn't find a TV schedule. A large built-in bookcase, which was the better option anyway, was filled with hardbound and paperback novels and nonfiction books "*For our Guests.*"

Some of the books were almost as old as The Pomo House itself, but I did find a relatively recent mystery.

The dust jacket copy of *Point Deception* by Marcia Muller said, in part: "In a remote spot on the rocky Pacific coast two families were found riddled with bullets ... a new killing revives a community's fears and suspicions ..."

I hoped the book might provide a little insight into the character of Appa Bay's coastal residents.

The book kept me up until the wee hours of the morning. After reading the last page, I fell into a deep sleep and almost didn't get up in time for my first breakfast at The Pomo House. But I did have a better understanding of the kind of people who make the rugged north coast their home. In a way they reminded me of many of the independent-minded people who choose to live in Nevada.

CHAPTER 5

"Hayes called early this morning and left you another message," Vanessa Jimenez said. She served me a stack of fresh blueberry pancakes surrounded by homemade miniature sausage patties. This morning she was efficiently dressed in blue jeans, an unadorned t-shirt, and a denim apron. Her long black hair hung loose around her shoulders.

"It would have been nice to talk to him," I said, perhaps a little too sharply. I was torn between taking the first bite of the very aromatic breakfast and expressing more displeasure with the missing Hayes Moreno.

"He insisted that I not wake you," she said evenly.

"Oh!" I opted to take that first bite and almost forgot about Moreno. But not quite. "I get up pretty early. What time did he call?"

"A little after five."

"Five?"

She nodded.

"Rather thoughtless of him to call at that hour."

"He knows I get up about that time."

"Oh." Another hint that some history existed between the two of them. "What did he have to say for himself?"

"He wants me to convince you that you shouldn't leave Appa Bay until he has a chance to talk with you face to face." She filled my coffee cup.

"Did he indicate when that might be?"

"No."

"Okay, give it your best shot—convince me I should stick around." I put a small piece of sausage between two bite-size pieces of pancake, dragged the mini-sandwich through the syrup, and stuck the whole thing in my mouth. It was a moment to savor, a moment I really didn't want interrupted.

She looked out the picture window at the fog, which was just beginning to disengage itself from the coastline. "I don't know how to do that," she said, "how to convince you."

I swallowed. "This breakfast is a good start," I said, trying to lighten the mood. "Did Hayes say anything else?"

"Uh, no." She placed the coffee pot on a cast iron trivet. "But that's Hayes—cryptic, mysterious, and always someplace other than where you want or need him to be. Ask me, I'd say he spends far too much time marching to the beat of our ancient drummers."

Well, Moreno was paying for my time, so if he wanted me to sit around and wait for him to come back from wherever he'd gone, then that's what I'd do ... for a while.

"Any suggestions how I might spend my day?" I asked, gesturing toward the window with another dripping forkful of syrup-smeared pancake and sausage. In the process I lost a plump blueberry to the wood plank floor.

"Sorry." I started to reach for it.

"Don't worry about it." She quickly stooped and collected the wayward bit of fruit. She stood, swept her hair behind her neck, pulled out a chair, and sat down next to me. Her back was plumb-line straight, her hands rested one atop the other at the edge of the table.

"If you're into sightseeing, Mr. Rolfe, you could drive down to Mendocino. Some interesting stores and art galleries there. And Fort Bragg's very colorful."

"What about around here? I've never been in Appa Bay before."

"Sort of like watching paint dry," she said.

I laughed. She didn't.

"Forgive me," I said.

"For what?"

"For laughing. I mean, you're trying to be helpful and I must seem ..." I laughed again in spite of myself. "Sorry. I just can't get this image out of my head of everyone standing out in the street looking at all the buildings being painted."

This time *she* laughed. Not a reactive pseudo laugh, but a genuine, infectious, eye-crinkler. "I am too serious, aren't I?"

"Don't know you well enough to comment on that, but I do have hard evidence that you're an exceptional cook."

"Thank you."

"Seems to be endemic to these parts."

"Oh?"

"Stumbled on the Wirok Café last night. A real treat."

"Ah, you met Annalee Mackey. She used to have a very popular bistro off Union Square in San Francisco that earned four stars year after year."

"Really? She said she was from Frisco—"

"—don't let her hear you call it that."

"Yeah, well, San Franciscans piss me off sometimes, getting all huffy about people who call their precious city Frisco. They should read a little history." He glanced around the kitchen, turned back to Vanessa. "Anyway, I assumed she'd had a small restaurant or diner someplace in the *Frisco*, maybe out in the avenues or south of Market."

Vanessa laughed. "Last night you were fed by Annalee the cook. Some of us have been treated to the gourmet cooking of Anne Lee Mackey, a cordon bleu chef. Two entirely different people."

"Why did she close down a top-notch San Francisco restaurant to move up here?"

"She's never said, as far as I know, but I've heard that her ancestors owned land around here many, many years ago."

"One of those getting back to one's roots things, maybe?"

"Could be."

She pushed her chair back to get up from the table, but I stopped her with another wave of my fork. "Is there a library in town?"

"I suppose you could call it that." She gave me that good laugh again. "Actually, it's one room in the back of the City Hall building. You can usually find a few current novels and nonfiction books; copies of the *Appa Bay Sentinel, Wirok County Gazette,* and *San Francisco Chronicle;* plus a terminal to connect with the main county library in San Tomas."

"Sounds good. Think I might just drop by and have a look around." I sopped up the last of the syrup with the last tiny piece of pancake. My hastily-conceived interim plan was to do some inconspicuous research on the gaming situation in Appa Bay and Wirok County while I waited for Moreno to finish doing whatever the hell it was that he was doing.

"Sorry, no library today." This time she made it to her feet and started collecting my dirty dishes. "Sunday. The whole town's closed down except for two churches and two saloons. Sort of the yin and yang of coast life."

She offered more coffee, but I declined. "Besides, our so-called library is only open on Monday, Wednesday, and Friday afternoons," she added.

"Maybe I'll take a nap instead." I thought it was funny; her expression didn't change.

"It's what most people do around here on Sunday afternoons." On her way to the kitchen, she stopped and used an elbow to point across the hallway. "If you're looking for something really stimulating, Mr. Rolfe, I do have the Sunday papers in the sitting room."

She said it straight-faced, but I thought I caught a glimmer of mischief in her eyes. This was not a woman to be taken lightly.

"Thanks," I said with what I hoped was the right amount of sincerity. "I appreciate the suggestions."

Actually, I still liked my library idea better than going to one of the saloons, reading the newspapers, *or* taking a nap. I went back to my room and called to find out if the main county library was open on Sunday (it was), then used my laptop and MapQuest to locate San Tomas. It was about a 30-mile trip inland.

* * *

The driver either wasn't very good at tailing people, or didn't care that I knew he was there. The dusty dark-colored Ford Explorer became a fixture in my rearview mirrors before I cleared the city limits of Appa Bay. Or maybe he was just on his way to San Tomas also.

It made no difference to me either way, although if someone *was* following me, I'd be curious to know who ... and why.

For the time being, I was more interested in the drive from Appa Bay to San Tomas -- a curvy, two-lane asphalt road that cut through rolling hills dotted with clumps of live oaks and grazing cows.

I made the most of the Cayman's road-gripping suspension and just might have exceeded the speed limit a couple of times ... or more. There was the added enjoyment of watching the driver of the SUV struggling to keep up, if that was what he was doing. Regardless, I was relatively certain he wasn't enjoying the drive half as much as I was.

Tough!

Once I reached the San Tomas city limits, the Ford dropped back even farther. By the time I found a place to park and was out of the Porsche, there was no way to tell where my road companion had gone.

Standing in the shade of a huge bay laurel, I could see three dark-colored Explorers angle-parked around the central plaza. They all looked suspicious.

I couldn't help but laugh at my overactive imagination. But experience and an annoying little itch between my shoulder blades wouldn't allow me to let go entirely of the notion that I'd been followed.

And I had no intention of wasting time trying to determine if one of the curb-parked SUVs was the one that followed me from Appa Bay; I memorized the location of each of them by make and color.

The uneasy feeling stayed with me as I cut across San Tomas's tree-filled town central plaza. The library, town hall, and police station sat on one side of the square; shops and restaurants lined the other three sides. All of the businesses seemed to be enjoying a steady stream of afternoon tourists.

In the library, reference section's back-issue newspaper files yielded a wealth of information about the Federated Indians of Temkut Rancheria, and how they came to be involved in the long process of planning, financing, and building a casino-hotel-conference center at Appa Bay.

I wondered why Moreno hadn't supplied me with some of the same background information when he'd invited me to come to the coast. At least he'd told me about the death of Councilman Benito Petrucci, which, according to today's newspaper, was still "being investigated."

Looking back through earlier editions of the *Wirok County Gazette*, I learned that a couple of years ago a small group of Temkuts had managed to get a commitment of funds to purchase more than 300 acres of prime grazing land and secure an option on another 1,500 surrounding acres southeast of San Tomas.

The ambitious original plan was to build a large gaming and resort complex near a congested intersection that connected the Sonoma-Napa wine country, the Pacific Coast, the entire San Francisco Bay area, and a back route to US 80 and points east—Sacramento, Lake Tahoe, and Reno.

At the same time, the Temkuts had started the long process of being recognized as a legitimate tribe, which would allow them to transform the acreage into a full-fledged reservation.

While I knew Nevada-based venture capitalists were investing in Indian gaming, it still surprised me to learn that Twin Arrows Investments had fronted the nearly $25 million for the land purchase and options. That seemed a lot of money to risk on a rag-tag band of Indians that had no official status in the eyes of either the Feds or the state.

Before the Temkuts could establish their nation within a nation, overpowering opposition from private land owners, environmental groups, religious congregations, and card room and horse racing interests forced them to abandon the bucolic grazing land site near San Tomas.

In what looked to me like a calculated PR ploy, the Temkuts turned over the development rights of the 300 acres to a land trust so the land would remain agricultural in perpetuity. In another highly publicized gesture of good will, they donated almost $2 million of Twin Arrows money to endow a chair in Native American studies at Wirok State University.

"We intend to take the high road in this venture," tribal chairman Frank Ross was quoted as saying in one newspaper article. "Despite what has been done to the coastal tribes over the centuries, we are going to show you the people we really are."

Enter Appa Bay, which owned nearly 400 acres it had purchased in a failed attempt to attract a name-brand outlet mall. The city council told the Temkuts, and investor Twin Arrows, that they were open to a casino proposal. This proved even more attractive to the tribe since the acreage connected to a rugged 60-acre oceanfront tract the Temkuts had managed to hold onto for several decades

And that sort of brought me up to date. For a tribe that supposedly was illegally terminated by the Bureau of Indian Affairs in the late 1950s for lack of members, the Temkuts now seemed to be doing quite nicely for themselves.

The whole scenario created a huge pool of potential suspects in the death of Benito Petrucci, depending on just how deeply involved the city councilman was in the overall Appa Bay-Temkut land transfer arrangement. Or maybe someone popped him for personal reasons. All that was for the Appa Bay police to work out.

I was more curious about which or how many of these entities and individuals might be involved in whatever it was Moreno wanted me to investigate and counsel him on.

I could imagine all kinds of nefarious undertakings with respect to the Temkut-Twin Arrows plan to build a gaming-hotel-convention center complex on a prime location overlooking the Pacific Ocean.

But that was all speculation. My expertise was in solving crimes connected to the risky business of gaming—players, operators, and manipulators—usually desperate and dishonest people. As best I could tell, none of these had yet come into play as far as the Temkuts and Appa Bay were concerned.

What I needed now was Moreno himself, in person, telling me what the hell it was he expected from me.

* * *

As I turned onto the San Tomas-Appa Bay road, a dusty dark blue Explorer Sport Trac—one of those SUV/pickup crossbreeds—was parked on the berm near the first "Speed Limit

55" sign. Someone was on the far side of the vehicle, but I couldn't get a look at whoever it was. Maybe he, or she, was just watering the roadside weeds.

I watched the truck in my rearview mirrors. After I'd put about a quarter of a mile between us, the person came around to the driver's side, climbed into the vehicle and pulled onto the road.

The SUV driver maintained that separating distance for the next few miles. When we hit a long, clear, straight, stretch of road, I considered stabbing the brakes, dropping into first gear, doing a whisky-runner's U-turn, and trying for a middle-of- the-road meeting with my tail.

My less impetuous self asked, "Why?"

I had no true involvement—good or bad—with anyone in the area, and might never have one if Moreno didn't show up soon. So why cause an unnecessary ruckus?

I accelerated through the next curve, switched on my under-hood radar detector, and kept an eye out for any California Highway Patrol or Wirok County Sheriff's Department cruisers.

About five miles out of Appa Bay, the SUV was but a mere speck in my rearview mirrors. While I was looking for a place to pull off and hide so I could follow my follower into town, the driver turned off onto a side road and disappeared into the coastal hills.

I congratulated myself for not doing something stupid when I'd first seen the SUV as I was leaving San Tomas. A confrontation then could have been embarrassing. I told myself it was probably all a coincidence that didn't even involve the same vehicle going and coming.

Appa Bay was even quieter now than when I'd left earlier in the day. I drove through the town, covering most of the side streets, before returning to The Pomo House. As I was getting out of the Cayman, I heard the distinctive grinding sound of an overhead garage door either opening or closing.

I looked to the rear of the property just in time to see the back end of a dusty dark blue Explorer Sport Trac disappear behind a closing door of the B&B's two-car garage.

CHAPTER 6

Instead of going directly to my room, I went looking for Vanessa Jimenez. I wanted to know—right now—whose Ford Explorer had just pulled into her garage.

It didn't take long to find the proprietress of The Pomo House—she was standing in the open area between the registration desk and dining room, looking as if she were expecting me. Her expression was impassive. I knew mine wasn't.

"Let me guess: another strange phone call from the mysterious Hayes Moreno," I said.

"No, he's here."

"Really? When did he arrive?"

"A few minutes ago."

"Nice!" I angrily and pointedly looked past her to the dining room, then the sitting room. "So where is he?"

"In the kitchen."

"Anxiously awaiting my return, no doubt."

"I don't know. Maybe. He's eating."

"Eating?" I was ready to turn Mr. Moreno inside out. "Did he say anything?"

"Said he was hungry."

"Swell!"

I walked past her and pushed against the swinging door that separated the dining room from the kitchen. She followed me through the doorway.

Hayes was standing, his long, lanky frame bent over a butcher block-style center island. He was spooning food into his mouth from a large soup bowl. For some reason I'd envisioned him having adopted a long braid hanging down his back since leaving Vegas, but in reality his coal black hair was cut full and didn't even cover his neck.

He chewed for a moment, swallowed, and said, "Portuguese fish chowder. You should try a bowl, Zach." He pointed past me with his spoon. "Vanessa is an excellent cook."

"That's old news," I said as evenly as I could manage.

He nodded. "Get him a bowl, Vanessa."

"No, I don't want any chowder," I said, moving toward him. "What I want is for you to tell me where the hell you've been."

He gave me an enigmatic smile. "Following you."

"Following me?" I stood glaring at him across the butcher block. "So that was you in that damn Explorer?"

"Yup!" He lifted another spoonful of chowder to his mouth. "Why?"

"A horse wouldn't have been able to keep up."

"Damn it, Hayes, I'm in no mood for jokes."

"Suppose not." He wiped his face on a dishtowel. "Let's go into the other room. We'll talk." He picked up the chowder bowl.

"Oh, no, you don't!" Vanessa said sternly. "No food in the sitting room. If you want to finish your chowder, stay in the kitchen."

Hayes looked at me, looked at the almost empty bowl of chowder, and then looked back at me. "Do you mind?" he said, pointing to the food with his spoon.

"I've waited this long," I said. "What's another lovin' spoonful?" I expected him to ask Jimenez to leave the room. He didn't. I was almost certain now that there was a lot more to their relationship than I'd originally suspected.

Hayes looked at Vanessa expectantly, apparently saw what he wanted to see, and ladled more soup into his bowl.

"Hayes, speak to me," I said. "Why the hell weren't you here when I arrived? Why did you follow me into San Tomas and back without letting me know it was you? And most of all, damn it, why did you *really* ask me to come out here in the first place?"

"Didn't you give him my message?" he asked Vanessa.

"I did what you asked," she said.

He looked at me, shrugged his shoulders, and continued to eat.

"Your message didn't explain a damn thing, Hayes," I said.

"There were some folks I needed to meet with."

"Go on."

He thought for a moment before responding. "I also wanted to know what you would do if I wasn't around."

"What does that mean?"

"You're from Vegas."

"Yeah, so? I mean, you knew that from the git-go."

"Never know what people from Vegas are going to do."

"Or Indians from California."

Vanessa laughed. "You two are something else."

I sighed. "She's right, you know."

"Maybe," Hayes said.

"What 'maybe?' You called, asked me to come, and I came. Let's get on with it."

"May have been a mistake."

"See ya." I turned, nodded to Jimenez, and started to leave the kitchen. "I'm outta here. Get my bill ready, please."

"Wait!" he said, losing some of his chowder to his shirt and face in the process. He wiped his chin and the counter with the dishtowel.

"That's all I've been doing since I got here, Hayes ... waiting for you to get off the dime and talk to me."

He scooped the last of the chowder out of the bowl and stuffed it into his mouth. As he chewed, he carried the bowl and spoon to the sink and set them down. There was a throat-clearing sound from Vanessa. He glanced at her, shrugged, rinsed off his dishes, and set them on the drain board.

"I need to show you some things," he said.

"That's what you said when you called me."

"Yeah, well, now's the time." He nodded toward the backdoor to the kitchen. "Let's go."

"Don't think so. At least not until you tell me why you followed me to San Tomas and back."

"Told you that a few minutes ago."

"No you didn't, Hayes. You gave me some cockamamie story about my being from Vegas, which is where I've been from for a long time, as you damn well know."

"Sorry."

"I might accept *sorry* if there wasn't a murder involved. I don't like dead bodies, Hayes, particularly murdered dead bodies, particularly murdered dead bodies when the killer is still unidentified and at large." I let him think about that for a moment, then added: "Is that clear enough for you?"

He looked at Vanessa, who shook her head.

"Hayes, talk to the man," she said. "Otherwise, I'm going to go help Mr. Rolfe pack and you'll be back where you were before you called him."

We moved into the sitting room and sat down. Rather, Hayes and I sat in a couple of the steer hide armchairs on either side of a rough-hewn oak coffee table. Vanessa stopped at the doorway and leaned one shoulder against the doorjamb.

"Do you know Greer Raebeck?" Hayes asked.

That stopped me for a moment. I couldn't imagine where he'd picked up that name. In fact, it had been quite some time since I'd even thought about the chestnut-haired Ms. Raebeck with the Sophia Loren eyes. I felt a twinge of sadness. A couple of years earlier we'd shared a passion for driving and working on fast cars, which had evolved into a more personal passion. But neither of us had been ready for a long-term commitment. Eventually, we stopped calling one another. Perhaps if...

I looked up and realized Hayes and Vanessa were still waiting for my reply.

"I know the name," I admitted.

"Sure you do." His tone was accusatory. "And you no doubt know she works for Twin Arrows Investments."

Another surprise. "That I didn't know." It seemed unlikely that Greer would be working for one of the new-age gaming corporations. And why hadn't Mike Rollins mentioned that when we talked since he was very much aware the once-upon-a-time relationship between Greer and me? But even if she did work for Twin Arrows, so?

"Did you check out Twin Arrows?"

"Of course. You asked me to, I did it. The Nevada Gaming Commission Control Board said they were no better, no worse than any other gaming corporation. A few broken regulations here and there, and one major beef with a competitor that cost them a big chunk of dough. But then, my understanding is that any gaming company approved to do business in Nevada is most likely to pass muster in California."

"Talk to Ms. Raebeck?"

"No, nor anyone else at Twin Arrows. Why?"

"Did you know she's one of the partners?"

Surprise number three. "Okay, enough already!" I moved to the edge of my leather chair and leveled an index finger at Moreno. "You were either at the *Las Vegas Sun* when the Corbin Alexandre story broke, or you found it in the files later on," I said. "Either way, *you* apparently know Greer Raebeck worked for Alexandre and that I was involved in that whole thing with Corbin, the Chinese, and the syndicate."

Alexandre and several independent casino operators had hired me to find out who was buying up smaller Nevada casinos, at premium prices, in cash, in what appeared to be a move by someone to become the czar of all Nevada gaming. It turned out to be a syndicate move, using an unsuspecting San Francisco Chinese group to front for them.

When Hayes didn't respond, I withdrew the accusatory finger. "What else do you know, or think you know?"

Moreno leaned back and crossed his legs. "I hear you and Ms. Raebeck played share-the-teepee at one point."

"We enjoyed each other's company for a while. But Greer and I haven't seen or talked to each other in a long, long time."

"But you *do* know where she got the money to invest in Twin Arrows," he said.

"Haven't the slightest. Could have won it in a high-stakes poker game, for all I know."

"It came from the Alexandre estate, after he was murdered."

I didn't believe that, or what it implied. "Are you accusing her of embezzling or stealing the money?"

He laughed. "You are a very suspicious man, Zach Rolfe, which is why I like you ... and trust you."

"Trust me so much you avoided meeting with me and then like a sneak, followed me to San Tomas today."

"You're from Vegas."

"Yeah, yeah! We've done that dance a couple of times, Hayes. Tell me something new."

He looked over at Jimenez. "Could we have some lemonade or iced tea?" He gave her a mischievous smile. "Here in the sitting room?" She cocked her head and raised one eyebrow. "Please?" he asked softly. She shook her head ever so slightly and went into the kitchen.

Moreno moved to the edge of his seat. "Seems Alexandre's widow, Jane, along with Alexandre's former silent partner, Quinn, laid a considerable sum of money on Ms. Raebeck. Apparently it was in appreciation for her dedication in uncovering Alexandre's killers and for later restructuring his casino operations so they were once again competitive and profitable."

"Good for her," I said, and meant it. Not bad for a former instructor in the Humanities at the University of Nevada. Hayes's comment also reminded me that I never did learn Quinn's full name. "Are you suspicious of Raebeck for a specific reason?"

"Too many coincidences," Moreno said. "You ... her ... Twin Arrows."

"Nevada is a very incestuous state when it comes to politics, business, and gaming." I was still trying to accept that Greer was a founding partner in a company like Twin Arrows.

"No different than California," added Vanessa. She set glasses of cold lemonade on the rough-hewn oak coffee table that separated Hayes and me. This time she sat down on the soft leather-upholstered couch that took up most of the space along the back wall of the room.

I took a sip of my drink—obviously made with fresh-squeezed lemons. For some unexplainable reason I found it difficult to stay pissed at Hayes with her around. Still, I had a feeling there was more to this Greer Raebeck thing than he was telling me.

"Do you feel okay yet with my being here?" I taunted.

"Probably as safe as any Redskin feels around any Round-eye." He sipped his lemonade, started to set it on the floor, looked up at Vanessa, and then used a coaster on the coffee table. "If you hadn't gone off to the library in San Tomas, my guess would have been that you were in some way part of the problem rather than here to help find a solution."

"What I found in San Tomas," I said, "was all the background stuff on the status of Indian gambling in California, stuff you should have given me in the first place."

He grunted and stood up. "Let's go out to the garage."

* * *

Parked next to Hayes Moreno's dirty Explorer was an immaculate red Mazda Miata, maybe two or three years old. I had no difficulty guessing who owned and drove the sports car.

Hayes opened the Sport Trac's tailgate and pulled out a well-worn cardboard file box. He thumbed through several index tabs before taking out a multi-folded document that he opened and spread across the floor of the SUV. It was an elaborate, hand-drawn schematic that in some ways resembled a series of detailed family trees. He waved one hand across the document, from left to right, indicating that he wanted me to take a closer look.

I bent over the detailed drawing and saw Twin Arrows Investments prominently positioned at the center, with a myriad of lines radiating out to individuals, corporations, rancherías, Indian casinos, gaming commissions, county boards, city councils, state legislatures, individual politicians, and on and on and on. Many of the entities were interconnected, creating what looked like a huge spill of spaghetti.

Greer Raebeck's name was there, in large block letters, but then, so was mine, as was Moreno's and Jimenez's, and a whole host of other people. I saw Benito Petrucci's name had a red line through it.

I straightened up and looked at Moreno. "Who put all of this together?"

"I did," he said.

Vanessa cleared her throat.

"Uh, Vanessa and I," he amended.

"So, having put this together, what makes you think you need me?" I said.

"Some of it's real, some of it's speculation," he said. "I want you to help me separate the good guys from the bad guys before the coastal tribes get massacred again."

CHAPTER 7

Northern California – 1834

"They will kill us if we steal their horses."

"We are already dying," said Moh-reh. "This is our last chance to go from this evil place."

"But the mission land is our home."

"No, it is not, Wah-nuh." He peered through the tall grass toward the split-rail corral, where several horses were barely visible under the light of the quarter moon. "The home of the Wiroks is the land as far as you can see in every direction, from the mighty waters to the mountains where the sun comes from every morning."

Wah-nuh looked out in all the directions where Moh-reh pointed. "I have not been to these places."

"No, and that is a great sadness. But once all the land was open to The People. We could roam from here to whenever we wanted. That was true from the first day of time. But since the days of my father's father, the Round-eyes have come from many far away places to claim the land as their own. They have killed the trees and fenced the land. They have made us work for them and till the land. They have beat us and killed us. Everything is for them and nothing for Wirok."

"Hernando, we are no longer Wiroks. The padre says we are now neofitas of the Mission San Rafael Arcangel."

Moh-reh grabbed his companion roughly by the shoulder. "Do not call me by that Spanish name. Just because the padre sprinkled water on my head from a church bowl and put a new name in his book does not change me from Moh-reh to Hernando Moreno. Moh-reh is an honorable name in our tribe. I will keep it forever."

Wah-nuh nodded, then shook his head unhappily. "Our brothers wonder, Hernan- uh, Moh-reh, why you do this dangerous thing. The padre says the Mexicans will give us the Nicasio lands and many sheep and horses. Isn't that enough?"

"Enough? They only give us back what was once ours to use freely. They have taken the best and leave us the rest. And even that they say we must share with the Miwok and Pomo."

"They are good people," Wah-nuh said.

Moh-reh grunted heavily. "Yes, but what of the Mexican rancheros? They are already taking some of the Nicasio land for their cattle. And for this the padre expects The People to give thanks to his god."

"There is a lot of land, Moh-reh, as far as the eye can see in every direction."

"No! You have not listened to what I have been saying. The time is gone when we were free to hunt and fish from the mountains to the great water. No more. I spit on this two-faced gift from the white man!"

"It is not good to talk that way about the padre and his god," Wah-nuh said.

Moh-reh pulled his friend closer. "Forget the padre and his Great White Father." He looked around. "It is time. Go tell the others. Give the sound of the tukkuuli when everyone is ready." He waited patiently after Wah-nuh departed. When he finally heard the muffled hoot of a horned owl, he crouched and hurried toward the corral.

The sudden arrival of the Wiroks in the middle of the night agitated the corralled horses. The animals snorted and tapped their hooves in the dust. Moh-reh and his band slipped into the enclosure and soothed the horses before a single whinny was sent out into the darkness. A portion of the split-rail fence facing open land was quickly dismantled and the wood rails set aside. Each man grabbed the manes of two horses and with an animal on either side of him, ran toward the coastal hills.

The next morning the village of nearly sixty Wiroks, which had never possessed a horse, now had almost two dozen studs, mares, and colts—a mixture of riders and workhorses.

The women began weaving harness from tule and creating horse-drawn travois that would carry the tribelet's belongings to their new home. Grain and dried fish were gathered in bundles, while stone and bone tools, small utensils made from gourds, and *hunting charms fashioned from shells were all carefully packed in woven baskets.*

As the village hoypu, Moh-reh had made the decision to move the village farther north along the coast. There, they would take up the true ways of The People—gathering, hunting, fishing, and making baskets. He was weary of tilling the land and harvesting crops, first for the mission, now for the Mexican land grant owners. It was time to go back to the land, to tread lightly, to leave no footsteps, to always apologize to the spirits in animals and nature whenever The People disturbed them, in whatever manner.

* * *

Moh-reh was dreaming of collecting huge abalone from the rocks in a cove near where he would soon move his people. He heard a shout and wondered how this could be when he had gone off alone to gather the succulent mollusks at low tide. Then his eyes popped open. He sat up abruptly. The harsh movement awoke his wife. Together, they heard more shouts. Then the air was filled with screams of fear and pain.

"Keep the children here," he told his wife. "I will see what is happening." He stepped out of his redwood bark home to catch the first glimpse of dawn. The dim light silhouetted several caballeros riding through the village, firing long guns and swinging swords. The Mexicans! The Mexicans had come for their stolen caballos.

Moh-reh looked around for a pole or club he could use to defend his family. He had no weapons other than a fishing spear, a small bow, and a few lightweight arrows meant for birds and small animals. The People had never had a need for battle weapons. They did not fight among themselves, or with outsiders. When the Spanish soldiers came with the friars, their numbers and weapons had been overwhelming. The Wiroks had been forced to work for the Spaniards, who became their masters. They had done what they were told to do, and prayed to the new god Dios.

When the Spaniards left and turned the mission lands over to the Mexicans, nothing changed other than it was someone else they now worked for.

Moh-reh knew the raid on his village was happening because of him, knew that it was because he had stolen the Mexicans' horses. He should have made his people work faster, longer hours. They should have left the village two days earlier. But that was not their way, and now the Mexicans had come not only for their caballos, but to take the lives of the ladróns who had taken the animals.

He found a pole that had been cut for a travois and tested its strength by striking it against a huge nearby live oak. The length of redwood sapling vibrated in his hands, but did not splinter.

As Moh-reh stepped in front of his home, a caballero came charging toward him, espada held low, the point aimed chest high. Moh-reh used one end of the pole to deflect the sword, then spun around and used the other end to strike the rider in the head. He was both surprised and proud when the Mexican fell from his horse and landed hard on the ground. He was even more surprised when the man did not rise, or even move.

Moh-reh grabbed up the rider's espada and called out to his wife. She stuck her head only part way out their redwood-bark kótcha. He could see she was trembling, her eyes filled with fear.

"Take the children. Run!" he ordered.

"Where will I go, husband?"

"Follow the stream to the big water. Run low and fast. Do not allow the children to cry out."

"You will come, too?" she asked.

"Yes, when I can. I will find you."

Moh-reh quickly pulled his wife, six-year-old son, and five-year-old daughter from the house and shielded them as they ran around to the backside and disappeared into the woods. When he looked back again at the village, several kótcha were burning, as were the sweathouse and roundhouse.

With the espada in one hand and the redwood pica in the other, Moh-reh moved toward the center of the slaughter. He'd gone only a few feet when a terrible pain tore through his left shoulder, knocking him backward. As the espada slipped from his grasp, he looked down and saw a ragged hole in his flesh, blood streaming from it.

Stunned, he looked up to see a Mexican only a few feet away hurrying to reload his musket. Slowly at first, then with greater speed, Moh-reh charged the man. He pushed the smaller end of the pike out in front of him, clamped the other end under his right arm, and held tightly to the shaft with his hand.

The Mexican dropped the long gun and raised his arms to defend himself, but he was too late. The pica bounced off his sternum, entered the soft flesh under the chin, and drove him to the ground.

Moh-reh pulled the pike from the gurgling wound and staggered. The smoke was blinding, burning his eyes. He gagged on the stench of death. All around him were bodies, shot or hacked apart with no apparent concern for age or sex. Women were shot down with sucking babies at their breasts; naked children were slain or crippled as they escaped from their burning kótchas.

Moh-reh wept and stumbled toward the center of the village, encouraging those who still stood to run for the woods.

He hoped to find Wah-nuh among the survivors, but the husband of his first sister had been cut down in front of his kótcha, a crucifix clutched in one hand.

"Their god did not help you, my friend," Moh-reh said. He peered into the conical redwood bark house, but the sight of more bodies prevented him from going in.

"Pagano!" a voice called out. Moh-reh spun around. A gray-bearded Mexican held an espada high over his head with two hands. "Ladrón de caballos!" the man cried as he brought the sword down full force. The blade glanced off the side of Moh-reh's head and buried itself in his right collarbone. The momentum carried both men to the ground.

The Mexican scurried to his feet, but Moh-reh, with both arms disabled, could not move. The Mexican planted a foot on Moh-reh's chest, twisted and pulled at the short sword until it came loose, then spat in the Wirok's face before moving on to find more heathens to kill.

* * *

Moh-reh's family, along with a few other women and children who had escaped the massacre, returned to the village two days later. Slowly, one by one, they buried the remains of their husbands and friends, erecting small wooden crosses supplied by the mission padre and some of the neofitas.

The padre insisted that the graves be marked with the Wiroks' Christian names.

Because Moh-reh's six-year-old son was the oldest village male to survive "The Horse Thieves Punishment," he was selected to be the new headman. While he had been given a Wirok name at birth, the church and other entities listed him as Moreno, Adán Moreno.

CHAPTER 8

"Benito Petrucci," I said, pointing to the chart on the tailgate of Hayes Moreno's Explorer. "Let's talk about him some more."

"He's dead," Moreno said.

"Yeah, yeah! You made that clear from the beginning, and I still don't like it. But what is it you're *not* telling me?"

"I don't know what you mean." He glanced quickly at Vanessa and back again to me. Her impassive expression didn't alter. "Nothing's changed with the Petrucci shooting since we talked on the telephone."

"Does that mean there was something going on before you talked to me, or before he died?"

Hayes shrugged.

"Damn it, Hayes, tell him!" Vanessa said.

"Okay, okay!" He boosted himself up and sat on the floor of the SUV. "A few days before Benny was shot, we found out he had Indian blood."

"Petrucci?" I said. "I thought good old Christoforo Colombo stuck to the east coast of the New World."

"From a Native American point of view, 'good' isn't exactly how we would describe the so-called discoverer of the New World," Hayes said and took a deep breath. "Had a couple of drinks with old man Petrucci one night after a city council meeting. Told me how his Italian-born great-great grandfather packed his clothes, a few hundred grape cuttings, and came to California during the gold rush. Didn't find gold, but he did find himself an Indian wife—Patwin tribe. Together, they planted a lot of vineyard acreage in this part of the country."

"Okay, so your dead city councilman was part Indian. Some problem with that?"

"Not in any ethnic sense," Vanessa said. "Anyone around these parts who claims to be a full-blooded Indian would have a lot of proving to do, and even then would still be suspect."

"The thing that got to us," Hayes said, "is that the records show Petrucci had registered as a member of the Patwin band, which is a division of the Wintuns."

"Which means?"

"The Patwins operate the Putah Creek Casino and Resort, thirty some miles northeast of here in northern Solano County," Vanessa said.

"So what are you thinking, conflict of interest? Spying? What?"

"Don't know what to think," Hayes said. "I'd planned to question Petrucci some more about all that, but before I could arrange it, we found him lying face down and dead in his own front yard."

"Can we go there?"

"Where, to the murder site?"

"No, to the Patwin casino."

Hayes looked at me as though I'd said something so outlandish he couldn't even begin to comprehend it.

"Well, can we?" I insisted.

"What the hell do you think that would accomplish?"

"Damn if I know," I said. "But strange as it may seem, I've yet to set foot inside a California Indian casino. If your Councilman Petrucci was linked to the Putah Creek operation, then what better place for me to look around to get an idea of what's going on out here on the left coast?"

"You thinking of going over there alone?" Hayes said.

"If I have to, but I was hoping you'd go with me ... provide a little guidance, make some introductions, fill me in on who's who. That sort of thing."

He scooted out of the SUV, looked at Vanessa, and said, "Can't do it."

Moreno started to walk away. I grabbed him by the upper arm and spun him around to face me. He started to take a swing at me, then let the fist drop down by his thigh.

"What the hell's going on, Hayes? I'm here because you asked me to be here. So, for the absolute last time, do you want my help or don't you?"

He shook off my hand, looked at Vanessa, and said, "Bad idea."

"Don't pull that the stoic Indian brave stuff on *me*, Hayes," she said. "You're in deep shit, if you'll pardon the expression, and you better grab the hand this man's holding out to you. If you don't, there's a good chance you, the casino, and Temkut Rancheria are all going to go under."

Hayes turned away, kicked a back tire of the SUV, and was silent.

"Well?" Vanessa prompted.

He turned back to us, nodded in my direction. "I can appreciate why you want to see things first-hand," he said. "But if I go with you, they'll run us both off before we even get inside the casino."

"Why's that?" I asked.

He scuffed a boot toe at the garage floor. "Well, the thing is, I may have made a couple of uncomplimentary remarks about Putah Creek in the past."

"Hah!" Vanessa exploded. "That has to be one of the grossest of gross understatements of all time."

Moreno lowered his chin to his chest, and mumbled, "Yeah, well, whatever."

"Okay, I got the picture," I said. "But I still need to go there ... or go to one of the Indian casino-resorts in the area that has an operation similar to what you're planning."

Hayes looked at me, slowly shaking his head.

"You don't have to go with me," I said. "All I need from you is a briefing and then I'll do it on my own. Or do you think that would be too difficult for a former Nevada Gaming Commission inspector?"

"*I* could go with you," Vanessa said.

There was a challenge in her voice that I knew wasn't meant for me, even though she was looking in my direction.

"That sounds cozy," Moreno said.

"I'm not looking to move in on your woman," I said. "You can get that idea out of your head right now."

"She's not my squaw," he said.

"And she never will be if you keep talking like that," Vanessa said and turned to me. "Tomorrow morning?"

"Works for me," I said.

"Right after breakfast."

Vanessa and I left Hayes standing alone in the garage and went back inside the inn.

* * *

We didn't get away for our Monday trip to the Putah Creek casino as early as planned. A couple of e-mail messages from Vegas clients kept me on my iPhone for part of the morning, then Vanessa had to deal with a carpenter who was renovating one of the B&B's rooms.

Since all of the inn's guests except me had left by late Sunday morning, Vanessa suggested that we catch lunch at a small, new casino that was on the way to the more grandiose Putah Creek resort complex. Vanessa said the layout of the Kotcha Rancheria Casino was typical of many of the smaller Indian gaming operations in Northern California.

"Thanks for volunteering to come along," I said. "Much more time around Hayes last night and I might have popped him one."

"I could see that," Vanessa said. "Not that he didn't deserve it ... from both of us."

We were riding in her red Miata, having decided that to take the Porsche, with its Nevada plates, might not be in our best interests. I was surprised when she asked me to drive. "I get to see more when I'm a passenger," she said.

As the Kotcha casino came into view, I wasn't impressed. At first I thought they were in the process of building a hotel or huge motel behind the casino proper. Instead, it was a concrete, layered parking structure that dwarfed the casino building itself. If the garage was built to accommodate huge crowds, they had to be showing up on the weekends because we were able to park just a few spaces away from a pair of elevators that carried us down to the casino.

We entered what was essentially one huge room under a sort of double Quonset hut-like structure. Almost one-half the inside was given over to bingo, while the rest of the floor space was filled with electronic slot machines. In one corner, far from the main entrance, was a small saloon-styled eatery.

"*Kotcha* is Miwok for house," Vanessa said as we sat down.

"And what did a Miwok house look like way back when?"

"Well, it sort of depended on what was closest—either slabs of redwood bark stacked in a conical shape, or a larger, round dwelling constructed of thatched grass."

I looked around. "Doesn't look like either one of those, either outside or in here."

She laughed. "No, I'm afraid naming the casino *kotcha* is something of a misnomer."

"Or maybe an inside joke, since it rhymes with *gotcha*."

She hit his arm with the back of her hand. "That's terrible."

"What can I get you?" came a voice from behind us.

When I turned around to answer the bartender, I saw a continuous row of embedded electronic poker machines winking and blinking at me from the top of the polished wood bar. There was barely enough room between the machines to set down a drink glass or small plate of hors d'oeuvres. Sadly, this was what was happening in Nevada casinos also. But then, were the machines any more intrusive than a rack of keno slips and marker, along with keno runners telling you another game was about to start?

The bartender had to lean far over the bar and the machines in order to hear our orders. We both went for house special club sandwiches and diet Cokes, which seemed a safe route to go.

"What do you think?" Vanessa asked as we waited for our orders to be served.

"About what?"

"The casino, of course."

"Smoky. Hurts my eyes in here."

She nodded her agreement. "Officially, we're not in either California or the U.S., so anti-smoking laws don't apply."

"Swell! What about just wanting a healthy atmosphere for the players and workers?"

"I think it's a defiance thing," she said. "But what do you think about the casino as a casino?"

"I suppose 'efficient' would be the best description. If it's being run properly, it probably does exactly what it was designed to do—make money for the tribe that owns it."

"Is it what you expected?"

"Gambling is gambling, Vanessa. Makes no difference whether it's a one-table poker game in the back of a saloon, or the Bellagio on the Vegas strip with an orchestrated water ballet. The trappings don't change the primary purpose."

"I think our casino will be much nicer than any of the existing ones," she said.

"Still won't change its basic purpose."

The bartender interrupted us, stretched over the poker machines again to hand us our orders, and gave us a tab. No comp drinks here.

After we'd taken our first bite of the surprisingly tasty sandwiches, Vanessa half turned and looked out at the casino floor, which was filled with flashing lights of every possible color.

She said something that I missed because of the cacophony of computer bells, whistles, chimes, and electronic semi-tunes. She moved closer and repeated what she'd said:

"The money's going to make things a lot better for many Indian families."

"I understand the goal," I said, "but never forget that when someone wins at gaming, someone else loses."

She took another bite of her sandwich and nodded. "Maybe it's the end of a long, long losing streak for us."

I'd assumed, because of her name that she was Hispanic. She'd just let me know otherwise. "Food's pretty good here," I said, trying to get away from the negative philosophical track I'd unintentionally taken. She didn't respond and we finished our lunch in silence, watching and not watching an Italian soccer match on the televisions suspended from the ceiling over the back bar.

Back on the road, I found her little roadster to be nimble and more than up to handling the narrow, twisty back roads that we chose for the two-hour drive to Putah Creek.

I've always admired Mazda's venerable small sports car. Yet, for whatever reason, this was the first time I'd ever actually sat in one, either as driver or passenger.

It wasn't a Porsche, but then, it didn't try to be. Essentially, it was pure, inexpensive fun. It had the capacity to let me sit back, put my hands at 10 and 2 on the steering wheel, and be entertained mile after mile.

The Miata actually reminded me of an MGA I once owned. While the Miata was a modern-day vehicle throughout, there was a definite link to those two-seater British sports cars from the 50s and 60s. It was top down, devil-may-care driving at its best.

"I can't get a fix on Hayes's thinking, or exactly what he wants," I said as we crested a small hill.

"Ah, you noticed that," Vanessa said. "I often think he takes the inscrutable Indian thing a bit too far." She seemed to be over the mild funk I'd regrettably put her into.

"Have you told him that?"

"Oh, yes! Many times. And you can see just how much good *that* has done."

"Okay, so tell me, what can we expect at the Putah Creek Casino?"

"In what respect?"

"Well, I was wondering what had prompted the uncomplimentary remarks Hayes mentioned."

"That!" She laughed and held one hand above the windshield and allowed her palm to rise and fall in the slipstream. "The Patwin Band got into the gaming business about 20 years ago with a small bingo operation on their Rancheria. That was a couple of years before the U.S. Supreme Court recognized the so-called inherent right of Indian tribes to offer gaming on tribal lands." She laughed again. "I don't think there's an Indian alive who hasn't memorized *those* words."

Vanessa pulled her hand down, reached behind the seats, and retrieved a small portfolio. "Anyway," she continued, "the

Putah bingo operation kept outgrowing itself every few years. They kept tacking on additions, expanding the hall, tacking on more additions, and spreading out in all directions. By the time the California Gaming Compact was signed in 1999, the place was one huge, sprawling mess."

"And Hayes was involved in this?"

"No, not directly. This happened before he moved back to Appa Bay permanently. He was on some advisory board that I can't even remember the name of now. Its purpose was to take a look at all existing Indian gaming facilities in California and write a report for the legislature. Unfortunately, Hayes told a few reporters what he thought of the Putah Creek facility before the advisory board turned in its findings."

"Apparently his remarks upset a few people."

"Hah! That's certainly a mild assessment of what happened. But let me read you something and you can judge for yourself:

She pulled some papers out of a portfolio, flipped through them, and then placed one sheet on top.

"After giving the reporters his idealized view of how he thought Indian casinos should look and be operated, Hayes said, and I quote:

"'Putah Creek, for example, is a nasty, overcrowded, and run-down casino. Since they opened the new parking lot, too many people are crammed into the small, older casino. I'm afraid if there were an emergency and people needed to escape, there could be serious and tragic consequences. There are a lot of broken slot machines and it seems there is never enough cashier staff. The patrons are rude and the staff is unfriendly. This is not a fun place to gamble and it does not make a good impression for Indian gaming.'"

She cocked her head at me and said, "So what do you think?"

"I think possibly Hayes Moreno needs to be *more,* not less, inscrutable."

She laughed and pointed to a sign about a quarter mile ahead of us. A large, garish billboard announced we'd arrived at the Putah Creek Casino and Resort.

"Looks like something more than bingo now," I said.

"Oh, yes. Much more." She consulted another sheet of paper: "'The most recent $205 million investment at Putah Creek Casino and Resort offers patrons 65,000 square feet of casino floor space, 2,200 slot machines, and 110 table games. In addition, there is a 1,000-seat facility for bingo, a 500-seat entertainment auditorium, a half-dozen new restaurants, a 225-room hotel and spa, a multi-story parking garage for 1,925 vehicles, and an 18-hole championship golf course.'"

"Big time operation," I said. "And the Temkuts are planning what, a Kotcha or a Putah Creek?"

"Similar to Putah Creek, only larger," she said. "However, we'll have an oceanfront setting ... the only one in California."

"And right now, we're where, in terms of San Francisco and Sacramento?" I asked, turning to enter the three-level parking structure that looked quite a bit like the one at the Kotcha Casino.

"About equidistant from the two," she said.

"Good positioning."

We parked and took an elevator down to the hotel lobby. The décor was lush, but not gaudy—something in between California casual and Las Vegas glitz. My initial impression was that a lot of careful thought and quality materials had gone into the design and construction.

"I could use something cold to drink," I said as the elevator doors opened.

"Sounds good."

As we started toward the main casino entrance off the lobby, a very unfriendly hand clenched my upper arm from behind and brought me an abrupt stop.

"You will have to leave the premises," said a gruff, no-nonsense voice.

The voice's owner started to turn me around, but I braced myself, and spun out of his grasp in the opposite direction. While he was still surprised, I brought my clenched hands down hard on the still-outstretched arm of a typical security type in a burgundy, broad-shouldered, narrow-hipped blazer. The move left us almost forehead to forehead.

"Politeness counts a lot with me," I said and looked around to find Vanessa. She was standing between two female security people, who wore similar, female-tailored burgundy blazers. Neither had a hand on her.

"Would you care to start over?" I asked my transgressor. While he was trying like a good soldier to pretend his arm didn't hurt, I moved over to stand near Vanessa.

"You are not welcome here, Mr. Rolfe," he said. "Now please leave."

"Wow! I didn't even hear the drums or see the smoke signals announcing my arrival."

Vanessa snickered. "You have the wrong Indians," she said.

"Oh, sorry!" I looked back at the security man. "Has someone mistakenly put me on the Gaming Commission's list of card-counters or slot mechanics?" I asked. "Is that why I'm not welcome?"

"I was told to prevent you from entering the casino and to escort you off the premises, sir," he said. "That's all I know."

"And do you want to try that again by yourself, or are you thinking of calling for reinforcements?"

"I will request backup, if necessary."

"What do you think, Vanessa, shall we go peacefully?"

"That's probably the wisest course of action," she said, still smiling.

"Then I shall retreat ... and live to fight another day."

"Do you really want to see the operation, or are you here for some nefarious reason, Toby?" asked a new, female voice from behind me.

Toby? Damn few people know that nickname, and fewer still are actually close enough friends to use it. It's reserved for special people, and special times. Then I recognized the voice.

"Greer Raebeck," I said, turning around. "It's been a long time."

The background information from Hayes saved me from what could have been an embarrassing situation. Greer was just as beautiful as ever, her chestnut hair cut a bit more severely to go with a very expensive, light-weight, mauve business suit. I smiled, remembering the see-through blouses that were once her trademark. I didn't know whether to offer her my hand, or try for a friendly hug and a light kiss on the cheek. These things can be difficult with ex-lovers.

She solved my dilemma by dismissing the security people with a nod of her head and stepping up to face Vanessa. "I've heard a lot about you, Ms. Jimenez." She offered her hand. "I'm Greer Raebeck, a partner in Twin Arrows Investments."

"So I understand," Vanessa said, shaking the hand in a very businesslike manner.

CHAPTER 9

"Why the bum's rush if Twin Arrows is involved in both the Putah Creek and Appa Bay casinos?" I asked Greer when we were comfortably seated in her top-floor office. One-way window–mirrors provided a panoramic view of the entire main gaming floor. I was surprised at the amount of action at both the slot machines and the table games—much more than I would have expected for an early Monday afternoon, and certainly relatively much more than at Kotcha.

"The unfriendly greeting wasn't my idea," Greer said. "In fact, I probably wouldn't even have known about it if I hadn't seen you as I was coming across the lobby."

"Twin Arrows—*your* Twin Arrows—does operate the casino, doesn't it?" I said. She didn't even blink at my lame and uncalled for attempt at sarcasm.

"Yes, but each of our management agreements is different, tailor-made according to individual tribal-state compacts. For instance, the Patwins' had a pretty good security system in place for their old casino and bingo hall before we came on the scene. It seemed a good idea to allow them to continue with that gaming service ... with a little input from us, of course."

"Of course." I looked down on the gaming floor. There wasn't anything I could see that would set it apart from a large, well-run Nevada casino. "Are you here all the time?"

"No way!" She shook her head emphatically. "I just happened to come in from Tahoe today for a meeting with the Patwin council."

"Lucky us."

"Look, what goes on between the tribes is strictly their business. We merely provide upfront development money in return for agreements to operate their Class III gaming over a stipulated period of time."

"How long did it take you to memorize that little piece of boilerplate?"

She laughed. "I spend much too much time in lawyer-scrutinized meetings."

"So in other words, Twin Arrows is only involved in the casino-style gaming—tables games, slots, that sort of thing."

"Exactly. The tribe continues to be in charge of the bingo and any player-against-player games."

"And you no doubt have an option to renew your contract."

"Certainly. So, it's obviously in our best interests to make sure our operations are successful."

"Our unfriendly reception," Vanessa said to me, "could have been the result of those earlier negative comments Hayes made about the Putah casino."

"Hayes Moreno?" Greer said.

"The very same," I said. "Why?"

"He's a strange one."

"I wouldn't disagree with that. And he definitely was not kind in what he said about the Patwin's previous gaming venture. But that doesn't explain how Putah Creek security knew we were arriving when we did. They appeared to be waiting for us."

"Any idea why?" Greer asked.

"Haven't the slightest," I said and looked at Vanessa, who shook her head. "Whatever, there's definitely a very efficient communications network at work here and I'd like to know who all's involved in it ... and to what end."

"It's not Twin Arrows," Greer said. "You have my word on that."

"Then you don't mind if we take a tour of the facilities?"

"Not at all. In fact ..." She interrupted herself by glancing at her watch. "Sorry! I was going to offer to take you around myself, but I have another one of those lawyer-scrutinized meetings coming up in a few minutes. Will you forgive me?"

"There's nothing to forgive," I said.

"I can get someone else to be your escort, if you'd like."

"It's really not necessary."

She gave me a slight nod. We both knew I could find my way around most any casino without the assistance of a guide.

"Should I be concerned that a former Nevada Gaming Control Board investigator is giving our casino the once-over?"

"In no way."

"Then perhaps I'll see you later, although these damn pow-wows can..." She looked at Vanessa. "Sorry! That was not appropriate."

"No offense taken," Vanessa said. "I'm very much aware of how much time Indians can take to make up their minds about almost anything ... and how frustrating it can be."

"Thank you. That's very gracious of you." She took her eyes off Vanessa and looked at me. I could see she wasn't comfortable with the situation. "It would be nice to sit and chat ... if we get the chance," she said.

"If I see anything I think you should be aware of, I'll be sure to let you know." With that, Vanessa and I excused ourselves and took the private elevator back down to the main level.

"You and Ms. Raebeck were *very* close at one time," Vanessa said.

It wasn't a question so I didn't treat it as one. "Long ago and long over. Do you see that as a problem in my working for the Temkut Rancheria?"

She tilted her head to one side and gave me a wide-eyed innocent look. "That, fortunately, is for Hayes to work out, not me. And he seems to have already come to terms with it."

"Good. Let's have a look around and see what the Putah Creek Casino and Resort has to offer the gamblers of Northern California."

For a little more than an hour we moved from table to table, game to game. I was tempted a couple of times to place a bet, but didn't. Everyone has his or her own thing when it comes to casino gambling. Mine is to have an excited crowd, spirited betting, and a potpourri of happy noises. It's a combination that shuts out the real world and allows me to concentrate on the dream world of thirty straight passes at the craps table, hitting a progressive slot machine for a million bucks, or breaking the bank at 21 or baccarat.

None of this was going to happen on a Monday afternoon in this rather remote locale.

* * *

"Well, did you see anything suspicious?" Vanessa asked when we finally got back to the private elevator to Greer Raebeck's office.

"It's a casino," I said. "No better, no worse than any others I've been in. There's the expected array of state-of-the-art electronic slot and video poker machines. The tables offer blackjack, craps, pai gow, baccarat, and several kinds of poker. And the high rollers and whales get the VIP treatment."

"Whales?"

"Players who make extremely large wagers—a thousand, ten thousand, one-hundred thousand dollars per round."

"Whew!" Vanessa said. "It makes me blanche just to look at a dollar slot machine." She glanced out at the casino floor. "Do you think Twin Arrows' games are honest?"

"No reason to think otherwise." I took in the entire operation with a 360-degree sweep of my hand. "This is a very elaborate and expensive operation. I don't think Ms. Raebeck and Twin Arrows are going to risk a multi-million dollar investment and their operating rights by getting involved in card sharps and rigged machines."

"I suppose you're right."

"And my guess is that the Patwins also wouldn't want to lose their gaming rights by knowingly becoming involved in cheating the customers."

"But it seems to me it would be very tempting."

"Not really. Remember: the odds are always in favor of the house. It's usually the players who try to cheat."

"So you're telling me casinos are *never* dishonest?"

"Usually only with the government—state *and* federal taxes ... it's called skimming."

She gave a nervous laugh. "Tribal councils are considered governments, too, you know."

I pointed us in the direction of the nearest lounge. "So I understand, but they're supposed to be *partners* with the operators, not tax collectors. I would hope corporations like Twin Arrows appreciate the difference."

"Me, too. But there's still a lot of cash floating around these casinos."

"True. And sometimes casino operators aren't happy with the built-in favorable odds. They can manipulate the house advantage to the point where it can come pretty close to being dishonest."

"And you can determine all of that by just observing?" she asked.

"What do you mean?"

"You didn't play any of the machines or games, so how do you know they're honest?"

"Well, first, I have a long-standing rule not to risk my money—or in this case, Temkut money—on the tables in any casino I haven't had a chance to cruise through at least once. It's like any investment—look before you leap."

"Makes sense ... if you know what you're looking for."

"As for the machines? Who knows? Can't really tell anything about them unless you can take them apart and examine the innards."

She didn't say anything while the waitress took our order. Neither of us was all that hungry, so we settled on one quesadilla to share and two Diet Cokes.

When we were alone again, she said, "You were so quiet while we were making the rounds, I thought maybe you saw something that made you think everything wasn't on the up-and-up."

"No, that's just me, I suppose. Don't talk much when I'm working."

"Maybe you're part Indian."

I looked at her. She wasn't smiling.

"Do you think Twin Arrows is doing a good job for the Patwins?" she asked.

"They're not going to let me look at the books any more than they're going to let me look inside their machines," I said.

"But from what I can see, it's an impressive, first-class operation all the way."

"Would you say that if Ms. Raebeck wasn't involved?"

"Yes."

"And that's what you're going to tell Hayes?"

"Yes."

"So, are we going back to Appa Bay now?"

"Yes."

"And you're sure you're not part Indian?"

"Absolutely."

"Good, because your one-word answers were beginning to make me think otherwise again."

I laughed. "Guess I'm not much fun when I'm working."

"I'm not complaining, just curious." She watched as the waitress placed our order on the table. After taking a sip of Coke, she picked up a wedge of quesadilla and aimed one point at me. "The thing is, if the Temkuts are going to get involved in all of this, I want to know as much as I possibly can about gambling."

"Gaming," I said.

"What?" She took a bite of the quesadilla.

"It's called *gaming*. It's become the *gaming* industry because of all the bad connotations surrounding the word *gambling.*"

"Looks like gambling to me," she said. "You put down a dollar and you either get another one like it, or you lose it. That's gambling. Gaming is something kids do on computers and in arcades."

"Can't argue with your logic. But you'll probably get along a lot better with the Twin Arrows people and the State Gaming Commission if you don't use Temkut Rancheria and gambling in the same sentence."

"Oh, I know what to say, how to say it, and to whom to say it." She picked up another piece of our snack. "I just wanted to hear your thoughts on the subject."

I was about to ask if she could provide additional background on the apparent rivalry between the Patwins and Temkuts when I saw Greer coming toward us.

"Well, did we pass inspection?" she asked.

I gave her a worried look and indicated she should pull up a chair. "A few irregularities, but probably nothing that would close down the casino," I said.

Frown lines started to form before she realized I wasn't serious. "So what do you really think, Toby?"

I was surprised to hear her call me by that name again, and it caused Vanessa to give me a sharp, questioning look. I got the impression Greer was signaling me that there was something else she wanted to discuss, but not here and now.

I ignored Vanessa's reaction and said, "Very classy facility. Heavy Nevada overtones, but that's to be expected."

"And you, Ms. Jimenez, what did you think?"

"I hope our casino will be as impressive."

"Thank you. We try to keep improving the product as we move along."

I was expecting Greer to dismiss herself, but she didn't, so I asked if she would join us for a drink.

"I should be going," she said, "but ..." She looked around, caught the eye of our waitress, and ordered a Duff Gordon brandy. "Have one with me, Toby? For old times' sake?"

"No thanks." Maybe it was my imagination, but I got the impression the invitation didn't include Vanessa. "It's a long, twisty drive back to the coast." I turned to Vanessa: "Something else for you?"

"I think a trip to the ladies' room is all that I need right now," she said. "I also want to call The Pomo House and make certain everything is all right. So, if you'll excuse me?"

When Vanessa was out of sight, Greer said, "Smart woman, that one."

"I agree, but what makes *you* think so?"

"She sensed I wanted a few minutes alone with you."

"Sort of sensed that myself when you called me Toby."

"It's been a long time, hasn't it?"

"And apparently a lot has happened with you during that time."

"You didn't know about Twin Arrows?"

"Not until last evening. Moreno told me ... or accused me ... or challenged me."

"Sorry."

"Yeah, well, what can I say? It would appear Mrs. Alexandre and Quinn set you up quite nicely after Corbin was murdered."

"They were very generous," she said. "But the idea to get involved in the development and operation of Indian casinos was something I came up with on my own."

"Mike Rollins says you've had a few ups and downs."

"Do you know any gaming operation in Nevada that hasn't?"

"No, but I don't think that's what you wanted to talk to me about." I watched her sip her brandy, trying to remember how long it had been since we'd shared a drink. "Do you have to get back to Tahoe tonight, or are you going to be around for a few days?"

"That depends." She glanced round the room, then looked back at me. I assumed she was checking to see whether Vanessa was returning to the table.

"Why *are* you here, Toby?"

"Consulting."

"No, seriously."

"Seriously, Hayes Moreno hired me to come take a look at some things concerning the Temkuts' casino involvement."

"What kind of things?"

"I don't know ... he hasn't told me yet."

She shook her head. "I don't think you're being totally honest with me."

I held up my right hand. "I swear I'm telling you the truth, the whole truth, and nothing but the truth."

"Okay. But I don't mind telling you that we're very much concerned about what happened the other day in Appa Bay," she said. "That thing with the councilman, Benito Petrucci."

"Concerned enough to back out on your deal with the Temkuts?"

"No, not at all. But I do need to know what's going on over there in Appa Bay."

"Talk to Moreno."

She reached across and took my hand. "I've tried that, without much success. But now that you're involved, it would be very comforting to know that I could rely on you as a source."

"Sorry, Greer, I already have an Indian casino client—Hayes Moreno and the Temkut Rancheria."

"But–"

Vanessa was suddenly hovering over the table, her face a map of deep concern. "We have to go," she said. "Now!"

"Okay," I said, slipping my hand from beneath Greer's. "What's the problem?"

"Grady Nolan's been shot."

"Grady Nolan?"

"Another of our city councilmen."

CHAPTER 10

"Is Hayes there?" I asked as Vanessa and I walked toward the Putah Creek garage.

"Yes, he's the one who told me about Grady."

"Did he say what happened?"

She stopped inside the garage and put the fingertips of one hand up against a concrete pillar in order to steady herself. When I tried to take her arm, she gently shook me off. All I could do was wait until she was ready to talk again. In the meantime, I watched the tears flow down her cheeks.

"Okay," she said, turning back to me. She used a tissue to wipe away the moisture from her cheeks. "We can go on now."

I wondered what deep emotional attachment to the Appa Bay councilman had brought on the tears. I walked with her in silence, deliberately not asking any more questions. She no doubt would tell me anything she wanted me to know when she was ready.

She offered me the keys to the Miata again. As I was backing out of the garage, she lightly touched the back of my hand as I started to up shift into second gear and said, "On our way back, pretend this is your Porsche."

I have no idea what the record might be for driving from Putah Creek Casino to Appa Bay, but my guess was that we beat it by several minutes. Vanessa said nothing during the entire trip, nor did I.

We stopped first at The Pomo House, but there was no one there except the high school girl who filled in for Vanessa when she was away for a day or so.

I waited in the small reception area while Vanessa telephoned the tribal offices, the newspaper, police headquarters, and the hospital, trying to locate Hayes, or to learn more about the Grady Nolan shooting. She came up with nothing.

"I'll take a tour around town and see if I can spot Hayes, or his Explorer," I said. "I'll keep checking in with you, if you like."

"I think I'd rather go with you," she said. "Just sitting around here waiting to hear from Hayes ... or *anyone* ... is going to drive me bonkers."

This time we took the Cayman, but that certainly didn't do anything to help us find Hayes Moreno.

"Grady and his wife, Nettie, raised me," Vanessa said, looking straight out the windshield. "I was five when my real parents were drowned in a Russian River flood." She took in a deep breath and let it out slowly. "They both worked on the Nolan ranch."

"I'm sorry."

"Not your fault." She turned to look at me. "Nettie died just last year. Cancer. Now Grady's gone. Can't imagine why in hell anyone would want to shoot him ... or Benny Petrucci, for that matter."

"Wish I had some answers for you," I said. "But then, I've never been able to understand why anyone *ever* feels the need to shoot another person."

She nodded, and kept nodding ever so slightly as she looked out the passenger side of the car while I drove and retraced the handful of streets that made up the town of Appa Bay.

As we were about to pass the Wirok Café for maybe the third time, I angled into the curb and parked. "I don't know about you," I said, "but I'm getting hungry."

Vanessa turned to look at me; the slightest hint of a smile broke through her sadness. "We didn't get to eat much of that quesadilla, did we?"

"It didn't look all that good anyway."

We entered the small café and took the only available booth. Before we could get settled, Annalee Mackey slipped into the seat next to Vanessa and took her hand.

"I'm sorry, dear. I know how much Grady meant to you."

"Thank you, Annalee." She gave the café owner a kiss on the cheek. "It's really difficult to accept, you know?"

"I know, dear. Senseless. Damn senseless."

"Do you know what happened, I mean, exactly?" Vanessa said.

"All I know is that Grady got shot. Ain't been nobody in here that's known any more than that." She looked across at the empty counter stools. "Sort of thought you'd be the one they would have told first."

Vanessa shook here head. "I've been over to the Kotcha and Putah Creek casinos with Mr. Rolfe. When I called back to check on the inn, I got Hayes. He didn't tell me anything other than Grady was dead."

Annalee looked across at me and raised one eyebrow. "You're the fella from Nevada, right?" She tossed a look over one shoulder toward the front of the café. My glowing yellow Cayman, its front license plate once again evident, was in the same parking slot as before. "Salmon special," she added. "Saturday night." Without waiting for a response, she turned to Vanessa. "*He* stayin' at The Pomo House?"

Before Vanessa could answer, the front door swung open and Hayes Moreno came in. He walked straight to our booth and announced: "Saw the Porsche."

"How nice," I said. "Where in hell have you been, Moreno? We've been looking all over town for you."

"Been around ... here and there ... things to do." He sort of oozed himself onto the seat next to me.

"Tell us about Grady," Vanessa said. "You were very abrupt on the phone. What happened ... and when?"

"Sorry! I wasn't thinking when you called from Putah Creek. Should have known better, seeing how close you were to the Nolans." He reached across the table to take her hand, but she shied away and wouldn't let him touch her.

"Hayes, stop beating around the bush and tell us what you know, if anything," I said.

He glared at me and tried a nicer expression on Vanessa and Annalee. Neither of them was buying it.

"Okay," Hayes said. "What I've been told is that it happened early this morning. Grady was fishing off the old pier with his cousin Harley when someone shot him twice in the back. No more than six inches separated the two hits. Same as Bennie Petrucci."

Vanessa pulled in a sharp breath. "You didn't say anything about Harley being shot, too." I could see she was struggling to keep from crying again.

"He wasn't. Whoever did the shooting didn't fire one shot at Harley."

"The cousin see anything?" I said.

"Nope. Grady fell into Harley's lap and by the time he got around to taking a look, there was nothing to see."

"Small caliber again?" I asked.

"Nothing definite yet from the coroner, but he said it looked to be a two-twenty-three or two-forty-three."

"Probably fairly common calibers around here, I would think."

"Good guess. Anyone who does any hunting probably has a rifle of one or the other of those calibers."

"And they *all* hunt," Annalee said, making a face. "Some kinda man thing, I'm told." She scooted out of the booth and went to the cash register to take care of a customer who was waiting to pay.

Moreno shook his head, Vanessa smiled, and I cocked my head as I looked from one to the other.

"Annalee doesn't understand about Indians and hunting," Vanessa said.

"Didn't sound to me like she was referring to only Indians," I said.

"No, probably not. I over-react some times."

Annalee came back and looked down at us. "You folks gonna be orderin' anything? Otherwise, I need to get back to lookin' after the payin' customers."

"Turkeyburger will work for me," I said. "And iced tea."

"Crab salad and a diet Coke," Vanessa said.

"Just a glass of water for me," Moreno added.

Annalee snorted. "You know where the glasses and water tap are." She swung around and headed for the kitchen.

"Don't think she likes me too much," Hayes said and went after his glass of water.

It gave me a moment to think about the .223 or .243 rifle rounds that had been used to kill the two Appa Bay city councilmen. If the small caliber ammo and rifles that fired it were fairly common, it was going to be damn difficult, if not impossible, for the police to find the murder weapon.

"Most hunting rifles are bolt action, right?" I said to Hayes when he returned with his water. He nodded. "But you said the entry wounds were relatively close together," I added.

"True, and I know what you're thinking ... almost impossible with a bolt-action. There are a few semi-automatics around, though." He nodded to himself. "If I thought on it a while, I know I could place a few Ruger carbines, almost as many Remingtons, and maybe even a Colt or two."

"And the cops know this, too?"

"Don't know why not. And if they don't, the information's not too difficult to come by."

"Or maybe it's not someone local," Vanessa said, "which seems more likely to me."

"Why?" I asked.

"Because the Nolan and Petrucci families have been in these parts for a long, long time."

"So?"

"Well, there may have been some heated arguments here and there over the years, but I never heard of any disputes hot enough or long enough to provoke a murder."

"Two murders," Hayes said.

"You know what I mean," she snipped.

Hayes sipped at his water and stared off at something in between the café's front door and a place so far away no one else could see it. He nodded ever so slightly as if satisfied with some answer he'd found, then pivoted so he could see both Vanessa and me.

"I'm curious: did you learn anything worth knowing at Putah Creek?"

"The Temkuts are still pretty much out of favor over there, and one in particular," Vanessa said with a wry smile.

"That'll probably *never* change," he said.

"And we ran into Greer Raebeck," I added, before he could ask.

Moreno gave me a twisted grin. "I wish I could have been there for *that*."

"Forget it, ghost man," I said. "Unless you know something I don't, I seriously doubt that she or the Twin Arrows organization had anything to do with killing your two councilmen."

"Now why doesn't that surprise me?"

"That they're not the source of the problem?" I said.

"No, that you would come to that conclusion, considering your history with the lovely Ms. Raebeck."

"Hayes, stop it!" Vanessa said. "That kind of talk isn't going to get us anywhere." She started to say something else, then saw Annalee headed our way.

"Think you'll be wantin' anything more?" the café owner asked after serving Vanessa and me our food.

"That's it," Hayes, the big spender, said without waiting for us to respond.

"Oh?" She tapped his water glass with one finger. "Sure you don't want to be overdoin' it, Mr. Moreno."

"If there's something you know about Twin Arrows that you haven't told me, Hayes, this would be an excellent time to start sharing," I said.

"You know everything I know."

"Wish I could believe that ... I really do."

He swallowed the last of his water and got up from the booth. "I got to get back to the office, make some more calls, write a story, and get on with what I was doing before all this happened."

I reached out and grabbed his wrist. "Sit down, Hayes. I need you in one place for more than a few minutes. And just what *were* you doing before today's shooting?"

He tried to pull away, but didn't force the issue. "I really do need to file a story," he said.

"Your deadline at the *Sentinel* isn't until Wednesday," Vanessa said. "It's not going to take you *that* long to write your story."

He sat on the edge of the booth seat. "I'm talking about the *Chronicle*," he said. "For tomorrow morning's paper."

I looked at my watch. "You still have plenty of time to make the home edition, good buddy, so just sit back while Vanessa and I finish our food. I'll even treat you to another glass of water."

He picked up his glass, tipped it, looked down at the few drops in the bottom, and then sat it back down on the table. He looked out the front window of the café again, sighed, and said:

"What do you know about a Washington-based lobbyist outfit called Lurton-Bales and Associates?"

"Not a thing. Should I?"

"Not necessarily, I suppose, but it would be damned helpful if you did." He tried without success to shake the last traces of water out of the glass. "The thing is, the rancheria has a meeting Thursday to sign a contract with them to help get the casino up and running."

"Isn't it a little late to be doing a background check?"

"I pushed for a month's delay in signing anything with them," he said, "but too many tribal members are champin' at the bit to make this thing a reality, like right now."

He shook his head slowly from side to side several times before continuing: "I don't know what happened to that fine old Indian tradition of considering things for a long, long time before acting."

Another head shake.

"Anyway," he continued, "Lurton-Bales came in, put on an over-the-top dog-and-pony show, and said they could almost guarantee a casino for Appa Bay before the year was out. That's all it took. Several of the tribe biggies pushed for an immediate vote."

"What did Twin Arrows have to say when they learned you're about to hook up with these big DC flacks?"

"They were none too happy." He picked up an unused fork and took the last bite of Vanessa's salad. She glared at him and tossed her own fork down on the table.

"And all this happened when, before or after the first councilman was shot?" I asked.

"Just before, at the last tribal council meeting."

Watching them, I realized that if I didn't start eating I was going to lose out on my only substantial meal of the day.

"The thing is," Hayes said, "Lurton-Bales claim they have another tribe talking to them about a casino in these parts. Sort of a squeeze play ... and Frank Ross, the council president, doesn't want to be called out at home base. Most everyone else agrees with him. Except me."

"And no repercussions from Greer Raebeck?"

"Not yet, unless ..."

"The murders?"

He shrugged. "I think that's why I brought you here. Besides, you've seen her more recently than I have."

"She didn't mention Lurton-Bales to either of us." Vanessa nodded her agreement. I took a large bite out of the turkeyburger, chewed, and pointed a finger at Moreno. "I'm going to tell you one last time, Hayes—I'm not in the business of solving murders."

"I got that, Zach. But you know the gaming industry ... and a lot of people involved in it."

"Let me guess: you want me to dig up the identity of the other casino that the hot-shot Washington lobbyist firm of Lurton-Bales is using as a carrot to get the Temkuts to go along with them."

"Exactly!" He picked up Vanessa's water glass and drained it. "Now, I'm out of here. Places to go ... things to do."

"Then let's all get out of here," I said.

"You're not invited."

"From now on, buster, where you go, I go."

Vanessa was already halfway out of the booth. "And that goes for me, too," she said.

Moreno grabbed the untouched half of my turkeyburger, took a big bite out of it, kept his grip on it, and stomped off toward the door.

I tossed enough money on the counter to cover our food, plus a generous tip. I hadn't planned to put this meal on my expense account, but with half my food going out the door with Moreno, he sure as hell was going to get the bill.

CHAPTER 11

Northern California—1851

Adán Moreno's gelding stepped into a hidden gopher hole at full gallop, twisted around, and crashed to the ground with such force that the rider was thrown another 10 to 15 feet away from the animal. By the time the dazed vaquero got to his feet and brushed himself off, the calves he'd been chasing were out of sight behind a hill. The rest of the cattle herd continued to move lazily northwest in the direction of the stream, prodded along by Moreno's cattle herding companion, the Pomo Eli-yah.

Moreno limped back to his fallen horse, which was still down and writhing in pain. He saw the animal's right foreleg was shattered, a jagged and bloody portion of the cannon bone protruding through the skin.

The day had started poorly. He had heard things in the barn when he was saddling his horse, things he was not supposed to hear. The words of El Patrón and his friends at first made him uneasy, then fearful. He was thinking about those words when his horse stumbled and went down. If he had been paying more attention to where he was going...

Moreno knew that this cow pony was not going to get up again. He also knew that he would suffer a severe beating by El Patrón, if not something worse. Only one moon ago a Wirok at another rancho had been hung up by the wrists and whipped almost to death for allowing a wolf to carry away a newborn calf. Now, Moreno had lost one of his master's horses. It would not matter that it was an accident.

Moreno studied the wounded horse and wished he had a rifle to put the animal out of its misery. But rancho owners did not allow their Indian captives to carry anything more deadly than a knife, and then only while working.

Just as Moreno slipped his blade from its deerskin sheath and bent down beside the horse's head, the other rider came up rapidly and stopped on the other side of the fallen horse.

"What has happened?" Eli-yah demanded.

"The horse put his foot in a gopher hole, I think."

"The leg is very bad, no?"

Moreno used his knife to point at the bloody fracture. The Pomo nodded his understanding of the problem and of what needed to be done.

"You will tell El Patrón that I had no part in this, Adán," Eli-yah said.

Moreno was not surprised that Eli-yah would think of himself first. The Wirok and Pomo had never liked one another and although they had suffered similar bad treatment by the Russians, Spaniards, Mexicans, and now Americanos, they were no closer spiritually than they had been before the white man arrived.

"I will tell El Patrón nothing," Moreno said. With one swift motion he sliced through the horse's jugular.

Eli-yah dismounted and glared at Moreno across the body of the dying cow pony. "How will you explain that you have returned without El Patrón's horse?"

Moreno wiped his knife clean on the grass, stood, and faced the Pomo. "I will not return."

"They will come after you," Eli-yah said.

"Yes." Moreno slipped the knife into its sheath.

"They will beat you."

"No! I cannot allow that to happen. I will fight them."

"They will kill you."

"I am already dead," Moreno said. He made a sweep of his hand across the horizon. "My people were once free to roam this land, day or night, season to season."

"No more," said Eli-yah. "The white men say it is their land."

"Who gave them this land that once belonged to everyone? Who gave them the right to make us their slaves?"

"They have guns," Eli-yah said, as if Moreno were a child. "They have the law."

"Their law. Where is Wirok law? Miwok law? Pomo law?"

"The padres say new treaties are being signed with the white men from Washington," Eli-yah said. "We will have our own lands again."

"Do you know where we can find this place they call Washington?" Moreno demanded. "Have you seen one of these treaties?"

"No."

"If they showed you a treaty in the language of the Americanos, could you read it?"

"No."

"Yes! That is the truth, Eli-yah. The padres tell us many things, but they speak the language of the Spaniards and Mexicanos. They do not use our language; they do not use the language of the Americanos. How will we know what is in these treaties?"

Eli-yah hung his head and murmured, "We must trust the padres."

Moreno grunted. "There is no white man we can trust. That is our history. That will not change for us until we change it."

"I do not like the way you talk," Eli-yah said, mounting his horse. "I will take the cattle to the corral."

"What will you tell El Patrón when he asks, 'Where is Moreno?'"

Eli-yah looked toward the herd. "I will tell him I do not know."

"Those are not words he will want to hear."

Eli-yah nodded sadly.

"Tell him about the horse. Tell him I ran away. That should protect you."

"You do not mind if I tell him those things?"

"Go, Eli-yah. Be safe!"

When the Pomo was gone, Moreno checked once more to make certain the horse was dead. Then he started walking toward the Wirok village by the lake.

Moreno's mother, wife, and two children still lived in a small house he built for his family before he was taken captive by El Patrón and forced to work on the white man's ranch. He knew *that when his son was old enough, El Patrón would come and take him also to work on the rancho. And if his daughter was attractive in the eyes of the white men, she would be taken also to service them in bed.*

* * *

"Will the white men come for you?" Loretta Moreno asked her husband.

"I think so." He bit into the leg of a squirrel that his wife had roasted over an open fire.

"And you will go with them?"

"No."

"I do not understand."

"If they come, they will kill me. It is what they do." He threw the leg bone into the fire.

"When will they come, Adán?"

"Soon. With the next sun, I think."

"Many men?"

"Not many. El Patrón will bring only one other white man with him, maybe two. I am not thought to be a man who causes trouble.

"I am afraid."

"I know," he said. *"But it is time to stop being a slave to every new tribe of white man who comes onto our lands."*

"They are strong," she said.

"We must be stronger." He pulled his knife from its sheath and began sharpening the steel blade on a flat stone.

"Is that your work knife?" Loretta said.

"Yes."

"You have never brought it home before."

"It is not allowed."

"You will use it to fight El Patrón?"

"Yes."

"Your knife is not as strong as their guns."

"I will first use as many arrows as I can, then use the knife for as long as I am able to stand."

Loretta Moreno picked up the stone knife she used to skin the squirrel, stood, and straightened her body. "I will fight at your side."

Moreno reached out and took his wife's hand. He gently pulled her back down to the ground next him. "No, you will take my mother and our son and daughter and hide on the far side of the lake. You must do this early, before the sun starts to steal away the night."

Loretta Moreno stood, looked down at her husband, and said with great sadness in her voice, "I will not see you again after this night." She turned away, walked slowly to the doorway of their small house, and went inside.

Moreno looked down and continued to sharpen his knife.

* * *

Throughout the night the men of the village came to Moreno as he waited for El Patrón and his men to arrive. They came singly and in pairs, carrying whatever weapons they possessed, from stone knives to sharpened pikes. Moreno tried to send them back to their homes, to their families; he did not want others to die because of his pride and stubbornness.

But the Wiroks, whether mere boys or old men barely able to move, would not listen to he pleas.

"Too many of The People have died for no reason at the hands of the white man," said the husband of Moreno's sister.

"It is true," Moreno said. "But I am the one who killed the horse of El Patrón. None of you should die for that."

"I am told the horse fell and its leg was broken," said another man.

"No matter. The horse is dead. El Patrón will not care why."

"We care," said the husband of Moreno's sister. "We will fight to protect you from him. We will fight so you and your children can enjoy the land the white men in Washington will give us in the treaties."

"We will get no land," Moreno said.

"The Indian Agent said the treaties will give us land to call our own," said Roberto Warner.

"There is no land," Moreno said.

"You put your mark on the treaty paper in front of the Indian Agent," said Warner. "We were told the head men from many other tribes did the same."

"Yes. They did that."

"Then why do you say we will get no land?"

"Because the white men who look for gold in the hills do not want any land given to The People," Moreno said. "I heard El Patrón and his friends say that this morning at the rancho. Those men laughed. 'No land for those dirty, stupid Injuns,' they said."

"But we will have the treaties," Warner said.

"The white men who make laws in Washington will not approve the treaties," Moreno said. "The white men at the rancho said the treaties have been put on a shelf."

"What shelf?" asked another.

"A place where no one will look for them," Moreno said.

"That is not right," said Warner.

"I have not told you everything," Moreno said. "The Californios are offering gold to Indian hunters for every one of us they kill."

"The Indian Agents will not allow this," said Warner.

"The agents do what they are told to do."

There was a long silence. The men shifted around, looked at one another.

"We must fight for our land," said the husband of Moreno's sister.

"What land?" Moreno said. "The white men take it all for themselves."

"Someday our children or our children's children will find a way to take back from the white man what is rightfully ours," said Warner.

"Perhaps," said Moreno. "At this time we can only fight for our lives and the lives of our families."

Just after the full roundness of the sun could be seen on the eastern horizon, El Patrón and two other white men rode into the *village on horseback; each carried a long gun. They began firing into the Wirok homes.*

When not one Wirok came out, El Patrón shouted, "We are here for Adán Moreno." He waited a short time, then he and his men started firing into the houses again. Again there was no response. "If Adán Moreno does not surrender himself, we will level the–"

An arrow lodged in El Patrón's throat, two more struck him in the chest. He slid from his saddle and fell heavily to the ground. A second rider took two arrows in the side. When he tried to turn his horse, a well-thrown lance knocked him from his saddle. Loud Wirok cries scared the third man's horse, which rose up and threw its rider. Moreno and the men of the village came from their hiding places and swarmed over the fallen man, their weapons raised and threatening.

Moreno went to El Patrón and stood over him. The man, close to death, looked up and glared at Moreno.

"You should not have beaten us," Moreno said softly. "You should not have made us your slaves. You should not have come to take the land of The People."

Late the next day, a detachment of Army regulars led by a Capt. William P. Lennox entered the area to round up and punish the Wiroks for the killings. Unable to find anyone in the village, they leveled the huts and set fire to them. On their way back to the fort, the frustrated troopers massacred every Indian group they encountered, most of whom were Pomos.

CHAPTER 12

Vanessa rode with Hayes and I followed in the Porsche. It was a short trip—before I could shift out of second gear, Hayes had me in the driveway of a small one-story stucco and redwood building. A non-illuminated sign in front said: *Appa Bay Urgent Care Center. 10:00 AM—6:00 PM. After Hours Call: (707)555-9911.*

"Morgue!" Hayes announced as he cut across a freshly mown lawn toward the back of the building.

I caught up with Vanessa at the double-door entrance and we followed our leader down a short hallway to another pair of swinging doors.

On the other side was a small morgue. A guy in scrubs, whom I took to be the coroner, was looking at a corpse lying face down on a stainless steel drain table; a sheet covered the body from the waist down. A man standing opposite the examiner, scowled at Hayes, then at us.

The room was so small Vanessa and I were stopped halfway through the double-wide entry, the doors resting against our butts. She squeezed past me and gasped when she saw the lifeless body, two small entry wounds visible between the shoulder blades. She started to wilt. I clamped my hands on her upper arms and held her in place.

"Don't think you should be here, Ms. Vanessa," the coroner-type man said.

"Is that Grady?" she whispered.

He gave her a sad, sympathetic nod.

She turned to look at me. "He's right ... I don't want to see this." She slowly backed out of the room, turned, and headed back the way we'd come.

During the moment it took me to decide whether or not to follow her, the third man in the room leveled a pudgy forefinger at me. "Who the hell are you?"

"It's okay, Chief," Hayes said. "This is Zach Rolfe ... he's working with me ... and the rancheria."

"Big deal!" He looked me up and down. "Probably another one of those Nevada fast-talkers the casino people keep trying to stuff down our throats."

Before Hayes could reply, the chief waved a dismissive hand at me and gave Hayes a sharp nod. "Get him the hell out of here. This is an official investigation, for crissakes!"

Hayes started to say something, but I intervened. "It's okay. I've seen more than my share of dead bodies."

I found Vanessa outside, sitting sideways in the Porsche, her legs sticking out the open passenger door. Her forehead rested in her palms; her body shook with soft sobs.

I stood there, not sure what to do, what to offer. After a long moment, she looked up at me, sniffed, and wiped away the tears with a curled forefinger on each hand.

"I kept telling myself that they'd made a mistake, that it hadn't been Grady who'd been shot," she said. "Then there he was ... on that table. I couldn't see his face, but I knew ... I knew it was him."

"Can I get you something? Take you somewhere?"

She nodded. "Home."

I waited until she pulled her legs inside the car, then shut the door, went around to the driver's side, and slowly drove us back to The Pomo House.

* * *

Vanessa thanked me and disappeared into her living quarters at the inn. I considered going back over to the morgue, but decided there wasn't much to be accomplished in that part of town, at least not with the negative attitude the chief of police seemed to have for all things connected with Nevada. Instead, I opted to do a little research from my room.

It was too late to be making phone calls, so I pulled out the laptop and mini-printer. Because of the remote location I was afraid I might have to use a slow, long distance dial-up connection to hook into the Internet. Fortunately the Pomo House had DSL service. After a couple of minutes of searching around for the directions to link up to the B&B's network, I was able to set about trying to find whatever I could about Lurton-Bales & Associates.

I was surprised by the amount of posted material, very little of which shed a positive light on the D.C.-based lobbyist.

The fly in the ointment was a guy named Felix Crandal, who moved into Lurton-Bales a few years back with a couple of lucrative Indian tribe accounts, finessed the founding partners into becoming little more than fronts for their own company, and then restructured the firm into his personal lobbying/political consulting fiefdom.

Currently, as so often happens with petty tyrants, it appeared he'd unwittingly positioned himself to be hoisted on his own petard in the not too distant future.

One report claimed Crandal, through Lurton-Bales, collected an outrageous $35 million in fees from various casino-operating Indian tribes that sought his help to stay in business. None of this had occurred in California ... yet.

While Crandal was successful more often than not in his influence peddling efforts, there were those who claimed greed won a no-contest battle over ethics before the bell ever sounded for the first round.

One particularly incensed tribe claimed it didn't know that just before Crandal hit them up for a $3.8 million retainer, he'd been actively working on behalf of rival tribes in the same region to shut down their casino. The earlier campaign put about $2.9 million into the Lurton-Bales coffer.

The exploitive Mr. Crandal essentially made wikiups full of money by sticking it to a tribe, then made even greater piles of wampum by promising to undo the damage caused by "unknown parties."

I realized that reports about greedy Washington lobbyists may be the Capital's equivalent of the dog-bites-man story, but Crandal appeared to have taken the tale to a new level of avarice and duplicity.

What I needed to know was whether this guy Crandal was just another Washington super-sharpie, or a very dangerous person. More to the point, was he someone who was willing to have a couple of city councilmen kept permanently from seeking re-election when serious money hung in the balance? And that wasn't the kind of information I expected to find on the Internet.

The next morning, before breakfast, I was back on the phone to Mike Rollins at the Nevada Gaming Control Board.

"If your Temkuts are thinking of bringing Crandal into their camp, they're either very rich or very stupid," Rollins said.

"That bad, huh?"

"Lurton-Bales, or rather, Felix-Crandal–with-one-L, is on our permanent black list. No way is he allowed to have a business relationship with any casino in Nevada other than being a customer, and even that's frowned upon."

"Care to tell me what brought this about?" I got comfortable so I could type the more important parts of conversation into the laptop.

"Couple of years back, your Mr. Crandal put together a sort of anti-gambling coalition up at Lake Tahoe."

"Tahoe? I never heard anything about that."

"We squashed it pretty fast," Rollins said. "Don't think it got any press mention outside the immediate area."

"Never thought the Californians would get that uppity about gaming on the South Shore ... too many of them have gaming-dependent businesses."

"Yeah, well, this was the North Shore ... and no Californians involved," Rollins said. "Strictly a Nevada operation."

"That must have been a first ... and probably a last."

"Well, I'm fudgin' a bit. It was more a coalition to control the growth of gaming in the area, not one to actually end it."

"Why even that?" I asked. "The North Shore's never been able to turn itself into a major gaming attraction."

"Well, rumor has it that one of the major hotel chains had plans to go into the North Shore, build a huge resort multiplex— skiing in the winter, lake activities and wilderness outings in the summer."

"And gaming."

"Of course. And gaming."

"So who didn't like it?"

"Some of the South Shore marginal casinos. Guess they figured that a mega-resort operation on the North Shore, along with the drain from the California Indian casinos, would do them in."

"So they hired Crandal."

"They hired Lurton-Bales, but it was Crandal who showed up to create and run the `Keep Tahoe Beautiful' campaign."

"And you shut him down?"

"We found the evidence. State's attorney general put a stop to the petition-signing operation before they'd collected a single signature," Rollins said.

"What happened to the casinos?"

"Fined them each one hundred thousand dollars for their stealth lobbying efforts."

"But you banned Crandal for life?"

"If I'd had my way, I'd have thrown his ass in jail and erased his name from the prison system database."

"Now you've got me *really* curious," I said.

"My suggestion would be that if you see Felix Crandal anywhere near your clients, shoot first and make sure you won't have to answer any questions afterward."

"That's a tad harsh, isn't it?"

"That son-of-a-bitch kidnapped the wives of a couple of casino owners who didn't want to help finance the coalition."

I heard Rollins take a deep breath before he continued.

"He had them locked up on an old schooner out in Crystal Bay. There was a late spring three-day freeze and one of the women died. He threatened to kill the other one if she told, but she was so angry she told anyway."

"So why isn't Crandal in jail?"

"The woman couldn't identify him or the two men who did the actual kidnapping," Rollins said. "We knew it was Crandal ... we just couldn't prove it."

"Thanks, Mike. You've convinced me. I seem to have a big, nasty problem on my hands."

"Is Lurton-Bales already on the scene?"

"They're sort of in and out of here. All I know is that a couple of weeks ago the Temkut Council decided to hold a vote on giving them a contract for lobbying and P-R."

"Shit! You've got your work cut out for you."

* * *

When I finally made it out to the dining room for breakfast the next morning, the high school girl who worked part-time at The Pomo House served me. When I asked about Vanessa, the only answer I got was a shrug.

I dawdled over my coffee, hoping Vanessa or Hayes might show up. No one came in except a young couple that appeared to be honeymooning; they certainly had no eyes for me.

Back in my room, I looked into my e-mails, then packed away the laptop and went outside to check the garage at the back of the property. Vanessa's Miata was inside, but there was no sign of Hayes's Ford Explorer.

I decided that if the information wouldn't come to me, I'd go to the information. Within a short time I'd traveled ten-plus miles and was parked outside the *Wirok County Gazette*. It was time to play my old newsman card.

CHAPTER 13

I'd called the *Gazette* from Appa Bay. The editor, Mark Trimble, had been abrupt and monosyllabic—typical newsman phone etiquette: act like you're too busy to be bothered, yet hang in there long enough to make certain you don't lose out on a good story.

I sort of sucker-punched him right at the beginning by telling him I was Zach II's son. My old man spent all of his working life as an itinerant reporter, and a damn good one at that. He'd worked for newspapers throughout Nevada and California—weeklies and dailies, big ones and small ones, good ones and bad ones. A lot of the older working editors and reporters in the Southwest either had known him or were aware of his admirable, if sometimes inflated, reputation. I took a chance that this might be the case with Trimble; and it was.

"Worked with your old man for a spell some years back," Trimble told me over the phone. "At the old *Sacramento Union.*"

"We only lived there about a year," I said.

"Sounds about right."

"He'd let me take the local sports results by phone at night and feed him the info for round-up stories."

"Hah! I remember doing that, too. What a pain in the ass."

"I was a kid … thought it was something special."

"Ever do anything more with that?"

"Sports?"

"No, not that. Newspaperin'?"

I gave him a quick bio—"J" School at the University of New Mexico, newspapers, and the AP.

No problem after that. He told me he would see me if I drove over to the county seat, but declined to give me any information over the telephone. I timed my arrival in San Tomas to be at the newspaper's offices about the time I assumed Trimble would have put the next day's edition to bed.

He was putting on a fresh pot of coffee when I arrived.

"Got time to go for a drink?" I asked.

There was a slight hesitation before he said, "Nope, but thanks. We can talk here."

I got the impression that turning down a drink was a relatively new thing for him. I didn't press the invitation. And the coffee turned out to be pretty good, for newsroom coffee, that is.

"It's not only a damn shame that South Shore casino owner's wife got killed, it was pointless," Trimble said. He ran a hand through the thinning, kinky gray-blond hair that covered most of his scalp.

"Aren't most killings pointless?" I asked.

"Suppose." He blew into his coffee cup, took a sip, and winced as the hot liquid hit his lips.

It was nice sitting in a newspaper city room once again, even one as small as this one. Every now and then I missed the news business and wondered where my life would have gone if I'd stuck with journalism and not joined the Nevada Gaming Control Board as an investigator. Ah, the old unanswerable paths-not-taken question.

"Anything in particular that made the South Shore killing more pointless than any other murder?" I asked.

"Didn't say it was *more* pointless. It's just that those guys pushing the anti-mega-resort petition didn't have much of a grasp on human nature."

"How so?"

"Know as well as I do, Rolfe, people are always going to gamble, one way or the other. Like in that movie, 'Build it and they will come.'"

"That was baseball," I said.

"Same difference."

"A lot of people think there are already too many casinos ... that the competition is going to turn the gaming industry into a knock-down, drag-out, survival-of-the-fittest battle. A free-for-all."

"Maybe," Trimble said and let his eyes search the ceiling. "Don't think that's right around the corner, though, do you?"

I laughed. "I've been involved in the Nevada gaming scene for a long time, Mark, and I'd say you've got things pretty well pegged. But what makes *you* think casino gaming hasn't reached the saturation point?"

He cocked his head to look at me, took a deep breath, let the air out slowly, and returned his gaze to the ceiling.

I stole the moment to look around the uncharacteristically quiet newsroom. The next day's edition was history, as I'd projected. The staff was gone and scattered—chasing down new stories, lolling in nearby bars, picking up children and/or spouses, maybe even heading home.

I mentally reconstructed the room as it might have been earlier in the day, a nostalgic attempt to slip myself back into the familiar atmosphere of an active city room—desk phones ringing; cell phones snapping open and shut; editors and reporters talking, shouting; monitors stalled on unfinished stories or resource web sites; contacts refusing to talk, or talking too much.

"Got a story in tomorrow's edition," Trimble said, interrupting my comfortable reverie. "Know what it says, Rolfe?" He didn't wait for an answer. "Says Nevada casinos pocketed record profits again last year. A record! Does that sound like the Indians are making them hurt over there? Or that the big California casino-resort complexes are going to run everybody else out of business?" He lowered his chin to his chest and looked over his half-rims at me. "Don't think so."

"And you're right." I gave a quick glance at a fractal screensaver gyrating next to me, blinked, and added, "Not only that, I'll bet the figures your story quotes are only for gaming revenue. If you add in the corporate take from gaming-related hotels, bars, and restaurants, the bottom line is going to be even more outstanding."

"Guess things have truly changed since the days when the crime syndicates ran everything."

"Oh, yeah! The Nevada casinos are pretty much like any other public company today—quarterly results and stockholder reaction are first and foremost. They're no longer remote desert locations set up to launder money from illegal mob activity back East."

"No wonder I can't get a cheap room or meal over there anymore," Trimble grumped.

"You got it. But believe me, Mark, the corporate types who run the casinos today are just as hard case in their own way as their mob counterparts were before them. Some say there are still middle-of-the-night burials out in the desert, although I have my doubts about that."

"Glad I'm here and you're there," he said.

"Yeah, well, right now I'm here, too. At least for the short term."

Trimble's phone rang. He held up a hand to forestall my saying anything further, draped a headset across his sparse curls, spun around 180 degrees, and poised his fingers above a computer keyboard. He said nothing after "hello," grunted a few times, and typed faster with two index fingers than most people type with all ten digits.

"Got it!" he said and returned the headset to a hook on his desk. "Sorry 'bout that. Our Sacramento stringer picked up a couple of political rumors he wanted to pass along, but didn't want them sitting in someone's e-mail inbox until tomorrow."

"No problem." I was about to pick up where I'd left off when a twenty-something gal rushed into the newsroom, grabbed something from a desk drawer, and was out the door again without giving us a single glance.

"God, what I wouldn't give to have that kind of energy again," Trimble said. "Anyway, you were saying?"

"I was just going to comment on the growing number of Nevada gaming interests that have sizeable stakes in the Indian casinos, not only here in California, but elsewhere across the U.S."

"And why not?" He stood, picked up his coffee cup, pointed to mine, and when I shook my head, headed across the room to pour himself another cup. I watched him wend his way between the half-dozen desks that cluttered the cramped newsroom.

"They're the ones who know the business, right?" he called from the door of the coffee room before backtracking to his desk.

"Hell, I'd be willing to bet that if I started a three-card monte game on the corner outside this building, I could keep it going indefinitely ... even if one of the tribes opened a full-blown casino right across the street."

"They might want a cut," I said with a laugh.

He slouched down into his chair. "Yeah, and then some sharpie from Nevada would probably try to muscle in on my action."

"And your cut would get smaller and smaller."

"But that wouldn't discourage the players from coming to my table, would it?" He stared into his cup and shook his head. "Never a shortage of suckers ready to gamble away the grocery money."

I nodded my agreement. "Cutting up the pie into smaller and smaller pieces could lead to some serious problems."

"Seems to me it's more a matter of expanding the bakery." He thought about that for a moment, nodded to himself, and added, "But maybe that's not what you came to see me about."

Trimble snagged a nearby chair with the toe of his shoe and rolled it close so he could prop both feet on the seat cushion.

"No, you're definitely on target," I said.

"Since you came all the way from Appa Bay, we must be talking about the whopping big casino the Temkuts want to build on that prime oceanfront property they own," Trimble said.

I nodded and started to prop my feet up on the closest paper-cluttered desk, then glanced at Trimble, who shrugged a go-ahead. We were now old newspaper buddies.

"Surprised you didn't get your information from Ed Harkins at the *Appa Bay Sentinel*," Trimble said. "Ed's a good man, pretty much on top of everything that happens over that way."

"Too close to home base," I said. "I haven't been there long enough to get a handle on who's beholden to whom."

Trimble barked out a laugh. "Ed's an old-fashioned newsman, Rolfe. Doubt he's ever been *beholdin'* to anyone."

"Under the circumstances, that's good to know."

"Something like that's *always* good to know." He tipped his cup to sip the last of the coffee and dribbled several drops on his shirt front. "Damn! My wife's going to get all over my case again." He wiped at the stains, to no avail.

"Anyway," he continued, "considering Ed's a few years older than me, good chance he also knew your Dad."

I looked around the room, saw we were still alone, and took my feet off the desktop, careful to avoid a computer monitor framed in pink Post-it notes. "Tell me this, Mark: have you heard anything about a D.C. political consulting outfit called Lurton-Bales & Associates?"

"You mean Felix Crandal—Crandal 'with one L'?"

"So he's been in touch." I said.

"Not really ... I just try to keep up with the scuttlebutt out of Washington." He tipped his empty coffee cup, stared into it, shook his head, and let the chipped cup settle back on his desk.

"Locally," he continued, "I only know that the Temkuts are supposedly thinking about hiring a lobbying outfit." He dropped his feet back onto the floor also, tried once again to wipe the coffee stains from his shirt, and released a small burp. "Caffeine! Supposed to stay away from it. Can't."

"Hayes Moreno just told me that the Temkut Council has already agreed to call a tribal vote on signing up with Lurton-Bales."

"Shit! When the hell did that happen, and why didn't someone let us know?"

"The way it sounded to me, the Temkuts made their decision at the last council meeting, what, a couple of weeks ago? Don't you have someone over in Appa Bay?"

"Yeah, Harkins. But I haven't heard boo from him about this, or from anyone else." He picked up a copy pencil and scribbled something into a spiral steno pad. Probably a reminder to follow up on Lurton-Bales—it's what I would have done in his place. "Hell of a way to run a newspaper."

Trimble tossed the pencil aside and flipped through his over-stuffed *IN* box. "Let's see what those scoundrels are up to."

I was tempted to offer to make the search for him—my first newspaper job was to sort through the daily accumulation of press releases, handouts, and meeting notices and give the city editor the ones I thought might be pertinent. What power!

When Trimble finished going through the stack of paper, he shrugged and tossed everything back into the basket. "Those types usually generate a flood of puff pieces and fancy computer-generated presentations. Doesn't seem to be anything here from Lurton-Bales." He pushed the basket back to its corner. "Will be, though. Count on it. Truckloads of the shit."

"And probably damn little of it of any value to you."

He nodded his agreement, burped again, and pulled a bottle of Tums out of his desk drawer. "Sorry the Temkuts are doing this; wished they'd kept it all local."

"My sources tell me these Lurton-Bales people are not high up on the scruples ladder," I said.

"You suggesting they might be behind those councilmen killings in Appa Bay?"

"That's for the police to determine. I'm just looking into the nuts and bolts of the rancheria's casino proposal."

"You a P-I?"

"Gaming consultant."

"Uh-huh! Same thing, isn't it?"

"Mostly."

"And you're working with Hayes Moreno?"

"Guess you could say that. He *is* the one who asked me to come over here."

He gave me a wry grin. "Think the word *enigma* was invented for guys like him."

"That wasn't always the case." I told Trimble what I knew about Hayes when he was at the *Las Vegas Sun.*

"Heard he'd worked on a big daily once. Didn't know it was the *Sun.*" Trimble scratched his head, took another quick look at the drying coffee stains. "What the hell's he doing over here working for a country weekly, even if it is a pretty good one?"

"Told me it was so he could devote more time to helping his people, the Temkuts."

"He's certainly been doing that."

"Is that a criticism?"

"Don't think so." Trimble again penciled something into his notepad. "Temkuts, what there are of them, weren't much more than a ragtag lot a few years back. The Feds had scratched them from the official Native American rolls. No longer recognized as an official tribe. Then Moreno started showing up, calling meetings, getting the Temkuts organized."

"And now they're an official tribe once more and have managed to get the wherewithal to build a casino," I said.

"That's about the size of it."

"Do you think Moreno may have some kind of hidden agenda?"

Trimble thought about that for a long moment. "Suppose it's possible. Sure isn't always forthcoming with explanations." He grunted a laugh. "Sort of like what the movies led us to believe Indians were like in olden days."

"Don't think they made many movies about the coastal Indians," I said.

"Seen one Native American, seen 'em all."

I refused to react. His eyes held on me, probing, testing. Then I saw just the vaguest hint of a smile.

"Damn good section on the California coastal Indians over at the library, if you're interested," he said.

"Good!" I didn't tell him I'd already made one pass at the library. "I think I'll go over there now and do some serious research."

"Need directions?"

"Nope!"

"Didn't think so."

We shook hands and I started for the door, but before I got there, he said:

"Pick up anything interesting about those Lurton-Bales people, I wouldn't mind hearing about it."

I acknowledged his request with a wave of my hand and went out the door. He really wasn't expecting to hear anything from me, which would make it that much more satisfying if I could feed him an exclusive, or at least give him a day's jump on the major metro dailies.

* * *

After two hours in the library reading about the Coastanoans—a name the early missionaries ascribed to all the coastal tribes— and going through back issues of the *Wirok County* Gazette, I was angry. Not at Hayes Moreno, or anyone specific for that matter, but at man's continuing inhumanity to his fellow man.

It was the same old story—arrival of Europeans in a new land did absolutely nothing to enhance the lives of the indigenous inhabitants, who for the most part had been living a bountiful and peaceful life for thousands of years.

On the west coast of North America, the explorers and missionaries found small tribes of people who neither wanted nor needed walls, people who "trod lightly on the land, left no footprints, and always apologized to the spirits of the animals and to nature" when they disturbed either in any way.

The local Wiroks, and most other coastal tribes, had no pottery, made no fabric, planted no seeds, and kept no domestic animals. They were gatherers, fishermen, hunters, and basket makers.

When they were "discovered," the Wiroks shared what they had with the newcomers and quietly giggled at the unusual ways of these men who hid their bodies under strange, cumbersome coverings.

In return, the Wirok were given deadly diseases, cheated, enslaved, run off their lands, hunted and killed by the military, slaughtered by government-sponsored bounty hunters, forcibly converted to Christianity, dispersed, virtually abandoned, and now, perhaps worst of all, subjected to the machinations of Washington lobbyists.

I couldn't do anything about what had happened to the Wirok over the past two or three hundred years, but I might be able to do something to prevent this latest attempt to screw them over.

But before I could do that, I wanted to talk to Felix Crandal, or someone from the notorious Lurton-Bales outfit, and try to get some answers one way or the other as to what these high-flying lobbyists had planned for the Temkuts. And that would be without regard to whether or not it coincided with Hayes Moreno's secret master plan.

CHAPTER 14

Northern California – 1865

Esteban Moreno, jogging along the rim of a foothills wash, smelled smoke, stopped, and in one fluid motion dropped to his knees to stretch out prone on the cold, hard ground.

He snaked himself forward through the underbrush, using only his elbows, until he was well hidden in a dense copse of cottonwood trees.

Voices drifted up from the wash, now dry in the late autumn. Moreno wiggled through the trees until he saw the source of the smoke—a small campfire, where a trio of what appeared to be gold miners were sprawled around an iron pot, eating from tin plates.

Moreno knew he would either have to wait until the miners fell asleep to continue on, or backtrack to find another route and possibly lose a full night's travel.

He would not, could not go back—his brother had been hiding out with the Yahi for more than a year, sought by the white men for his frequent acts of rebellion. The most recent involved rustling a half-dozen sheep from one of the rancheros.

Now, Moreno was attempting to take advantage of an opportunity to end the exile, perhaps forever. He needed to find his brother within the next day or so and return him to the coast before the next full moon.

He carefully scanned the area to see if he could possibly sneak past the miners. A cloud-splotched waxing moon offered little light, making him wary of the terrain above the cottonwoods, and on the other side of the wash. Both appeared to be too steep for him to quickly —and quietly—circle around the camp and continue his trek eastward.

He knew that if the miners found him, they would kill him.

He had departed from his village four days earlier, traveling only at night to avoid being spotted by Indian-hunters looking to collect a $5 per head bounty from the state, or the *lowly 25 cents many white communities paid for "Heathen Injun" scalps.*

He accepted his situation and watched while the men finished their meal. He hoped that after eating they would immediately go to bed so he could continue his journey. But after the food was gone, the miners began drinking from a jug. Whisky.

More waiting.

By the time the last miner fell asleep, or passed out in a drunken stupor, the moon was gone from the sky, leaving only a dim glow from the still burning campfire.

He waited until the miners' fire was reduced to a few smoldering embers before leaving the protective cover of the trees. He moved toward the bottom of the wash, then stopped after a short distance, sensing that he wasn't the only living creature in the vicinity of the miners' camp. He flattened his body against the ground and listened.

Soon, from up the wash, three Yahi slipped into the camp. They split up and made short work of going through the miners' supplies and gear. Moreno watched the trio pack up all of the food, collect a rifle and a couple of loose knives, then leave the same way they'd come, disappearing into the now moonless night.

Moreno was about to follow the Yahi when one of the miners got up to relieve himself. Unable to navigate on legs made rubbery by the whisky, the man toppled over onto his companions, spaying urine all over them and himself. Shouts and curses were followed by rolling, tumbling bodies and flailing fists.

"I'll kill you, you sumbitch!" one of the miners shouted.

"Piss on me, willya? Where's my gun? Where's my goddam pistol?" yelled another voice.

"Go fer yer gun and I'll slit you from gonads to gizzard."

The melee ended as the men started crawling around the camp looking for their weapons. Moreno scooted backward until he was once again hidden among the cottonwood trees.

"Food's gone!" one of the miners growled, waving a heavy pistol the Yahis had missed.

"Redskins!" declared another. "Miserable damn savages come in here and cleaned us out while we was sleepin'."

Someone threw wood on the fire. When there was enough firelight, all three gave the camp a thorough searching. They uncovered one rifle and another pistol.

"Shee-it!" said one. "We gonna have to go back to Sacr'menta and get more supplies."

"Come sun-up, I'm goin' after them godless dirty filthy savages that done this to us." The other two men grunted in agreement.

Moreno watched the frustrated miners beat at the nearby underbrush and study the ground in the dim light.

"I ain't waitin','" one of them shouted.

To Moreno's surprise, the man started down the wash, going in the opposite direction the night raiders had taken. The other two miners followed him.

Once the white men were out of sight around a bend, Moreno hurried past the campground and took off running up the wash, going where he'd seen the Yahi disappear into the darkness.

He saw that the miners, like most white men, had little or no tracking skills – the Yahi had made no attempt to cover their tracks, and signs of their rushed departure were everywhere. He was able to follow their trail at an easy trot.

The sun was now up, making Moreno uncomfortable to be traveling in daylight. But he needed to make up the time lost at the miners' camp. Fortunately, he had to stop only rarely to double check a disturbed bush or a scuff mark in the soil.

The route climbed and took him across several rivulets, a large stream, and deeper into the foothills. Then, after crossing a small meadow, he lost the trail. He backtracked twice, each time reaffirming his conclusion that the Yahi raiders had entered and crossed the meadow, only to disappear into a dense forest.

As he searched for new signs of the Yahi, it occurred to him that losing their trail might be a good rather than a bad thing— he was probably in their home territory. He stopped looking, found a fallen tree, and sat down. If he were right, he had come as far as he needed to come— the Yahi would eventually come to him.

When the sun was about as high in the sky as it would go this time of year, Moreno heard the Yahi coming, slowly, almost in total silence. He did not move. In a blink he was surrounded by Yahi.

"Why have you come to our land?" asked a lean young man, aiming an arrow at Moreno's chest.

Moreno slowly arose from the fallen tree and signed for the Yahi to repeat his words. The Wirok and Yahi spoke much the same language, but dialects were quite different, as were many descriptive words. He listened with great care as the young Yahi repeated himself.

"I seek my brother, Adán Moreno, a Wirok, who has lived with you for many moons."

The Yahi said nothing, did not react nor lower the arrow. An older man stepped forward and spoke quietly to his companion, who finally lowered his arrow and pointed it at the ground.

"What is your name?" asked the second Yahi.

"Esteban Moreno."

The older Yahi motioned with one hand, a member of the group turned and disappeared at a run back into the forest. "We wait here," he said.

Moreno sat back down on the fallen tree, but the wait was not long. The runner returned, exchanged a few words with the older Yahi, who told the whole group they were leaving.

"Come!" said the younger Yahi, pointing only his bow at Moreno. The threatening arrow had already been returned to its deerskin quiver.

Moreno accompanied the Yahi a short distance into the woods, where they came upon a small encampment. There, standing among a group of women and children, was his brother.

The two men raised their right hands in greeting, then embraced.

"What news do you bring?" asked Adán Moreno.

"The white ranchers have invited all The People to a peace-making feast at the next full moon," said the younger Moreno.

"Do you trust them?"

"I am told this is happening in other places, with other bands of The People."

Adán thought for a moment, then asked: "Have you talked with any of The People who have attended these peace-making feasts?"

"No, brother, but the white men say they want the bloodshed between them and The People to end."

"I, too, have wanted that for many moons. But I am a fugitive. The white man's laws have forced me to live with the Yahi."

"The white men talk of something called an 'amnesty,'" Esteban said. "They say all of The People who have broken their laws will be forgiven if they come to the peace-making feast."

"Do you believe them, Esteban?"

"I want to believe them, brother. I want to stop hiding from bounty hunters. I want to stop seeing our people starve and die because they are not allowed to fish or hunt or make fire without permission."

"Maybe the white men have decided they too no longer want those things for The People," said Adán.

"You will come back with me?"

"Yes. Even if things do not change, we will get to eat a filling meal."

* * *

Adán and Esteban Moreno, tired and dirty after their long journey, paused at the end of the dusty trail and gazed out across a huge pastureland-turned-campground.

Everywhere they looked were gatherings of The People— twos and threes, small family groups, and even what appeared to be entire villages.

Adán slowly raised an arm and made a sweeping gesture across the full breadth of the horizon, taking in the rolling, tree-

splotched hills that created a backdrop for all those who had come for the peace-making feast.

"I did not think so many of The People would come here this day," Adán said. He shook his head and sighed. "I know this land. Once we caught the antelope here, snared the rabbit, and found eggs of the birds to feed our families."

He turned to his brother. "This should be our land; the land of our children and our children's children."

"That time is gone, brother. It is not to be."

"We are the only ones not dressed in the white man's clothes," Adán said sadly. "Our time is no longer."

When they checked in, they were directed to a large roped-off area. It was reserved for tribal leaders, ranch owners, town dignitaries, and military officers. They were told the gathering would last at least a week.

The Morenos entered the designated area, but stayed close to the perimeter and closely observed the preparations that had been made, and were in the making, for the so-called peace-making feast.

Several beef and lamb carcasses were being barbequed over open pits, filling the air with the pungent aroma of roasting meat. Close by a large barn, huge tables created from rough-hewn logs were laden with seafood, vegetables, fruits, and sweets.

They watched with pleasure as tribes of The People chanted and performed ritual dances in colorful, full costume. But the playing of loud, war-like marches by uniformed white bands was disturbing, as were demonstrations of roping and branding by wildly yelling cowboys.

The People continued to arrive for the feast from every direction, most all of them traveling by foot since very few could afford to buy or keep a horse or mule.

"It is strange that the white men allow us to walk among them and be this close to their women," Adán remarked at one point.

"Perhaps it is a sign they really want to live in harmony with us and the land and the animals," Esteban said.

* * *

Late on the second day of the festive event, a small band of Rumsen arrived, having traveled for several days from far south of San Francisco. Esteban noted that they avoided offers of food and drink and came directly to him and his brother.

"We have come to warn you," said the headman of the Rumsen. "This is not a safe place for you and your people."

"What makes you come here to tell us this thing?" Adán asked. "You live many days from here."

"True," said the Rumsen. "But we come because for many years the Rumsen have traveled here to take your young women as wives, and the Wirok have gone south to take our young women to bear your children."

"That is true," said Adán. "Our bloods are mingled, which is good for all."

"That is why we come to tell you about another peace-making feast, one that in truth was an ambush, a lie the white men used to kill many of The People who had done them no harm."

"You saw this?" Esteban asked.

"No. My sister's son was invited to attend the feast when he went to trade with the Modoc, many days north of here. The white men poisoned the food and the Modoc became suspicious of the smell and taste. When the Modoc refused to eat, the white men took their guns and killed all but five. My sister's son was one of the few who escaped."

"We have been eating this food for two days," Adán said. "None of The People have become ill."

"That is good. We come only to tell you what we know," said the Rumsen.

Adán Moreno nodded solemnly. "I am glad your sister's son is safe."

The Rumsen, without eating any of the food at the lavish feast, quietly left the area, one by one. When they were gone, Esteban led his brother to a secluded area.

"I am worried, brother, that I may have been wrong about the true reason for this peace-making feast. I fear The People may be in danger."

"Is it what the Rumsen told us, or are there other reasons that make you fearful?"

"I have been watching the soldiers," Esteban said.

"They have done nothing that I have seen," Adán replied.

"Watch them," said Esteban. "Every time one of The People leaves the feast to go into the woods, a soldier follows."

"Do they not both return?"

"I am not sure. I only saw this after the Rumsen told us their story."

"We will both watch," said Adán.

Several times the Morenos saw Wirok leave the feasting area, probably to relieve themselves in the woods. Each time a soldier left his post and followed. After a few minutes, the soldier would return, but not the Wirok.

"I must find out for myself," said Adán.

"I will go with you," said Esteban.

"No, you must stay here. If I do not come back, you must warn as many of The People as you can."

Esteban started to object, but was silenced by a stern look. "This is not going to be a good day," he said.

As Adán started toward the woods, Esteban saw a soldier come out of the barn and follow his brother, keeping a fair distance between them.

* * *

Adán knew the soldier was behind him. He walked toward the river, picking up speed in small increments. The soldier did the same.

When Adán reached the river, he pretended he was going to squat behind a tree. When he heard the soldier approach, he jumped up and dove into the water. He stayed under as long as he could, swimming down stream. When he came up, he looked back and saw the soldier at the bank, a bayonet protruding from the end of his rifle. Just then, Esteban jumped out from behind a tree and struck the soldier in the head with a large rock.

"I told you to stay at the table," Adán called as he waded toward the river bank.

"I was afraid the soldier would kill you."

"I am not too old to defend myself," Adán said, moving toward the shore. *"This is a very dangerous game we are playing, brother. Are you sure no one saw you leave the feast?"*

"I took much care." He helped Adán climb up the river bank.

"We must warn the others."

"It may be too late," Esteban said. *"Many soldiers were coming out of the barn when I left. Most of the ranchers and men from the town were also holding rifles and pistols at their sides."*

Before the Morenos reached the open area of the feast, shots rang out, first only a scattered few, then with increasing rapidity.

They crawled to the edge of the woods and watched with great sadness as The People were massacred, individually and in terrified groups. Only a very small number escaped the slaughter and disappeared into the trees.

CHAPTER 15

"What I want," I told Hayes Moreno, "is the name of the go-to person for Lurton-Bales, the person the Temkuts are dealing with on a day-to-day basis."

"Why?" Moreno asked.

We were sitting at one of the knotty pine tables in the dining alcove of The Pomo House, sipping coffee while Vanessa fixed breakfast for us. Outside the picture window, the early morning sun was filtering through the oak and bay laurel trees.

"Why? Because I want to talk to him, or her. That's why."

"Well, originally we were told it would be Josh Bales."

"And you believed that?"

He gave me a puzzled look.

"Thing is," I continued, "it's been my experience that only *really* big money clients get hands-on attention from the principals of the Lurton-Bales of this world."

"And your point is?"

"My point, Hayes, is that I don't think you've told me everything there is to tell."

He thought about that for a moment. "Yeah, well, we almost fell for it … the Josh Bales lure. Then I did some digging: Bales is figurehead … trust fund baby whose daddy bought him a partnership in a going concern. His job's apparently to go out and use his good looks to charm the stupid Indians … do a little name-dropping to impress them."

"And I'd be correct in assuming that the daddy involved is former U.S. Senator Julian Bales?"

"You got it, man."

"And you don't like the son because of his background, or because he doesn't know what he's doing?"

"Both," Hayes said.

"Maybe you haven't given him a chance."

"She-e-e-it, Zach! A man's got to show up more than once for you to decide if you're gonna give him a chance, let alone like him."

"But you said Bales was the local contact."

"*Supposed* to be the local contact. We haven't seen hide nor hair of him since that first visit."

"What about Felix Crandal?"

"Who's Felix Crandal?"

"Hayes, I'm getting a little confused here."

"You're confused? How the fuck do you think I feel?"

"You did tell me that the Rancheria was ready to sign with Lurton-Bales, right."

"Yep. Argued my head off against it. Tried to get the council to hold off and take a second look, what with Petrucci and Nolan getting shot ... killed."

"Speaking of that, police come up with anything yet?"

"If they have, they sure haven't shared it with the press, or anyone else that I know of."

"So, if not Crandal or Bales, who *was* here representing Lurton-Bales in the negotiations?"

Vanessa came in with a tray of French toast, fresh fruit, and a pile of bacon. She put the food in the middle of the round table, poured us more coffee, and took a seat so we were sort of facing one another.

"Now that's what I call a sumptuous breakfast," I said. Hayes said nothing as he scooped food onto his plate, poured syrup on his French toast, and started eating.

"The person you need to talk to," Vanessa said, "is a very snotty know-it-all with an unpleasant Texas drawl, one Terence Wadkins."

Hayes looked up and glared at her.

"He one of your guests?" I asked, uncertain just how many other people were staying at The Pomo House. I'd seen a few cars around, but no one else had showed up for any of the meals when I was present. But then, I hadn't been keeping any kind of a regular schedule. I pulled a rasher of bacon onto my plate, forked a piece of French toast, and topped it with strawberries and blueberries. I filled the tines of my fork with a combination of everything and stuffed it into my mouth. Delicious!

"Mr. Wadkins did stop by when he first came to Appa Bay," Vanessa said. "He gave The Pomo House a cursory glance, called the accommodations 'quaint and said he would find a place to stay over in San Tomas, or perhaps Putah Creek." She squinched her nose and took a large sip of water, as if washing out a bad taste.

"Better off without a guy like that," I said.

"The whole tribe would be better off without him, or *anyone* from Lurton-Bales," Hayes said, looking from his empty plate to the center platter.

"You've had enough!" Vanessa said. She pushed the platter in my direction.

"Well, I think I need to go have a chat with Mr. Wadkins," I said. "What's he like?"

"An asshole," Hayes said.

"The world is full of them, so I'll need something a little more descriptive than that."

"He was sort of in and out of here," Vanessa said. "Best I can do is tell you he was about six-one or so, had a deep tan and gel-styled red hair."

"That'll work."

"And, Zach?"

"Yeah?"

"He looked like he could handle himself, physically I mean." She pushed the rest of the bacon onto my plate. "Wouldn't surprise me if he had a portable Bowflex in the back of the black Caddie Escalade he was driving."

"No steer horns on the hood?"

She laughed, but there was a deep furrow between her eyes. "Let me make a couple of calls," she said. "Maybe I can track him down."

"No need," Hayes said. "He called in to the tribal office and gave them a contact number in case they need to talk to him. He's at Putah Creek Resort. Suite 801."

"Wanna go with me?" I asked Hayes.

"Told you, I'm not welcome over there."

I looked at Vanessa, who gave me a negative shake of her head. "Have to pull some stuff together so my accountant can do the quarterly tax returns." She got up and started clearing the table. "I also have some guests checking in late this afternoon."

"Okay. I'll go have a little fun on my own."

"Say hello to Greer Raebeck for me," Hayes said, giving me a smirky grin. Then he looked at Vanessa and winked.

* * *

This time when I stepped into the Putah Creek Casino and Resort no one intercepted me. I used a house phone to call Greer, but was told she was in a meeting. Left a message. Then I tried Terence Wadkins' suite, and struck out again. Didn't leave a message.

I went down into the casino and changed a couple of twenties for singles since I wasn't keen on having to cash in chits if I didn't have to.

The casino was much busier than when Vanessa and I had visited, perhaps because it was hump day and people were getting a head start on the weekend. The larger crowd provided me with good cover, although I didn't really think I needed one. Greer Raebeck had sort of put her stamp of approval on me.

I made the requisite tour through the electronic slot machines, burning up dollar bills almost as fast as I could pull them out of my pocket.

During my stint with the Nevada Gaming Control Board, I'd come across numerous slot machine operators who thought payouts were supposed to be anything from occasional to exceedingly rare occurrences. Whoever was in charge of the Putah Creek slots had made payouts an endangered species.

While I dallied with the slots, I also watched the table action. The players' expressions told me they weren't doing any better than I was.

On the other side of the tables, however, I didn't expect to find any indication as to how the play was going. Dealers, pit bosses, and other casino floor people are trained to remain as expressionless as possible—win, lose, or draw.

Ah, but not so on this shift. Something was upsetting the status quo. It didn't take me long to isolate the 21 table that was apparently causing the ripple of concern among the house people. I watched in fascination as the standard veneer of impassivity rapidly peeled away. The pit boss's eyes narrowed and there was an ever-so-slight tightening of the lips.

I played the last "credit" on my dollar machine and started to leave when the machine's electronics made a fake coin-dropping sound. I'd hit three plums for a pay of 14 credits—a big $14 return on a mere $40 investment. I reluctantly played off the payout, pushed the button to give me a credit chit, and took off toward the cluster of 21 tables.

As best I could determine, I was the only player who'd noticed a change in the body language of the house people. What seemed to have their attention was a $50-minimum-bet table.

This early in the day, I was surprised to find all six player positions occupied at a high-stakes game.

I watched the play for a few minutes, but didn't see anything out of the ordinary on either side of the table. What did give me pause was the third base player—he was a perfect match for the description Vanessa had given me for Terence Wadkins.

Now I really wanted to know what was happening at that table to make the staff get all antsy. I suddenly had a very strong need to play a few hands of 21—at that particular table. Only a couple of problems: I was low on cash, and there was no open seat.

A quick trip to the cashier solved the first problem but the transaction cost me an exorbitant house "handling" fee to tap into my bank account for a thousand bucks.

Not long after I returned to the table, one of the players got up and left, his face flushed with anger. I quickly slid onto his stool at first base, a slot I try to avoid when gambling on my own ... better to see what cards the other players are getting before having to make my own decision. But when running an investigation, it's an excellent spot to watch all the action, from first to last card dealt, how the winners are paid, and the chip collection style of the dealer.

I bought ten $50 red chips, which made a dinky stack by comparison with the stacks in front of the other players. Mr. Wadkins-Look-Alike was doing *very* well—a tumbling mountain of chips rested in front of him, in a variety of colors. Not knowing what the Putah Creek's chip color scheme was, it was impossible to guess where he stood cashwise. The red chips alone must have added up to at least a couple thousand dollars, and there were half again that many black, light blue, and gold chips.

The casino was using a single deck, something that isn't seen much these days. Today, most casinos throughout the world use a "shoe" containing from two to four decks, which makes it much more difficult for card-counters to have an edge.

The Putah Creek dealer uncharacteristically gave each player and himself the first card up, followed by a down card to everyone but himself. Only after the players were satisfied with their cards, or had gone bust, did the dealer give himself a second card.

It's a much more house-oriented system than most casinos use. Problem is, if you double down and hit 21, you lose twice as much if the dealer declares a blackjack at the end instead of at the beginning.

The trick to protecting your investment is to remember not to double down if the dealer has a ten-counter showing.

This dealer, who had a six showing, gave me a pat hand of 19 on my first deal. The next player took a hit and went bust on 22. The following player, like me, stood pat. Two more broken hands and the dealer confronted the big winner at third base.

He wasn't a typical player—he'd peeked at his hole card only once and hadn't touched it or his up card—a ten—since. He dipped his chin slightly to call for a hit, nodded his satisfaction with the four he received, and waited calmly for the dealer to take a second card.

The dealer drew a 10, took another hit, and came up with a four-spot for a total of 20.

There were loud groans from the other players, and from a few people who had stopped to watch the action. I quickly checked the facial expressions of Mr. Third Base, the dealer, and the pit boss. Everyone seemed perfectly satisfied.

The 20, of course, wiped me out and gave player number three a draw. The third base player slowly used his four-of-clubs to flip over his hole card, a seven of spades.

A very nicely played 21.

The dealer glanced nervously at the pit boss, who nodded ever so slightly, then matched the one gold chip resting in front of third base.

By then I'd managed to identify the Putah Creek chip colors, at least at the $50-table – $50, red; $100, black; $500, light blue, and, gold for $1,000, the maximum bet for the table. I guestimated the potential Terence Wadkins had somewhere between $15,000 and $20,000 in chips, showing. Who knew what he might already have pocketed?

If some sleight of hand or non-kosher event had taken place, I sure didn't see it. My intuition said there was a good chance I might be going blind.

I doubled my bet, like any sucker hoping to get even, hunched over the table, and waited for my new cards. I kept my head down, but not so low that I couldn't keep a close watch on every move by every player, and the dealer.

I caught what was happening three rounds later.

That wonderful aphorism about the hand being quicker than the eye is a lot of bullshit. As any magician could tell you, it's all a matter of timing and distraction. Both were being demonstrated by experts at this 21 table.

I watched with grudging appreciation as this player-dealer team of card mechanics repeatedly took both the casino's and players' money, including mine.

Numero Uno of the duo was the bubble-peeking deuce dealer. Without pattern, he would use the slightest possible pressure to ascertain the value of the deck's top card. He then dealt only seconds, while keeping the top card either for himself, or to break one of the players.

Numero Dos was the Maybe-Wadkins at third base, and at the cash receiving end of the dealer's manipulations. A basic flaw in what they were doing, whether they realized it or not, was that they were getting greedy—there simply were not enough big spenders at the table to support their action.

As a result, the winnings of Mr. Third Base were upsetting the table's win/loss percentage. And while this was making the pit boss edgy, he stayed out of it. It seemed the cheating dealer had the complete confidence of the house.

Apparently no one else was seeing what I was seeing. Not even the eye-in-the-sky behind the overhead skylight. Everyone was concentrating on the action at third base, where the player was ever so nonchalant, at times giving the impression he'd much rather be someplace else.

Under different circumstances, I might have said something. But about the last thing I wanted right now was to call attention to myself. Also going against me was the fact that the dealer was an expert at one of the most difficult scams to spot— there's no physical evidence.

When it came time for the dealer to take his mandatory break, I was certain Mr. Third Base would play a couple more hands as a cover, then fade into the crowd.

Wrong again.

I watched as he used his seemingly unconcerned style of play as a diversion to his performance as one of the most adept hand mockers I've ever seen—he palmed and substituted cards in no set pattern and managed to give himself a substantial winning edge.

It was amazing because he had to be aware that his winnings, without question, made him the focus of house surveillance.

Hayes Moreno and the Temkuts might be covering my legitimate expenses, but certainly not my stupidity. I stopped doubling up after another losing hand.

The finale to this high-wire act came when the original dealer returned. Mr. Third Base played two more hands, won the first, lost the second. He asked for a chip rack, collected his stash, and slipped off the stool. He generously toked the dealer with two $100 chips before departing.

A class act all the way.

I played one more hand, lost, and got up to tail the big winner. A quick count told me I'd dropped about $500, which Mr. Third Base now had in his chip caddy.

I headed first for the cashier's cage, assuming my quarry would be cashing in his chips. But there was no sign of him. I altered course for the main entrance, which took me past the bank of hotel elevators. He wasn't there, either.

Looking back into the casino, I saw him in the middle of an aisle of rainbow-flashing electronic slots, playing a quarter poker machine. The caddy of chips from the 21 table rested loosely in the crook of his left arm.

I couldn't resist. I walked down the aisle, bumped him slightly, excused myself, and continued on past him. He didn't even look up.

Moving on down the aisle, I looked back over my shoulder to keep him in sight. He stayed with his machine.

I cashed in my chit and chips and bought some quarters in case I had to cozy up to a slot machine in order to cover my surveillance.

As I was leaving the cage, Mr. Third Base suddenly appeared, stood in line to get cash in for his winnings. He moved with the crowd, looking neither left nor right.

Nice! Now I was stuck with a $10 roll of quarters bumping off my thigh while I tailed this guy to find out whether or not he was Terence Wadkins.

I lingered near the cashier, watched the exchange of chips for cash, and silently counted 29 $1,000 packets of Ben Franklins, plus another stack of loose green.

His take appeared to be just a little shy of $30,000.

"Zach?" a female voice called out as I was about to follow Mr. Third Base.

I looked around to see Greer Raebeck headed my way, dressed in the sexiest business suit I'd ever seen: the lapels of a black pinstripe jacket were cut back severely to reveal a transparent scoop-neck blouse that hung loosely over a lace camisole; the pants, with just a hint of bellbottoms, had ankle-to-hip slits on both sides.

I gave her an exaggerated head-to-toe appraisal when she was only a few paces away.

"That must have been a *very* interesting meeting you were in," I said.

"Talent booking," she said. "Never want the agents to think the talent is more of a draw than the games and the people who run them."

"I'm sure you made the point elegantly."

"Why, thank you, Zach." She slipped an arm through mine and guided me in the direction of a casino café. "I did get the message that you'd called." She glanced at her watch. "I'm starving, but maybe you've already had lunch?"

"Nope."

"Then how about a late, late lunch? My treat."

"I accept your generous offer."

There was a long line waiting to be served, but Greer steered us past everyone, and with a smile and a nod to the hostess, continued on to an isolated booth. A discreet gold tent card in the middle of the table said *Reserved*.

"Are you here alone?" she asked.

"Not now."

Another smile. "I mean, did Ms. Jimenez come over with you again?"

"No, this is strictly business."

She questioned me with a tilt of her head, but said nothing and motioned for the waiter.

"There's a house special I think you'll enjoy," she said.

"Order away." After the waiter was gone, I said, "I'm trying to locate a guy by the name of Terence Wadkins. I was told he's staying here."

"Terry? I think that was him leaving the cashier's cage when I spotted you."

"Thought so. I need to talk to him, or someone from the Lurton-Bales den of lobbyists."

"Sounds serious."

"Possibly."

She toyed with her salad fork for a moment, looked around the room, and said: "You won't like him."

"Oh?"

"He's a slick, fast-talking con man. And a bully."

"Interesting. Did you know he also cheats at 21?"

"Yes, unfortunately. But I'm sort of caught between a rock and a hard place where Lurton-Bales is concerned."

"You mean Twin Arrows is linked to them in some way?"

She closed her eyes and chewed at her lower lip. After a moment, she said: "Zach, I'd trust you with my life … again … but this isn't something I can share."

"Are you sure?"

"Yes. Very sure."

"Okay, then tell me about all that wonderful talent you were interviewing."

At least I got her to laugh, and then we did the chit-chat thing until we were served a colorful platter of what she enthusiastically declared to be authentic tapas.

In between describing each of the two-bite-size Spanish appetizers, she told me about the trials and tribulations of interviewing talent for the smaller entertainment rooms of the casino.

"You should hear some of them; they either can't stay in tune, or think a couple dozen four-letter words in a row are funny."

"Are they all that bad?"

"No, not really. We get some very talented people—from agents, through recommendations, and those who cinch up their belts and make a cold call."

"And today, how did that go?"

She wiped a smear of sardine from one corner of her mouth and nodded enthusiastically. "Quite well, actually. A trio of folksingers from LA who actually knew how to harmonize, and a very talented jazz pianist from the Bay Area."

Then her face turned somber and she looked past me, suddenly into thoughts she wasn't ready to share. I prodded.

"Is Lurton-Bales muddying the waters in some way?"

"I'm not in a position to answer that, Toby."

That ended the small talk; in fact all talking. When we were finished eating, I reached over and gently placed a hand atop one of hers. "I'm available to help."

"I know." She took in a deep breath, let it out slowly. She turned her hand over and interlaced our fingers. "Do you think that if we'd worked at it a little harder we might—"

"Do you really want to go there?"

She put her executive face back on, and we left the restaurant.

"Do you want me to see if I can locate Terry?"

"No, I'll take care of it."

She gave me a quick peck on the cheek and was gone. I watched her hips sway provocatively as she walked away across the thick, multi-colored carpet, and I wondered if maybe we *should* have gone there.

But I needed to find Mr. Wadkins, who once again didn't answer his room phone.

As I started another tour of the casino floor, I spotted Wadkins at a different 21 table. It was only when I got closer that I noticed the table wasn't in play.

He turned, slid off his stool, and walked straight up to me.

"Outside, Mr. Rolfe," he said. He stepped around me and walked rapidly toward the front entrance.

I certainly wanted to talk to him, but I just as certainly didn't like being told what to do. And how was it he knew my name?

If I wanted to ask him some pertinent questions, then I needed to be where he was. So I followed him, having to trot to keep up. At the entrance, he slowed, waited for me, and then suddenly stepped around behind me. When I turned to face him, he narrowed his eyes and with a quick jerk of his head indicated I should keep moving.

As I stepped through the doorway, a black Cadillac Escalade pulled up and stopped, blocking my path. The back door of the huge SUV swung open.

"Get in!" Wadkins ordered.

I could see the second row of seats had been folded flat, but the black interior and darkly tinted window glass kept me from seeing if anyone was in the back of the overblown vehicle. I took a step back instead of forward.

"Not a good move," he said, the flat of one hand suddenly in the middle of my back. His other hand slid smoothly up under my arm pit and into my inside jacket pocket to relieve me of my cell phone.

"But I promised to call Mom," I said.

"You're a smart ass."

His palm was suddenly replaced by a hard, smaller, rod-like object that I wasn't about to argue with.

"Get in!"

I hesitated, obviously a moment too long. Next thing I was nose-plowing the thick, rough carpet of the Caddie, my arms and legs flying in four different directions.

By the time I got all my limbs under control again, the door had slammed shut behind me and I was staring into a pair of trim black-stockinged ankles.

CHAPTER 16

"You really didn't have to go to all this trouble just to have an after-lunch date," I told Greer Raebeck as I scooted around to sit cross-legged in front of her. The SUV's interior lights softly accented her features. I rubbed my skinned nose and stretched my neck.

"Wadkins does get a little carried away sometimes."

"Yeah! You should speak to him about that."

"Sorry. I didn't want anyone seeing us leave the casino together." She patted the seat beside her; I got off the floorboards to accept her invitation.

"We've already been seen together; we have a history of being seen together."

"Don't be flip," she said.

"Flip? I don't think so. I've been over here twice in the past three days, and each time we've talked openly. Why the sudden need to play hide-the-PI?"

Greer turned her head, looked out the tinted window. "I was thinking back to when we first met … *ancient* history."

"There is that, but right now I'd like some kind of explanation as to what's going on between you and Terence Wadkins."

"You mean romantically?"

"No, damn it, not *romantically*. Although you did seem comfortable calling him *Terry*."

"And that upsets you, Toby?"

"Stop tiptoeing around the question, Greer. Why is it that one minute Wadkins is Mr. Nasty-ass, and the next minute he's helping you set up this CIA-like snatch?"

"What do you know about Lurton-Bales, and Felix Crandal in particular?"

"I've done some homework," I hedged.

"Where? Mike Rollins at the Nevada Gaming Control Board? Mark Trimble at the *Wirok County Gazette*? A few casino owners? The major daily newspapers? The Internet?"

I nodded. "All of the above."

"Then all you've done is collect a few minor facts and read a lot of supposition. But you haven't even scratched the surface."

"What more do I need to know other than Crandal's a hard-nosed, winner-take-all lobbyist out to make some big bucks by dabbling in the Indian gaming industry?"

She sank back into the soft leather car seat, pulled her feet up off the floor and curled them under her. "He's ruthless, Toby," she whispered.

"And Terence Wadkins works for Crandal, right?"

"Yes and no. Terry works for Twin Arrows Investments, but Crandal thinks he works for him, for Lurton-Bales."

"Are we talking industrial espionage?"

"No, we're talking about protecting one's ass and assets."

"So Wadkins' cheating at your 21 tables is all part of a scam, a sort of show-but-don't-tell game, is that it?"

She sucked in her lower lip. "As I said before, Terry goes a little overboard sometimes. He and his dealer friend may think the money they've taken off the tables is theirs, but when the time's right, they're going to get a rude awakening. Till then, I let him do his thing, let him think he's getting away with it."

"I could take him down a notch or two if you'd like."

"Maybe later." Greer said. "Right now I need to find a way to keep Crandal from luring so many Indian tribes into the gaming business that it bankrupts all of them, and Twin Arrows right along with them."

"Does that include Hayes Moreno and the Temkuts?"

"Unfortunately, yes."

"But the Temkut Rancheria casino would be a direct competitor to Putah Creek," I said, more than a little confused.

"Competition is healthy, as long as it's legitimate. Always has been and probably always will be. What we're worried about are people like Crandal who are looking to pull several million out of the pot by victimizing both the Indians and their backers."

"Like the Temkuts?"

"Like the Temkuts," Greer said.

"So why hasn't Twin Arrows done something about the likes of Lurton-Bales?"

"We need proof, Toby."

"Come on, Greer, when has a lack of truth ever stopped Nevada gaming interests from finding a remote hole in the desert for anyone they found threatening, or even objectionable?"

"We're not talking Nevada, we're talking California."

"Same difference as far as I can see. Not only that, I think the corporations that now control gaming are more ruthless than the syndicates ever were. The mobs needed a way to launder all the cash that came in to them from the rackets—high-jacking, prostitution, numbers, whatever. The only corporate goal is to make certain the shareholders get quarterly dividends. The end is still justifying the means."

"And then comes along an equal opportunity guy like Crandal," she said, "who sees nothing wrong with robbing the rich and poor alike. He gives only to himself, and to a few money-grubbing politicians who make certain that enabling legislation is always in place."

She sighed, stretched, and looked very attractive.

"Give me an example," I said to keep from making a move I was afraid we'd both regret.

"A favorite ploy," she said, "is to take a multimillion-dollar lobbying fee from some tribe that is having trouble getting a casino up and running, then secretly accept another huge fee from people who want to block the same casino."

"That's more than hedging one's bet, it's downright dishonest."

"Oh, that's not all of it. Sometimes, through a lobbyist partner, Crandal will contract with another Indian tribe that wants to establish a casino in the same area as the first tribe and then double his take."

"So why hasn't Twin Arrows exposed this guy for what he is?"

"Don't think we wouldn't like to. We've a lot of money at risk out there. But so far, no one has been able to come up with any evidence that will hold up in court. Also, and that's a very big *also*, Crandal's insulated his operations by using off-shore accounts, and by getting cozy with some very powerful politicians in Washington."

"Does Hayes Moreno know all of this?"

"It's been explained to him, just as I've explained it to you. But I think he sees himself as Geronimo or Cochise, out to defeat the white man."

"And it hasn't been going that well for him, is that it?"

"Exactly!" Greer gave me a self-satisfied look.

"Which apparently is why he hired me."

"I would say that pretty well covers it, Toby. Only I wish I'd thought to call you first."

She gave me a smile that was very familiar, a smile that I was once willing to do almost anything for. "Too bad. I already have a client," I said.

"Can't blame a gal for trying," she said.

"So what now?"

"I'm going to drop you off in San Tomas. I don't want to risk being seen bringing you back to Putah Creek."

"I can appreciate the need for caution, but my car's in your casino garage."

"There's an hourly shuttle that runs between San Tomas and the casino." She fished around in her purse and pulled out a book of tickets. She tore out one and handed it to me. "One shuttle ride, compliments of Putah Creek Resort and Casino. Please come visit us again."

"Oh, swell, aren't I the lucky one."

"Sure you don't want to work for us?"

"Told you before, I have a client."

"So you did. So you did. Which means it probably wouldn't be a good idea for you to come visit us again, other than to collect your lovely yellow Porsche."

"Any particular reason?"

"It might not be healthy."

"For me or for you?"

"Both of us."

She leaned over and gave me a light kiss on the cheek just as the Escalade pulled to a stop. She nodded at the door, I stepped out onto the sidewalk in front of a small, ornate bus stop decorated with posters advertising upcoming events at Putah Creek.

"Wadkins has my cell phone," I said.

"You can pick it from my secretary when you come to retrieve your cute little yellow Speedster."

"Cayman."

"Whatever." She started to close the car door. "Have a nice shuttle ride."

I gave her a little salute, she slid the door closed, and the Escalade was gone.

I was about to sit down on a spring-loaded seat in the bus shelter when a silver van pulled up to the bus stop. Assuming it was the shuttle back to Putah Creek, I stepped out to the curb. The rear door slid open to reveal the muzzle of a very nasty assault weapon aimed at my midsection.

"Get in!" growled a voice from behind the gun. "Now!"

Greer hadn't been as circumspect as she'd thought.

* * *

This time, instead of nicely filled-out black stockings to look at, I got a black hood pushed down roughly over my head, followed by plastic shackles for my wrists and ankles.

Another difference: these people didn't seem to want to talk, nor did they offer me a nice cushioned seat inside the van.

Was getting kidnapped twice in one day any kind of a record?

No one said where we were going, or why. In fact, no one said anything. I returned the favor.

The driver seemed not to care that he was carrying extremely valuable cargo. Me! He must have hit every available pothole, and corners were taken without regard to my being unable to hold on, had there been anything to hold on to.

I rolled around into almost every portion of the van floor before I managed to wedge myself into one corner. Both the floor and sidewalls were covered with industrial-type carpeting, which felt grimy to the touch and had an oily, machinery kind of smell, but it did provide a small amount of cushioning; very small.

My snooping around obviously had upset someone—the Temkuts, the Pomos, Lurton-Bales, Twin Arrows, Appa Bay. Wirok County, or someone I'd yet to come in contact with. I wished I'd been a little more prepared for their reaction, whoever it was.

The immediate problem was to find a way out of my present predicament.

We drove for a long time, perhaps an hour, maybe longer. I almost fell asleep a couple of times, but was able to shake it off. This definitely wasn't the time or place to be taking a cat-nap.

The van eventually slowed, made a couple of sharp turns, the last of which rolled me out of my safe-haven corner and made me painfully aware of a number of sore spots. The driver stayed in low gear for a steep incline.

A long moment after the van stopped, the side door slid open. Impatient, insistent hands pulled me out and stood me in loose gravel. The restraints were removed, but the hood stayed in place.

I was shuffled along, stiff and sore, through the loose stones, which I guessed were part of a driveway. We paused, then started up substantial wooden steps, through a doorway, and into a building. The ever-present large hands gripped my arms on both sides.

We crossed a large expanse of marble or tile flooring and took two steps down onto a level covered by very plush carpeting. After a few feet, we stopped. The hood was jerked off my head, taking a few hairs with it.

It took a moment for my eyes to adjust, to see that I was facing a huge expanse of tinted glass.

Outside, beyond a redwood deck almost large enough for a tennis court, the late afternoon sun hung low in the sky. Dim winter rays reflected off what I assumed to be the Pacific Ocean.

I started to turn my head to take in the rest of my surroundings and was backhanded into continuing to look out the picture window.

My peripheral vision soon picked up movement to the left, which evolved into the backlit figure of a tall, broad-shouldered man. He stood there for a moment, apparently studying me. I couldn't see his features well enough to be certain.

"My apologies for bringing you here like this, Mr. Rolfe."

The hands on my arms relaxed, but remained in place. Two kidnappings, two apologies. Now wasn't that just perfect.

"I'm Felix Crandal."

I held perfectly still, tried to put a face on him from the photos I'd seen.

He moved closer. "It would have been nice if we could have met at The Pomo House, perhaps, and enjoyed a few of Ms. Jimenez's savory snacks. Or maybe dined on fresh-caught salmon filets and shared a bottle of chilled sauvignon blanc at the Wirok Café."

I waited.

He stopped in front of me, a couple of feet away. The photos I'd seen were obviously from a few years back—slightly sagging jowls, combined with a road map of red and blue veins on his upper cheeks and across the nose, made it obvious he was doing considerably more rich dining and drinking than was good for him.

"As things stand," he said, "I don't think intimate dining and socializing is in either of our horoscopes, wouldn't you agree?"

I couldn't have cared less. A quick, body-hugging uppercut freed me from the guy holding my left arm and caught Crandal square in the solar plexus. As the air whooshed out of him and he doubled over, I clipped him solidly with a right cross that also spun me out of the loose grip of my other captor.

I ducked, pivoted in place, and drove the heels of both hands into the two very confused faces watching me.

The sprawling entryway's double cut-glass doors were very visible, even in the fading light … and only about 30 feet away. The thick carpet gave me good traction and a jump-start on my still-stumbling captors.

I reached the double doors just in time to see a slug shatter one of the curved, beveled panes at about ear level.

"Not in the goddam house," a labored voice coughed out behind me.

I agreed, but didn't wait to say so. Rushing out of the house, my main concern was what the hell was I going to do now?

CHAPTER 17

I didn't need Hayes Moreno or any other Temkut guide to tell me in which direction to head; I was certain we were somewhere north of Appa Bay.

That made it simple: stay close to the shoreline and, for as long as it would last, keep the fading dusk light off to my right. I slapped my pockets to find my cell, came up empty. Raebeck, or Wadkins, had it. Both it and the Porsche were at Putah Creek. Just dandy!

I had no way of knowing just how far south I would have to travel before I found Appa Bay, or came on some other coastal community. But that was the way it was going to be.

One thing I did know: Crandal's people would come looking for me. I'd made fools of them, and that never goes over well with muscle-bound types. Also, Crandal never had a chance to interrogate, threaten, or do whatever it was that prompted him to have me snatched off the street and delivered to him in such an unfriendly fashion.

I loped along the edge of the two-lane asphalt road that pretty much followed the coastline. Here and there lights flicked on in homes scattered just off the road, both shoreside and on the opposite up-slope. Some were mere cabins, others looked to be substantial residences.

It didn't seem wise, though, to go knocking on doors looking for help, or asking to use a phone. I had no idea who knew who in the area.

Traffic was light in both directions. But the vehicles coming up behind me concerned me the most. I looked back over my shoulder every two or three paces, and when I saw headlights coming, scrambled off the road into whatever cover I could find.

Each jump launched a new squadron of mosquitoes. As I crouched low to stay out of the headlight beams, I could hear other creatures scurrying about through the leaves and pine needles. I was able to put up with the bloodthirsty insects, but I didn't want to even think about what would happen if I stumbled into a skunk's den.

I eventually got the timing down so that I spent as little time in the brush as possible.

Far behind me I saw a four-light grouping, probably a pair of rollbar-mounted driving floods and a set of very bright headlights. Other rays of moving light shot out from both sides of the vehicle. The vehicle's occupants were obviously searching for something or someone. There no doubt in my mind that someone was me.

The oncoming light-o-rama truck kept its headlights on high beam as it met other cars; no courteous dimming by this guy.

I had to get off the road.

Unable to see the coastline, and not wanting to jump off the road and free-fall into the ocean, I crossed the blacktop and scampered up into a grove of very scratchy pine saplings.

I waited, slapped at mosquitoes, waited, and slapped at mosquitoes; and waited, and slapped at more mosquitoes.

I risked pushing a small limb aside to check on the progress of the truck, and quickly let it fly back into place. The quad lights were now about 100 yards to my right. It was a monster four-wheel-drive duallie pickup, creeping along, half on the road, half on the berm. Two guys standing in the truck bed were using high-intensity, hand-held spotlights to sweep back and forth along both sides of the road, punching the beams into the bordering vegetation.

I pressed my face down into a soft pile of old pine needles and tried to become one with the earth. It seemed to take forever for the sound of the truck to arrive and move past me. Once certain it was a good distance down the road to my left, I slipped out of my uncomfortable hiding place and scurried down to the road again.

I continued moving south, prudently keeping to the side of the road facing traffic, and constantly looking several yards ahead for a new place to hide if it became necessary.

The truck was now just a diffuse glow of white light, punctuated by a pair of red taillights. I knew I was still at extreme risk. At any moment the truck could reverse course. Even a complete dolt would have to realize I couldn't have gotten too much of a lead while traveling on foot.

If I could manage to stay out of their sights when they eventually came back, I might stand a chance of getting away. Wishful thinking said they might decide I'd lit out cross-country. Reality said otherwise.

Just then the pickup's brake lights came on. The driver made a broken U-turn and once again the four beams were coming my way.

The hillside next to me was too steep to climb. I ran across the road into a broad private pull-off area in front of a large barn-like garage. Not a particularly good move. Now I was hemmed in by the building, a massive gate, and six-foot redwood fencing running off in both directions.

A look down the road told me the magnum pickup was moving much faster than before, the spotlights continuing to probe both sides of the road. Within seconds I'd be trapped.

I tugged at the garage doors. Locked. The gate was no more accommodating. The rattle of the truck's diesel engine was now deafening. I flattened myself against the gate only a blink before the outer edge of the spotlight oozed through the shrubbery.

The diffused beam danced over a foot-long piece of horizontal pipe with a large spike driven through it. A sliding latch.

A tug at the spike, the gate swung back, I stumbled through, closed the opening just before the full splash of light spread across the fence and garage doors. The pickup didn't change speed.

I caught a quick breath, held it, and listened until the diesel clatter was lost in the distance.

Light suddenly filled the yard behind the gate. I scampered back through the gateway and raced off down the road.

Someone secured the gate without stepping through the entry to see who or what had unlatched it.

Almost an hour later I came to a commercial campground nestled in a small cove. As I hid near the entrance and debated whether to go in and look for a telephone, car lights swung down and around the tight curve and lit a small roadside sign: *Anchor Bay ¼ mile*.

I pushed on, hoping my burning feet would carry me the distance.

At the top of a grade and around another curve, I found a small cluster of buildings. Almost all of them were businesses of one kind or another, but the only one open was the Fading Fog Tavern & Grille.

Before giving the bar a try, I trudged up and down both sides of the road to check out the whole community. The only other thing of interest was another road sign: *Gualala 3 miles*.

No way. I knew my loafer-clad and probably blistered feet were not up for that. My calves and thighs were also sending out distress signals.

Worse, I now knew I should have gone north when I left Crandal's place. Gualala was a good 25 miles south of Appa Bay. That knowledge explained why the big pickup hadn't come for me sooner – they must have gone north first.

A fairly new Dodge crew-cab pickup and an old rusty Volvo station wagon were the only vehicles parked outside the tavern. Neither seemed threatening.

It cost me $3.00, plus tip, for an Anchor Steam beer I didn't even want just so I could get change to make a call.

"Where's the payphone," I asked the bartender.

"Don't have one …haven't had one in here for a year or more. Have to use your cell."

"Don't have one … with me."

He shrugged.

"Where you need to call," said a solitary drinker a few stools down.

Good question. Who the hell could I call to come get me? Had to be someone I could be sure wouldn't call Crandal and tell him where I was stranded.

Moreno? He was becoming more and more of an enigma the longer I was in the area. And Vanessa Jimenez was pretty close to Moreno, or so it appeared. As for Greer, she'd made it clear she preferred to keep a lot of distance between the two of us.

I opted to take a chance on Vanessa. Maybe if I asked real nice she would bring some clean clothes from The Pomo House.

"Appa Bay," I tardily said to my benefactor.

He pulled a smartphone from a pocket of his chambray shirt and said, "Give me the number."

Guess I didn't look too trustworthy.

* * *

She'd tried twice—once on the phone and again when she arrived—to find out how I'd ended up on the coast, on foot. I'd put her off the first time, then gave her an edited version of my forced meeting with Crandal and subsequent escape.

"Did you tell Moreno you were coming over here to pick me up?" I asked Vanessa after I'd settled into her top-down Miata.

"I got the impression you didn't want me to tell anyone," she said. It was not a particularly friendly response.

"True. But the two of you seem close."

"Look, he's not my boyfriend, or anything like that," she said without looking over at me.

"I wasn't trying to be nosy."

"Good!"

I leaned over and looked at the odometer. I figured Crandal's place was maybe four or five miles from where Jimenez had picked me up in Anchor Bay. I didn't want to miss seeing its location on the way back north.

"You have a problem with the way I'm driving?" she snapped.

I pulled back. "No way." I explained why I was checking the instrument panel.

"Why didn't you just ask? I know exactly where Crandal's staying."

"You've been there?"

134

"Once, if you think that's important."

"It could be."

This time she looked at me, gave me an assessing once-over, then turned her eyes back to the road. "Crandal threw a big open house not too long ago. Invited anyone and everyone who had even the remotest connection with the Temkut Rancheria's proposed casino."

"You don't sound impressed."

Instead of answering, she raised a hand and wiggled her fingers toward a well-lighted, imposing house sitting on a promontory overlooking the ocean.

It was too dark to make out the details, but the number of lights flooding the grounds and in the house left little doubt that it was a huge estate.

"His?" I asked, "or Lurton-Bales'?" I put one hand on top of the doorsill and the other on the seatbelt buckle, ready to jump ship if she slowed even the tiniest bit as we approached Crandal's place.

"They're leasing it," she said, holding her speed. "Belongs to some guy down in Silicon Valley."

I relaxed into the seat. "Hefty expense."

"What do they care? The tribe will end up covering the cost, of that and lot more."

"You're not a fan of this casino thing, are you?"

"Not true. Native Americans have been kept poor for a long, long time. I might have wished for some other way for us to get out from under hundreds of years of poverty, but right now, it's casino time."

She raised both hands from the steering wheel and held them in the air above the windshield. "So be it!"

"For some reason, you're not convincing me the Temkut casino has your full support."

She took the wheel again just before entering a sweeping "S" curve, then looked across at me.

"Two people are dead, Mr. Rolfe, one a very special person in my life. At the same time, the whole community is having to associate with a lot of very unsavory people. I can only hope that in the end it will all have been worth it."

"Point well taken. And speaking of taken, are we headed back to The Pomo House?"

"We can do that. Or if you want, we can drive over to Putah Creek to get your car."

"No, the car can wait. Considering the events of the day, I'd rather go someplace Crandal and his people can't easily find me, at least for tonight."

She was silent for a long moment. "Know just the place."

A few miles later, Vanessa turned off Highway 1 and headed inland on a very narrow, bumpy road that hadn't been treated to fresh asphalt for a long, long time.

We cut off onto an even narrower dirt road and came to a stop at a split-rail fence.

"Give me a hand," she said.

She got out of the car and walked to the fence; I followed. She removed one of two rails, I removed the other. We drove through, then replaced the rails. She parked the Miata behind a stand of second-growth redwoods, well out of sight of the fence and road.

"Short walk," she said.

"Damn well better be or you'll have to carry me."

I painfully followed her to a thatched-roof log cabin set beneath the largest bay tree I'd ever seen. The bole had to be close to eight feet across.

"Hunting lodge," she said. "Belongs to the tribe."

The inside was one huge room, with six cots divided along two of the walls. A kitchen of sorts took up most of another wall and was equipped with a sink and hand pump, a couple of Coleman stoves, and an open cupboard holding cooking utensils, plus a set of heavy-duty, off-white dishes. A two-door closed cupboard hung over the cooking area. A five-foot square, rough-hewn table and four rustic chairs sat in the middle of the room.

Vanessa opened the cupboard. Four shelves were filled with tin and glass food canisters and a variety of canned goods.

"Enough for a banquet," she said.

"I'm impressed."

"Thank you, Mr. Rolfe. It's not quite up to Pomo House standards, but it should do for tonight." She pointed back at the stored food. "Are you hungry?"

"Been too busy to notice until now," I said. "But a little food wouldn't hurt. What's good on those shelves?"

"How about stove-top cornbread and minestrone soup?"

"That would sit well, thank you."

I started toward the cupboard, but she waved me off. "Go sit down at the table. "You've had a bad day."

"Don't you have to be getting back?"

"Let me worry about that, okay?"

"If you need help, just ask."

"I'd rather you told me about your day – how you ended up stranded on the coast, and whether you found out anything worthwhile."

* * *

She made just enough food for the two of us, and even found a bottle of zinfandel lying on its side behind a couple of tall, spaghetti-filled glass canisters. It may not have been up to Pomo House standards, as she said, but under the circumstances, it was perfect.

"So, you're no longer welcome at Putah Creek Casino," Vanessa said, "Terence Wadkins isn't who he claims to be, and Felix Crandal probably isn't ever going to be included in your circle of friends."

"That's a fairly accurate summary." I swallowed the last of my wine from one of the coffee cups.

"So what now?"

"First, I thought maybe you could bring a decent set of wheels for me to drive when you come back to pick me up tomorrow. Might as well leave the Porsche in the Putah Creek Casino garage. Now that I've created enemies, a screaming yellow Cayman is much too conspicuous."

She gave me a puzzled look.

"What?"

"What's wrong with me driving you to get a different car in the morning ... after we have breakfast? It's beautiful out here in the morning."

"Why, Ms. Jimenez, I'm shocked."

She laughed and got up to clear away the dishes. Sore as I was, I joined in.

As we cleaned and put away the dishes, she bumped into me a couple of times, sort of hip to hip, and each time said, "Oops." Then as I was cleaning off the camp stove, she leaned against my back and reached over my shoulders to return the cornmeal to the cupboard.

I twisted around in her arms, slid my hands up and across her shoulders. "Have you had a little too much wine, Ms. Jimenez, or are you flirting with me?"

"Yes, Mr. Rolfe." She planted her lips against mine and ran her hands up the back of my neck.

"One cot or two?" I whispered when our lips parted.

"One."

CHAPTER 18

Sometime in the wee hours, we pushed two cots together, listened to a lilting cricket-and-owl duet, and made love again.

When I awoke, Vanessa wasn't in our double-cot bed. I glanced around the small cabin, saw her at the kitchen counter, nude. She was humming, busy with something that smelled just as appetizing as she looked.

The morning sun put her in silhouette, a lithe, curvaceous, and animated silhouette that signaled she was enjoying her morning while cooking in the buff.

I slipped off the cots, walked over to the counter, and wrapped my arms around her bare waist.

"Is this a Temkut thing?" I asked.

"What?" She leaned her head back against my shoulder.

"Cooking in the nude?"

"I'm Miwok, not Temkut."

"Does that make a difference?"

"Probably not. It was just too nice a morning to get all bound up in clothes."

"I should have come down to your kitchen at The Pomo House much earlier in the mornings, I think."

She gave me an elbow in the ribs.

"How do you like your eggs?"

I laughed and looked over her shoulder, expecting to see a box of powdered eggs rather than the real thing. "Where the hell did you get fresh eggs?"

"Threw a few supplies in the car before I came to get you ... just in case. Eggs, chicken-apple sausage, juice, bagels."

"You are definitely a woman of surprises." I pushed aside her long black hair, kissed the nape of her neck.

"That was nice," she said before turning her head to return the kiss.

We ate breakfast outdoors, nudist-park style, sitting on towels spread across the bench seats of a well-worn, rickety redwood picnic table. The cabin-wide back deck had an unobstructed view of tall trees, wild shrubs, and the quiet traffic of birds and small animals going about their morning routines.

"What now?" Vanessa asked, pouring more coffee for the two of us.

"I don't know, maybe stay right here, enjoy you and nature, and wait for lunch."

"That's a lovely thought, but not very practical."

"It also wouldn't be very practical to go back and placate my bruised ego by going one-on-one with Crandal." I sighed. "Even though that's exactly what I feel like doing."

"Is there a 'but' in there someplace?"

"Absolutely. But a foolhardy confrontation isn't going to accomplish anything."

Vanessa put her elbows on the table and rested her chin on the backs of her hands. "So?"

"So, right now I need to know what Felix Crandal and his bunch of Washington-based flimflam artists *really* have planned for the Temkuts and their casino."

"Isn't that what you've been doing?"

"I thought so, but getting abducted tells me that I need to take a hard look at this whole thing from a different perspective. My guess is that everything Lurton-Bales has been feeding your tribal leaders, the public, and the politicians is a gussied up banquet swill, better known as bullshit."

"And?"

I sat there running the cast of characters and their interrelationships through several scenarios. I was deep into plots and subplots when I sensed restlessness on the other side of the table.

I peered at Vanessa across the rim of my cup and slowly sipped the last of the coffee. "I need a different car."

"Okay. And again ... *and*?"

"I need to go places, see people, ask irritating questions. The Porsche's too obvious. Besides, as you know, it's stuck over in the Putah Creek Casino garage."

"Take me back to The Pomo House and you can use my car."

"The Miata? Your *red* Miata?"

"Yes."

"If a yellow Porsche's too obvious, your Miata would be like waving a flag, a red flag. Besides, I bet there's not a soul within a hundred-mile radius that doesn't know that car and who it belongs to."

"Point taken." She stretched her arms high above her head, interlocked her fingers, and twisted from side to side at the waist.

I tried looking beyond her to the forest of trees, but it didn't work. There was simply no doubt about it – Vanessa Jimenez was one of the most striking women I'd ever had the good fortune to meet. … and share a cot with.

"I could go back to town and find something ugly for you to drive," she said, bringing her arms down and folding them across the main source of my distraction.

"Yes, the uglier the better," I said, thankful she'd returned us to where we'd been in our conversation. "Would you mind?"

"No problem. You can tell me what you have planned while I tidy up the cabin. Then I'll be on my way."

"You've got a deal, only I'll help with the chores."

The basic problem with helping a beautiful nude woman wash dishes, put things away, and generally straighten up a relatively small living space is that you can't avoid running into one another now and then. Bump, take hold, hold on.

The cots were the last thing we put back in place.

* * *

We shared a cold, outdoors shower under a sprayhead fed by plastic pipe fastened to the trunk of the bay laurel. That accomplished without dalliance, we dried each other with the towels from the picnic table bench seats.

Vanessa had, as requested, brought me a fresh set of everything from my room at The Pomo House. While I dressed, she changed into clean jeans and t-shirt she'd packed in a small travel bag.

She said it would probably take her a couple of hours to get back to Appa Bay, find a suitable nondescript vehicle, and return to pick me up.

After she left, I picked out a slim paperback from a shelf of faded and tattered books and settled in on the back deck with a large bottle of Pellegrino she'd left behind for me. The book, *A Run in Diamonds*, was a fast-paced caper novel by a guy named Alex Saxon.

Memories of my evening and morning with Vanessa, the warm sun, the solitude of the outdoors, and a good book almost kept me from hearing a vehicle pull into the parking area out beyond the cabin grounds.

I assumed it was Vanessa returning, but I needed to be sure before dashing out into the open. I slipped the paperback into a rear pocket, a location these books were originally designed to fit, and moved quickly and quietly off the deck.

Going around to the side of the cabin, sticking close to the outer wall, I came to the front just as Vanessa came through the opening in the foliage.

"Any problems?" I asked, stepping out into the open.

She looked at me and laughed. "You been hiding there ever since I left?"

"Naw! Been reading on the back deck." I patted my rear pocket. "Good book. Think anyone would mind if I took it with me? Got me hooked and I need to know how it turns out."

"No problem with the book, no problem getting you something to drive." She turned and pointed toward the parking area. "Come see."

I heard the cooling pings of the engine before I saw the dirty, dented, beige-over-rust, crew-cab Dodge pickup. It looked to have been around for a decade or more.

She made a sweeping presentation hand gesture toward the truck. "May not be much to look at, but she's tight, with a hot Hemi engine that won't quit."

I've known some women like that, but didn't think this was the time and place to mention it. I settled for, "Thank you, ma'am. Couldn't ask for more."

"I was also thinking," she said, "you could use the cabin as a base if you want."

That had its plusses and minuses. "How many people know about this place?"

"Probably most, if not all, of the Temkuts, plus any number of other Native Americans. Probably some non-Indians also."

"Might cause a problem or two if someone came out here unexpectedly."

"If I let the tribe secretary know you're using it while you're working for Hayes, she'll just tell people it's not available."

"She know you and I have been out here?"

She shook her head. "Not everyone gets permission first before coming out to use the place."

"That's what I was afraid of. And speaking of Hayes, any idea where I might find him?"

"I tried to call him while I was back in town, but Ed Harkins at the *Sentinel* said Hayes was with Chief Chubb, working on a story. And I know there's a tribal council meeting that starts around six o'clock this evening. The tribe's supposed to vote on whether or not to hire Lurton-Bales."

"Well, Hayes is first on my list of people to see and question." I took Vanessa's hand and did a walk-around of the truck. "You done good."

"I thought so." She leaned a hip against a front fender. "You want to wait until dark before heading back?"

"Nah, I'm not trying to hide. I just didn't want my yellow Porsche or your red Miata making it obvious where I was at any given time."

"Then what say we go. I should get back to The Pomo House and take care of a few things before my neglect puts me out of business."

* * *

She was right: The Dodge was a sweet-running truck, as far as trucks go. A mile or so before we hit the outskirts of Appa Bay, I suggested she get in the back seat and sort of keep a low profile until we reached The Pomo House. She obviously saw the wisdom in my suggestion and crawled over the seat and kept her head below the window line until I got her home. Before she got out, she paused just long enough to lean over the seatback and give me a kiss on the cheek. Then she was gone before I had a chance to thank her again, and not just for the truck.

First stop in my search for Hayes Moreno was the *Appa Bay Sentinel.*

Also, I figured it was time, maybe past time, to meet Hayes' boss face to face. I was curious whether he was the real thing, as Mark Trimble over in San Tomas claimed him to be.

The only person in the small, cluttered newspaper office was a bald guy with a large handlebar moustache who looked to be in his mid-seventies.

"Ed Harkins?" I asked.

"That's me. Who wants to know?"

"Zach Rolfe."

"Oh, yeah. Moreno's friend."

"Right. He around?"

"Nope! Chief Chubb called earlier, said they had some info on the slugs they took out of Benito Petrucci and Grady Nolan. Hayes went over to talk to him."

"Ballistics report?"

"That'd be my guess. I took the call, but Chubb wouldn't give us any details over the telephone. Sometimes think he watches too much 'CSI' and 'Criminal Minds.'"

"Mind if I wait around a while for Moreno to return?"

"Don't mind. Sittin's free, long as you don't pester me. Tryin' to write an editorial." He turned back to his keyboard.

"About the casino and the killings?"

He lowered his chin and glared at me over his half-frame glasses.

"Right! No pestering."

I read the previous week's edition of the *Sentinel*, scanned today's edition of *Wirok County Gazette*, and leafed through several copies of *Sunset* magazine. Pleasant enough, but I was getting antsy. Time to move on.

I looked back at Harkins as I opened the door to leave. He raised a hand but his eyes continued to dance between the monitor and keyboard of his computer.

I walked from the *Sentinel* office to the hardware store, picked up a pre-paid cell phone, and continued on to the Wirok Café. I tried to call Hayes, had to leave a message for him to call at the new cell number.

The noon rush was over at the cafe, so I had no trouble finding an empty stool at the far end of the counter. I wanted to keep a watch on the door, and have a little privacy so I could ask Annalee Mackey a few questions.

"Ah, you're back again," Annalee said, clearing the previous customer's dirty dishes from in front of me. "Guess I haven't poisoned you ... yet."

"Is there a lunch special?" I asked, looking up from the menu.

"Crab cakes. But don't get your hopes up – they're gone. If you're really hungry, and not here just to do a little more pokin' around, could fix you a fried Pacific oyster sandwich on lightly toasted focaccia, with a side salad of tomatoes and oregano dressing."

I glanced at the menu again, then back at her. "Must have missed that one. Sounds good."

"Prefer not to put *everything* on the menu, Mr. Rolfe."

"My appetite is in your capable hands, Ms. Mackey."

That earned me the briefest of smiles. She looked toward the front of the café. "Don't see that sunflower-yellow coupe of yours."

"Been doing a little strolling about town. Good for the circulation."

"Uh-huh. So is capsaicin, but a little caution is always a good idea."

"Is there some kind of message there?"

"I'll go prepare your lunch," she said.

"Seen Hayes Moreno today?" I called after her. All I got was a shake of the head.

I was question-ready for her return – what did she know and when did she know it? Or was she making an educated guess about something? But our conversation was over, at least for the day. Annalee disappeared into the kitchen. Her assistant served

145

my lunch and collected payment for the meal, which was succulent and flavorful, with a noticeable touch of cayenne pepper in the paper-thin breading on the oysters. Capsaicin, indeed!

I was more cautious than usual as I walked back to where I'd parked the pickup. I used the cell to call the *Sentinel*, but Hayes still hadn't returned. He had, however, e-mailed his story to Harkins. The editor didn't have time to give me all the details, but he did say ballistics had matched the slugs that had killed the two city councilmen. They were from the same weapon.

I pondered taking a trip to the police station, but seriously doubted the chief, or anyone else, would tell me anything.

Well I needed to go someplace, anyplace, where I might find Hayes Moreno. Before I could turn the key in the ignition, my new cell rang.

"We need to talk," Hayes said.

"Tell me about it."

"I'll meet you in Vanessa's garage, behind The Pomo House, in about a half-hour."

"Maybe a little clue ..."

He was gone.

Okay, the garage, in about a half-hour. I put in a call to Greer Raebeck.

"We need to talk," she said.

"Tell me about it."

"I'll meet you in the casino garage, where you left your Porsche. Soon as it turns dark. Alone!"

"Maybe a little clue ..."

She was gone.

No one wanted to tell me anything. But at least I now had someplace to go. Two someplaces.

CHAPTER 19

Northern California – 1878

"Do you understand what you're signing, the obligation involved?" the rancher said to Nuñez Moreno. The white man stood with one foot resting on a wood slab bench outside the door of a weathered clapboard bunkhouse.

Moreno leaned against the building, did not reply immediately, did not move, nor blink an eye. He did not want to be the person who had to answer El Patrón's questions.

Nuñez Moreno was neither head man of the Temkuts, nor an elder of the tribe. His father's brother had been their leader for many, many years. But his uncle was very old and ill, had heard the hoot of the great horned owl and was ready to travel west to be with Coyote.

The tribe had said, "Nuñez, you are the only one among us who can read and write American. You must meet with El Patrón."

Moreno looked at the single sheet of paper Señor Guthrie Kendall had signed and handed to him. It was beyond his skills.

"I do not understand this paper and all of its words," Moreno said.

"It's a simple document," Kendall said, "a quitclaim deed that says you and your people now own these nine acres in exchange for payment in kind."

Moreno took in the information and considered it. "Tell me about the land again," he said.

"The property extends from my fence here, to the rise of the hills due east, and between the two gullies that run north and south of here."

Moreno looked out beyond his employer as Kendall made a sweeping gesture across the landscape. What he saw was an uninviting expanse, dotted here and there with a few live oaks. It bordered neither bay nor inlet, yet was often flooded by hillside run-off that cascaded through the two bordering gullies during the rainy season. The wild grass and mustard plant that grew there every spring were now reduced to tan, broken stalks, and the mostly barren hills were made even more unattractive by fecal droppings from cattle and sheep that still grazed the acreage in search of edible stubble.

"And no one will be able to take this land from The People?" Moreno asked, wanting to add "again," but knowing better than to make such an offensive remark.

It is yours," Kendall said. "File the deed with the county, pay the taxes every year, and the land is yours ... forever."

Moreno was suspicious. Pay taxes? With what? He had never so much as touched one of the new silver dollars the Americans clinked in their pockets. It was like the Dream-Ghost dances that gave hope, but did not always come true.

But the Temkuts were being offered land, and he was well aware of his tribe's history: Like most coastal Indians, they had been chased from their tribal lands nearly one hundred years earlier. They were kept from returning, first by the padres, then by Spaniard, Mexican, and Californio land grant owners, who clung to their vast rancheros as if their God had created the land just for them.

His people had scattered, some into Spanish Mission settlements to be beaten into accepting the white man's god, others into the hills to be slain by miners, others into the grasslands to be hunted down by cattle ranchers, and still others into the inland fertile valleys where they were shot and killed by farmers.

Moreno knew of these happenings from listening to the stories told over and over in the roundhouses and sweat lodges of The People. And he told his own stories of the grim bounty hunting sponsored by the state, and the internment camps where cruel soldiers taunted, beat, and killed The People for simply breathing the air.

A few years earlier, Moreno had led a small group of Temkuts in their escape from one of the camps. They had sneaked out on a Saturday night while the guards were passed out following a long bout of drinking. They stealthily made their way back to traditional village sites, only to find that whites had stolen the lands of their ancestors.

Nuñez Moreno, his wife, and several other runaways went to work for Señor Kendall, who had proved to be more generous than most of the other ranchers in the area.

Now, El Patrón was offering to "sell" them these nine acres. If true, Moreno envisioned his tribe establishing a village, perhaps returning to some of their old ways.

But the dream shattered with thoughts of the real world.

"We have no money to pay you for this land," Moreno said sadly. He was surprised that Señor Kendall did not know that Indians were almost never paid in hard cash. Payment for working as ranch hands and domestic servants came in the form of food, hand-me-down clothing, and occasionally permission to build a shack, tend a small garden, and perhaps raise a few chickens on a landowner's property.

"I'm not asking your tribe for money," Kendall said. "The quitclaim says 'payment in kind.' That means in exchange for your services. In this case, for past services. If you sign, the land belongs to you, the Temkuts."

"Then you are giving us the land?" Moreno said.

Kendall laughed and kicked at the bench. "You know damn well I don't give away shit, Moreno. You and your people have worked hard for me. You've earned this land, probably more."

Moreno was not convinced. This would be the first time since the white man's arrival on the coast that any of The People had been offered an opportunity to regain use of land their ancestors once roamed at will.

"It's time for hard-working, peaceful Indians to be given the right to legally own land, just like other men," Kendall said.

Moreno more than agreed, and wanted to say so. But he held his tongue. He wanted to accept that the Temkuts, through their collective sweat and pooled resources, were entitled to this land El Patron was offering ... provided they paid the taxes.

"It is good," Moreno said, still wary as he signed his name to the deed.

* * *

"And what is that?" asked the man who said he was from a museum in a place called England.

"Fish trap," said Nuñez Moreno, picking up the device woven from sandbar willow.

"Do your people still use these?"

"No, we are not allowed to go to our traditional fishing places," Moreno said.

"Will you sell it to me?" the man asked.

Moreno nodded and they agreed on a price. The museum man had already bought two conical seed baskets, a cooking basket, a couple of small serving bowls, and a large seed parching tray, all made from gray willow.

"No!" Moreno's wife objected when the Englishman picked up a hazel wood cradle.

"We can make more," Moreno told her in the old language. "He is paying with silver dollars and it is almost time to pay the tax money to the county."

That evening, the men gathered at the village roundhouse to discuss the growing interest in their baskets by collectors, souvenir hunters, and museums.

"We need to make more new baskets to sell to the white men," said Francisco Reyes. "If we do not, the white man's money will go to the Pomos and Miwoks."

"We are a small village," said Moreno. "Our women can make only a small number of baskets."

"Then the men must make baskets also," said Salvador. "The white men pay many dollars for our large carrying baskets, and those decorated with feathers and olivella beads and abalone shell."

I agree," said Juan Calisto. "Many of us know how to weave the rough baskets, but we must go to our wives, mothers, and grandmothers to learn how to craft the very fine baskets."

"Some of us must continue to work on the farms and ranches or Los Patrónes will become angry and maybe take our land away from us," Moreno said.

"It is our land now," said Salvador. "You signed the paper with Señor Kendall."

Moreno did not disagree, but he had a lingering fear and distrust of the white men who controlled everything surrounding the Temkut village—the land, streams, and coastal waters.

* * *

"Rutherford the Rover"
First Sitting President
To Visit California

Nuñez Moreno sounded out each word of the newspaper headline as he waited to be paid for the latest batch of Temkut baskets he was delivering to the trading post.

He was pleased that the coastal tribes had been able to create a thriving mini-industry in basket production. Both collectors and the trading posts continued to pay fair prices, in dollars.

Moreno read the words on the newspaper a second time but still wasn't sure what was being said. It did seem that the head man of all the Americans was coming to California.

"Does your President come here, to San Tomas?" Nuñez asked as the trader counted out silver dollars for the basketry.

"Nope," said the San Tomas trading post owner. "'Round these parts, he's supposed to stop at Truckee, Sacramenta, Redding, Frisco, and Oakland."

He went on to explain how President Rutherford B. Hayes was embarking from Washington on a 71-day, 9,000-mile Western expedition on behalf of James A. Garfield's 1880 run for the presidency.

"Señor Hayes will no longer be your head man?"

"Nope! And can't say as I'll miss him. Too many fancy ideas for my tastes."

"I would like to see a President of the United States," said Moreno. "I would like to ask him many questions about what has happened to The People."

"Just bet you would," said the trader. "But don't go gettin' all worked up 'bout it. Don't think he's gonna have much time for Injun bellyachin'."

"How many days?" Moreno asked.

"Till he gets to Californy?"

"No, how many days to the closest of those white man villages where Señor Hayes will visit?"

"Reckon that depends. Lotta land and water between here and any of those cities."

Moreno knew the trader was not going to give him an answer, even if he knew. He would have to find someone else to tell him more about this Rutherford B. Hayes, tell him exactly when the President of the United States of America would come to California, tell him how many days it would take to travel to the closest city where he could see the head man of the whites.

* * *

Nuñez Moreno took his village's only two riding horses for his trip to Sacramento. Along the way, his Miwok, Pomo, and Patwin brothers provided him with directions, cautioned about dangerous miner encampments, and kept him supplied with dried fish and mudhens, boiled and mashed buckeye nuts, and meat from fresh kills.

He made it to Sacramento the day before President Rutherford B. Hayes' train arrived from Tahoe.

Moreno caught only a glimpse of the President at the train station, then again at the governor's mansion, prudently staying to the rear of the crowds. But he talked to other Indians and read, as best he could, from the numerous pamphlets distributed during the visit. He became convinced that Señor Hayes understood the problems of The People, and wanted to help them.

Most impressive was learning that President Hayes strongly supported educating Indians in "the white man's ways" so they could "take their place in mainstream American society," according to one newspaper. This was Moreno's dream also.

One pamphlet he saved to take home told of the President's backing for a new school for The People – the Carlisle Indian Industrial School in a far off place called Pennsylvania. If the child his wife now carried turned out to be a son, he would do everything possible to send him to that new special school.

* * *

The clouds roiled in off the ocean and shouted rain. Facing what promised to be the first big storm of the season, Nuñez Moreno rode down from the coastal hills, a deer slung across the back of the horse that trailed behind him. He'd trapped the animal with a well-placed wood fiber snare, then carefully slit its throat to drain the blood.

He planned to give the deer to his wife, who would skin the animal, cure the meat, and turn the hide into a soft, warm blanket for the child that nestled deep inside her. Perhaps she carried the son he would one day send off to the Carlisle Indian School in the state of Pennsylvania.

When the storm clouds released their burden, the rain washed over Moreno, streaming through the holes in his well-worn clothing. It was a blessing as it healed his body, eased the knotted muscles, cooled the white swelling in his joints.

The night was coming as fast as the clouds and he scurried to find a sheltered camp site near the edge of a small lake. He was not sure whose land he might be on and did not want to be chased off, attacked, or perhaps have his life threatened. He knew there were still those who would kill him with no more thought than shooting a rabid dog.

Moreno did not build a fire, making his evening meal the last handful of roasted acorns he had been given during his long trip to Sacramento.

He was still a good half day from his village near San Tomas. He had rehearsed several times how he would share with his wife and other members of the tribe the encouraging news he had learned in Sacramento. It was good to know the head man of the Americans wanted to improve the lives of the Temkuts and all other Indian tribes. He saw a better life for his children in the future. He was happy.

When Moreno awoke the next morning, flies were everywhere in the sun, coming at his face, jabbing in a steady drone at his eyes. He kept brushing them away with a twitch of his hand.

He sat up—the valley lay flat around him. The morning heat came up off the ground and hung in a low dense haze all the way to the distant rim of the coastal hills. The sky was a brilliant blue, not a single rain cloud in sight.

He could feel the sweat moving in his long hair. He ran the flat of his palm back over his scalp, then used it to swat at the unrelenting flies. Flies!

He jumped up, fearful that the insistent, biting insects might spook his horses and leave him to travel the remaining distance by foot. But the horses were calm, their hobbles slack, as they grazed on the sparse vegetation beneath the trees.

After refreshing himself in the lake waters, Moreno retrieved the deer carcass from the tree limb where he'd stowed it for safekeeping during the night. When he had his few belongings lashed to the second horse, he mounted up and headed west at an easy gait. His surroundings were once again familiar and he was secure in the knowledge that he would soon be home.

* * *

Francisco Reyes came running out of a small grove of live oak, waving his arms at Nuñez Moreno, who reined his horse to a stop.

"It's gone! It's gone!" Reyes shouted. His dust-covered face was streaked with trails of tears. He raced back and forth in front of the Moreno's horse, pounding at his thighs with his fists.

"Calmly, my brother. Tell me what is gone."

"The village! Our village! Gone!"

"The storm? A flood?"

"No-o-o-o!" Reyes dropped to his knees and pressed his face into outstretched hands. "No-o-o-o!"

Moreno climbed down from his horse, went to his friend, and knelt down beside him. "I need to understand, Francisco."

Reyes looked up at Moreno. "I have been waiting here for your return. Six days! I thought you would never come back."

"Six days?" Moreno was even more confused. He had been gone only two days more than a week.

"They had papers, Nuñez. Said we must leave."

"Who had papers?" Moreno demanded.

"The Sheriff ... and ... and men from ... the ... the iron horse. We could not read the papers ... they had guns ... said we had to go."

"There is no railroad ... no trail for an iron horse to come near our village."

'Soon!"

Moreno spun around and swung himself back onto his horse. He tossed the reins of the horse carrying the deer to Reyes. "Follow me home," he said.

Reyes stood but could not raise his eyes to meet those of Moreno. "There is no home, Nuñez. Everything is gone ... burned to the ground."

* * *

"We paid the taxes on time, every year," Nuñez Moreno said to Guthrie Kendall outside El Patrón's hacienda.

"I know, and I'm sorry."

"You said it was our land forever."

"Yes, and, again, I am sorry, Nuñez. I truly believed the legislature would make Indian landowning legal."

"And the railroad men, they do not have to pay us for our land, for destroying our village?"

"They have convinced the courts it is public land," said Kendall.

"Public land?" Nuñez said loudly. "What is this public land the iron horse men speak of? Are we not part of the public of this land?" He made a sweeping motion across the visible horizon with an outstretched hand. "We were living on this land long before you white men arrived."

"I know. I know." Kendall said.

"Where is the land for us? Where are we to go? Where are we to live?" Nuñez said.

CHAPTER 20

I drove the battered pickup around to the back of The Pomo House and pulled up next to the garage. I was no more than a minute or so late for the meeting the elusive Hayes Moreno had specified.

But there was no sign of Hayes or his Ford Explorer, and the garage door was closed. I was about to go find Vanessa and ask if she'd heard from him when a loud creak came from inside the garage.

I slapped both palms against one of the door panels and shoved upward. No movement. I peered into the dark garage through the row of windows at the top of the door, but even standing on tiptoe all I could see was the top of the Explorer. Then a splash of daylight from a doorway at the rear of the garage brightened most of the interior.

I dashed around to the back only to run square into a fist that staggered me and left me holding onto the side of the building to keep from falling. My nose hurt like hell; I could feel blood running down over my lips and chin.

By the time I recovered, whoever had clobbered me was crashing off through the woods. It didn't seem worthwhile to take up the chase. Besides, I had a gut feeling the intruder wasn't into something as simple as burglary.

I eased through the open door my attacker had used to escape, keeping low and trying not to stumble over anything. I found a wall switch, flipped it on. A single overhead bulb eliminated most of the shadows. I laid a hand on the hood of Vanessa's Miata—cold—and then did the same with the Explorer—warm. The SUV's interior lights were on, but no one was visible inside.

After edging my way between the two vehicles, I found Hayes sprawled face down on the garage floor beneath the Explorer's open tailgate. Whatever it was he needed to talk to me about was going to have to wait—he was out cold; a trickle of blood oozed out from under his head onto the concrete floor.

I crouched down, checked his pulse, and kept my head on a swivel. Just because one person had taken off running didn't mean there wasn't someone else lurking out of sight in the garage. Hayes's pulse was thready. I rolled him over and found a jagged two-inch slash on the left side of his forehead.

I pulled the emergency release cord for the overhead door, pushed it up, and ran for the house. Vanessa was in the kitchen, stirring something in a large pot.

"Call 9-1-1," I yelled at her. "Hayes has been hurt."

She grabbed the phone, punched in the three digits, and gave the location of the B&B.

"You don't look so good yourself," she said as she hung up the phone. She reached out to touch my damaged nose, but I grabbed her hand and pulled her along behind me out through the door and along the path to the garage.

I was hoping we'd find Hayes sitting up on the Ford's tailgate, swearing into the air. No such luck. He was just as I'd left him.

Vanessa plopped down beside Hayes and gently placed his head in her lap. She crooned to him in soft, rhythmic words I didn't understand, nor did I need to—she was doing what she believed needed to be done.

When the EMTs arrived, accompanied by a police cruiser, they gave Hayes a thorough examination.

The EMTs and the cop queried Vanessa as to what had happened, but paid no attention to me. She had no answers for them other than what I'd told her. I started to add something, but they ignored both me and my battered nose.

The EMTs loaded the still-unconscious Hayes onto a stretcher, pushed him into the ambulance, and drove away. The cop hung around to look into the garage and check out the area leading back into the woods before taking off.

"That was strange," I said to Vanessa.

"What?"

"I might as well have been invisible."

"You're not one of them ... Temkut," she said.

"All three of them?"

"Yes."

"Helluva way to run a railroad."

"Don't worry about it." She turned and started for the house. "Need to get my purse." She stopped, looked back at me. "Can I get you something for your nose?"

"Nope. It's used to being in the wrong place at the wrong time." I put my index fingertips gently on either side of my nose, wiggled it gently. It was going to be sore for a few days. "Want me to go with you, or follow you with the truck?" I asked.

"I think I'd like you to come with me, please."

* * *

Hayes was conscious when we arrived at the Appa Bay Urgent Care Center. The on-duty doc said he appeared to have a concussion, that they probably would send him over to San Tomas for x-rays; either way, he would be kept overnight for observation.

"Got there a little too late to see who cold-cocked you," I told Hayes.

"Too bad 'cause I didn't see who it was, either." He rose up on one elbow. "Musta been hiding in the garage when I pulled in."

Vanessa placed a hand on his shoulder and gently pushed him back down onto the pillow. "You need to lie still and get some rest." She brushed the hair away from his eyes and kissed him on the forehead next to a new but bloody bandage.

He gave her a weak smile. "Hey, don't go messin' with my warrior image."

An attendant came in, checked Hayes's chart, and rolled him out toward the ambulance loading dock.

Vanessa tried to follow along, but was told she would have to travel on her own over to San Tomas.

As I watched Hayes disappear down the hallway, it occurred to me there was something wrong with this whole scenario. I tried to separate the afternoon's events from my underlying displeasure with Hayes for being so secretive, and for being less than honest with me since I arrived in Appa Bay.

"I don't want to go over to San Tomas," Vanessa said. "Hospitals depress me something fierce."

"Couldn't agree more."

Outside, I had my hand on the Miata's door handle when it finally came to me what was wrong with that poignant little scene in the ER.

"Damn!"

"What's wrong?" Vanessa said.

"He's lying!"

She gave me a confused, questioning look across the seats of the open roadster. "Who's lying?"

"Hayes."

"I don't follow you," she said. "Lying about what?"

"Didn't you notice the bandage when you kissed him on the forehead?"

"Of course. Why?"

"I wasn't thinking, can't believe I could have been so back-country stupid,"

"Zach, will you please tell me what you're talking about?"

"That guy didn't sneak up behind Hayes and clobber him; he was facing whoever it was that hit him."

She looked at me for a couple of beats, nodded, and said, "I see what you mean ... he has to know who it was that attacked the two of you."

"Exactly!" I turned around and headed back toward the Urgent Care Center.

"Zach! Where are you going?"

"If that ambulance hasn't left yet, I'm going to make that son-of-a-bitch tell me who knocked him out and did serious damage to my nose."

Vanessa ran to catch up with me, grabbed my arm, and pulled me to a stop. "You can't do that, Zach. He's really hurt. Let them take him to get the x-rays."

I pulled loose from her hand. "When I get through with Hayes Moreno, he's going to need another set of x-rays."

She took my arm again, this time with both hands. "I understand why you're angry, Zach, but let it go for now. We'll go see him first thing in the morning."

"Sure, and find he's pulled off another one of his infamous disappearing acts?"

"From the looks of him, I really don't think he's going anyplace tomorrow or maybe for a couple of days."

"Then maybe I'll just follow the ambulance to San Tomas and baby-sit him until he's feeling better."

"Are you serious?"

Was I? Yeah. More or less. I sure as hell wasn't going to lose Moreno again, not if I could help it. However, it wasn't practical to stay at the hospital for what ever time it might take for him to be declared fit enough to be released.

"You're right!" I took her hand, which was getting to be a habit, and started us toward the parking lot. "Let's get out of here, go someplace with a better smell."

* * *

"Want me to fix a bite to eat?" Vanessa said after she'd help me straighten my nose and put a big piece of tape across it. "Then maybe afterward we could..."

She put a hand on my chest, spread the fingers wide, and slowly moved downward until her palm came to rest on my belt buckle. She tilted her head and gave me a wide-eyed, expectant look.

"That's the second nicest thing that's happened to me all day," I said. "And very tempting, although kissing might prove to be a bit of a problem." She gently touched the tip of my nose and smiled her understanding. "Unfortunately, I have a lot to do before the evenin' sun goes down, little lady."

She laughed and I knew it was all right. I glanced at my watch: 5:10. The Temkut council meeting supposedly started at five. And it was still a few hours before it was time for my requested after-dark meeting with Greer Raebeck at the Putah Creek Casino.

"Think there's any chance I could get into the Tribal Council meeting this evening?"

"Not without Hayes," Vanessa said. "And maybe not even *with* him."

"Even if I just sit in the back, listen, watch the vote, and don't say anything?"

"Don't think so."

"Could you get me in?"

"I'm not a Temkut, remember?"

"Okay, then maybe a sandwich or a bowl of soup. After that, I'm outta here, off for other parts."

"Want me to go with you?"

"Think you better stay here. It's getting a bit dicey out there."

After we did the dishes and tidied up the kitchen, Vanessa renewed her offer to go along. Again, I declined, thanking her with a caress of her cheek that easily could have escalated into something much more sensual had it not been for my damn nose.

I drove the Miata around to the garage and put it away for Vanessa, then gave the garage interior a thorough examination. I also went through Hayes's Explorer, looking for who-knows-what. Nothing.

The woods didn't yield any clues, either. Would have liked to check with the Appa Bay police to see if the cop had come up with anything, but I knew from the way I'd been treated earlier there wasn't going to be any cooperation there.

It was still too early to head for the Putah Creek Casino, so I called Ed Harkins at the *Appa Bay Sentinel* to find out where the Temkut council met.

"Heard you're the one who found Moreno," he said.

"True. Get that from the cop or the EMTs who showed up?"

"Came in a round-about way. Usually find out what's going on hereabouts, whether the Temkuts tell me or not."

"What about the Council meetings?"

"That's different. If they don't tell me what they discussed, then chances are I'm never going to find out."

"But Moreno's a member of the Council."

"And what makes you think that gets me anything special?"

"Got it. So where *does* the Council meet?"

"Won't let you in," he said.

"So I've been told. Any harm, though, in knowing the location?"

"Reckon not. They've taken over an abandoned Pentecostal church just north of town, near the Rancheria headquarters. Usually gather about six."

"Thanks."

"If you learn anything, I'm a great fan of reciprocity."

I gave my word and went looking for the old church. There was no missing it, not just because of the architecture, but for the number of vehicles parked in a field next to the building. Looked like the whole tribe had turned out for the vote. I found an inconspicuous place to park the Dodge pickup on the other side of the street, about a half-block away in the direction of town.

It was a little past six and I wished I'd asked Vanessa or Harkins how long the meetings usually lasted. I still needed to get to Putah Creek by eight o'clock.

Well, they might not let me in, but they couldn't keep me from checking to see who had attended after the meeting broke up. I settled back, tuned the radio to a local "soft rock" FM station, and watched the doors of the paint-challenged building.

CHAPTER 21

Frank Ross tapped his gavel twice on the rickety, collapsible table and looked around at the other members of the Temkut Rancheria Council. When the hubbub failed to lessen, the chairman pounded the table harder, but still only twice, as was his custom.

"Ladies! Gentlemen!" shouted Ross. "Let's get this meetin' going. We got some things to discuss, a vote to take, and we don't want to be here all evenin' like last time."

"Won't take long if you got word that construction's gonna start soon on the casino," said one of the tribe members seated up front.

"Billy, that'll happen *when* it happens. I keep tellin' you that and you plain don't listen."

"I've *been* listenin' to you, Frank, and the rest of the council. And I've been listenin' to all those Nevada fellas that've kept comin' around here for almost three years now. Still haven't seen a single shovelful of dirt come out of the ground."

Others began to shout similar comments and complaints, taking the noise level a few decibels higher than it had been before Ross started the meeting. He used his gavel over and over again, in double raps, but the plastic tabletop didn't have what it took to send out an attention-getting call to order. Frustrated, Ross stuck a thumb-middle finger combination between his lips, took a deep breath, and let loose with a long, loud, shrill whistle. Wren Childers, the Council secretary, clapped both hands over her ears.

The room became church-quiet.

"This kind of behavior isn't getting us anywhere," Ross said in a normal voice. With exaggerated theatrics, he used both hands to raise the gavel to shoulder-level, then place it gently on the table in front him. Wren and Lawrence Drucker, the tribe treasurer, both smiled.

"I know you're not going to like what I have to tell you now, but here it is: the North Coast District Office of the

163

California Coastal Commission has notified us that our plans for the Temkut Casino and Resort are in conflict with the California Coastal Act of 1976." Before the swell of murmurs could grow into a din again, he raised one hand, palm facing outward, to quell the protests.

"Not only that, but word from the Coastal Commission's executive director is that there is slim to no chance that an approval will ever be granted."

Ross's hand went up again in anticipation of the protests. The gesture was unnecessary – he had their attention.

"Our legal guys have already told the Coastal Commission for the umpteenth time that we have an inherent right to offer gaming on tribal lands, as set down by the U.S. Supreme Court in 1987. Also told those bozos how things work under our gaming compact with the State of California."

"Right!" someone shouted.

"Yes, 'right,'" Ross repeated. "However, the Commission's executive director isn't convinced that our compact supersedes the jurisdiction of the Commission when it comes to protecting the coast's environment."

A chorus of catcalls and boos resounded through the nave of the former church.

Ross's raised palm silenced them once again.

"I know, I know," he said. "Seems like no matter how much we try to convince people that we have a right to proceed with our plans, another monkey wrench gets tossed into the works."

"Isn't that why we're voting on whether or not to hook up with this Lurton-Bales bunch?" said Drucker. "Didn't they say they'd handle all that kind of government and political red tape for us ... for a god-awful huge fee?"

"So they claim," said Ross. "Maybe we should go ahead with the vote and get things movin' in that direction." When no one objected, he continued: "As you've all been notified, the board members have recommended that the Federated Indians of Temkut Rancheria retain Lurton-Bales Associates of Washington, DC, as lobbyists and public relations counsel."

"How much?" someone yelled.

"That's the second stage," Ross said. "Right now we're simply voting on whether or not to start negotiatin' with them."

"Vote!" several people yelled.

"Okay," Ross said. "Those in favor of entering into negotiations with Lurton-Bales, raise your hand." About one half of the people in the room raised their hands. "Those against?" The number of hands in the air appeared to be about the same.

Ross turned to, the secretary. "Did you get a count, Wren?"

"You gotta be kiddin'," she said.

"Okay, everybody, we're gonna have to count hands. Those in favor?" He raised his own hand with the others and waited for the secretary. When she nodded, he said, "Those against?"

After a moment, Wren Childers said, "Tie!"

"Shit," Ross mumbled, then turned to the waiting crowd. "Wren says it's a tie." He held up a hand to quiet the groans and mumbles. "Anyone want to change their vote?" When no one responded, he sat down.

"Where's Moreno?" someone shouted.

"Don't know," Ross said. "He was supposed to be here."

A man in the back, wearing an EMT uniform, stood. "Moreno's at the hospital in San Tomas." He sat down again.

"What the hell happened, Lawrence?" Ross asked the EMT. "Not another shooting, like Petrucci and Nolan."

Lawrence Herrera stood again. "Naw. Got a hit on the head by someone over to The Pomo House. Arthur took him on over to San Tomas for x-rays." He sat back down.

"Lawrence, will you please tell us what happened?" Ross shouted over the vocal noise of the crowd.

"Already told you," Herrera said.

"Who did it?" asked a woman sitting next to Herrera.

"Don't know," Herrera said.

"Was Vanessa Jimenez there?" Ross asked.

"Yup. Her and that guy from Nevada that's staying at her place."

"Either of them get hurt?"

"Don't think so. Have to ask Charlie Longtree. He was the duty cop."

Most of the audience was standing now, many of the people crowding around Herrera.

"Okay, okay, everybody," Ross shouted. "Let's calm down. Nothin' more we can do here tonight. I say we adjourn the meeting. We'll meet again when our vice chairman gets out of the hospital." Most the people were headed for the door before he could do a double tap on the table with his gavel.

"Wish I knew what was goin' on around here," Wren said.

Ross expressed his agreement with a hands-out shrug.

"So when we gonna start buildin' the casino?" Billy Leaphorn asked, still sitting in his seat.

"Billy, go home, will ya?" Ross said.

CHAPTER 22

Sitting on your duff for almost two hours, particularly on a truck seat, makes you appreciate just a skosh what stake-out cops go through. If something didn't pop soon, I'd have to abandon this gig and take off for Putah Creek for my meeting with Greer Raebeck. Maybe I wouldn't get kidnapped this time.

I mean, whoever came up with that thing about how Native Americans don't talk much obviously never got to listen in when a tribe was involved in trying to set up a casino. At least, that's what I thought the meeting was all about. They'd been at it supposedly since 6 p.m. By the time I got to Putah Creek, it would be well past dusk.

My fingers were on the ignition key when the building doors spread outward and people came straggling out of the old church, talking and shaking their heads. I got the feeling things had not gone well. I wondered if Hayes's absence had prevented them from making a decision on whether or not to hire Lurton-Bales.

In the parking lot, all four doors of a big, black BMW swung open at the same time. I chastised myself for not having spotted the Bimmer during my earlier drive-by. Suddenly there were my good buddies Felix Crandal and Terence Wadkins, plus the two musclemen who had kidnapped me and probably the ones who had chased me in the pickup with its array of spotlights.

Crandal reminded me of a big city executive, newly arrived at a dude ranch: the cuffs of his white, starched, button-down shirt were rolled up a couple of turns; glossy black, tasseled loafers gleamed at the bottom end of a pair of too-short, too-new blue jeans.

The Lurton-Bales bunch stood by the BMW until Frank Ross came out of the building, then Crandal and Wadkins walked rapidly over to the chairman. Crandal moved like the stiff jeans were chafing his butt and balls. The trio exchanged greetings and continued to talk as Ross headed for a white Ford Escape hybrid with a big Temkut Rancheria logo on the side. The tribal chairman didn't seem pleased with whatever it was Crandal was saying to him.

My first thought was that if the Lurton-Bales people were in town, there could be a direct connection to what had happened to Hayes. Was the attack on him specifically timed to keep him from attending the meeting and having an influential voice in the proceedings?

I saw a couple of other vaguely familiar faces among the Temkut, but I was primarily interested in Ross's reaction to Crandal and Wadkins. The lobbyists were talking up a storm, using more hand gestures than a gospel minister. Ross simply kept shaking his head right up until the time he got into the mini-SUV and drove away. I wasn't sorry to see the Lurton-Bales guys ignored and unhappy, but I sure wished I could have heard what they were saying in that parking lot.

Crandal stalked back to the BMW, Wadkins trailing behind like an out-of-favor puppy. The two of them, along with the pair of jerks, got into the car and headed north, Crandal driving. I waited several seconds, then did a u-turn and followed them. I stayed a cautious distance behind them since the Bimmer wasn't a car I was likely to lose in this part of the country. After a few minutes I saw the left turn signal blinking; I slowed so I wouldn't catch up to them before Crandal made the turn even though I was relatively certain they wouldn't be suspicious of my loaner truck.

As I drove past, they were onto the crushed stone driveway leading to the big redwood showplace where I'd been an unwilling guest. That was as much as I needed to know. A quarter-mile down the road, I turned around and headed back the way I'd come.

It was getting late and time to find out why Greer Raebeck was being so secretive about needing to see me.

* * *

The Dodge pickup got me to the Putah Creek Casino in good order. It still wasn't quite dark so I did a slow tour of the garage. The Porsche was just where I'd left it, but there was no sign of Greer. I parked one level up and walked back down. I found a spot to hang out in the shadows, my car between me and the elevator.

The casino's exterior lights were so bright it was difficult to determine at what moment the sky actually turned dark. Just as I looked at my watch to confirm an educated guess that the time was near, I heard the chime of the elevator. Within seconds Greer stepped out into the garage.

I didn't move or call out as I watched her walk confidently in the direction of my bright yellow Porsche. I still found her a very attractive woman and had to acknowledge a small pang of regret. When she was about halfway to the car, she stopped and looked at her watch before glancing around the garage. She hadn't given me a chance to tell her during our brief telephone conversation what I would be driving, or where I would park.

I was about to step out into the light to let her know I was there when the elevator chimed again. I stepped back and watched while she turned to look in that direction. The doors slid open and a pair of security guards stepped out, their shoulders and biceps straining the burgundy blazers.

"Ms. Raebeck!" one of them called out, waving a sheaf of papers in his hand. "Just a moment, please!"

Greer raised a hand to acknowledge them, did a double-take, spun around, and started running toward the Porsche.

The two guards started running also, twenty or so feet behind her.

I pulled the Cayman's keyless fob from my pocket and pressed the button to unlock the doors. When she got even with me, I grabbed her arm and pulled her hard against me.

"Wha...?"

"Here!" I slapped the key fob into her hand. "Start the car!"

She scrambled away from me and into the aisle, just ahead of the first guard. He reached out for her at the same time he came even with me. I sucker-punched him in the right temple and kicked his legs out from under him.

The second guard was too close to avoid his fallen buddy and stumbled head-long into my right fist. Two down and time to make tracks.

A screech of tortured rubber caught my attention. And there in the aisle was the Cayman, sliding to a reverse stop, the dual exhaust pipe poking into the shoulder of one of the fallen guards. The passenger door swung open for me.

"Wanna drive?" Greer yelled.

"You're doing fine!" I leaped into the coupe; she stomped the accelerator and I was pressed hard against the seatback. Before I could fasten my safety belt, the insistent beep-beep-beep of the seatbelt warning device assaulted our ears.

One level down, we sped out into the night and raced along the tree-lined casino driveway toward the access road.

"Which way?" she yelled as we came to the "T" inter-section.

"Left!" I yelled over the irritating beeps. "San Tomas!"

The outside tires moaned loudly as she made the skidding turn without letting up on the accelerator. Once she had us lined up with the road, I said, "Take it those weren't any of your people." I struggled to get my seatbelt fastened before the damn beeper short-circuited my brain.

"Good guess," she said.

"What made you suspicious? You couldn't possibly know the entire staff by sight."

"True ... but I do know the security color of the day. They should have been wearing medium blue blazers, not burgundy. We switch every other day."

"Glad you're on my side ... at least I think you are."

"Look, I apologized about the thing with Wadkins. And if it'll help, I'll do it again: I'm sorry."

"I'd rather sulk," I said.

She reached over to touch my cheek with her fingertips and I involuntarily pulled back.

She glanced my way, did a double take, and said, "My God, Toby, what happened to your poor nose?"

I was about to explain when she laughed. I slumped down in the seat and glared out the windshield. "You just better hope that calling me over here was for a good reason."

"Now, now! Don't pout." She reached down and started digging around in her purse with one hand while keeping the Porsche nicely on the road with the other "Remember when I told you there was a connection between Twin Arrows and Lurton-Bales?"

The Porsche's speedometer ranged between 80 and 90 mph as we made tracks for San Tomas. I'd initially pointed us in that direction, thinking that if someone took up the chase, they'd most likely think we would head for Appa Bay. I also considered the possibility of making a surprise visit to Hayes Moreno at the hospital.

"Yeah, I remember your comment about Twin Arrows and Lurton-Bales. You said something about trusting me with your life, but not with that information."

"Sorry. I had no choice … then." The lost hand came up out of her purse with a thin, clear CD jewel box. She held it out to me.

"What's this?"

"Something I'd like you to look at."

"Is it tied in to the way with those two bogus security guards were chasing you?"

"I certainly have to think it is."

"Yeah, well, you also made it clear before that you preferred to keep a lot of distance between the two of us."

"True."

"Well, Ms. Raebeck, here we are, about as snug as two people can get without being in a rug together." I glanced over at her; she looked straight ahead through the windshield.

"Ready to share now?" I asked.

"Some."

"Some? What's that supposed to mean?"

"It means things are in a state of flux."

"You mean like all fluxed up?"

"Ha." She pushed the speed up to an even 100. "I'd add the other 'ha,' but what we're all involved in here is no laughing matter."

"No, I think not. Certainly not with two city councilmen dead, Hayes Moreno beaten and in a hospital, and my pride suffering from having been bushwacked by the criminal hand of Felix Crandal."

"Toby, I swear to you, Twin Arrows is not responsible for any of that."

"So you've said before."

"And it's still true," she insisted.

"Okay, I'll accept that … for the time being. But you still haven't told me why it was so necessary for me to meet you at the Putah Creek Casino tonight."

She backed off a little on the speed as we saw the lights of San Tomas making a bright spot on the horizon ahead of us. "I received an e-mail early today telling me—telling Twin Arrows—to back off on our plan to provide financial support for the Temkut casino and resort. Like immediately."

"Who sent it?"

"It wasn't signed. And the e-mail address of the sender proved to be bogus."

"And?"

"I'm none too fond of extortion … in any guise," she said.

"Did you respond?"

"Couldn't. Not only was the address phony, it was one of those irritating no-reply-possible things."

"Is there a copy of it on the CD?"

"Yes, but I don't think it'll do you any good. I had my IT people try to track down the sender. Untraceable. Anyway, I downloaded it, along with some other material, for you to take a look at."

"So no idea at all who it might have been from?"

"Not a clue. If you look at the major players, the Pomos may not be too happy that we're also funding the Temkut project, but they were aware a long time ago that there was going to be competition popping up here. As for Lurton-Bales, can't see them closing a potentially lucrative pocket before they get a chance to stick their hand into it. And while there are a number of groups that do what Twin Arrows does, we pretty much stay off each other's turf."

"I'm still not clear as to why you came to me, though, Greer. I've told you more than once that I have a client … Hayes Moreno … and I'm not going to drop him for you."

She had the Porsche all the way down to a sedate 65 as we passed the *City Limits* sign. "I understand that, but that shouldn't keep you from getting back to me with anything that might tie in with what I've told you, should it? I mean, as long as it's not in conflict with what you're doing for Moreno."

"Know where the hospital is?" I said.

"Of course."

"Let's go there."

She made a couple of turns and there it was, the Wirok County Hospital. She pulled into the parking lot, which was two-thirds empty, and parked my highly recognizable yellow Porsche between two hulking SUVs.

"You haven't answered my question," she said as she handed me the keys.

"I'll do what I can. Okay?"

"Works for me."

Inside the hospital, I used a house phone to call Hayes's room.

"Sorry, sir, Mr. Moreno is no longer a patient here."

"What?" I said more sharply than I should have. "Where'd they send him?"

"I have no idea where Mr. Moreno is, sir. He checked himself out a little more than an hour ago. About 10:30. He seemed to be in quite a hurry. He even forgot to take his envelope of personal belongings."

"That's just dandy," I said and hung up.

"Not here?" Greer asked.

"Nope. Gone. Checked himself out and they don't know where he went."

"Now what? Are you going to go look for him?"

"With a vengeance." I started for the door. "Want to come along, or do you need to get back to Putah Creek? I'll take you wherever you want to go."

"If you don't mind, Toby, I'd appreciate a ride out to the Wirok County airport. Twin Arrows has a Beechcraft King Air there and a pilot on standby. I'm getting out of Dodge and heading back to Lake Tahoe. I'll see if I can find out what's happening from there."

"Sounds like a good idea to me." I drove her to the airport and waited to make sure both the plane and pilot were there.

"I'll let you know what's up when and if I find Moreno," I said after she'd checked out everything.

"I'd appreciate that," she said. "And, Toby, please take care of yourself."

"You, too." I waved and headed west for Appa Bay.

CHAPTER 23

Hayes Moreno was on his way back to the hospital to retrieve the envelope containing his personal belongings when he saw Zach Rolfe's yellow Porsche pull into the parking lot. He spun around and walked rapidly away in the opposite direction.

What he needed more than anything was to get back to Appa Bay. As soon as possible. That required making a call. But with his cell phone in that damn hospital envelope, a pay phone was his only hope. It took two gas stations and an all-night convenience store before he found a working phone, then sweated bullets when it took every loose coin in his pants pocket to call his cousin, Esteban Lupin, who lived in San Tomas.

"Esteban? Hayes. Hayes Moreno."

"Yeah, like how many other guys named Hayes live around here, you know?"

"Okay, okay. The thing is, I'm stuck here in San Tomas without wheels and I need a ride out to Appa Bay. Can you do that for me?"

"What you doing in San Tomas, bro, bar-hoppin'?" asked Lupin, who managed a Big-O tire store and preferred to be called Stephen. "Or did that Explorer of yours finally gasp its last gasp?"

"Can you drive me to Appa Bay or not?" Hayes wanted to remind his cousin that he didn't drink, but wasn't in the mood to go there. "I know it's late, but…"

"No problem, bro. Tell me where you are and I'll be there in minutes."

Hayes gave his cousin his location, hung up, and started pacing in a tight circle, certain that Esteban would be his usual self and take forever to get off his duff and drive downtown. Probably caught him sitting around in his underwear, watching TV. But, for a change, Esteban was true to his word and within a short time a pale blue crew-cab Chevy S-10 pulled up to the curb, rockabilly music blasting out from the cab. Two rows of large yellow lettering spread across the side of the truck: *Big O Tires /*

Stephen Lupin, Gen. Mgr. / 1022 Putnam St. / San Tomas, CA / (707) 555-4949.

Hayes climbed into the passenger seat, nodded his thanks, and immediately turned down the volume on the radio.

"Hey, bro, what the hell happened to you?" his cousin asked when he saw the bandage on Hayes's head.

Hayes waved off the question.

"Embarrassed, huh?" Esteban said. "Should stay out of those roundeye bars."

"Esteban, I don't–"

"No *Esteban*, man. It's Stephen!" Then he started laughing. "Don't sweat it, Hayes. Just flapping my lips. We all know you don't do the booze thing, okay?"

Hayes forced a small smile and sat back in the seat.

"Where's the Explorer?"

"Pomo House … I hope."

"You still bunkin' there? Not that I blame you. That Vanessa lady is one fine lookin' woman."

Hayes glanced at his wrist to check the time, but his watch wasn't there. Probably with his wallet, cell, and truck keys, in the left-behind manila envelope. "Keep your thoughts about Vanessa Jimenez to yourself," he said.

"Ooh! So it's that way, is it, bro?"

"No, Esteban … Stephen … it's not *that way* or any other way with Vanessa. She's just good people and a good friend."

"Wish she was *my* good friend."

"Knock it off, man, and tell me what time it is," Hayes said.

"Right there, bro," Esteban said, pushing a finger against a button next to the radio's digital readout. The numbers switched from the station call letters to show *10:48.*

"Shit!" Hayes mumbled.

"You late for somethin'?"

"I'm late for two somethings … was supposed to be at the tribal council meeting at six, but there's nothing I can do about that now."

"So where we headed, bro?"

"The hunting lodge. Another meeting there … at ten."

"The meetin' after the meetin', huh? Esteban said with a laugh.

"It's not funny."

"Yeah, well, I don't know if you've noticed, man, but you're more than a tad late for that ten o'clock confab."

"Tell me about it."

Hayes slumped down in the seat and closed his eyes. His head continued to hurt, but that wasn't information he cared to share with his cousin.

They rode the rest of the way back to Appa Bay in silence; rather, they didn't talk; Stephen turned the volume back up on the rockabilly.

"Mind waiting a moment until I make sure I have another set of keys?" Hayes asked when they pulled into the driveway of The Pomo House.

Esteban laughed. "Big bump on the head, no watch, and no car keys. Very, very suspicious, bro."

"Damn it, Esteban, I…"

"Don't have to tell me nothin', cuz, but people will start talkin', you know?"

"Not if you keep your mouth shut when you get back to San Tomas. Anyway, I owe you one."

Esteban was still laughing. "Don't owe me nothin,' bro. Worth every minute just to see the ever-cool Hayes Moreno all ruffled. Don't recall ever seeing that before."

A digital salute was all Hayes could manage before going inside to retrieve an extra set of keys for his SUV. When he returned, he waved a parting *thank you* to his cousin before going to get the Explorer out of the garage. He noted that Vanessa's Miata was gone. If he was fast, and lucky, he might get there before the tribal meeting broke up.

Once on the coast road, he drove much faster than was prudent, keeping a watchful eye more on the dashboard clock than on the speedometer. He was keenly aware that by the time he reached the tribal hunting lodge, he'd be close to an hour and a half late. He hoped the others hadn't given up on him and gone home.

He almost drove past the entranceway to the lodge, braked hard, turned in sharply, and slid to a stop on dry pine needles. The split rails were down and off to one side; he could see three familiar vehicles parked under the trees—Frank Ross's Escape hybrid, Vanessa's Miata, and a silver 6 Series BMW convertible that Greer Raebeck kept at Putah Creek for her personal use.

The meeting wasn't over.

"Hayes!" Vanessa Jimenez cried out when he entered the lodge. "What're you doing here?" She ran across the dusty, plank floor to confront him. "You're supposed to be in the hospital." She took his arm and walked him over to the rough-hewn dining table where Frank Ross and Greer Raebeck were sitting across from each other.

"Not too difficult to get out of a hospital, *if* you can find your clothes," Hayes said. "Like a jerk, I forgot to pick up my personal belongings before I left." He went around the table and sat down next to the tribal chairman. "Thanks for waiting for me."

Hayes looked across at Vanessa and gave her a what-are-you-doing-here shrug.

"I know this is supposed to be a Rancheria casino thing, but I thought I should come out and tell everyone you wouldn't be here," Vanessa said.

"Then we sort of got to talking about this and that and the time got away from us," Greer said. "Otherwise, we'd probably have been gone."

Ross put a hand on Hayes's shoulder. "It doesn't please me to know there has been more violence," he said. "Ms. Jimenez says your friend Rolfe thinks you really do know who struck you down. Is that true?"

"We're guessing it was one of Crandal's people," Greer said.

"Nope. Good guess, but nope. Believe it or not, it was Lance Chubb."

"The Appa Bay police chief?" Greer said.

"None other." He turned to Vanessa. "When I found him in the garage, he'd taken my schematic out of the Explorer and was reading it on the tailgate. I asked him what the hell he thought he was doing; he jumped up, shoved me, and hit me with something; his pistol, I think. Next thing I know, I'm in the Urgent Care Center."

"He must have taken the diagram," Vanessa said. "I looked for it when I got home, but it wasn't anywhere in the Explorer or the garage."

"Don't know that he's going to learn anything from it," Hayes said. "Just a lot of inter-connecting lines to all the names and entities involved in getting the casino started. And a few notes on my suspicions."

"What does your Mr. Rolfe think about our situation?" Ross asked.

"I didn't think you knew about him," Hayes said.

"He hasn't tried to hide himself," said the tribal chairman. "Saw him parked on the street near the meeting hall earlier this evening." He looked over at Vanessa. "That old Dodge pickup you borrowed for him is almost as conspicuous to most of us as his yellow sports car."

"It's what he wanted," she said.

"Sorry, Frank," Hayes said. "I felt we needed another set of eyes, someone who has a good grasp on the Nevada gaming scene."

"I have to admit that Rolfe's good," Greer said, "but haven't I been helping you with that sort of thing?"

"Wanted someone who doesn't have a stake in what's going on around here," Hayes said.

"Still should have shared that information with the tribe," Ross said.

"Didn't expect everything to get so damn complicated … or dangerous," Hayes said.

"Perhaps we should take all this to the sheriff in San Tomas," Ross said.

"Not so sure that's the best course of action," Greer said.

The heavy main door to the cabin creaked open; they all turned to see who their unexpected visitor was. Hayes was surprised when Greer jumped up and pulled a small pistol from her purse.

* * *

I'd caught a glimpse of an Explorer racing out of town just as I arrived from San Tomas. Since I wasn't sure it was Hayes's SUV, I went on up to The Pomo House. Both his Ford and Vanessa's Miata were gone. The next question: where are they?

If they'd wanted a bite to eat while they discussed things, I was sure they would have stayed at The Pomo House. Unless they didn't want me popping in on them, which was exactly what I'd had in mind.

All the restaurants were closed and the bar would have been too public. I drove past the old church where the tribe held its meeting, but there were no longer any vehicles in the parking lot and there were no lights on in the building. The next logical place was the hunting lodge, particularly if Hayes was hiding from someone.

There were four vehicles parked on the lodge grounds, all of which I recognized except for a flashy BMW convertible.

I didn't knock, simply barged in, which wasn't too bright on my part—everyone appeared startled, except Greer, who was standing at table with a pistol in her hand.

"Are you going to shoot me just because I didn't knock?" I said. "And what the hell are you doing here anyway? Thought I put you on a plane to Tahoe not too long ago." She flushed a bright red and slipped the pistol back into her shoulder bag.

I walked over and sat down next to Vanessa, Greer on the other side of me.

"Toby, sorry about the subterfuge of having you take me to the airport. I couldn't tell you I was coming out here," Greer said.

"Seems there're a lot of things people can't seem to tell me." I looked across the table, glared at Hayes, and stuck my hand out toward Frank Ross. "Zach Rolfe."

He took my hand in a firm grip. "Hayes should have introduced us long before this."

"Yes, he should have. He also should have told me who clobbered him earlier today, and why."

"It was Lance Chubb, the chief of police," Vanessa said. "Or so Hayes claims."

"Nice. Something personal between the two of you, Hayes, other than the traditional cop-reporter mutual distrust?"

"He doesn't like me, but that's not what this was all about," he said. "Remember that diagram I showed you?"

"Yeah. The one with all the lines connecting all the players. What about it?"

"Chubb took it."

"So what else is happening here?" I said. "How long have the four of you been cahoots with one another? And why wasn't I told, Hayes?"

"Toby…"

"Zach…"

"Mr. Rolfe…"

"Let's do it one at a time," I said. "Maybe it'll make more sense that way."

Ross held up a hand to silence the others. "Mr. Rolfe, I am sorry that Hayes brought you into this situation without fully informing you about all the people involved. I am also sorry that he did not see fit to consult with me before securing your services."

Hayes stood, his hands stretched out in front of him. "Frank, I apologize. I did what I thought was best for the tribe."

"The tribe decides what is best for the tribe," Ross said. It was not a statement to be challenged. He motioned for Hayes to sit down, then turned to me: "It took several years for my people to gain official recognition and to become the Federated Indians of Temkut Rancheria."

"I've done some reading about that over at the San Tomas library," I said.

"Good. Most outsiders don't take the time." He looked across the table. "Ms. Raebeck is one of the few exceptions. Anyway, our next move was to find a way to survive financially so we could provide jobs and homes and schools for tribal members. Like many tribes in California, we decided to build and operate a gaming casino. We came a little late to that decision, which has had both its good points and its bad."

"And things obviously haven't been going too well of late," I said.

"It went well in the beginning," Hayes said. "And we knew it wasn't going to happen overnight."

"But the process has gone on far longer than it should have," Ross said. "About the same time we began to suspect that someone was throwing a monkey wrench into the works, Ms. Raebeck came to us with the same kind of suspicions."

"Initially, I … Twin Arrows that is … thought perhaps the Temkuts had decided to go with another financial group," she said. "You know, deliberately slowing things down to make us think it wasn't going to work out."

"And?" I asked.

"Not so," she said. "Since then we've been working together to try and find who's sabotaging the operation."

"And you've found out what?"

"Damn little," Hayes said. "That's why I called you in to help."

"Without telling Mr. Ross, here, or other members of the tribal council."

"Probably not my best move," he said.

"Hmmpf," Vanessa grunted.

"So the casino project's going nowhere, you have two murders on your hands, the Lurton-Bales people appear to be up to no good, and now the police chief is skulking around beating up Hayes and sneaking off with what might be an implicating document. Is that about it?"

"Unfortunately, no," Ross said. "Now the California Coastal Commission is giving us big time trouble."

"The Coastal Commission?" I said. "What the hell's their stake in Indian gaming?"

"Not the gambling," Hayes said. "The land."

"It's your land, isn't it? Sovereign tribal land?"

"Maybe, maybe not," Ross said. "Depends a lot on whether you are an Indian or a white man." He looked at Vanessa and

Hayes for acknowledgement and received two quick agreeing nods.

"It is almost impossible to count the times The People have been chased from their land, given less desirable land, and chased off again," Ross continued. "Every time the white man thinks Indian land is valuable, he takes it—sometimes violently, sometimes by law … white man's law."

"And the Coastal Commission wants to take your land?" I asked.

"No, they can't take it," Hayes said. "But they think they can tell us how we can or can't use it." He paused. "Basically, they say it's illegal for us to build a casino and resort on coastal land."

"Any suggestions?" Greer asked.

"Yeah. I think maybe you're not even close to identifying the real source of the Temkuts' problem," I said.

"We were just discussing the possibility of going to the Wirok County sheriff to see if we can get him to intervene," Ross said.

"Or, before you do that, we can sit here, all night if necessary, until each of you tells me everything you know about this whole situation, from the time the notion of a casino was first put into words, up through what's happened today. Then maybe I can do what Hayes asked me to come here to do."

CHAPTER 24

Northern California – 1910

"My people are homeless," said Nuñez Moreno. "They are driven from place to place by the white man on whose property they seek refuge."

It was the second time in Moreno's 55 years that he had traveled to Sacramento. This time he sat in a small, cramped conference room before a California Senate subcommittee on Indian Affairs. He was uncomfortable in the itchy store-bought suit he had ordered through the trading post. The suit was too large, the shirt too small, and the stiff shoes hurt his feet. But he was determined not to be distracted by minor irritations.

When none of the committee members spoke, Moreno continued, "The Washington government does not help us. Our children are not wanted in the local schools. We have no medical care for our sick. We have no implements, no lands for farming. My people are willing to work. Give us a place, any place, to make our own way and we will be happy."

"I thought all of that was taken care of five years ago," said one of the committee members.

"Yes, yes," said the chairman. "In 1905 Congress ratified the so-called 'lost' treaties of 1851. Passed a lot of legislation, dubious legislation I might add. Then they sent the Bureau of Indian Affairs on a fool's errand to buy up property hither, thither, and yon for tribes of landless Indians, for God's sake. Waste of public funds, if you ask me."

The chairman turned in his high-backed leather chair and waggled a finger at an aide. "Where's that BIA report, the one about buying tracts of land for Indians?" The aide pulled a bound report from a pile of similar documents and handed it to the chairman.

"Ah, yes, here it is," said the Senator, running his index finger down the length of one page: "Thirty-six new reservations and rancherías in sixteen Northern California counties." He

glanced at the other two members of the committee, seated on either side of him. "Never have been able to get that straight: just what the hell is a 'rancheria' again?"

"Very small parcels of land," said the Senator to his left. "Supposed to provide home sites only for small bands of homeless Indians."

"Ah, yes," said the chairman. He turned his attention back to Nuñez Moreno. "And you're here to tell us that this did nothing to help the…the…" He glanced at his notes. "The Temkuts? And if not, why not, Mr. Moreno?"

"According to your own report, Senator, the BIA's investigator visited sixteen counties in Northern California. What that report doesn't say is that not once did he step foot into twelve other counties, including Wirok County, where my tribe has made its home since long before the time of the white man. There, my people continue to live, wishing only to enjoy the same kind of peace they had for centuries. If they cannot have that simple life, then what is left for them?"

"Yet you seem to be an educated man, Mr. Moreno, to have stepped away from that simple life you speak of," said the chairman. "You obviously read and write, have knowledge of arithmetic, and possibly are aware of a certain amount of history. Is that not correct?"

"Yes, Senator, that is correct. I was fortunate. The owner of the land that employed my family saw fit to send me to Indian school."

"And are there not others among the Temkuts who enjoy that same kind of education?"

"There are some, Senator. Perhaps a half-dozen."

"I see." He paused. "I would think that those of you with an education could find good jobs, save money, and help your tribe buy land." He waited for Moreno to respond. After several seconds, he said, "Does not what I say make sense?"

Moreno continued to sit in silence.

"I would like an answer, sir. After all, you came to us."

Moreno sat straighter in his chair, took a deep breath, let it out slowly, and said, "What you say makes sense, Senator, *provided there were those who would hire us for other than common labor, and provided there were those who would allow us to own land."*

* * *

"Are we going to get our own reservation or ranchería?" Felipa Moreno asked her husband when he returned from Sacramento.

She set aside the basket she was weaving, one of a matched series for a museum in Europe. It was a special order that had come through the trading post,

"I know you are tired from your long journey," she said, "but the trader stopped by today and asked to speak to you. He is staying the night here in the village."

"I do not know if we will get land to call our own," he said. "They did not say when they would make a decision."

"Did they look kindly on your request?"

"Woman, you know as well as I do that very few white men look kindly on anything asked of them by an Indian."

"But the chairman did allow you to speak, Nuñez. That is something you never thought would happen."

"Yes, that is true. It is not often that members of unlisted tribes are allowed to make requests before such committees."

"Then perhaps that is in our favor."

Moreno grunted. "That chairman is not a friend of The People, particularly homeless Indians."

"Then why did they make him chairman of that committee?"

Another grunt. "Perhaps for that very reason." He plopped down in a wicker chair opposite his wife. "Did the trader say what he wanted to talk about?"

"I asked, but he said he would talk with you." She sighed. "He is like all white men: they do not discuss business with women."

The next morning Moreno was up early and went looking for the trader. He found the man feeding his half-dozen pack animals down near the stream. A bed roll was still stretched out under a tree; a coffee pot sat burbling near a small, rock-ringed

186

*bed of coals. He was having trouble getting one of the mules to
stand still while he put a feedbag on its head.*

*"Nuñez!" called out the trader as Moreno walked toward
him. "Hear you been up to Sacramenta talkin' to them politician
fellas. That right?"*

*"Yes." Moreno put his hand on the flank of the recalcitrant
mule, which immediately stopped moving and stood still. "When I
came home last night, Felipa said you had something you wanted
to talk about."*

*"Yeah, guess I do, Nuñez." He tilted his head up, sniffed the
air. "Gonna start rainin' soon."*

"That's what you wanted to talk to me about?"

*"Well, it's part of it. I mean, you know it's doggone
impossible to get into this valley after the rains start."*

"I know."

*"Yeah. The road out yonder gets to bein' one big ole river
of mud. And even when it's dry, the trail between the road and
here gets plumb more dangerous every year, Nuñez. I mean, what
yer needs is one of them new type roads that's good all year."*

*"I wish we had one of those, too," Moreno said. "I talked
to the man who owns the land about putting in a road, but he said
it isn't somethin' that's going to do him any good."*

*"Reckon I see his point. Sort of a dollars and cents thing."
He checked to see if the mules had finished their oats. "Thing is,
that's sorta the way it is for me, too. Dollars and cents. Just can't
justify keeping these mules and feeding them to come in here just
once every two months. Everyplace else I go I can use a wagon.
Carries more and only means two animals."*

*Moreno pulled at his chin with one hand. "Guess you're
saying you're not going to be comin' into the Moloku Valley
anymore. That it?"*

*"Suppose so. And I do feel bad about that, Nuñez. I like you
and your people. You're good Injuns."*

* * *

*A few days later, Moreno rode into San Tomas on a day he knew
the BIA agent would be at his office in the county seat.*

"What can I do for you, Nuñez?" Bernard Eldred said. He didn't bother to get up from his chair.

"Need the BIA to build us a road," Moreno said.

"Whoa, Nellie! Don't think I've ever had anyone come in here with that one before. What makes you think we should build the Temkuts a road, even if we could?"

"Well, Mr. Eldred, you know we have only this one road into our valley," Moreno said.

"True, but there isn't all that much traffic into and out of Moloku Valley, unless things have changed considerably since the last time I was out that way," Eldred said. "And there's already a pretty good road that goes part way in."

"Can't use it when it's raining or been raining," Moreno said. "It's just too muddy and slippery. Pack animals can't keep their footing. And the rest of the way into the valley is just a trail. Wagon won't make it through even when the weather's good."

"The trader gets through to you, doesn't he?"

"He says no more, Mr. Eldred. Costs him too much to keep up a pack train to carry goods in and every other month or so, and even then, only during the dry months."

"That's sort of his problem, isn't it? Maybe you Temkuts should talk to another trader."

"Did that. Can't find anyone interested. All say the same thing. The bad road means they can't make enough money off us. So what we need is a good, solid road that the rains won't wash out."

"That's gonna cost a lot of money, Nuñez."

"Doesn't have to. We looked into it already." He paused, remembering the conversation he'd had with a civil engineer in San Tomas, and how proud he'd been when the man complimented him on his plan. "Should take 600 or so man-days of labor, which we'll contribute. Without pay."

Eldred shook his head and laughed. "Now that's a plan I might be able to sell. Washington always likes projects that don't cost them any money."

"I didn't say it wouldn't cost any money," Moreno said. "We would need money for tools and materials, and provisions to feed the men and horses."

"How much?"

Moreno pulled out a sheaf of papers and placed them on the desk between the two men. "Got it all worked out right here. Should be pretty close, according to Jacob Daniels, a civil engineer in town."

"Hm-mm," Eldred mused, stroking his long, full beard as he glanced through the figures. "That Daniels fella has a pretty good reputation. You say these are his figures?"

"Yes, sir."

"Well, Nuñez, tell you what: I'll put all this in my monthly report to headquarters. We'll just wait and see what happens."

"You might also put in your report," Moreno said, "that if the Temkuts had a good road that could be used every month of the year, they could pretty much support themselves. Maybe even build a school. The valley's real good for growing fruit and we have some timber that needs thinning so better use could be made of the land. With the fruit and the timber, the valley would attract a lot more traders. Create some competition. Get a regular business going."

"So, you'd take on cutting the timber, planting the orchards, picking the fruit, and doing the selling?"

"Yes, sir, every bit of that."

"Must say you sure have all this worked out real good." He folded the estimate papers neatly and stuck them into his satchel. Have you talked this over with your landlord?"

"Mr. Chalmers?"

"Yes."

"Only the part about our building the road. He has no objections provided it doesn't cost him anything."

"Good. I'll let you know one way or the other when I hear back from Washington."

* * *

A little more than two months later, toward the end of August, BIA headquarters sent word that it would "pay for the materials *and sustenance for men and animals, and lend all necessary tools to build a 8.9-mile, all-weather, wagon-worthy road through the Moloku Valley, provided it meets all Wirok County standards, with construction to start the following year, immediately after cessation of the spring rains."*

Nuñez Moreno immediately set the tribe to work thinning the dense stands of trees, stacking the logs, and clearing land to plant more fruit tree seedlings, mostly apples, pears, and plums. When the new road was completed almost a year later, in late July, the Wiroks were ready to start a thriving trade in lumber logs and fresh fruit. And by the end of harvest season, the women were set to can fruit, jams, and jellies, and to make cider.

BIA agent Bernard Eldred and the Temkuts landlord, Jared Chalmers, rode in on the first wagon to use the new road into Moloku Valley.

"This went far better than I ever expected," Eldred said. He climbed down from the wagon to face Nuñez Moreno, and virtually the entire Wirok tribe. "The BIA is proud of you."

"Thank you," Moreno said. He stepped aside, then followed Eldred and Chalmers as they moved out to inspect the orchards and timberlands. Neither of the men spoke to him again until they returned to the loading platform that had been built to handle the loading and unloading of traders' wagons.

"One small formality before we christen this a going operation," Eldred said. He motioned for Moreno to follow him and Chalmers over to the loading platform. "All we need is your signature on this document and you're on your way," he said to Moreno.

"What is this?" Moreno said, looking down at a bound document of several pages.

"Generally, it spells out the terms of the overall operation."

"May I read it first?" Moreno said.

"Of course, of course. Take your time. In the meantime, maybe Mr. Chalmers will join me in a mug of that cider your women have prepared."

Moreno had already started reading; tears of grief formed in his eyes as he came to a statement that followed a page of legal whereas and wherefore paragraphs:

"The funds derived from the sale of timber and other products produced by the Temkut Tribe on the Moloku Valley land owned by Jared Chalmers shall be conserved for the benefit of the Temkut Indians rather than given to them outright since their simple life unfits them for business.

"Gross proceeds of this venture shall be divided thusly: two-thirds for the land's owner, Jared Chalmers, and one-third for the tenant-farmer members of the Temkut Tribe of Indians."

CHAPTER 25

By the time I left the Temkut hunting lodge, I'd interrogated Frank Ross, Hayes, Vanessa, and Greer to the point where they didn't even want to look at me anymore; maybe even punch me out. I wasn't sure which.

But I did have a better handle on the background leading up to the tribe's initial decision and subsequent efforts to get involved in the gaming business. Like every other Native American tribe across the country, they needed income to provide their people with homes, schools, and businesses.

What I didn't come away with were any additions to my slim portfolio of hard facts. But the questioning had put things into better perspective. And a couple of suspicions had come to mind that I preferred not to discuss with any of them, at least not for the time being.

When I announced on my way out that I had places to go and things to do, each of them, except Ross, offered to go with me. When I declined, their individual expressions exhibited a variety of non-verbal responses—Greer, relief; Vanessa, disappointment; Hayes, puzzlement. Ross gave me an enigmatic smile, which I found the most satisfying.

It was now too late to do anything other than go back to The Pomo House and see what other pertinent facts I might discover while surfing the web with my laptop. About halfway there I was bit badly by the hunger bug. Because of the hour, the only source of relief I could think of was Vanessa's kitchen. I hoped she wouldn't be home yet because I wasn't up for more conversation, with her or anyone else.

There was an unfamiliar Corvette with Arizona plates in one of the guest parking spaces, but Vanessa's Miata wasn't in sight. I checked the garage. Empty. And so was the refrigerator in the kitchen. All I could scrounge up was half a glass of milk and a solitary, leftover piece of apricot pie, not one of my favorites. I hoped she was out shopping, for the guests, if no one else.

Later, while deep into a series of articles about the power wielded by the California Coastal Commission, I heard a very light tap-tap on my door. I quickly crossed the room and pulled open the door. No one there. On the floor by the doorway was a small, napkin-covered wooden tray containing half a bagel topped with fried egg, tomato, and onion, plus a still-steaming pot of herbal tea. The offering was greatly appreciated, but I wondered why Vanessa hadn't wanted to hand-deliver the tray.

The next morning I was up early, returned the tray and dishes to the kitchen, and was gone before anyone else was stirring. As much as I appreciated Pomo House breakfasts, part of my plan was to start my day by eating at the Wirok Café. Even at that early hour, I had a long wait to even get a stool at the counter.

"What got you up with the chickens this morning, Mr. Rolfe?" Annalee Mackey asked as she stopped in front of me to take my order.

"Sort of that old thing about the early bird getting the worm," I said, glancing at the menu.

"Afraid we're fresh out of worms." She gave me a mock look of regret. "Perhaps I could talk you into a salmon, Swiss, and mushroom breakfast quiche. Got one almost ready to pop out of the oven."

"Works for me. And some sourdough toast on the side."

"You got it. Coffee?"

"Green tea?"

"Wimp!"

"Can't help it, Annalee."

She leaned over the counter toward me. "Know what ya mean. It's what I drink, too." She reached under the counter and pulled out a copy of the *Wirok County Gazette*. "Here, give you somethin' to do while I go scare up your quiche."

A quick glance at the headlines told me there wasn't much going on in California, the U.S., or the world that hadn't been going on the day before. But the day's editorial and the Op-Ed page definitely caught my attention. Mark Trimble, the editor, had taken issue with the California Coastal Commission for

attempting to prevent the Temkuts from building their casino and
resort:

> *One little piece of Wirok County oceanfront
> property—less than five acres—has never been
> listed as belonging to anyone other than Temkuts,
> not since the first non-Indian set foot in what is now
> Wirok County—Russian, Spaniard, Mexican,
> Californio, or Californian.*
>
> *The Temkuts have been fine stewards of that
> small parcel of land, even in times when they didn't
> have the wherewithal among them to purchase a net
> to fish the waters of the Pacific, let alone buy a boat.*
>
> *True, the adjacent four hundred acres sold to the
> Temkut Rancheria by Appa Bay have considerably
> expanded the size of the Temkuts' holdings. But
> when you consider that 500 years or so ago this
> entire continent was freely available to native
> peoples, 405 acres is not a very sizeable chunk of
> real estate.*
>
> *We think it would be wise of the California
> Coastal Commission to closely study the plans the
> Temkuts have put forth for their casino and resort.
> From the beginning up through the present we have
> been unable to find one aspect of this project that
> would despoil any part of our beautiful and
> wondrous California coastline. Indeed, the
> Coastanoans, as all California natives were once
> mistakenly called by the Spaniards, have been more
> conscientious stewards of the land than any of the
> white men who stole the land from them.*
>
> *While we are not proponents of legalized
> gambling, whether casinos, card rooms, pari-mutuel
> betting, or even the lottery, we do believe that
> Native Americans have been denied far too long the
> right to prosper on their own, to use their land in*

any appropriate manner for the benefit of their people.

An Op-Ed piece alongside the editorial, signed by a group calling itself "Concerned Citizens for the California Coast," expressed a considerably different opinion with respect to the Temkut Rancheria Casino & Resort:

> *The California Coastal Commission is right to take on the issue of bringing the Temkut Rancheria's casino proposal in line with existing coastal land use and environmental rules.*
>
> *When Californians endorsed the tribal casino initiative in 2000, they didn't realize they were opening the door to a lightly regulated gambling industry fueled by Nevada casino interests.*
>
> *There's a huge difference between the public's political perception of tribes being able to open casinos on their own reservations, and then, in partnership with others, being able to secure property to build Las Vegas-style casinos and resorts with little regard for community zoning and environmental restrictions.*
>
> *There is no question California tribes are exercising a right they won in the 1988 passage of the Indian Gaming Regulatory Act and California's Proposition 1A. Nor is there a question that we, as a nation, failed to treat tribes with respect and honor.*
>
> *Regardless, there is growing public concern about the need to limit Indian gaming and stop the severe erosion of local control.*
>
> *The California Coastal Commission, by insisting that its long-standing rules and regulations be adhered to by* everyone*, is taking the lead in this battle against the moving target of tribal gambling.*

"Pretty interesting reading, dontcha think?" Annalee said. She was using a pair of potholders to serve me an aromatic quiche in a small, hot, ceramic dish. Her teenage helper-of-the-day brought my toast and tea.

"Which part of the page, I asked, "left or right?"

"Mark Trimble makes some good points," she said. "Problem is, don't think he's got the pulse of the public on this one."

"How's that?" I brought a forkful of the quiche to my lips to test its heat. Still on the border of tongue-searing.

"Trimble may be thinkin' more about future advertisin' revenue than about what's gonna happen to the county."

"Like your losing or having to give up the Wirok Café?"

"You gotta good memory, Mr. Rolfe. Say that for you."

"Sort of like my appetite," I said. "I try to pay close attention to both." This time the quiche made it past my lips. I savored the flavors swirling in my mouth. "Delicious!"

"Thank you."

"I still think you should seriously consider expanding to take advantage of the growth that's going to take place."

"Well, if your memory's as good as it seems to be, then you'll recall what I said the first time we met…"

"You said you like your business the way it is, and you like the town the way it is."

"You got that right, bub." She looked across the counter toward the back booth and nodded and smiled at someone who was out of my line of sight.

"Should I take that to mean you're one of those Concerned Citizens who wrote the Op-Ed piece in the *Gazette*?"

She gave me one of those wouldn't-you-like-to-know looks and walked back toward the kitchen. I finished my quiche, tea, and toast, left enough cash on the counter to cover the bill and a generous tip. I glanced at the person in the back booth, but didn't recognize him. I waited a moment before leaving, but Annalee didn't show herself again.

I spotted a newspaper dispenser on the sidewalk a couple of cars past the Porsche, walked over, dropped in a couple of quarters, and pulled out a copy of the weekly *Appa Bay Sentinel*. I was curious whether Hayes's boss, Ed Harkins, was also running an editorial this week to counter propaganda from the Concerned Citizens for the California Coast. There was no Op-Ed piece and Harkins' current concern was whether there was going to be a good crab season this year, something that wouldn't occur for several months.

I decided it was past time to make another attempt at a personal visit with Harkins at the *Sentinel* since I'd only talked to him previously by telephone, and got sort of a brush-off the first time I stopped by. I was ready to use Mark Trimble at the *Gazette* and my old man as "Pass Go" cards, but neither was necessary.

* * *

"Ah, Mr. Rolfe! Hayes said you no doubt would drop by. Been thinking we should have a meaningful face-to-face talk." Harkins tilted forward in his creaking wood desk chair, stood, and stepped away from his cluttered desk, hand extended. "I was kinda busy last time you came by."

"Sorry I haven't stopped in again until now," I said, shaking his hand. "And I've yet to thank you for directing me to The Pomo House."

"Mighty fine-looking woman, that Vanessa Jimenez." He let go his grip and ran the hand across his bare scalp, then touched each end of his waxed four-inch handlebar moustache. "Hear she's a dandy cook, also."

"Couldn't argue with either point." I said. I glanced away to take a closer look at his dimly lit office; it could have been lifted *in toto* from the set of an old movie called *Ace in the Hole*, where the local editor wore both a belt and suspenders because he didn't want to take any unnecessary chances.

Harkins pulled a ladder-back chair up close to his rolltop desk, used an arm to sweep a couple of telephone books onto the floor, and motioned for me to sit down. We sat in unison. "So watcha been able to do for the Temkuts?"

"Damn little."

"Don't surprise me none." He ran a hand back and forth across the flat of his rolltop desk, scattering copy paper here and there, and finally came up with a pair of tortoiseshell-like half glasses. Once he had them settled on his nose, he tilted his head back to peer through the lenses, nodded, and pulled a newspaper from atop the desk.

"Seen this?" he asked, handing me the paper. It was open and folded to today's editorial page of the *Wirok County Gazette.*

"Read it at breakfast at the café," I said. "Interesting."

"*Interesting*, like a piece of art you don't want to tell the truth about, or *interesting* like a cautionary Chinese comment about your future prospects?"

"Perhaps someplace in between."

"Ha!" He slammed a palm down on his desk. "Trimble said you reminded him of your old man. He's right. Need a job?"

I laughed. "Doubt if there's enough happening around Appa Bay to keep both Moreno and me busy."

"Moreno? Hell, I don't see him enough to remember from week to week what he looks like. More trouble than he's worth, that one."

"Well, thanks for the offer, but I think my newspapering days are all in the past." I slapped the *Gazette* against my open palm. "But I've never given up my penchant for asking a lot of questions. For instance, what's your take on Trimble's editorial and the companion Op-Ed piece?"

"Mark Trimble is an idealist. It's still a giant leap between the way things should be and the way things are, and need to be."

"So you don't favor the Temkuts building their casino and resort?"

"Did I say that?" Harkins gave me a wry smile. "I mean just because I like my town the way it is doesn't mean I'm anti-Native American."

"Heard that like-things-the-way-they-are sentiment once already this morning. Couldn't get a definitive explanation there, either."

"Get enough people around here to trust you, Mr. Rolfe, and you might find that's the prevailing attitude."

And suddenly it came to me that with all the baddies who had descended on Appa Bay and on the Temkuts—to lie, cheat, and steal in hope of getting in on a piece of the action—the real villain or villains might be hiding within the confines of the town itself—a town that couldn't make up its mind whether it wanted to remain a tranquil coastal village or bring back bigger than ever the booming, hot times of a bygone era.

CHAPTER 26

Reporters, at least those who've been assigned to a police beat, know more than a little something about how murder investigations are conducted, sometimes quite a lot.

One of the first things you learn is not to get on the wrong side of the investigating officer. In the case at hand, that was Appa Bay Police Chief Lance Chubb, nephew of the mayor and alleged assailant of the guy who was supposed to be my Indian guide through this coastal quagmire.

Hayes Moreno was certainly no Sacagawea. I wasn't even sure he was still on my side, if he ever was.

Another question nagging at me was the situation with the murders of the two city councilmen. That was police business and for the most part, I preferred to let it stay that way. But a little concrete information as to what was going on would be nice. The secondhand bits and pieces I was getting from Hayes and others just weren't cutting it. Specifically, I wanted to know whether or not the police had a hot murder suspect. And if they did, how might that person, or those persons, be tied into the overall Temkut gaming and resort plans?

As I ticked off the names of the people I'd met thus far, and weighed their value with respect to obtaining any useful information, at the top of my list were the two EMTs and the cop who'd showed up to take care of Hayes after I found him knocked unconscious in The Pomo House garage.

They were all Temkuts, according to Vanessa, which probably meant I would need someone they trusted to open the door for me. And even that might not work with the cop since he was under Chubb's thumb.

The pair of EMTs held a little more promise. My guess was that if they were anything like most people in that line of work, they were pretty damn independent and probably didn't give a rat's ass whose toes they stepped on in order to get done what needed to get done – whether taking care of minor accident victims or tending to the dead and dying at a major catastrophe. Or maybe even a couple of murders.

Another assumption was that the one person who really wanted to get all of this straightened out, and appeared to truly have the best interests of the Temkuts at heart, was Frank Ross, the tribal chairman. Whether he would talk to me or not was up for grabs. If he hadn't already put me on the wrong side for being Hayes's unauthorized operative, maybe I could make him a member of the trusting posse Editor Harkins said I needed to round up.

I got the feeling Harkins was more pissed at Hayes than he was at me.

* * *

It still wasn't noon when I called Vanessa on my cell to ask her how I could get in touch with Ross.

"What do you want with Frank?" she asked.

"Not quite sure. Just a private little man-to-man chat to see I if can get a feeling of what's going on around here through his eyes."

"Thought you gave him and the rest of us a pretty thorough grilling—is that the right word?–out at the hunting lodge."

"Talking to someone with other people around just isn't the same as getting up front and personal," I said. "Sort of like the difference between one-on-one and group therapy."

"Do you think he didn't tell you everything pertinent?"

"Might be a thing or two all of you left out of what you told me as an outsider. I need to find out if there's something he knows, or maybe doesn't know that he knows."

"That's rather cryptic ... and not very informative."

"Sorry you think that."

"No, what I think is that you're not being totally up front with *me*, Mr. Zach Rolfe." There was a brief pause. "Am I a suspect in some way or the other?"

"Wouldn't be too cool of me to tell you that if you were."

"Uh-huh! Well, to answer your first question, Frank owns a small arts and craft gallery in the center of town, across from the hardware store. It's called Temkut Treasures."

"Thank you kindly. I promise to bring you up to speed as soon as possible."

"Uh-huh! Doubt if you ever do that totally for *anyone*. However, you can do me one favor."

"If I can."

"Be careful."

"The absolute second rule in the ever-popular 'Beginner's Guide to PI Snooping.'"

She laughed. "What's the first rule?"

"Don't get caught."

* * *

Even though it was close to lunch time when I parked in front of the small, clapboard, eucalyptus-shaded Temkut Treasures store, there was very little activity up and down the main drag of Appa Bay. A few cars were parked nose-in toward the buildings along the two or three blocks that made up the "downtown," but that was about it.

A few reed-woven baskets of various sizes and designs were displayed on a slat bench outside the store. A small hand-printed sign hanging from a string in the middle of the door glass said "Open." I picked up the largest of the baskets, rotated it on my palm until I'd seen the entire circumference, then turned it upside down. There was no tag to tell me the price, the name of the basket weaver, or whether it was an authentic Temkut design. One thing was obvious, though—the workmanship was excellent. That much I'd learned from an anthropology major I'd dated while attending the University of New Mexico many years ago.

Another thing I knew for certain: the basket hadn't been imported from China.

I expected the tinkle of chimes or a buzzer to announce my arrival when I opened the door, but there wasn't a sound, not even the creak of a weary hinge or loose board.

More baskets were neatly displayed on tables, on the floor, and on shelves. Framed black and white photos of what I assumed were Temkut people and places lined the walls. Some of the images were faded and difficult to make out, others were sharp and detailed. There were both snapshots and scenes that looked to have been arranged by a professional photographer. They covered, in no particular chronological order, an historical perspective ranging from the past couple of decades to what I would guess were the late 1800s.

I was about to take a closer look at a variety of smaller items arranged in a pair of antique display cases when a voice interrupted:

"Are you basket shopping, Mr. Rolfe?"

Frank Ross stepped through a doorway filled with multi-colored stringed beads that hung from the lintel to almost the floor.

"No, not really," I said.

"I didn't think so," Ross said. "I didn't take you to be a collector of Indian artifacts."

"Actually, I do have a small collection of Indian baskets and pottery, all from Southwest tribes, though."

"In this instance, I'm pleased to be wrong. Please forgive me."

"No need for an apology," I said. "And I'd like to add that the craftsmanship here is as good as anything I've ever seen."

"Thank you. We like to think our basketry is as good as you'll find anywhere in the West. As for pottery, we can't even pretend to compete with the Arizona and New Mexico tribes. That's a skill our ancestors never really developed."

"I'll let you in on a little secret, Mr. Ross: I'd be hard-pressed to come up with *any* such skills brought down through the ages by *my* forefathers."

"You should not denigrate your ancestors, Mr. Rolfe, even in jest." He tilted his head to one side and gave me an appraising look before continuing. "As for the present, I don't think it was the modest collection of basketry outside my store that brought you in here today."

"No, and I wouldn't insult your intelligence in an attempt to dispute that."

"Good." He came around from behind the counter, pushing a couple of stack stools in front of him with one foot. He lifted one from the other, handed the top one to me, and sat down on the other.

"Not very comfortable," he said, "but if our talk is extended, I'll close up and we can go down to the café."

"Fair enough." I handed him one of my business cards, which he stuck into his shirt pocket without looking at it.

"So, Mr. Rolfe, what is it you think I might know that I don't know that I know?"

I laughed. "She called you, didn't she?"

"If you're referring to Ms. Jimenez, yes, only she texted me. Thought I should be aware that you were planning to stop in to see me."

"Ah, smart phones, the modern day jungle telegraph."

"Beats the shit out of running barefoot through the woods wearing nothing but a scratchy loincloth," Ross said without a hint of a smile.

"Okay, then tell me this: from your perspective, were the two murdered councilmen, Petrucci and Nolan, solidly behind your efforts to build a resort and casino?"

"Yes, from the very beginning."

"Word is that Petrucci may have been backing off," I said.

"I think that word is false, Mr. Rolfe. Someone is trying to make people look in the wrong direction for reasons those two men were killed."

"And what's your take on why they were killed?"

"I have been unable to find a reason for their terrible deaths. I have never wanted anyone, white or Indian, to be harmed in any way as a result of the Rancheria seeking to derive income from gaming," he said.

"There's no one who has gotten angry, threatened to stop your efforts to build the casino and resort, anything like that?"

"There have been some spirited discussions, both within the Temkut community and between our people and the townspeople. But we have always been able to come to a reasonable compromise whenever there were differences, or least I thought we had."

"That's good to know." I needed to shift positions on the stool, but didn't want to be rude. Ross was right, though: the seat wasn't very comfortable. "Still, I've recently gotten the impression from some non-Temkut locals that there may be an undercurrent of discontent with the Federated Indians of Temkut Rancheria's casino plans."

He looked at me for a long moment, ran the fingers of both hands through his hair, and finally said, "Anyone other than Ed Harkins and Annalee Mackey?"

"You don't miss much, do you, Mr. Ross?"

"I try not to."

"And?"

"Do I think either of them capable of murder? No. They grouse a lot, but I cannot see either of them picking up a gun and killing someone."

"There are people who will do such things for a price," I said.

"True. But we are talking about misguided people who want to see things remain the way they are forever, or even more unrealistically, go back to the way things were in another era. But down deep, they know these things do not happen, can not happen. So why would they resort to deadly violence?"

"I recall that at the lodge no one knew for certain who brought the Coastal Commission down on your heads. Could it have been Harkins and Mackey, or someone like them?"

"Yes, that they might do. But we have no proof."

"Then maybe you can help me with something else—I know there is one Temkut on the police force. Are there more than that?"

"No, just Charlie Longtree. Perhaps a token, perhaps not. Why do you ask?"

"I would very much like to find out what's happening with the murder investigations within the Appa Bay Police Department."

Ross thought for a moment. "I don't think it would be fair to ask Charlie to leak information about what the police are doing."

"You think he's that loyal to Chubb?" This time I shifted to find a comfortable spot on the small wooden stool. "I mean, Hayes Moreno says it was Chubb who clobbered him."

"So Hayes has said. But I cannot emphasize too much the extent of Charlie's loyalty to his job, and to the police department," Ross said. "His presence on the force has saved a number of our people from being mistreated for minor offenses."

"Okay, I won't wiggle the wigwam where Officer Longtree is concerned. But what about the two EMTs who came to The Pomo House when Moreno was attacked?"

Ross looked at me for a long time before answering. "Good boys, Arthur and Lawrence. Good at their jobs and dedicated when it comes to helping the tribe. Do you think they also might know something they don't know they know?" There was a slight mischievous twinkle in his eyes.

"That's exactly what I think, Mr. Ross. EMTs get in the middle of stuff, see and hear things. But they're so much an integral part of the crime landscape that people don't pay much attention to them as long as they're doing their job."

"And you would like me to speak to them, ask if they'll cooperate with you?"

"That might be very helpful in trying to find out what the hell's going on around here."

"Ah, good, it has been a short meeting and we no longer have to sit on these damn uncomfortable stools." He stood, rubbed his ass, and said, "I will speak to them."

"Thank you."

We shook hands and I headed for the door. "Will you give me a call me after you talk to the EMTs?"

"You will hear from me, Mr. Rolfe," he said. "I promise."

"Jungle telegraph?"

"Perhaps something more contemporary."

"Good. My e-mail address is—"

He held up one hand and with other pulled my card from his shirt pocket. "It's on here, I believe."

* * *

I'd just tapped the key fob button to unlock the Porsche's doors when a voice behind me said, "Step away from the car, Mr. Rolfe."

I turned to see Chief Lance Chubb walking toward me from the building next door to Temkut Treasures. I wondered how long he'd been waiting, and if he'd overheard any of my conversation with Frank Ross. He hitched up his heavy-duty service belt and stopped in front of my car. He gave me an insincere smile as he put one highly polished black chukka boot on the painted front bumper of the Porsche. The whole scene was kind of a cliché, but I had a feeling Chubb got a good portion of his posturing from TV and old movies.

I wanted to tell him—not too politely—to get his damn boot off my car, but to what end? Instead, I did my painful best to look pleasant and said, "Afternoon, Chief. Something I can do for you?"

He looked up and down the street, which was still pretty much deserted. "Been checking on you, Rolfe." He slid the sole of his boot down the face of the bumper and moved away from the front of the car. I could see the trail of grime where his boot had been.

"If there's something you wanted to know, all you had to do was ask."

"I wanted to hear from other sources," he said.

"Ah! And what did you find out, Chief?"

"I'm told you're a private investigator, a snoop."

"That's absolutely correct," I said. "No secret there."

"And while you're licensed in Nevada, that's not the case in the State of California."

"That's also correct."

"So what're you doing here?"

"I'm staying at The Pomo House."

He took in a deep breath, blew it out slowly, then rolled his shoulders. "I already knew that, so don't get cute. I want to know *why* you're here."

"Tourist."

"I told you, don't be a smartass." He slowly moved his right hand back until he could rest it on the butt of his pistol. I didn't find it threatening, just silly. "You're here because of Hayes Moreno." He said *Hayes Moreno* like it was a pair of dirty words.

"That's true. He invited me to come over to Appa Bay."

He looked up and down the street again. "Not much to see here, so maybe it's time you ended your visit and went back to Vegas." He looked down and watched while he spread his feet about eighteen inches apart, as if following a memorized diagram for a particular kind of police encounter. When he looked up again me, he was scowling. All we needed was a little Dimitri Tiomkin music from "Gunfight at the OK Corral."

"Are you making a play to run me out of town, Chubb?"

"There's nothing here for you, Rolfe." He stepped closer. "And it'd be a good thing if you forgot Moreno's wild ass claim that I slugged him at The Pomo House. Never happened." His face was now within inches of mine. "If you do stick around, and I hear that you're doing any kind of PI work, or anything else suspicious, I'm going to throw your ass in jail." He poked a stubby forefinger into my shoulder. "Got that?"

I was bored with the game. "Got the message, Chief." I started to turn away, but he grabbed my arm. I'd let him get away with the finger-poking, but that was extent of my generosity.

"Look, Chubb," I said, "if you're going to arrest me on some trumped-up charge, do it and get it over with. Otherwise, I've got other things to do."

He held on and squeezed a little harder, his thumb digging into my bicep.

"If you think I'm going to get physical with you, Chief, forget it." We stood staring at each other. Another silly game. "Look, just knock off the playground bully routine."

"Or?"

"Or nothing, Chubb. We're just standing out here wasting each other's time."

He gave me an exaggerated up-and-down look. "I don't think you're all that tough, Rolfe."

"I have no idea how tough I am, Chief. I mean, I might be able to take you in a fair fight, but you've got a badge and a gun. I have neither."

"Maybe that's something you should keep in mind, Mr. Rolfe."

"Not the kind of thing I ever lose sight of."

He let go, shifted his feet, and dropped his right shoulder slightly. He couldn't have been more obvious about setting up to take a swing at me.

"Back off, okay?"

His hand came off the holstered pistol and cut in quickly toward my midsection. I spun away from the blow, which merely grazed my shirt. I grabbed his wrist with both hands, twisted his arm up behind his back, and applied just enough pressure to keep him facing Temkut Treasures.

"No gun, no badge," I whispered in his ear. "But I do have a witness."

He looked up. Frank Ross was there watching us through the glass pane of his front door.

I dropped Chubb's arm, stepped back, and waited for him to do whatever he might think was necessary. He stepped toward Temkut Treasures, his back still to me. Since that seemed to be that, I got into the Porsche, backed from the curb, and drove away. In the rearview mirror I watched him walk slowly in the opposite direction; he didn't look back at either Ross or me.

I wondered if the encounter was his idea or if someone else had sent him to convince me that I should pack up and go home.

It was a thought worth exploring.

* * *

"I don't know what I can tell you, man, you know?" said Arthur Pinola. "But Frank said I should talk to you, so I'm talkin'."

We were sitting on the running board of Appa Bay's only fire truck, inside a converted barn that still had an active horse stable attached to one side of the building. Opposite us was the EMT ambulance. Both vehicles glistened with wax and you could see your reflection in the profusion of chrome accessories.

"Do you make all the emergency runs?" I said.

"Nah. We have two paid full-timers, Lou Galindo and me, plus three, no, four trained volunteers."

"So who made the run with you to The Pomo House when Hayes Moreno got clobbered, Galindo?"

"No, it was, uh, Lawrence. Lawrence Herrera."

"He here today?"

"Nah! Probably at work at the hardware store."

"So how do you get hold of him when there's a call, by cell phone?"

He held his hands out, palms up, to either side of him and looked at me like I'd just dropped in from another planet. "Direct pager, man! A cell's way too slow and reception's not all that great out here in the first place." He lowered his hands and shook his head from side to side. "It's not like any of them's a million miles away, you know? I mean, take Lawrence, he's only across the street."

"Guess I should have figured all that out on my own," I said. "Is that the store the mayor owns?"

"Yep! Joey Tobin."

I laughed.

"What's so funny?" He gave me a quizzical look.

"Small towns," I said. "Everybody's related or connected in some way or the other."

"Joey Tobin's not a Temkut, if that's what you're thinkin'."

"No, I was thinking how Tobin is Chief Chubb's uncle and how Herrera works for Tobin and how the dead councilman, Grady, raised Vanessa Jimenez and on and on and on."

"What can I tell you, man? Like you said, it's a small town."

"So it is," I said. "Anyway, I spoke to Frank Ross because I knew you and Herrera, along with the cop, Charlie Longtree, showed up when Moreno got popped in the nose at The Pomo House.

"You were there, right?"

"Yeah. But what about the shootings of the two city councilmen, Petrucci and Nolan? Did you and Herrera make those calls also?"

"Yep! Real sad. Known both of them since I was a kid. Nice guys."

"So have you heard anything from the cop, Longtree, about how the murder investigation's going?"

"You know Charlie?"

"No, Frank told me who he was."

"Charlie don't say much about his work."

"He ever say anything about Chief Chubb?"

Pinola grunted and rolled his eyes toward the ceiling. "If Chubb wasn't Joey Tobin's nephew I don't think he'd be able to get a job doin' much more than pumping gas."

"That your opinion or Charlie's?"

"Everyone's."

"My impression's that he's something of a bully, and apparently not too bright," I said.

"You got him pegged just right," Pinola said. "You know, the town paid to send him off to the police academy in San Francisco. Big waste of money. Should have sent a couple more guys to learn how to be EMTs."

"Did Chubb graduate?" I didn't really care other than he might have a little more cop knowledge than I'd assumed he had.

"He stayed for the whole course. But he didn't graduate."

"So he's not much of an investigator?"

Pinola cocked his head to one side and gave me a squinty-eyed look. "I wouldn't ask him to help find someone's lost dog."

"So you don't think he's done much with the murders?"

"Charlie says all the evidence has been turned over to the sheriff's department in San Tomas."

"Think Charlie would talk to me?"

"Nope."

"Okay. So what about you? Any ideas about who killed the councilmen?"

Arthur Pinola dry-washed his face with the palms of both hands, then got up and paced back and forth the length of the fire truck.

"I don't know who did it," he finally said. "But I have my suspicions."

"And?"

He stopped, turned his head away from me, and let out a big breath. "Nope, won't say. Wouldn't wanna make someone look guilty who really wasn't, you know?"

I nodded, giving him as much time to think it through as he needed.

"But you know what?" He pulled a piece of toweling from his back pocket, and polished away at a real or imagined smudge on the rearview mirror of the fire truck.

"What?"

He studied the back of the chrome mirror for a moment, grunted his satisfaction, and stuffed one end of the towel back into his rear pocket. "Benito Petrucci and Grady Nolan weren't killed by no outsider. Huh-uh!"

"What makes you say that?"

He took a long moment before answering. "Just … just a feeling, man. Can't say anymore than that."

I wasn't convinced. "They get on the bad side of someone local for some reason?"

He slumped back against the front tire of the fire truck and squeezed his eyes shut. "I … I don't know."

"Or won't say?"

"Whatever, man."

"Have you discussed any of this with the Frank Ross?"

He shook his head negatively.

"Why not?"

"He hasn't asked."

* * *

I left the fire station, walked across the street to the hardware store to talk with Lawrence Herrera. He was busy with a customer, and then another customer. I did a tour of the store while I waited. It was quite large—much larger than I would have guessed. The main floor seemed to contain everything one would expect to find in a well-stocked hardware store. There was a mezzanine toward the rear, with a sign at the foot of the stairs that said *Sporting Goods, Office, Restrooms.*

I climbed the stairs and while I was inspecting an extensive array of hunting rifles, a man came out of the office and walked over to me.

"May I help you sir?"

"Not really," I said. "Just getting acquainted with the store."

"New in town?"

"Visiting."

"Oh? May I ask from where?"

"I live in Las Vegas," I said.

"I see. Are you involved in the gambling business over there?"

"Not specifically," I offered as a deliberately non-specific answer. "Why, do you get a lot of those kind of folks here in Appa Bay?"

"A few," he said. "A few." He studied me for a moment, as if considering whether to continue to take our conversation in this direction. "As it happens, the local Native Americans are looking into opening a resort and casino."

"Interesting."

"Yes, it's certainly been that."

I was relatively certain I was talking to Joey Tobin, owner of the hardware store, the town's mayor, and Chief Chubb's uncle. "Probably have an effect on your business if it gets built."

"Oh, no doubt about that."

"Enough to bring in a Home Depot or Lowe's as competition?"

He laughed, but not humorously. "Not that kind of effect. Don't think it would cause a squirt in population growth. Just get a different kind of folks coming in and going through town, that's all."

And now I had three stalwart citizens who admittedly were not all that keen on what a casino would do for their town. "When does the local tribe expect to build their casino? Any time soon?"

"Hard to say at this point." He scratched his head. "Might never get built."

"Any specific reason for you to think that?"

"Nope. Some things happen and some things don't."

I nodded and started moving toward the stairs. "I'll keep a watch in the newspapers. See what happens."

"You do that," he said. "But don't think we're big enough to get that much attention by the media, one way or the other." He turned and went back inside the office.

When I got back to the main floor, I saw the store was empty of customers and went looking for Lawrence Herrera. I found him in the nail department, restocking the shelves.

Herrera was reluctant to talk to me, and was even less helpful than Pinola had been. However, he did sort of agree with his EMT partner about the murders being committed by someone local.

Herrera was nervous, though, which hadn't been the case with his EMT partner. He repeatedly looked up at the mezzanine office window as he talked to me, and continued to stock the nail section with a variety of brads, finishing nails, and box nails.

Ever so often I saw Tobin looking out the window at us; at one point he looked concerned and acted like he might come down to find out what we were talking about. As a result, I didn't push Herrera as hard as I might have under other circumstances.

While I was convinced the two EMTs had a lot more information than they were willing to share, I was going to have to find another way to get to them. Perhaps another talk with Frank Ross. Or maybe it was past time—way past time—to put some heavy duty pressure on Hayes Moreno.

When I left the hardware store, my favorite baddy, Terence Wadkins, was leaning up against the driver's door of the Porsche. Why the hell had people suddenly taken to being so physically attached to my screaming yellow Cayman?

With Wadkins, though, I wasn't going to be as circumspect as I'd been with Chief Chubb. But just as I got close enough to say something without shouting, Wadkins said.

"Crandal would like to talk to you."

CHAPTER 27

"You know, Wadkins," I said, "the last time your Mr. Crandal wanted to talk to me it got uncomfortably complicated—shackles, kidnapping, being shot at, and a long hide-and-seek chase along the coast road, not one of which is on my list of fun things to do."

"Crandal said to tell—"

"I have damn little interest in what Crandal said to tell me." I raised both arms and waggled my hands wildly at him. "Now git!"

Wadkins backpedaled and stared at me like I'd gone mad, which is exactly what I wanted him to think. "He … he wants to apologize," he said.

"About what?"

"About what happened out at the coast house the other night."

"What's he think," I said, "that I'll be willing to listen to some *cockamamie* story about how it was all a big mistake and then let it go at that?"

Wadkins shook his head. "I don't know what you're supposed to think, Rolfe." When he had about fifteen feet between us, he stopped shuffling backward. "I told you what he wanted me to tell you. Said he just wants to talk. Wants me to take you over to meet with him at the Wirok Café."

It was daylight and the café was about as neutral and as public as any place you could find in Appa Bay. So, I figured, what did I have to lose? If another big silver van pulled up in front of the café just as we got there, this time I wasn't going without a fuss … a damn big fuss.

"Lead on," I said.

Wadkins turned around, looked back over his shoulder at me, and just stood there. I assumed he was waiting for me to catch up and walk with him.

"Just head off toward the café," I said. "I'll follow along behind and keep a little distance between the two of us, if you don't mind."

At the café, I could see that the street was clear of any suspicious vehicles, and only a couple of people were in view. Wadkins held the door open for me, but refused to budge when I indicated that he should go in ahead of me. The door closed with Wadkins still standing outside. I didn't know whether that was to keep me from leaving or to keep other people from coming in.

Crandal was sitting in the farthest booth from the door, facing the front of the café. He kept his eyes on me as I walked toward him. I passed three guys eating at the counter, none of whom looked threatening. I nodded to Annalee Mackey, who was standing behind the cash register. Her eyes flicked back and forth between Crandal and me. She picked up a couple of menus and followed me to the booth.

"Wadkins cause you any problems?" Crandal said.

"He's still standing, isn't he?" I sat down across from the Lurton-Bales head honcho and studied Crandal while waiting for him to tell me why I was here. The bruise I'd given him high on his left cheek only added to the physical dissipation I'd caught only a glimpse of at the coast house.

Before he could say anything, Annalee arrived at the booth and handed us each a menu. "Didn't ever expect to see the two of you fellas doing the lunch thing," she said.

"Any special reason for that?" I said.

"I'd like to order," Crandal interjected before she could respond.

My assumption was that he didn't want anyone listening in to our conversation. So I gave Annalee my best smile and said, "What's the lunch special today?"

"Gone!" she said, her eyes still switching slowly between Crandal and me.

"How about a salmon burger on an English muffin?"

"Can do that. What to drink?"

"Iced tea."

"Okay. And for you, Mr. Crandal?"

"Just double that, Annalee," he said.

That they called each other by name was a bit of surprise. I didn't take Crandal for the kind of high-powered Washington, DC, lobbyist who would frequent a small-town café often enough to be known by name. But then, there was a lot of shit going on around Appa Bay that I didn't understand. Yet!

Once Annalee was out of earshot, Crandal said, "That thing of bringing you up to the house in the back of a van was an error in judgment."

"The uppercut and right cross weren't."

His left hand moved toward the bruised cheek, but was quickly withdrawn and dropped gently to the table top.

"Point taken," he said. "Now maybe we can have the talk I was hoping for then."

I gave him what I hoped was a serious look of disbelief, then made an exaggerated survey of the entire diner, with special emphasis on the front door and window.

"What's the problem?" he said.

"Just wanted to make sure your bodyguards weren't nearby, ready to take a shot at me if I don't answer all your questions."

He inhaled deeply, held his breath for a moment, apparently along with his temper, then exhaled sharply between compressed lips. "I apologized to you once, Rolfe. That's it. Now let's get on with it."

I gave him a little twisted nod of the head and said, "My assumption is that you want to know why I'm in Appa Bay and whether I'm going to cause you any grief. Is that it?

"I wouldn't have put it exactly like that, but, yes, that's the general idea," he said.

"Well, let me ask you a question first, Crandal: What is it you think you can do for the Temkuts in the nation's capital that they're not capable of doing for themselves?"

"I, uh, thought I was one who called this meeting," he said.

"Yeah, well, you're just sitting there not saying anything of real interest so I thought as long as I'm here, waiting to have lunch, I might as well try to fill in a few gaps."

"I assume you do know who I am, being a private investigator, and all of that?"

"Skip the talking-down-to crap, Crandal. I'm in no mood to sit around trading sarcasms with you. We each have good intel on the other, so either answer my question or get to the business of why you really sent Wadkins out to round me up."

He steepled his fingers under his chin and thought for a long moment before answering. "Lurton-Bales is extremely successful in helping Indian tribes that want to get into the casino business. We steer them through and around all the federal, state, and local legal obstacles that often stand in a tribe's way."

"Save the sales pitch for someone who needs to be impressed. The consensus of those who keep track of such things is that you've collected something in the lofty neighborhood of $100 million over the past decade from various Indian tribes throughout the U.S. Those same in-the-know-people say your efforts aren't always as transparent as they should be."

"I don't intend to sit here and let you insult me, Rolfe."

"Then don't try to snow me. Just tell me what it is you want from me, or I'm out of here."

I realized both of us were talking louder than we should have been. Crandal raised an accusatory finger and started to answer, then saw Annalee bringing our food.

"You boys aren't going to get into a tussle, are you?" She placed our plates and glasses in front of us.

"Only verbally," I said. "Sorry if we were getting a little loud."

"That casino thing seems to get all kinds of people doing that in here," she said.

"Oh? So who else has been getting into noisy arguments about the Temkut casino?" I asked.

"Well," she said, "not too long ago—"

"Thanks, Annalee," Crandal said, cutting her off for the second time. "I have several more things to discuss with Mr. Rolfe and I'm running a little late. Okay?"

She gave Crandal the kind of look a woman might give her husband for cutting her out of a conversation. "Sorry!" she said sharply. "Didn't mean to intrude." She turned around quickly and went back behind the counter to take care of her other customers.

"Regardless of what you actually can or can't do for the Temkuts," I said, "I'm told you signed a memorandum of understanding with the tribe."

"There's no secret about it."

"Care to tell me how much money is involved?"

"No, although I'm sure your friend Hayes Moreno will provide you with that information if you really want to know."

"Possibly." One never knew about Moreno. I took a big bite out of the salmon burger. It was moist and garnished with a thin slice of red onion and the tartar sauce had been applied with restraint. I chewed happily while waiting for Crandal to get to the reason for buying me lunch.

"What was Moreno's purpose in bringing you over from Vegas?" he said.

"It would seem we each need to have a good heart-to-heart with Moreno rather than clashing egos here in the lovely little Wirok Café." I took another bite and wondered whether Crandal was going to eat or not. I drifted off into a scenario where he got up and left without ever touching the salmon burger. My dilemma was whether or not to ask for it to be wrapped up to go.

"What would it take to convince you to return home to Nevada?"

I refocused and saw that he was leaning across the table to make his mini get-out-of-town-or-else pitch.

"You aren't trying to bribe me, are you?" I said.

"I'm saying, Lurton-Bales could make it worth your while to toss your bags into that yellow Porsche and point it east."

I couldn't help myself—I kept looking from my almost-disappeared sandwich to his virgin salmon burger. I was even beginning to crave the half-sour pickle on the plate next to the nicely toasted muffin.

Knock it off, I told myself.

"You know, Mr. Felix Crandal, if I had any evidence, or even thought that you truly were here in the best interests of the Temkuts, and that everything was moving along in a copasetic

219

manner, I'd get myself out of these parts in a jiffy. I really would. But—"

"But what?" This time that accusatory finger made it to within a few inches of my face. "I defy you to come up with one iota of evidence that we are not who we say we are or will not do what we say we will."

"Yeah, well, you may have your memorandum of understanding, but something tells me a fair number of the Temkuts are still restless about your proposal."

His face turned crimson and he looked like he was about to shout something nasty. I watched as he slowly brought himself under control. He stretched his fingers, then wiggled them like they were stiff from arthritis. He even started to pick up the salmon burger but before he actually touched it, he withdrew his hands and placed them on the table next to his plate.

Thank God!

"What would make you think there was any kind of problem?" he said evenly.

"Well, for one thing, I was outside after the Wirok Council meeting broke up last Thursday evening, as were you and your people."

"So?"

"So, it looked to me like you pretty much got the cold shoulder from Frank Ross, and some of the other tribal members weren't all that friendly, either," I said. "Not exactly the expected atmosphere that might surround a brand new business relationship."

"A little give and take," he said. "But no problem. Just par for the course in my business." He took a drink of his iced tea and pushed the sandwich dish toward the center of the table. Toward me!

Could I do it? I was beginning to see the act of taking his sandwich as a humorous prank. It must have showed.

"Is there something in all this you find funny, Mr. Rolfe?"

"What? Funny?" *Caught!* "No, not really. I was sort of thinking how ironic it is that here we are, two white men in the twenty-first century discussing which of us has the Native

Americans' best interests at heart. Guess that's been going on for a few centuries now, hasn't it?"

Crandal pulled a card from his wallet and tossed it across the table to me. "That's my cell phone number, Rolfe. If you decide to accept my offer, call. But don't wait too long."

"I suggest you not stand on one foot while waiting for that call, Crandal." I took the last bite of my salmon burger. "I'd also appreciate it if you would tell Wadkins that it would be wise if he kept plenty of distance between him and me."

He shook his head ever so slightly, lips a thin line, and slid out of the booth. I turned and watched him head toward the door. As he passed Annalee, there was some kind of non-verbal exchange, but from where I was sitting I couldn't catch the tenor of it.

When Crandal was finally out the door, I turned back around and finished my iced tea. His sandwich still sat there, untouched, but the fun had gone out of the make-believe abduction of his salmonburger, particularly after I realized he'd stuck me with the lunch tab.

Before I could ask for the check, Annalee came over and placed it on the table next to my plate.

"Guess he wasn't very hungry after all," she said.

"Nope."

"Didn't touch the sandwich, did he?"

"Nope."

"Want me to wrap it to go?"

"Yep."

"Not very talkative today, huh?"

"Guess Mr. Crandal affects people that way."

She cocked her head at me. "Spit it out, Mr. Rolfe."

"Seems to me Crandal did a rude don't-speak-unless-spoken-to thing a couple of times with you today. Some reason for that, Annalee?"

"I'll meet you at the cash register with your sandwich," she said. There was a hint of anger in her eyes.

I was seriously curious about what the connection was between Annalee Mackey and Felix Crandal. Whatever it was, I intended to look into as soon as possible.

To sort of get the ball rolling in that direction, after I'd paid for lunch and accepted the salmon burger in its little white Styrofoam container, I said to Annalee, "Crandal keeps a pretty tight hold over the group, doesn't he?"

"What?" Her expression shifted quickly from surprise to wariness.

"Never mind. I shouldn't have said anything."

I left her standing there, her eyes dancing with curiosity. But I wasn't the cat who was going to satisfy it. Rather, I tormented her a tiny bit more with what I hoped was the hint of a self-congratulatory smile.

My spur-of-the-moment probe had hit pay dirt—apparently somewhere out there in the wilds of Wirok County was a group trying to sabotage the Temkut effort to build a resort and casino, an enterprise with a magnificent and enviable view of the Pacific Ocean.

* * *

Sitting in my car, not sure where I wanted to go or who I wanted to talk to next, I decided to call Vanessa. She answered so quickly I barely got the cell to my ear. I wasn't sure her phone even rang.

"Any chance Hayes is hanging out there at The Pomo House?" I said.

"This is weird," she said. "I was just picking up the phone to call you, and here you are."

"Okay, you first—why were you going to call me?"

"Hayes popped into my kitchen a couple of minutes ago, stayed just long enough to ask if you were here, and then was gone again. I thought you might want to know he was looking for you."

"I'm not too hard to find," I said. "He has my cell number and the Porsche is certainly obvious enough to spot."

"I don't know what was up with him, Zach. He seemed really agitated."

"Okay. Thanks. I really appreciate your letting me know. If he calls back, tell him I'm going to take a drive by the locations where each of the two city councilmen was shot."

There was a long pause before she answered. I mentally kicked myself for not remembering her relationship to the second murdered councilman, Grady Nolan, who had raised her.

"Any particular reason you're going to do that?" she asked softly.

"Sorry. I shouldn't have been quite so blunt, considering the circumstances."

"No, it's okay. I don't want you or anyone else tiptoeing around me about what happened to Grady. Or Benny Petrucci, for that matter."

"I'll let you know if I find out anything."

"Thanks, Zach. Oh, yes, I was wondering: Did you get to talk to Frank Ross?"

"Yes. He was very cooperative."

"And?"

I had to ask myself, as I had previously, whether she was genuinely interested in finding a solution, or was part of the problem in some way. I decided to go with option *A*. At least for the time being.

"Seems to me that Frank Ross is the real thing," I said. "I think he's as much at a loss as anyone as to who's behind the killings. He's also genuinely perplexed by the escalating problems in getting the tribe's casino built."

"I could have told you that," she said.

"Yes, but—

"—but you needed to find out for yourself, right?"

"Right!" I shifted around and looked out behind the Porsche, caught a glimpse of a dirty Ford Explorer crossing the main street and heading down toward the waterfront.

"You still there?" she asked.

"Still here. Thought I just saw Hayes's SUV in my rearview mirror. But it's gone now. Anyway, Ross gave me intros to the two EMTs, Arthur Pinola and Lawrence Herrera, but I didn't learn much from either of them. The guy I'd really like to talk to is Charlie Longtree."

She laughed. "Charlie doesn't talk much. About anything."

"So I've heard." I looked around again to see if I could find any sign of Hayes.

"Let me see what I can do," she said. "My mom and Charlie's mom were pretty close. He hung out a lot at our house when we were in high school. I think he had a crush on me, but he'd probably rather die than ever admit it."

"Think he might talk to you?"

"I'll give it a try. What do you want to know?"

"Anything and everything he's willing to tell you about the murder investigations. But I'd settle for a little info on just how diligent Chubb is being at trying to find the shooter."

"I'll let you know one way or the other. Will you be back here tonight?"

"That's my plan."

"Maybe a special dinner, my part of the house?"

"Nicest thing anyone's said to me all day. I accept the invitation. Now, I'm going to go see if I can find Hayes."

I turned the Porsche around, found the side road I thought I'd seen the Ford go down and headed west, toward the ocean. The old fishing pier came in sight almost immediately, as did what looked to be Hayes's Ford Explorer; it was pulled up alongside a dilapidated shed. I drove over, took a look, and when I saw there was no one inside the vehicle, I parked next to it. A quick cross check of the license plate number and the info on Hayes in my notebook told me I'd found him, or at least his truck.

Appa Bay's abandoned ocean-fishing operation was apparently deserted, except for a flock of bickering seagulls. I peered in through the Ford's open driver's window, but didn't see anything other than a soft drink cup, too large for the built-in holder, leaning against the back of the seat, beads of liquid still showing inside the clear straw.

What had prompted Hayes to drive down here? And where in hell was he now?

I scanned the area several times before getting out of the Porsche. In addition to the shed, there were three or four other small structures set close to the water's edge, plus one large building, probably a fish-processing plant, that occupied most of one side of the pier. All of the wood buildings were gray and disintegrating from age, neglect, and vandalism; most of the windows had fallen victim to thrown stones and other objects.

This was the place where Grady Nolan was shot and it sort of gave me the creeps even though it was mid-afternoon and there wasn't a cloud in the sky. It was one of those moments when I thought the decision I'd made long ago not to carry a gun might have deserved a little more advance scrutiny.

The shed's rusting, paint-bare galvanized metal door was tightly shut; an open heavy-duty padlock hung from the loop of the hasp. Rather than go barging in, I took a stroll around the outside of the building. All I learned was that there was just the one door, plus a single multi-pane window next to it. Four of the window's six panes were covered with grime, the other two broken and showing glass shards like alligator teeth around the outer edges.

"Hayes!" I yelled through one of the broken panes. "You in there?"

No response. I edged closer to the window and listened. No sound of any kind. I tried again, louder:

"Hayes!"

Nothing.

I peered through the window, broken glass crunching beneath my shoes. There wasn't enough light getting through to see any farther than a short distance inside, and all that revealed was a crumbling wooden floor. If I was going to find out who was in there, I had to go inside.

I was regretting my "no gun" rule even more as I put a hand on the door knob, turned it gently, slowly pulled open the door, and fell backward as a damn seagull came flapping and squawking out into the open, giving my face a good feather-slap as it sailed by.

"Shit!"

I watched the indignant gull wing its way out over the water, banking neither left nor right. Maybe it had the right idea.

"Hayes Moreno, if you're in there, get the fuck out here before I have to come in there, grab you by your black Indian hair, and thump the daylights out of you."

Still no response. I went back to the Cayman, dug out my four-cell Maglite from behind the driver's seat, and went through the shed door, light blazing. It was one large, un-partitioned expanse, containing nothing but a couple of lopsided workbenches and lots of cobwebs. No wonder the gull was so anxious to escape.

So, while it *was* Moreno's Ford Explorer that I'd seen headed down to the pier less than twenty minutes ago, was he the one driving? And if not, who was? Was I simply being led on a wild goose chase? All I had at the moment were an empty vehicle and one freaked-out seagull.

I closed the door to the shed, left the padlock hanging in the hasp, and took off to do what I'd come to do in the first place—take a good look at the spot where Grady Nolan had been shot. I kept the flashlight in hand; it didn't have the range of a pistol, but maybe I could use it to give Hayes a well-deserved whack up along the side of the head if I found him.

At the end of the old pier, where Nolan had been fishing when he was shot, the area was still cordoned off with yellow police tape. Orange spray paint created a rough outline of where his body had dropped; his fishing rod and bait bucket were still lying nearby. Since there was nobody around, at least not within sight, I stepped over the tape and walked out to the end of the pier. If Chief Chubb or any of his cops found me poking around, I'd probably end up in the slammer.

I would have to do some fast talking if someone official wanted to know why I was nosing around where I shouldn't be. But then, it wouldn't be the first time.

I turned and looked back up at the shoreline, taking in the hodgepodge of buildings that were within shooting distance. The killer could have been hiding in any one of them, including the shed where I'd just been; I could see the window and door from where I stood.

Then I remembered the broken glass I'd stepped on when I tried to look inside the shed through the shattered window panes. Could the killer have hid in the shed and knocked out the glass from the inside in order to get a good bead on Nolan? Probably just wild speculation on my part, but it was worth a second look.

After another thorough search around the end of the pier, which produced nothing, I headed back toward the shore. At the shed, I picked up one of the larger pieces of broken glass from beneath the window and held it up to the shards that protruded from the frame. It certainly looked like the same glass to me.

I was convinced the window had been smashed from the inside after I went back in and couldn't find any glass fragments on the rough-sawn plank flooring beneath the window, not even a glint of a reflection from the flashlight's bright beam. As they say, it was an inside job, at least for misdemeanor window breaking.

Just before I turned off the Maglite, I caught a glint from something other than glass. I crouched down and saw the end of a brass shell casing that had almost dropped out of sight between two of the floor planks. I prized it out with my pocketknife, then used my handkerchief to pick it up. A .223—the same caliber as the rounds taken from the bodies of Nolan and Petrucci.

I carefully returned the casing to the exact spot where I'd found it; I didn't want to be accused of tampering with evidence. If possible, I *did* want to find some way to let Vanessa's cop friend Charlie Longtree know that it might be fruitful to give the inside of the shed a thorough investigation, or re-investigation, particularly in the area near the window.

I used the flashlight to make certain I hadn't left behind any telltale signs I'd been there. As I was crossing from the far side of the shed and getting ready to leave, I heard a car engine start up. I ran for the door and got there just in time to see the Ford Explorer driving off, headed back up the hill toward town. I couldn't see who was driving, but I intended to catch up and find out pretty damn fast.

I ran over to the Porsche, opened the door, and…

CHAPTER 28

My head was pounding like it had been run over by a truck and there was a God-awful taste in my mouth.

What the hell happened?

I felt myself rolling from side to side; not a lot, just enough to make me nauseated. I tried to brace myself, but couldn't get my arms to move. At first I thought I'd laid on them crooked and they were asleep—like when you have to get up to pee in the middle of the night and all your arms do is tingle instead of being there to help push you up off the mattress.

Then I felt the wetness in my clothes and beneath me.

Damn, Rolfe, this is pretty fucking embarrassing—you've peed yourself. How're you going to explain that *to the lovely Ms. Jimenez? Have to sneak out with the bedclothes, wash and dry them before she comes in to do the room.*

God, how I wanted my head to stop throbbing.

Wait a damn minute. If you're in bed at The Pomo House, how can you be looking up at a bright blue sky?

Okay, just how dumb can you be? Your arms aren't asleep, they're tied down.

I wiggled my fingers and stretched them out enough to discover that I was lying in a puddle of water. And under the water, wood; rough wood.

Twisting my head from side to side revealed that I was securely lashed to the bottom of a large wooden rowboat, which explained the rocking that was making me ill; I wanted to vomit. I could also hear the soft slap-slap of water against the side of the boat.

So where are you, Rolfe? Out in the bay? Adrift on the ocean itself?

I tried to raise my head to see over the gunnels but they were too high and I was lashed too tightly to the bottom of the boat.

How in hell did you let this happen to you, Rolfe?

In between the head throbs, I tried to think it through, tried to get a grasp on where I'd been and what had happened to get me into this stupid predicament.

There was a shed, and a pier, and something shiny. That much I remembered. And broken glass. Was that significant? No, not the glass. Something else. On the floor. A cartridge casing, brass cartridge casing. Caught between the floorboards.

The caliber was important. Yeah, .223. That was it, same as the rifle used to kill Grady Nolan on the pier. And Benny Petrucci in his front yard. Two city councilmen. Killed by who? By whom?

There was a heavy bump against the side of the boat that almost rolled me over. I braced as best I could and rolled back. Didn't dare allow myself to be tossed face-down into the water, which was getting deeper and deeper.

A dark-colored SUV. That image was coming through strong now. Hayes's Ford? Yeah, fucking Hayes. Driving away, headed back up into town. Couldn't let him get away. Ran for the Porsche; going to do the chase-'em-down thing. And...

And what? Can't remember a damn thing after that.

Someone must have clobbered me, and pretty damn hard. That much I could figure out from the headache. But how long had I been out? I looked up at what appeared to be a morning sky. Couldn't be. I went down to the pier in late afternoon. If I'd been hit hard enough to keep me out until morning, I should be damn near dead.

But who? And where'd they come from? Couldn't have been whoever was in the Explorer, unless there were two of them and one stayed behind.

Come on, Rolfe! Forget all that. Get your arms free ... get your ass out of this goddam leaky boat.

I twisted and squirmed, but whoever tied me must have been a Boy Scout at one time; no give at all. My efforts accomplished nothing other than to soak parts of me that weren't already wet from the sea water.

And it was getting warm. Uncomfortably warm. Where was that infamous California coastal fog when you could really use it?

In between futile struggles to get loose, I could feel the boat bobbing. Was I anchored out in the middle of nowhere? Maybe I was just drifting. But to where? I hoped it was with the incoming tide. Maybe someone would find me before I drowned.

Not the way my luck was running. I'd probably be dashed against the rocky shoreline, or drift out with the ebb tide to the open sea. Shit! Open water wasn't a familiar or friendly environment for a desert rat like me.

Forget that crap, Rolfe! Think positive!

Another bump against the side of the boat.

I didn't want to know what might be causing it. Even in far-off Nevada we read about the Great Whites that swim up and down the Pacific Coast looking for sea otters, seals, snorkelers ... and stupid PIs.

Screw it! There'd be plenty of time—maybe—to worry about sharks if this miserable goddam dinghy filled with water and sank.

Happy thoughts, right? Think about Vanessa, Greer, driving the Porsche ... off through the highways and byways of my convoluted mind.

And the case? Moreno, the Temkuts, Lurton-Bales. Everything running together, apart, and back together again.

I had no way of knowing how long I spent trying to reconstruct everything that had happened since I got that first call from Hayes more than a week ago. But to what end? Even if I did solve the damn case, who was I going to tell about it out here on the briny deep?

You can't just give up, Rolfe. You're not about to allow yourself to become floating carrion for the birds or pan-seared fish food.

I had to do something because the water in the bottom of the boat was now covering both arms and was up into my crotch.

Would the soaked rope make it easier to wiggle my hands loose, or would the water make the bindings even tighter? Couldn't remember.

The end of the boat where my head rested suddenly dipped and it felt like the boat was picking up momentum. Not a lot. But

I could feel I was no longer just sitting and bobbing on the water under an increasingly hotter sun.

I could hear something sloshing around near my head. I tried again to raise my head high enough to see what was happening, then sank back, exhausted.

"Relax, Zach. We're almost to the beach"

The comforting voice came from somewhere above and behind me. Or did it come from in front of me?

God? How far gone am I?

"You're in no danger."

Reading my mind? Did it matter? Couldn't identify the voice. Male? Female?

Something heavy clunked into the boat near my feet. I strained to no effect to see what had happened, who was speaking.

As I let my head fall back, a back-lit object loomed over me. I blinked my eyes, tried to clear my vision, squinted. All I got was a fuzzy shape hovering above. It finally registered—a head. Someone's head!

"What the fuck's going on?" I croaked through parched lips; pain radiated out into my chin and cheeks. I made another attempt, this time trying not to move my mouth to demand, "Untie me!"

"Let me get you to shore first. The footing's not too good here. If I fall, we're both shit out of luck."

"Hayes, is that you?" No response. "What the hell are you doing out here? Come to finish off the job?"

"Take it easy, Zach. We're almost there."

Much too soft a voice for Moreno. And much too kind.

I felt the boat scrape bottom, come to a slow, grinding halt. Nimble fingers immediately attacked the ropes that bound my arms and had me tied to the bottom of the boat. Before I could react, the hands grabbed my shoulders and helped me to sit upright.

Despite a long-sleeved shirt and blue jeans, I saw now that it definitely wasn't Hayes who had rescued me. Vanessa! I looked around, saw I hadn't been any farther out than the shallows of the boat harbor that served the old fish-processing facility.

"How the hell'd you find me," I said. "I could have been halfway to Hawaii."

"Fortunately for both of us, you weren't." She put an arm around me, helped me out of the boat, and held on as we waded our way onto dry land. "Need to get your head looked at and get some something on that sunburn."

I looked down at my bright red arms, but was afraid to touch my face. "What time is it?

"A little after noon." She stopped, caught her breath, and continued to walk us on up toward the buildings.

"I've been here, what?" I tried to count the hours on my fingers.

"Almost a full day," Vanessa said.

"Wow! That's scary."

"I'd have been here sooner, but a guest couple wanted to extend their stay and there was no one else around to take care of them."

"What made you come looking for me, especially down here?"

"When you called me late yesterday, you said something about seeing Hayes's Explorer headed down toward the waterfront."

"Oh, yeah. I vaguely remember doing that."

"Said you planned to come back and have dinner with me after you checked it out."

I nodded and looked around to see if there was someplace close to sit down. The knock on the head and the hot sun were taking their toll on me; I was weak and disoriented.

"Can you make it up there?" she asked when she felt me sagging. She nodded toward an overturned aluminum rowboat off near the shed I'd investigated just before being bonked.

"Give it my best effort," I said.

"When you didn't show up for dinner," she said, "I figured Hayes had caught up with you and the two of you had gone off investigating, or whatever."

She continued to walk and sort of drag me until we reached the upside-down boat. She lowered me down onto it, then sat beside me. "I fell asleep in front of the TV and when I woke up early this morning and saw neither of you were around, I tried calling your cells and didn't get any answers. I took off as soon as I was finished with my guests. Because of what you said, this is where I looked first."

"I remember now that I *was* planning to take you up on that special dinner. Hayes, or someone, sure as hell caught up with me first." I rubbed the lump on the back of my head. "Bushwhacked me and sent me out to sea."

She gave me a look.

"Okay, left me anchored in the harbor."

"Why do you think it was Hayes who attacked you?"

I pointed toward the shed behind us. "It sure as hell was his Ford parked over there when I arrived. Then it took off. Must have been him here, along with someone else."

"I don't think it was Hayes," she said.

"I appreciate your loyalty to the tribe, but I checked the plates—definitely Hayes's Explorer."

She pulled her purse out from under the boat, opened it, dug around inside, and came up with a couple of pills and a small bottle of water. "Take these," she said.

"What?"

"Tylenol."

"I prefer aspirin."

"Not for a concussion, you don't." She said it with such conviction that I wasn't going to argue.

After the tablets slid down and I finished the water, I said, "I'm telling you, it was Hayes's SUV. I checked the license plate."

"Maybe so," she said, "but I'm almost certain it wasn't him driving—he took my Miata when he left The Pomo House to go look for you. I came down here in that pickup I borrowed for you to use."

"Thought I left that thing at Putah Creek."

"Thing? That's a treasured Temkut vehicle. Couldn't just leave it over there."

"Yeah, well, I think we should take a drive through town and see if we can find Moreno," I said.

"I think I need to get you to the Urgent Care Center."

"I'll skip the urgent care stop, if you don't mind. But I definitely could use a soft bed and a few hours sleep."

She grunted and scowled at me before getting up to lead me to the parking lot. When I started for the Porsche, she snatched the keys out of my hand. "You're in no condition to drive, Mr. Zach Rolfe. We'll take the pickup."

"Why don't you take us in the Porsche?" I said.

"Would love to, but look at us. We're both soaked and filthy. Let's not insult your little yellow screamer."

We continued on to the paved parking lot where she'd left the beat-up Dodge crew-cab she'd previously loaned me.

"Dinner still warming in the oven?"

She laughed.

On the way to The Pomo House, she took a detour and stopped at the Appa Bay Urgent Care Center anyway; and she wouldn't take any argument about my not going in.

"You're going to have your head looked at, then off to bed for some rest. We'll worry about Hayes tomorrow."

The on-duty RN examined my eyes, head, and asked a lot of questions to test my memory, concentration, and thinking processes.

"Well, you've got a dandy of a bruise," she said, "but the skin isn't broken. What hit you?"

"Damn if I know."

"Are you going to be with him?" she asked Vanessa. When she got a positive response, she said, "Good. Make sure he gets some bed rest, with his head elevated about 30 degrees or so. And check his eyes and pupils every hour; they should be equal."

"No problem."

She picked up a bottle of tablets, tapped out a couple into a small, pleated white paper cup, and handed it to me, along with a regular paper cup of water. "Take these," she said.

"What are they?"

"Tylenol. I'll give you a couple more to take in four hours if your head still hurts. Okay?"

"She just gave me some of those a little while ago," I said, pointing to Vanessa.

"I did," Vanessa said.

"Good. He can take these two later, if he needs them. But nothing stronger than that. Got it?"

"Yes," Vanessa and I said together.

When we got back to The Pomo House, Vanessa helped me out of the truck and took me in to my room. She started to sit me on the edge of the bed, but I resisted.

"Not in these clothes," I said. "I promise to crawl straight into bed after I undress and take a shower."

"Don't worry about it," she said, pushing me down. Then with the gentlest of touch she explored the area where I'd been whacked on the head. "Yep, that's one dandy bump. Need to make sure the swelling doesn't increase." She rested her hand on my shoulder. "Now go get your shower. I'll be right here in case you get dizzy or nauseous. Okay?"

"Promise?"

"Promise."

I took her hand and kissed the back of it. "I really appreciate what you did. You're my hero."

"Glad I found you."

She started to take her hand away, but I didn't want to let go. Instead, I pulled her down to sit next to me; there was little resistance.

"You need to get some rest," she said.

"This is very restful." I kissed her lips; she kissed back.

"You need to rest," she repeated, then slowly started to unbutton my shirt.

I returned the gesture and then we were in the shower together and then in the bed together and then sort of resting together.

At one point I said, "Is my head elevated thirty degrees?"

CHAPTER 29

When I awoke later—much later—it took a moment or two to orient myself, to realize I was in my room at The Pomo House. Scrolling back, I remembered being in bed with Vanessa, who was now gone, along with our filthy clothes.

Floating in the boat…

Getting hit on the head…

Chasing after the Ford Explorer…

At least the clunk on the head hadn't affected my memory; everything seemed to be in place as I chronicled the previous day's activities.

I tentatively put both feet on the floor, tested my stability, and when it proved relatively sound, went looking for my watch. If the time it showed was correct, almost forty-eight hours had passed since I'd gone looking for Hayes down along the waterfront.

After performing the usual first-thing-out-of-bed rituals, I dressed and went into the main part of the B&B looking for my rescuer. No big surprise—she was in the kitchen, working with several pots and pans on a huge Wolf six-burner gas range.

"Feel better?" she said over her shoulder. She was wearing another of her trademark peasant blouses, along with blue jeans and sandals. A half apron, with "Chief Indian Chef" printed in block letters on the front, was tied around her trim waist.

"Much," I said, which was the truth. I walked over to where I saw two plates and silverware set out on the counter. A mouth-watering aroma filled the kitchen.

"Not exactly the setting I'd planned for this meal," she said, "but I wasn't about to toss it out. Decided it might make a nice, if somewhat heavy and late lunch for us."

"You'll get no argument from me. Smells like it will be delicious regardless of when it's served." I plopped down on one of the two leather-upholstered bar stools at the counter.

She came over and sat down beside me. "I think I know why you were unconscious for so long." She took the edge of my right shirt sleeve in her fingers. "Mind?"

"We getting undressed again?" I said.

"Behave yourself!" She pushed up the sleeve and lightly poked my triceps.

"Ouch!"

"Uh-huh! Saw a puncture mark and slight swelling there this morning when I was getting out of bed. Looks like someone jabbed you with a needle, probably after hitting you."

"No doubt a contributing factor to my nausea," I said. "Still bothering me."

"Maybe you'd rather not eat?"

"Not even a remote consideration. You've fixed this meal twice and I certainly don't intend to miss out on it the second time, no matter what the condition of my insides."

"Good!"

She served up the spiciest, most succulent cioppino I've ever stuck a fork and spoon into, accompanied by a broiler-toasted mini-loaf of extra sour French bread, laced with crushed garlic, butter, and asiago cheese. I really didn't want to go *anywhere* after that.

However, I did need to retrieve the Porsche, so after we washed the dishes and cleaned up the kitchen, we took off in the pickup, with Vanessa doing the driving just to be on the safe side.

"I tried to call Hayes again," she said. "Twice. No answer."

"You think something may have happened to him?"

"Only because of what happened to you down at the fishing pier." She tapped her fingertips on the steering wheel. "It's not all that unusual for him to take off, not tell anyone where he's going, and turn off his cell. But he seldom isolates for this long." Her tapping on the wheel changed to pounding. "Besides, this time he has my car!"

"He's a strange one, all right."

She didn't say anything further, but I'd heard disapproval and hurt in her voice. It bolstered my earlier suspicion that at some time in the not too distant past she and Hayes had had a thing for each other. And the looks I'd seen him give her made it obvious that he was ready and willing to resume that relationship; I don't think the feeling was mutual. But I'd learned long ago not to take for granted what a woman might want, or not want.

She drove us back down to the fishing pier in the old pickup. I took her to the shed and showed her the broken window and the brass shell casing.

"So tragic," she said. "Grady Nolan was a good dad to me. Don't think he ever did anything hurtful to another human being his whole life, physically or verbally."

"I take that to mean you're clueless as to who would have had reason to kill him, or Petrucci, for that matter."

She looked out the shattered window at the old pier where the second of the two shootings had occurred. When she looked back at me, her face was grim. "I wish I did know who killed Grady, Zach. I'd go after the bastard myself."

I reached out and took her hand. "Come on, let's go see if we can find Hayes, or even his Explorer, for that matter."

"And my Miata, too, if you don't mind." She managed a small smile.

"Ah, yes. And your Miata."

When we got to the Porsche, I handed her the keys after unlocking the driver's door.

"You're going to let me drive your prized little coupe?"

"Why not? I'm feeling much better, but I think I'll give it a little more time before I get behind the wheel again. Don't want to put any of the fair citizens of Appa Bay in danger." While she was familiarizing herself with the Porsche's controls and instrument panel, I said, "What about the pickup? You don't want to just leave it here, do you?"

"It'll be all right," she said. "I'll just give Frank Ross a call and he'll have someone come down and get it; it belongs to the tribe."

We had no trouble finding Hayes's Ford—it was parked on the main street, about halfway between the Wirok Café and the hardware store. The keys were in the ignition and the soft drink cup, now dried out, had fallen over on the passenger's seat. We walked the street, stuck our noses into every store that was open, and ended up back at my car without seeing Hayes, or talking to anyone who had seen him in the past 24 hours.

The next quest was to find Vanessa's Miata. After covering every paved and unpaved street in Appa Bay, she drove us out to the Temkut hunting lodge, which triggered fond memories of our night there, along with a little wishful thinking. And that's where we found her little roadster, parked on the other side of the gate, top down. But no Hayes, either inside or outside the cabin. Nor could I find any evidence that he, or anyone else, had recently been inside the cabin.

"Curious," I said, once we were back outside.

"What?"

"I just noticed there aren't any tire tracks behind the Miata, nor any footprints to indicate someone got out of the car after it was driven in here."

She came over beside me and looked around for herself. "You'd make a damn fine Indian," she said.

"Thanks."

"So what's your guess as to what happened here?" she said. "Extraterrestrials?"

"If so, then we don't have a problem," I said. "Once they find out how unreliable Hayes is, they'll bring him right back."

She laughed harder than the quip merited, but I assumed part of that was releasing some of the tension she'd been under. "Probably wouldn't have taken him in the first place." She spread her arms out to her sides. "What now?"

"To The Pomo House, unless you have some other idea."

"Not a one."

When we got back to where we'd left the Porsche, she said, "I'll drive you home so you can rest, then have someone bring me back out here later to pick up my car."

"No need," I said. "I think I'm now up to getting behind the wheel, provided we don't get into any wild car chases."

"Are you sure?"

"No, but if I know you're following along close behind me, I'll resist any temptation to play Bullitt."

"He drove a Mustang," she said.

"Well, good for you."

She smiled and handed me the keys to the Cayman, some disappointment showing in her eyes. She'd taken to the wheel of the car like she'd owned Porsches all her driving life. "If I hadn't been so worried about you, I would have *really* enjoyed driving your screamin' yellow car," she said. "How much does one of these little gems cost?"

"About double the price of a new Miata, plus a few bucks," I said.

"Guess I'm going to have to work a little harder keeping my place filled with guests … maybe a lot harder."

As she turned to get her car, I noticed something unusual about the surrounding area that I hadn't notices before. "Stop!" I shouted. "Don't move!"

She looked back over her shoulder and frowned. "What?"

"Look at the ground between the road and the gate. Do you see anything unusual, or am I carrying the Indian thing too far?"

Vanessa looked down for a moment, took a step back, crouched down, and studied the entire area leading from the coast road to the fence.

"I think you earned your merit badge in tracking this time," she said. "The whole pathway from the road to where my car is parked has been brushed with a tree branch of some kind to make it look like no one was, or had been here."

"Let's go look inside the Miata," I said.

When we got there, we saw nothing unusual other than the parking brake was off and the gear shift was in neutral.

"Looks like someone pushed the car in here," I said. "And I think you're right about someone sweeping the path clear of any footprints."

"To what end?" she said. "Knowing Hayes, it could be part of some elaborate practical joke."

I rubbed the back of my head where I'd been coldcocked. "I'm not laughing."

I waited while Vanessa got in, started the Miata, and backed out to where the Porsche was parked. I closed the gate behind her, took one more look around, and then got into my car.

Not long after taking off to lead our little trail party of two back to The Pomo House, I wished I'd taken her up on her offer to drive us to the B&B. The nausea hit, starting as a small rumble in my gut and making a spiked climb upward until I could taste its metallic presence in my jaw muscles. It caused several tear-producing gulps that almost made me pull over and stop. Then it eased, but it was still an uncomfortable ride back to the inn.

When we got there, a police cruiser was parked in the driveway, an Appa Bay cop leaning against the driver's door. I forgot all about the nausea as I watched Vanessa get out of her car, walk over to the cop, and give him a hug. I figured it had to be Charlie Longtree. Maybe we were finally going to get some kind of official word on what was happening with the murder investigations, and maybe a clue as to what was going on with Hayes.

After Vanessa made the introductions—it *was* Longtree— we went into the kitchen for a cup of coffee and to find out what light her long-time friend might be able to shed on the whole Appa Bay situation.

"The bullets that killed Nolan and Petrucci definitely came from the same rifle," Longtree said, once we were gathered around the kitchen counter. "But we haven't found the rifle, or been able to turn up any other clues."

"Do you think Chief Chubb is involved in any way?" Vanessa asked.

"In the investigation?"

"No, not that. I mean in the killings, the attack on Zach."

"Mr. Rolfe was attacked?"

Vanessa and I told him what had happened down at the municipal fishing pier.

"Look, Vanessa, the chief may not be one of the best cops in the county, but he's honest … and he's fair."

"What about his attacking Hayes?" I said.

"That's a lot of made-up bullshit. Moreno has his own agenda, whatever it is. I have no idea why he accused Chubb of ambushing him."

"What's your intuition tell you?" Vanessa asked.

"My intuition doesn't tell me shit about any of this. I mean, who knows why Moreno says what he says and does what he does? I sure as hell don't. What I'd rather have is a viable suspect or two."

"I would think any list of suspects would include both those who would benefit from a resort and casino being built, and those who would like the town to stay the way it is," she said.

"Guess that could cover most everyone," Longtree said.

"To that end, who else sits on the city council?" I asked.

"Joey Tobin, the mayor," Vanessa said, "plus Mildred Deacon, who's sort of our local postmistress, and T.C. Love, who owns the convenience store at the edge of town."

Longtree shook his head slowly from side to side. "Can't image Ms. Deacon or Mr. Love being involved in anything illegal, let alone murder," he said.

"I certainly agree with that," Vanessa added.

"And Chubb's uncle, the mayor?" I asked.

"He's a man with a lot of irons in the fire," Longtree said, "but that doesn't mean I would accuse him of foul play."

"Anything any of the surviving council members have to gain from the deaths of Nolan and Petrucci?" I asked.

"Nope," they said in unison.

"What about the families of the deceased councilmen?"

"Both widowers," Longtree said. "I don't know anything about any other family."

I looked at Vanessa, who had turned sad at the mention of Nolan being a widower. "Neither of them had any children or siblings that I'm aware of," she said.

Longtree scuffed at the kitchen floor with the toe of one boot, looked at Vanessa, then past her, and shook his head.

"What is it, Charlie?" she asked.

"Probably nothing to it, but I've heard some talk that both Nolan and Petrucci were kinda sweet on Annalee Mackey."

"Charlie, you've got to be kidding," she said. "Grady Nolan hasn't so much as looked at another woman since Nettie died."

"Maybe, maybe not. I'm just telling you what I heard."

"I don't know whether to laugh or cry," she said.

"Would that make her a suspect or would it put her above suspicion?" I said.

Vanessa glared at me. "Zach, how can you say such a terrible thing?"

"Look, people are dead. We're trying to find out who did it and why. So we need to know who all the players are in this supposedly quiet little town of Appa Bay. And we need to establish what their real relationships are to one another."

"Yup," Longtree said. "Of course there's the thing about Petrucci being part Patwin, but both the Temkut council and the city council looked into his Indian connections and couldn't find any conflict of interest. Besides, the city council's votes on the casino have been unanimous throughout."

"And what about Annalee and the mayor?"

"What do you mean?" Vanessa said.

"Well, the other morning when I was having breakfast at the café, seemed to me there might be a thing going on between the two of them. I mean, I didn't catch them holding hands or sneaking a kiss in the back, but something more was happening than just a call for the check."

Vanessa started laughing and shaking her head from side to side.

"Not going to happen, huh?"

"No way," she said.

I looked at Longtree, but his expression hadn't changed. "Well, you two know the home folks much better than I do."

Vanessa was still laughing.

"Okay, then let's look at this thing from a different angle," I said. "If the ultimate goal is to prevent the casino from being built, then why shoot just the two councilmen, then only rough up Hayes? And what about clobbering me and setting me adrift?"

"Doesn't make sense," Longtree said. "Although we know it wasn't Chief Chubb who slugged Moreno, and we don't know for certain whether or not Moreno attacked you, dumped you in a boat, and shoved you out into the bay."

"You should tell Charlie about that Wadkins guy," Vanessa said. "The one who supposedly works for both Crandal and your friend Greer Raebeck over at the Putah Creek casino."

"I know who he is," Longtree said. "What about him?"

"He keeps turning up, trying to play the tough guy. Without much success," I said. "But the mention of Putah Creek reminds me that I never heard back from Greer Raebeck about who the fake security people were that chased us the other night."

"I would like to hear this," Longtree said. "All of it."

I gave him a summary of my encounters with Crandal and Wadkins, told him about what I'd found at the old fish processing plant, and explained my relationship with Greer Raebeck.

"There you have it," I said. "It's up to you to figure out what to do with it."

He grunted and jotted something in his notebook.

"I'm going to make a suggestion," I said. "I'm going to chase down Greer and see what she has to say, and after I do that, maybe the two of you could come up with the name of someone who might profit by having the Coastal Commission come down hard on the Temkuts over the casino. You know, like something more solid than the old 'Protect the Coastline' rallying cry."

It took three phone calls before I located Greer in the Lake Tahoe offices of Twin Arrows. She was busy and the conversation went no further than to tell me she hadn't been able to identify the two bruisers who chased us out of the parking garage.

I relayed the information to Vanessa and Longtree, who had been conversing while I was on the phone.

"Neither of us can come up with a suspect as to who might have put pressure on the Coastal Commission," she said.

"We need to find Moreno," Longtree added.

"That's what we were trying to do before we came back here and found you waiting," Vanessa said.

"In fact, that's all I've been doing ever since I arrived here," I said. "And he's the one who called and asked me to come to Appa Bay."

Longtree gave me a nod of understanding, gave Vanessa a brief hug, and said he had to get back to the police station. After he left, Vanessa excused herself to take care of some Pomo House paperwork, and I went to my room, kicked off my shoes, got out of my shirt and pants, and made myself comfortable on the bed. I turned on the laptop so I could update my running notes, review everything that had happened thus far, and then try to figure out what to do next.

* * *

The slamming of a car door woke me. I struggled to get my eyes open and in focus, then jumped up and rushed to the window, almost spilling my computer onto the floor in the process. It was dark now, but not too dark to catch a glimpse of a pale blue crew cab pickup and Hayes's Explorer, along with someone untying a towrope that connected the two vehicles. There was a *Big O Tires* logo on the truck's door.

Then I saw Hayes walking rapidly toward the garage. This time he wasn't getting away without telling me what the hell was going on. But by the time I pulled on my pants, shoved my feet into a pair of shoes, and got through the door, he was pulling out of the driveway in Vanessa's Miata, the pickup truck close behind, both kicking up sprays of gravel as they accelerated away.

I rushed back to my room, grabbed my wallet and car keys, then headed out to see if I could catch up with Moreno. If that wasn't successful, I'd read enough of the advertising on the side of the *Big O* tire truck to know its home base.

* * *

After almost an hour of looking for and not finding Hayes in Appa Bay, or anyplace up and down the coast road, I took off for San Tomas. The *Big O* store was at the far east end of the main street. The pickup was parked in front of one of the three tire-changing bays, or at least a truck identical to the one I'd seen earlier outside The Pomo House. The inside and outside lights were on, but the front and bay doors were closed and locked. A *Closed* sign hung in the window.

I rattled the front door, pounded on the frame, and clattered my car keys against the window glass. A couple of minutes or so of this and I heard a faint voice yelling from somewhere inside the building.

"We're closed, goddam it! Can't you read?"

"Emergency!" I yelled. "Hayes Moreno's in trouble. Sent me to get you."

It took only a few second before a scruffy, overall-clad character came to the door.

"Who the hell are you?" he said, squinting out at me.

"A friend."

"Whose friend, 'cause I sure as hell don't know you."

"A friend of Hayes," I said. "Open the door."

"Maybe I'd better call the cops."

"Sure you want to do that? I mean, I did see you and Hayes steal a red Miata earlier this evening in Appa Bay."

"No, no, no," he said, turning the knob of the door's deadbolt. "Hayes had a key."

"Then where is he?"

"Thought you said he's in trouble."

"He is, or soon will be if you don't tell me where he is, Mr.—"

"Lupin." He took a couple of steps to his left. "Stephen Lupin." He rose up on his toes, looked down the street in the direction I'd just come. "I'm Hayes's cousin." He moved back to his right. "First cousin ... Esteban, really."

I reached out and put my hands on top of his shoulders, held him in place. "Okay, Cousin Esteban, or Stephen, where'd Hayes go after he left you?"

"Look, I don't want any trouble, okay?" His feet did a kind of shuffle.

"Okay. Tell me where he went."

Esteban thought for a moment before he answered. "To a house out on the coast road. North. Guy out there he wanted to follow."

"He give you a name?"

"No, sir." He looked left, then right, then back at me. "All I know is that the guy drives a big, black Escalade."

I released Esteban and stepped back. "Did he say why he wanted to follow this guy?"

"No, sir." He eased back toward the door. "Hayes doesn't tell me much. Doesn't tell anyone very much."

I gave him a big grin. "You sure as hell can say *that* again." I walked away, leaving him standing there, doing a little dance, somewhere between confused and relieved.

Inside the Porsche, I called Crandal, put up with a bunch of static from one of his bodyguards, and finally convinced the guy that it would be in his boss's best interests to take a call from Zach Rolfe.

"I thought we'd agreed to disagree, Mr. Rolfe," Crandal said when he came on the line.

"I need to know where your man Wadkins is," I said.

"He was here most of the day, but he's gone now."

"Thanks, but I sort of knew that. I checked your driveway earlier for his Escalade. It wasn't there. Any idea where he went after leaving your place?"

"No, I don't. Wadkins is free to go wherever he wants to go, Mr. Rolfe."

"Unless you have something for him to do."

"True."

"And on nights when you don't have anything for him to do, any idea what he does with his time?" I asked.

"I think he likes to play blackjack."

"At the Putah Creek Casino?"

"I really don't know, Mr. Rolfe. However, that *is* the closest casino around here, at least for now."

"I hope you're not sending me off on a wild goose chase, Crandal."

"I'm not *sending* you off anywhere. I gave you a little information that I didn't *have* to give you. What you do with it, or whether you believe it or not, is none of my fucking business."

I'd already turned the Porsche in the direction of Putah Creek and was accelerating out of San Tomas before I disconnected from Crandal.

CHAPTER 30

Things had not gone well for Hayes Moreno the past couple of days.

The bad run started early the previous day when someone stole his truck while he was working at the *Appa Bay Sentinel* office. He'd reported the theft, but by this morning, when the cops hadn't found it, he'd borrowed Vanessa's Miata—without her permission—to go look for the Explorer himself. After driving every street and lane in and around town, he finally found it mid-morning, parked in the center of town near Frank Ross's Temkut Treasures, a spot he'd already passed several times. The truck was unlocked, the keys were in the ignition, but it wouldn't start.

He called his cousin to come over from San Tomas.

"I've tried everything," Esteban said. "She jus' won't start. I think we need to take her back to my shop."

"Got no time for that right now," Hayes said. "I need to find a guy and ask him some questions." He looked up and down the street. "Do you mind driving me around for awhile to look for him?"

"In my truck?"

"Yeah. The Miata's a little too obvious."

"Okay, man, but I can't stick with you too long. Got things to do back in San Tomas."

"Deal," Hayes said. "We'll drop the Miata off at the tribal hunting lodge."

"You're not going to take it back to Vanessa's?"

"May need it later."

Esteban drove him around the rest of the day in the *Big O Tires* truck, but they could find no trace of Wadkins or his Escalade.

* * *

"Man, how long we gonna look for this dude?" Esteban complained. It was getting close to dusk. "I tol' you, I need to get back to San Tomas."

Hayes was disappointed. He'd really wanted to find Terence Wadkins—preferably alone—and do a little forceful interrogation as to why it had been Wadkins and not Chubb who had coldcocked him in The Pomo House garage and taken the schematic.

"Okay. Okay. Take me back to the lodge so I can pick up the Miata, then you can take off."

* * *

"Oh, fuck!" Hayes said as they pulled up to the lodge.

"It's gone, man. The Miata," Esteban said.

"Yeah, I can see that."

"So watcha wanna do now?"

"What I want to do is go dig a hole and hide in it. Vanessa's really going to be pissed."

"You think someone stole her car?"

"No, I think she probably went looking for me, found the car, and took it home."

"You gonna go tell her wha' happened?"

"Not if I can avoid it; at least not now." He slammed a hand down on the dashboard. "Let's go get the Explorer and tow it back to The Pomo House."

"You don't wanna tow her to my shop?"

"Not now."

When they got to The Pomo House, the lights were on in the kitchen; Hayes could see Vanessa working inside. He also caught a glimpse of Rolfe looking out the window of his room. He hurried over to check inside the garage while Esteban untied the tow rope. The Miata was right there, as he was both afraid and hoping it would be. He was glad it hadn't been stolen, but he knew Vanessa was going to be all over him like pitch on a tar stick for having taken it in the first place. To compound the problem, he'd decided to take her car again—and again without her permission—and keep looking for Wadkins.

As he and Esteban high-tailed it out of the parking area, spraying gravel from the rear tires of both the Miata and the *Big O Tires* truck, he was almost certain he saw Zach Rolfe in his rearview mirror, come running around the side of the house.

Too late, Zach!

A few minutes later he spotted Wadkins coming out of the Wirok Café, climb into his black Escalade, and drive away. He followed the big SUV, close enough not to lose sight of it, but not so close that the driver would become suspicious. What he wanted was to catch Wadkins alone and unaware.

Hayes knew Rolfe had had a couple of run-ins with Wadkins since arriving in Appa Bay, but those encounters hadn't resulted in anything, at least not in the way of providing information as to who killed the two councilmen. He also knew he shouldn't have told Rolfe and the others that it was Chief Chubb who had clobbered him the other night inside The Pomo House garage. It had been a spur-of-the-moment, sophomoric stunt just to make Chubb look bad, prompted solely be the fact that the police chief had been giving him a rough time about one thing or the other ever since he arrived in Appa Bay. Without thinking it through, he'd jumped at the chance to get even. He realized now that he should have at least told Rolfe the truth about Wadkins having knocked him out and making off with the diagram he'd drawn.

He was expecting Wadkins to drive back out to Crandal's place. Instead, the Escalade turned off onto the road that would take them in the direction of the Putah Creek Casino.

If the casino *was* Wadkins' only destination for the evening, then Hayes knew he needed to find some way to get into Putah Creek without being spotted. As far as he knew, he was still *persona non grata* there. Someday, he told himself, he might learn to curb his remarks about other tribes' casino plans and operations, but that wasn't going to do him any good right now.

When they got to the casino entrance, Hayes pulled off onto the shoulder of the road, stopped, and waited while Wadkins continued onto the long driveway that led up to the front entrance of the resort and casino. He watched as the Escalade rolled to a stop at the casino front door. Wadkins got out, handed the keys to a valet parking attendant, and walked through the gaudy entranceway into the casino.

Hayes waited a couple of minutes to make sure Wadkins wasn't coming back out, then drove around to the casino's three-level parking structure. He cruised the aisles, from level to level, looking for a suitable space to park the Miata, one that would keep it from being in the direct line of sight of the roving security patrols. He finally found the near-perfect place on the middle level, between a matched pair of huge out-of-state RVs, whose sides hung over the two white-painted dividing lines of the space between them. He backed into the narrow slot as far as he could—bumper to bumper with a car in the slot behind him—and left the Miata ready for a dash out of garage, if that became necessary. He had to climb over the door to get out of the roadster.

The next task was to get into the casino itself. And after that, find Wadkins.

And after that?

He really wasn't sure; he would simply have to wait and see. If Wadkins left the casino later, he'd follow; if the creep checked into a room for the night, he'd find a way to get into the room and do what he could to force some answers out of Wadkins.

As he walked toward the bank of elevators that connected the garage with the casino proper, it came to him that he should have brought along something to disguise his looks. But then, he hadn't known he was going to be here, and even if he had known, he wasn't sure what he could have done to keep from being recognized.

He was startled by the ping of a bell before recognizing it as the arrival of an elevator car. The doors slid open and a happy group of male and female twenty-somethings spewed out into garage, blocking his way.

"Good night at the tables?" Hayes said, just to be polite.

"Naw, lost our pants," said one guy.

"Panties!" corrected a gal clinging to his arm. "Lost our panties!"

"Yeah? I thought that would come later!" said another guy.

That put all of them into a near-hysterical laughing fit that Hayes wasn't in the mood to appreciate. While he waited for them to get over themselves and move on, he saw that one of them was wearing something that might keep the security people from recognizing him the minute he stepped into the casino—a brown camouflage desert hat with a broad brim and a neck-protecting flap hanging down in the back. All he had to do was talk the owner into giving it to him, or selling it.

"Hey!" he called out. Everyone stopped to look back at him. "You, with the desert hat!"

The wearer reached up, put a hand on his head, then pointed to his chest. "Me?"

"Yeah, you," Hayes said. "Wanna sell the hat?"

"Ya gotta be kiddin'."

"No, no," Hayes said. "I'm serious."

"How much?"

"Ten bucks."

"Nah," he said. "Just bought it today." He thought for a moment. "Twenty! Make it twenty and it's yours." He turned to his friends, seeking approval. Several of them nodded, gave him a thumbs up.

Hayes pulled out his wallet, found a twenty, and held it up. "You got a deal!"

The guy moved out of the crowd, took off the hat, and did a little pantomime show as he presented it to Hayes. "Deal!" He snatched the twenty from between Hayes's fingers, turned to his friends and yelled, "Food money!"

A couple of the guys waved and one gal threw Hayes a kiss as the group headed for their cars.

Hayes punched the button to bring the elevator car back, and while he waited, he examined the hat; more to see if it was reasonably clean than anything else. Inside, on the sweatband, was a price tag—$9.95. He grunted a short laugh and put on the hat. He looked at himself in the chrome of the elevator door and carefully tucked his long black hair up and behind the rear sun flap, then pulled the brim down low all around his head. It wasn't much, but it was better than nothing. Maybe no one would spot him, at least for a while. More importantly, spot him before he found Wadkins.

It didn't take long to find the Lurton-Bales gofer—Wadkins was hunched over his cards at a $100-limit 21 table, totally absorbed in the game.

Hayes wished he could grab the empty stool next to Wadkins, but there was no way he could sit in at a table with stakes that high, not even for one deal of the cards. He had to find someway to get close to Wadkins and coerce the guy into going outside with him. He assumed Wadkins eventually would have to go the john, so he'd just wait. If they tried to throw him out before that, he'd have to come up with a different plan, perhaps resort to simply staking out Wadkins' Escalade in the valet parking area.

In the meantime, he looked around for a simple cover while he watched Wadkins and the table action. Unfortunately, there wasn't even a slot machine close to the gaming table to use as a prop. A busy cocktail bar several feet in the wrong direction seemed to offer the only place to wait and not attract attention. He walked over, stood by a stool, and saw that if he stretched a little, he could keep an eye on Wadkins.

"What may I serve you, sir?" asked the bartender.

Hayes was going wave off the guy, then decided it would look better if he had some kind of drink sitting there. "Coke," he said. "Diet."

"Yes, sir."

Before the bartender returned, Hayes saw someone come up behind Wadkins, whisper in his ear, and then slide up onto the stool next to the gambler. At first he thought it was a man—medium-short hair, white blazer, and dark slacks. But the body movements made him reconsider. It was a woman. Greer Raebeck? Not with that hair, or those clothes. The woman was also too short to be Raebeck. He wished he could see her face.

He picked up his Coke, slid off the bar stool, and walked slowly toward Wadkins' 21 table, thinking to casually check out the new arrival, then return to the bar. He was almost there when a voice behind him said, "Lose your way to the Temkut Rancheria, Mr. Moreno?"

When he turned around, there was Raebeck and one of her security people.

"Spotted me, huh?" he said.

"What are you doing in the casino, Mr. Moreno?" Greer asked. "I thought you were aware that you'd worn out your welcome here a long time ago."

"Looking for a friend. He said to meet him here are the 21 tables. It's important, otherwise I wouldn't have come in."

"And have you seen this friend of yours?"

"I thought so, but I'm not sure," Hayes said. "I was just headed over to that twenty-one table when you stopped me."

"Care to tell me which person you thought was your friend?" she said.

"Uh, not really. He's a Temkut. I, uh, think he's been thrown out of here a few times. I don't want him to get into trouble."

"Never took you for the big brother protector type."

"Probably a lot you don't know about me Ms. Raebeck."

"Uh-huh!" She scanned the area. "Well, since we don't want any trouble, either, I'll have my people check the tables. If your Temkut friend's here, we'll find him."

Hayes shrugged, hands out, palms up. "That's the way it goes sometimes." He started to turn away. "Don't be too rough on the guy."

"No, no, Mr. Moreno, please don't go," Greer said. "I think we need to talk."

"Nah, I don't think so."

"George!" she said to the security man. "Take Mr. Moreno up to my office. And please make sure he doesn't leave until I say he can go."

"I didn't do anything," Hayes said. "If you call the cops, what are you going to tell them, you don't like me?"

"Who said anything about the cops?" Greer said. "I'm calling Rolfe."

"Shit!"

As George the Security Man escorted Hayes through the casino to the private elevator that would take them up to Raebeck's office, Hayes took one more glance in the direction of Wadkins' table. The person sitting next to him turned just enough so he could catch the profile. He wasn't sure, but it sure as hell looked like Annalee Mackey.

Maybe it is finally time for a meaningful sit-down with Rolfe.

CHAPTER 31

Northern California – 1950

He stood in front of the mirror in the small bedroom, brought his right hand up sharply into a military salute, and barked: "Staff Sergeant Randolph Moreno reporting for duty, sir." He scowled at his image, shook his head slowly from side to side, and brought the rigid hand back down alongside his thigh.

The space in the mirror where his saluting arm had been was now filled with the reflection of his wife, standing in the doorway of the bedroom. Frown lines wrinkled her forehead; a single tear tumbled over a lower lash and slid down across the roundness of her cheek.

"I don't want you to do this," whispered Loretta Moreno, her arms crossed tightly across her chest. "You spent three years fighting in a war on tiny little islands no one ever heard of, and you came home to me alive and whole. I don't want you to go away and risk your life again."

He turned to face his wife. "I told you, I have no choice. Our reserve unit is being activated. Things are not going well in Korea."

"I never wanted you to join up with that reserve unit in the first place, remember?"

"Yes, I remember. But it's brought in a little money every month, money we've sorely needed."

"Evil money," she whispered. "Evil, evil money they pay to buy your soul."

"Life would have been much tougher for us, Loretta, without the money from the Reserves. Have you forgotten already that no one was hiring Indians when I came home from Japan?"

"The government was supposed to help find you a job." She sat down on the edge of the small, sagging bed they shared. "But they didn't help. They were supposed to provide a low-cost loan so you could buy a home, but no job, no loan. Then there were those wonderful job-training programs, all in places where we

couldn't afford to live. The GI Bill was created for white men, Randolph, not Indians."

"I got paid the unemployment benefits. That helped."

"Oh, yes, the wonderful '52-20' program ... twenty dollars a week for 52 weeks."

"It kept us from starving."

"It helped make you feel sorry for yourself, Randolph, helped make you feel even more dependent on the white man's government."

"That's why I joined the Army Reserve unit in San Tomas." He sat down next to her. *"We needed the money."*

"We would have managed, Randolph. We would have found a way." She raised her arms even higher across her chest and clenched her shoulders. *"I knew from the moment you told me you were going to sign those reserve papers that it would bring trouble."*

"I know."

"But you did it anyway. And now they're going to take you away from me, away from your sons."

"Yes."

"Tell them no! Tell those white men in their fancy uniforms with all the gold decorations that they don't need Randolph Moreno to help fight another war. Tell those politicians in Washington that Randolph Moreno did his part for their country; tell them they should have learned a lesson, tell them they shouldn't have gotten their nation into a new war."

"They say it isn't a war, Loretta; it's a police action."

"Are men dying?"

"Yes."

"Then it's a war. When men fight and die, it's a war, Randolph. You know that as well as I do." She pulled even harder at her elbows. *"When we met, you were always quoting Chief Joseph: 'I will fight no more forever.' What happened to those feelings, Randolph?"*

"That was a long time ago, Loretta." He moved closer, reached out and tried to touch her. *"It's our country, too."*

"Very damn little of it. And we don't even own that for the most part. The white man's government owns it, holds it 'in trust' for us, they say, whatever that truly means." She flung out one arm and knocked his hand away, then shook a finger at him. *"Well, I'll tell you again, Randolph Moreno, I didn't trust them before and I trust them even less now."*

Moreno let his hand fall onto his thigh, took a deep breathe and let it out. "I know you're angry with me, Loretta, but there's nothing I can do."

She stared at him for a long moment, her eyes overflowing with tears. "We should run away, Randolph. Run away from the white man and all the troubles he causes."

"They would only come find me, lock me up, and keep us apart forever."

* * *

The three men stood outside the small market, squinting under the building's dim exterior lights, trying to count the loose coins in their outstretched palms.

"Don't look like we got enough for a six-pack," said Moreno. He looked into the palms of the other two men. "Whacha think?" He wiped his other hand down the side of the khaki army pants he continued to wear almost two years after the Korean armistice was signed

Wesley Warner raised his palmful of change closer to his face and used the index finger of his other hand to push the coins around until he had the nickels and dimes segregated into small groups. A single quarter rested in the center of his hand. He started to count, ignoring the three or four pennies resting at the heel of his palm.

"I got eighteen cents," said the third man, Delano Rojas.

"If you're gonna count pennies, then I got twice that," Moreno said.

"Guess I'm the winner," said Warner. "Fifty-five cents." He used the poised finger to move the pennies in with the other coins. "Actually, sixty-three."

Moreno closed his eyes and did the arithmetic. "Not enough!"

"Not enough what?" came a voice from the edge of the market's tiny parking lot.

Moreno knew the voice without even looking up.

"Not enough for what?" Loretta Moreno repeated, forcing her way between her husband and Wesley Warner.

"Uh, we were just going to buy some sodas, Loretta," Warner said. *"Want one?"*

Delano Rojas giggled.

"From the looks and smell of you three, I'd say you've had enough sodas for one day." She clamped her strong fingers onto her husband's elbow and turned him away from his two friends. *"Come on, Randolph, we're going home. There're things to talk about."*

"What things?" He tried to pull loose, but couldn't.

"Serious things." She turned toward the lot and started toward their battered and rusted '40 Ford pickup.

Moreno tried to follow, but only one leg made the turn. He stumbled and grabbed her arm with both hands.

"Goddam leg!" he yelled as he tried to regain control of the prosthetic leg the VA hospital in San Francisco had given him. He couldn't pivot on it to make rapid changes in direction without stumbling. This was particularly true after he'd had a few, no, actually, several beers.

"If you fall," she said, *"I'm going to leave you right there on the ground, Randolph. Maybe even pull your leg off and take it home with me. That way I'll at least know where some part of you is."*

"Come on, Loretta, that's mean. What's your problem?"

"You're my problem, Randolph Moreno. I need you home helping me get out firewood orders. They're backing up"

"Shit, can't the boys help with that? I'm tired."

"No, Randolph, you're drunk. The boys already chopped the wood and are doing their homework. I need you to load the truck and help me make the deliveries."

"But my leg—"

"I don't want to hear one more word about that damn leg of yours, Randolph. If you can stand on it all day long drinking

beer and rotgut wine, then you sure as hell can use it to do something that will bring a little money into the house."

"But—"

"No, the only butt I have any interest in is the one I want to see on the passenger seat of that truck."

Moreno straightened himself, blinked his eyes, and said, "I'll drive."

"Like hell you will!"

When they got home, Arnold Simms, the local Bureau of Indian Affairs agent, was sitting on the front step of the 30-foot by 30-foot clapboard, four-room shack the four Morenos had been living in since Randolph was released from the VA hospital several months earlier. Simms was married to Moreno's aunt.

Moreno looked first at the huge pile of split firewood at the side of house, sighed, and then nodded to Simms. "What brings you all the way out here from San Francisco?"

"Need to talk to you and Loretta."

"Do you want to come in?" Loretta asked.

"We can talk out here," Moreno said before Simms could respond. He didn't like the BIA agent. Never had.

"Randy, you shouldn't be hanging around with all those winos in San Tomas," Simms said. "You're a better man than that."

"Better at what? Even the Army doesn't want me anymore. No one wants a one-legged Indian."

"I know. I know," Simms said. "That's part of why I'm here."

"Someone found the rest of my leg?"

"Randolph!" Loretta said. "Let Arnold say what he came to say."

"You're aware of the Urban Indian Relocation Program, right?" Simms said.

"You tried to recruit me for it when I came home from the hospital, if I remember right. Whole bunch of promises about transportation to some big city where there were going to be lots of jobs. Temporary housing. Job training. Help to find a job. All that kinda shit."

"True. But you wouldn't go."

"That's for damn sure. Don't know how you got so many Indians to fall for that crap. White men never keep their promises to Indians. If they did, the Temkut reservation would cover thousands and thousands of acres, from the mountains to the sea."

"Yes, that's true enough, Randy,

"Instead, we have less than a full section, most of which is barren and so steep a goat can't get a good foothold to make little goats."

"Randolph! I want you to hear what Arnold has to say about what the white man's Congress wants to do now with our land."

"You know about the program?" Simms asked her.

"You know how efficient the Indian telegraph is."

Simms nodded and looked out at the scattering of houses and the scrub oaks dotted here and there.

"Wesley Warner and Delano Rojas signed up for that Urban Relocation thing," Moreno said.

"Randolph, that's old news," Loretta said. "Drop it!"

"The housing was in Los Angeles' worst slums," he continued. What I heard, the job training program never got started, and all those good jobs disappeared, went to white boys. Didn't do Wesley and Delano a damn bit of good. So they came home to the reservation. Figured they might as well starve and die among friends."

"Damn it, Randy, If you don't shut up and listen to what I have to say, then I'm taking off. Still have several rancherías to visit before I call it a night."

"None of Washington's programs for The People are worth a good—"

"Enough! Let Arnold say what he came to say."

Moreno leaned against the side of the house, stuck his hands in his pockets and shrugged his consent.

"It's this way," Simms said, "seems Congress has decided to abandon its trust relationship with a number of tribes, including the Temkuts. They think the people on certain

rancherías are ready for full assimilation into non-Indian society."

"Which means what in everyday words?" Moreno said.

"I'm afraid you aren't going to like this, Randolph," Simms said.

"Can't remember a single time when I've liked something you came to tell us."

"Maybe we should go inside," Simms said.

"Yes," Loretta said.

"No, damn it! Spit it out, Arnold," Moreno said.

"Congress wants to terminate, that is, put an end to federal recognition of many reservations and distribute the tribal lands, in fee, to individual tribal members. In exchange, Congress promises to improve the roads, water systems, sanitation facilities and vocational schools, and bring in electricity before the termination would become effective."

"What does 'in fee' mean?" said Moreno.

"It means we'd have to buy the land and pay the taxes on it, provided we could find the money to do either of those things," Loretta said. "It also means it's just another big land grab by white men."

"That come from the grapevine also?" Simms asked.

"No, I've been reading up ever since I heard something about this. Not all of us stand around drinking beer all day."

"Aw, come on, Loretta, that's no—"

"Go ahead, Arnold," Loretta said. "Don't mind him."

Simms took a deep breath, and said, "Well, the thing is, each tribe is being encouraged to vote for termination."

"I'm sure they are," Moreno said. "But my guess is that if the tribes don't vote in favor of this wonderful plan from the politicians in Congress, the reservations will be terminated anyway."

"Is that you or the beer talking?" Simms said

"Having Loretta put me down is one thing, Arnold. You try it and I'll make you sorry you ever opened your mouth. Besides, I know what I'm talking about."

"Then I think you should give this one a chance."

"Why? I mean you know as well as I do, Arnold, that Congress never ratified all those treaties from the mid-eighteen hundreds. And what was that, only eight and a half million acres that should have gone to California Indians up and down the state." He tapped Simms on the chest. "How do we know all this new legislation and all these new promises connected with termination won't get 'lost' again?"

"Times have changed, Randolph."

"Maybe for some people, Arnold. But nothing ever changes in the way white men treat the Indian. All I can do is hope that some day one of my sons or one of their sons will find a way to get back some of what we've lost since the white man came to steal the land of The People."

* * *

Randolph Moreno stumbled through the front door of his house, staggered across the room, and half-fell into one of the wooden chairs at the table. He slammed a fist down so hard the dishes rattled and one fork fell onto the floor.

"Randolph!" Loretta Moreno spun away from the smoking wood stove. "I told you I would not have you coming into this house drunk one more time. Now get out of here before I take the broom handle to you."

"Wesley Warner's dead!"

"What do you mean Wesley's dead? He was all right at the council meeting last night."

"Sheriff shot him not more than an hour ago."

"Oh, no," Loretta said, wiping her hands on her apron. "What happened? What god-awful thing were the two of you up to his time?"

"I wasn't with him. Maybe if I had been he wouldn't be dead."

Loretta walked over and sat down at the table across from her husband. "Poor Marrielle and all those children of theirs. What are they going to do?"

Moreno banged his fist on the table again. "Starve, woman! Just like all the rest of us. Sit here and starve while we wait *another two years or four years or whatever for the government to keep its promises."*

Loretta reached across and put her hand on Moreno's wrist. "What happened? Was Wesley acting up some how?"

"He was digging a well, tired of waiting for the water we were promised so we could grow vegetables and take them to town on the road that has never been built. That's all he was doing, Loretta – digging a damn well."

"That doesn't make sense. What business was it of the sheriff's?"

"Down to the store, they say the sheriff went out to Wesley's and told him to stop diggin'. Said it wasn't his land no more." He pressed the heels of both hands against his forehead.

"That's Temkut land! Always has been!"

Moreno removed his hands from in front of his face, looked across at his wife. "Not since the goddam Termination. Remember? All the tribal trust land was divided up among the members."

"Of course I remember; it was less than two years ago."

"Right. The BIA gave us the land, said it was now ours. All we had to do was pay the taxes on it, like the white people do." He took in a deep breath. "Well, Wesley didn't have the money to pay his property taxes. So when the sheriff told him the land had been sold at a tax auction yesterday, Wesley took off after him with a shovel; hit him once in the shoulder before the sheriff drew his gun and shot Wesley in the face."

"No, no, no!" Loretta stood, twisted the apron in her hands over and over until it tore and pulled loose from her body. "Oh, my God! What are we going to do, Randolph?"

Moreno walked around the table, held her in his arms, and whispered, "That's not all of the story, Loretta."

Her body went rigid. "What else? Tell me!"

He squeezed her to him. It took a long moment before he could speak, then, "The tax man sold our land, too"

Loretta Moreno wrenched herself loose and began beating her husband on the chest with her fists. She hammered at him until she fell to the floor exhausted.

CHAPTER 32

The Porsche was purring along at close to 90 when a green dot flashed on the dashboard telling me I had a phone call.

"Rolfe here," I said with a nod of appreciation to the unknown genius who made it possible for me to talk on my cell phone without taking my hands off the steering wheel. But I still wondered where the hell they got the name Bluetooth.

"Toby, Greer. I need to see you. As soon as possible."

"Gosh, didn't know you were still that hot for my bod."

"Don't be crude. This has to do with your Indian friend, Hayes Moreno. Where are you?"

"As coincidence would have it, I'm not too far from the casino. In fact, I just saw the lights of the Putah Creek sign up ahead."

"Good! When you get here come straight up to my office, okay?"

"Yes, ma'am."

"Stop that!"

"Not even a hint about what you're pulling me into?"

"Just get here. And please don't get distracted by anything you see on the main floor."

"What's down there that you think might distract me?"

The connection clicked off, telling me I wasn't getting an answer, at least not right now. A quarter-mile later I turned into the driveway leading up to the casino's parking structure. Once again I found a hidey-hole parking space and backed in. Why change a good habit?

As I walked to the elevator, I saw a familiar red Miata that was also poised in a ready-to-get-out-of-here-fast stance. I gave Greer a call to let her know I was in the garage, and when the elevator door slid open, there stood my good friend Terence Wadkins. He was so busy counting a fistful of $100 bills that he didn't bother to look to see who was blocking his way out of the elevator.

"Either get in or let me out," he said, still concentrating on the cash.

I didn't move. Something told me Greer's urgent call might well have something to do with Wadkins, too. He shifted to one side to avoid me, I shifted with him. We did this dance twice before he finally glanced up.

"What the fuck?" He quit trying to count his winnings and stuffed the bills into a side pocket of his houndstooth sport coat.

"It's nice to see you, too," I said.

"Let me off the damn elevator, Rolfe."

"No, don't think so." I put a hand on his chest and pushed him up against the back wall of the elevator car. Not too hard, but not in a friendly manner, either.

"This isn't funny, Rolfe."

"Who's laughing?"

He started to step around me one more time, but the door slid closed and there we were, alone together at last.

"It's a short ride down," I said.

"I hope you're having a good time." He turned his head away and feigned interest in a garish framed promo for one of the casino's upscale dining rooms. None of the food in the pictures looked real.

He stayed that way until we stopped at the casino level. When the doors slid open, a pair of the casino's matched security people were standing there, flanking the exit as I stepped out.

"Ms. Raebeck asked us to take you up to her office," said the one on my right.

"How nice." I had to assume they were wearing the right color blazers for the day. I pointed a thumb back at Wadkins, who looked like he was ready to bolt and run, given the slightest opportunity. "What about him?"

"She wants to see Mr. Wadkins also."

"What the hell?" Wadkins blurted.

"Come along nicely, Terence," I said. "It may be a very nice party."

One of the security guys nodded me toward Greer's private elevator, then sort of herded Wadkins along behind me. When we reached the mezzanine level, Greer was standing just outside her brass-studded, burgundy-leather office door, fist on hip, a grim look on her face.

"That one stays out here for now," she said, pointing to Wadkins. "And make sure he doesn't wander off."

Greer tilted her head toward the interior of her office, indicating she wanted me to go in first. One step through the doorway and I saw Hayes. I stopped short and she bumped into me.

"Oops," I said. "Didn't know you'd caged the wild thing."

Hayes gave me an I'm-as-surprised-as-you-are-look from his chair next to Greer's glass and chrome desk.

"Mr. Moreno agreed to stay and wait for you," she said, "after I found him stalking Wadkins downstairs."

Hayes shook his head. "No, I never told you I was looking for Wadkins. I said I was looking for one of my Temkut brothers. Besides, you told those guys outside to beat on me if I tried to leave before you got back. There was no agreement involved."

Greer walked past me and sat down behind the desk. She pointed to a chair opposite Hayes. "I need to know what's going on, or not going on, between the two of you," she said.

"You and me, both," I said. "Originally, my good friend there asked me to come over from Nevada to help him solve a casino problem. I get here and find out his tribe isn't even close to getting its casino up and running. Instead, I find myself in the midst of two murders, which is way beyond my comfort zone. Further, I've been accosted by the law and other people, and put in a boat to drown, all of which causes deep-seated resentments. To make matters worse, I can't be sure who, if anyone, is telling me the truth, which just plain pisses me off."

I looked at Greer and added, "And that last part includes you, Ms. Raebeck."

"I don't recall lying to you," she said.

"Let's just call it sins of omission, which also applies to Hayes, there."

"Okay," she said, "we can discuss that later. But first, I want to know, Mr. Moreno, what you were really doing in the casino downstairs. I want the truth, and all of it, not some half-assed story you think will get you off the hook for the time being."

"I was following Wadkins," Hayes said.

"Isn't that what I just said a moment ago?"

"Yeah, but you were just guessing."

Greer gave him one of those don't-push-me-too-far looks.

"Okay, so here's the deal," Hayes said. "I know there's some kind of hinky deal going on where Wadkins is supposed to be working for both you and Lurton-Bales." He paused, waited for a reaction, got none. "Anyway, it's a situation I find ludicrous because I don't think he has enough sense to be left out alone at night."

Another wait, but still no reaction from Greer.

"Regardless, I've been trying to find out which of his purported employers sent him out to clobber me at the Pomo House and make off with some research material."

"What?" I roared. "You told everyone the police chief attacked you. Now you say it was Wadkins?"

Hayes looked off into a far corner of the ceiling, then looked back, first at Greer, then at me. "We have a thing, Chief Chubb and me."

"That doesn't exactly explain your lie," Greer said. "Or why you think I might have put Wadkins up to attacking you."

He shrugged. "Suppose not." He gave each of us another look, sort of testing to see if we were going to push the issue. I knew that if Greer wasn't going to, I sure as hell was.

"So what'd you do, follow Wadkins here, hoping to get back your who's-connected-to-whom schematic?"

"It seemed a good idea at the time. Only now I'm being held prisoner in here and he's probably taken off for parts unknown."

"You're not a prisoner, Mr. Moreno," Greer said. "And my security people are keeping Terence Wadkins company right outside my office." She pointed at the door.

Hayes started to jump up, saw the pistol Greer was now holding, and slumped back down in his chair.

"Not a prisoner, huh?" he growled.

"A detained guest, then," she said. "Wouldn't you say that's an appropriate description, Toby?"

"I'm just listening," I said. "The two of you are very entertaining. Besides, you're the one with gun." I assumed it was the same pistol she'd had at the hunting lodge.

"If Wadkins is still here, is she out there, too?" Hayes asked.

"She, who?" Greer and I said in unison.

"The woman he was talking to at the twenty-one table where he was playing."

"Do you know who it was?" I asked.

"I'm not certain, but I got the impression it was Annalee Mackey," Hayes said. "All I know is that I saw this woman come into the casino, go straight to the high-stakes twenty-one table where Wadkins was sitting, lean over his shoulder, and start talking to him. He'd had eyes only for his cards up to that moment, then he stopped playing. I couldn't see her face. I was about to catch a good glimpse of her just as your security goons hustled me away. Next thing, I'm being pushed into the elevator for a trip here."

Greer used a rigid forefinger to stab at a couple of buttons on her desk; a huge flat screen monitor lit up behind her. She swiveled around in her high-back chair and looked up, as did Hayes and I. White-on-black CGI numerals showed the current time in the lower right hand corner.

"Is that the table?" she said without turning around.

"Yup!" Hayes grunted. "Wadkins was hovering at the middle slot."

"And she's not there now, I suppose," I said.

"Damn! They really trained you good over there at the Nevada Gaming Commission," Hayes said.

"Seems to me a *Las Vegas Sun*-trained journalist like you should have picked up on who Wadkins was making contact with long before this," I snapped back.

"Now, now, boys, I really don't give a good damn whose is bigger," Greer said. "Let's just get Wadkins in here and find out what he has to say about all this."

She picked up a small mobile phone and gave the order. The door to her office opened almost immediately and Wadkins was shuffled into the room by one of the security guys, a big, splayed hand in the middle of the Wadkins back.

"Put him in a chair in front of my desk,' Greer said. The guard pulled another chair from the corner of the room and roughly seated Wadkins about halfway between Hayes and me.

Greer manipulated the console of buttons on her desk and swung around once more to look at the flat screen monitor. There was the same 21 table, only the time was about one-half hour earlier and there was Wadkins, deep in conversation with a female standing next to him.

"Who's that?" Greer demanded.

Hayes and I said, "Wadkins."

Wadkins said, "Me."

"Geez," Greer blurted. "The fucking Three Stooges!" She sighed. "The woman *with* Wadkins, you dimwits!"

"Dunno!" Wadkins insisted. "She just came up and started gabbin' at me. Really annoying, you know? Damn near lost that bet."

I waited until I could see the face, as did Hayes. When it was clear who she was, Hayes and I looked at one another. I gave him a nod.

"Annalee Mackey, sure as hell," Hayes said.

"Don't know the bitch," Wadkins said and started to get up.

"Sit!" I ordered. "I'm sure Ms. Raebeck's men are still right outside the door." He melted back into his chair.

As we watched, Annalee Mackey and Wadkins continued their conversation for almost two minutes before Wadkins pulled an envelope from and inside jacket pocket and handed it to her. She said something to him that made him flinch, then he scooped up his chips, and left the table. Annalee watched him walk away, then got up and strolled off in a different direction. New players moved in, the game continued.

Greer turned back around to make it three pairs of eyes that were drilling into Wadkins. Waiting. Insisting.

"Wha...?" He looked at each of us in turn.

"Don't go stupid on us, Terence," I said. "You know damn well who that was standing next to you, bending your ear. Have you forgotten so soon that only a few days ago you took me to Annalee's café for a meeting with Crandal?"

"Maybe I did, maybe I didn't. Doesn't mean I know her."

"You've been eating breakfast at the café at least twice a week for the past few months," Hayes said. "And we just watched you hand her an envelope."

"Yeah, yeah! So?"

"So knock off the crap about not knowing Annalee Mackey and tell us why she came here to meet with you tonight," I said.

Wadkins did another survey of the room, crossed his arm on his skinny chest and leaned back in the chair. "No!"

I nodded at Hayes, who was already half out of his chair. We reached Wadkins at the same time.

"I would prefer you not beat the crap out of him in my office," Greer said. She leaned forward and waggled a forefinger at Wadkins. "These boys do not want to play nice with you, Terence, and I can't say that I blame them." She waited a moment but got no reaction. "If they want to drag you out of here, I'm not going to stop them. Do you understand me?"

"You got no right to treat me this way," he said to her. "I work for you."

"No, no, Terrence. You work for Felix Crandal. What you do for me, and the money I allow you to win at the tables, is just a distasteful little arrangement I have with Lurton-Bales to keep them happy until their so-called lobbying work is completed."

"Got that, Terence?" I grabbed his arm and started to lift; Hayes did the same thing on the other side.

"Let go of me!" He did his best to squirm out of our hands but remained in place about six inches above his chair. "If I tell you any more, he'll kill me."

"Who, that slime ball Crandal?" Hayes said. Wadkins nodded and went limp.

"Well, *we* may not kill you, Terence," I said, "but you're going to wish we had."

"Okay, okay. Just let go of me!"

We did and he collapsed inside his clothes. I thought he was going to disappear right before our eyes.

"The envelope I gave Mackey was full of cash," he said. "From Crandal."

"What's he paying *her* for?" Hayes asked.

"How'm I supposed to know?"

"Then guess, Terrence," Greer snapped. "And make it a good guess ... something that has a ring of truth to it."

"Look, all I know is that he was on the phone to Washington, talkin' to someone back at the Lurton-Bales head office, when he gave me the envelope. He said something about being pretty sure this would seal the deal with somethin' called the Coastal Commission." He raised his hands, palms up. "That's it! I swear!"

"And you've taken money to Annalee before? I asked.

"Yeah."

"What about taking anything from her to give to Crandal?"

"Sometimes. But ... but not tonight. Honest."

"You have someplace we can stash this piece of trash for awhile?" I asked Greer.

"Of course." She called in her security guys, gave them short, quiet instructions, and had them take Wadkins away. He seemed almost relieved to get out of the room with his skin intact.

"I also told security to run off copies of Annalee Mackey's photo from the computer files, circulate them, and see if she's still in the casino," she said.

"I doubt it," I said.

"Me, too." She looked over at Hayes. "So tell me, what's going on with the Coastal Commission?"

"I don't have the whole story, but I sure as hell intend to dig our every single detail. That is, if I'm free to go now."

"Go! Go!" she said, flitting fingers of one hand at him. "Just keep me informed. No more of this silent Indian shit."

Hayes started to leave the office, but I stepped in front of him before he could get a hand on the door knob.

"We're leaving together, friend. You still have a lot of explaining to do and I'm not letting you out of my sight until I'm satisfied that I have answers to all my questions."

He gave me a noncommittal, lopsided grin.

"If we don't find Annalee here, do you plan on looking for her back in Appa Bay?" Greer asked.

"You can count on it," I said.

"Keep me informed."

I nodded. "And I do hope you'll do the same for me, Ms. Raebeck."

CHAPTER 33

"I've got Vanessa's Miata," Hayes said when we reached the garage.

"So?" I herded him toward the aisle where the Porsche was parked.

"She's gonna be really pissed when she discovers that her car isn't at The Pomo House."

"You're just going to have to deal with that later because right now, you're traveling with me. No way am I letting you out of my sight tonight, or maybe for the next few days."

"Look, I can explain. I really can."

"Wouldn't that be nice." I picked up the pace so he had to half-jog to keep up with me. He kept trying to say something, but I ignored him until we were tucked into the Porsche and well clear of the casino garage.

"How long you gonna stayed pissed off at me?" he asked when we were on the road and I was settled into a nice comfortable 90 mph.

"Maybe for fuckin' ever. Me *and* Vanessa."

"Where we headed?"

"The Wirok Café. I want to know why Crandal was passing money to Annalee Mackey, if that's what was actually going on."

"Wadkins said it had something to do with the Coastal Commission."

"Yeah, but what? You're the local expert, or so I've been led to believe."

"I've got an idea or two," Hayes said. "But we're getting awfully close to the café's closing time." He tapped the dashboard clock with his forefinger.

"If she's not there, we'll go to her house. I assume you know where that is."

"No problem, man."

"And while we're on our way, you can tell me what you know—or think you know—about Crandal, Annalee, and the Coastal Commission."

"You probably know as much as I do about Crandal and Lurton-Bales, maybe more. As for the Coastal Commission, all I know is that Frank Ross found out that one of the board members is a blood relative of Annalee's … a cousin."

"Which means?"

"It means Annalee has roots in Wirok County that go back a long way."

"Is that supposition, Hayes, or something you know to be fact?"

"Fact, man. That's where I've been most of the time since you got here—digging into old records in the county and state archives. Even had a friend make a search in the Library of Congress."

"And?"

"Well, Anne Lee Mackey is a direct descendant of Guthrie Kendall."

"Kendall? Not a name I've run into since I got here."

"Probably because there aren't any Kendalls around here anymore," Hayes said. "But in the late eighteen-hundreds, Guthrie owned damn near all of what's now Wirok County. Came by most of it by marrying into a wealthy Hispanic family. The records indicate he was also pretty good at being at the right spot at the right time to buy up distressed property at bankruptcies, tax sales, and foreclosures."

"So, then he lost it, sold it off, what? And what does any of this have to do with our Annalee?"

"*El Patron* Kendall had only one son, who later had five daughters. And you know what happens when you start divvying up inheritances."

"The more descendants," I said, "the more ideas about what should be done with the money, or business, or, in this case, the land."

"Exactly! And as far as I've been able to find out, not a single Kendall descendant currently owns so much as an empty lot in these parts."

"Including Annalee?" I said.

"Yep! Including Ms. Anne Lee Mackey, and her spinster second cousin on the Coastal Commission board."

"All very interesting. And while I can appreciate the research you've done, what does any of it have to do with the Temkut casino?"

"That gets a lot more vague ... and complicated at the same time. What I do know for sure is that the Commission wields a lot of power when it comes to coastal property."

"Could they stop you guys from building your casino?"

"Not according to our attorneys; the tribe is a sovereign entity."

"I hear a 'but' in there somewhere."

"Yeah, well, the thing is, back in 1878, Kendall gave the Temkuts a quitclaim deed to forty acres that just happen to be smack-dab in the middle of where we want to build the resort and casino."

"The site with the oceanfront view, right?"

"Of course. Problem is, a railroad came along around 1890 and found, or manufactured, a way to cheat the land away from the Temkuts. Only the rail line never got built, the railroad company eventually went belly up, and for one reason or another, ownership of those forty acres fell into limbo ... until fairly recently."

"I'm guessing about the same time the Temkuts made it known they wanted to get into the gaming business."

"That's pretty much the idea," Hayes said. "I picked up the trail of someone nosing around in the old land records not long after the city council voted to sell the Temkuts the town's surplus acreage. The line of inquiry, according to the folks in the county recorder's office, is that if the railroad obtained the land illegally, then ownership should revert back to Guthrie Kendall, thus on to his heirs and beneficiaries."

"But you said Kendall gave the Temkuts a quitclaim deed to the land. Doesn't that carry some weight?"

"It would, if we could find the original document, or even a copy of it. So far, we've come up empty-handed. There's also the question of whether it was unconstitutional for the Legislature back then to make it illegal for Indians to own land."

I slowed as we hit the outer edge of Appa Bay, where the speed limit signs started showing much, much lower numbers than what I'd been driving.

"Well, I think we need to find out what Ms. Annalee's true interest and involvement is in all of this," I said. "Does she just want to stop your casino from being built, or is she looking to get her hands on forty acres of prime waterfront property, with or without a mule?"

* * *

The Wirok Café was closed when we got there, as Hayes had warned, despite my having kept the speedometer hovering near 100 while we were out on the open road. Hayes guided me to Annalee's house, but that, too, was dark.

"Any suggestions?" I said.

"We could wait until morning; catch her when she opens the café."

"There's been enough waiting, Hayes. We need to get this thing wrapped up so I can get back to Vegas and help people solve problems I actually understand."

"She could be anywhere."

"What's she drive?"

"An older Jaguar sedan, powder blue," he said.

"You're kidding."

"Nope"

"Well; that shouldn't be hard to find, provided she's hanging out around town someplace."

I drove, Hayes gave directions, and we both looked for Annalee's Jag. It took us less than twenty minutes to cover the whole town.

"That's about it," Hayes said when we reached the last building at the south end of town. "I don't know where else to look. Maybe she left Appa Bay."

"Let's take trip out to Crandal's digs," I said. "Maybe she went there."

"I suppose. But she seems to have kept their relationship under wraps, using Wadkins as a go-between."

"Can't hurt to look." I turned around and headed north.

We didn't even make to the next intersection before my mirrors were filled with flashing red and blue lights. "What the hell?" I pulled over to the right and coasted to a stop. Hayes twisted around and tried to see out the back window, although I didn't understand why—we were obviously being stopped by the cops. Since I couldn't come up with a reason for the pull-over, I figured it was just more harassment.

I was already reaching for the car registration when the cruiser sped past us without slowing.

"Follow him!" Hayes said, pointing.

"Why in hell would I want to do that?"

"We ... *I* need to know what's going on."

"What, you want me to help you play reporter?"

"No, no. Just follow him. That was Charlie Longtree driving."

"So?"

"He hates using the light bar ... says it makes him feel like a big show-off."

"But that's what—"

"That's Charlie ... don't try to make sense out of it. If he's using the light bar, something really big has to be coming down. Please, just follow him."

I popped the lever into first and took off ... reluctantly. Again we didn't get very far—Longtree's cruiser was nosed in at Mayor Tobin's hardware store on the opposite side of the street. The driver's door was open and he was crouched down behind it, weapon drawn and aimed at the front door. I slammed on the brakes and came to an abrupt halt about a half-block short of the action.

We saw more flashing lights coming from the north and watched as the Chief's SUV slid to a stop next to the cruiser. Neither Longtree nor Chubb had used a siren.

Chief Chubb jumped out of his vehicle, shotgun in-hand, and also used his door as a shield. He looked over to where we had parked.

"Douse your headlights!" Chubb yelled. "And stay back!"

"What the hell's going on, a robbery?" Hayes yelled back.

"Not sure, but it seems to be a lot more serious than that."

After I turned off the headlights, we both got out of the car and used it as a barrier to watch the action. Inaction, actually.

"Who all's in there?" we heard Chubb shout at Longtree.

"Just Tobin and Herrera, the guy who works for him."

"Lawrence Herrera, the part-time EMT guy?"

"Yup!"

"Who called you?" Chubb yelled.

"Lou. Said he'd found out something he thought we should know about."

"Did he say what?"

"Nope! Started to, then said Tobin was coming. Heard the two of them shoutin', then the line went dead."

"Anything happen since then?"

"Nope!"

"Guess we'd better go in," Chubb said. "Cover me."

I nudged Hayes and said, "Didn't think he had it in him."

"He has his moments."

We saw Chubb jump out from behind the SUV's door, run across the sidewalk, and smash himself up against the store's outer wall. He was about halfway between the front door and a display window. Then we heard a shot. Hayes and I ducked down behind the Porsche.

"Not good," Hayes whispered, rising up just enough to peek over the hood.

I was about to reply when a car came roaring out of the side street next to the hardware store, turned north, and accelerated past the two police vehicles. It was a light blue Jag sedan.

"Someone should go after her," I said.

"Her? Are you sure it's Annalee?"

"Whoever. The Jag should be chased down."

"Looks to me like they got their hands full over there."

"Then *I'm* going." I slid along the side of the car and opened the passenger door. "You coming?"

"Not unless you insist, man. I'd rather stay here and see what happens."

"Okay, but you better not disappear on me again, Moreno."

He nodded and dashed ahead to hide behind a pickup truck parked on our side of the street. I squirmed my way into the Porsche, settled into the driver's seat, and sped away.

After two or three miles, I kept expecting to see the backend of the Jag as I sped around the each bend in the road. But that didn't happen. There were no side roads that led anywhere, but that didn't mean the driver couldn't have turned off into one the residential properties along the way, although I doubted that. I had a strong feeling we were headed toward Crandal's place.

Then I knew I was right as I slid around a curve and entered the quarter-mile or so straight section that went past the Crandal manse. I caught the glow of taillights, then brake lights as a car turned left into a driveway.

By the time I reached the same driveway—Crandal's—the Jag was stopped, its front wheels almost on the first step of the wood steps leading up to house. I pulled in behind the Jag; the still-running car was empty, the driver's door hung open, and the headlight beams splashed all across the double-door entryway, reflecting off the cut-glass panes. One door was ajar.

I heard a shot as I turned off the Jag's ignition. Two of those in less than an hour were way beyond my tolerance level. I'd intended to leave the headlights alone, but sensing I might already be a target, why become a well-illuminated one?

I switched off the Jag's lights, closed the door, and was suddenly engulfed in total darkness. Not even a dim glow coming through in the glass doors.

And no sounds.

I ducked down, circled around the Jag, and rushed up the front steps. Keeping low, I pushed the door farther open and edged into the foyer. I could smell the gunpowder residue from a recently fired gun.

Still no lights; still no sounds.

I straightened a little so I could feel along the wall for a light switch; my fingertips found a panel of three, all in the off position. I decided it didn't really matter which one I hit. So I flipped on all three and dropped flat onto the floor.

It was like a stage setting—Crandal, a bloody bullet hole in the center of his forehead, was sprawled on the floor, his face less than a foot from mine; next to him was a chromed semiautomatic; and beyond that, Crandal's two goons, one on either side of Annalee Mackey, with firm grips on her arms.

"That son-of-a-bitch was going to cheat me out of everything," she screamed at me.

CHAPTER 34

"We had nothin' to do with any of this," one of the bodyguards said. "This one come chargin' in here shouting and swearing and demanding to see Crandal." He shoved Annalee out toward me, but didn't let go of her.

"I can believe that."

"When he came out of his office over there," the guy said, pointing to a room off the foyer, "she whipped out that little chrome thirty-two laying there on the floor and plugged him in the forehead. Bam!"

Annalee struggled to pull her arms loose. It wasn't going to happen.

"Best thing would be to call the sheriff," I said.

"Don't think so," the other guy said and pointed a Glock at me.

"Enough with the guns." The muzzle dipped a little but didn't go away. "Look, if we leave Crandal where he is, don't touch Mackey's gun, and you both tell the same story, there shouldn't be any problem with the sheriff. Okay?"

They looked at each other, whispered something behind Annalee's back, and then the one with the Glock said, "Okay, but what do we do with the broad?"

"Take her back into the living room, stash her on the couch, and keep an eye on her."

While they took care of our prisoner, I called the sheriff.

Through it all, Annalee didn't say a word.

* * *

Just before the deputies and coroner had finished up with Annalee, the late Felix Crandal, and the crime scene, Hayes showed up with Vanessa.

"Caught the report on my scanner," Hayes said, looking around the huge living room and out the wall of tinted glass where the moon was reflecting off the Pacific Ocean. "Nice digs," he said.

"I'd give you a guided tour, but…"

"What happened?" Vanessa asked. "Why'd Annalee shoot Crandal?"

"She said he was trying 'cheat her out of everything,' and then that was that," I said. "She wouldn't say another word, although I tried to get her to talk about it. My assumption is that Crandal had led her to believe he could get the land back for her, the land Guthrie Kendall ceded to the Temkuts."

"Why would Crandal get involved in something like that? He was being paid to help clear the way so the Rancheria could get its casino up running."

"There seems to be one helluva lot more to Crandal than is immediately apparent," I said. "But before we try to figure out all of that, what the hell happened at Tobin's store?"

"Lou Galindo said he was doing an inventory of the guns and ammo in the store when he came across an extra rifle in the rack where they keep all the new guns," Hayes said. "It was a used Remington two-twenty-three."

"Isn't that the kind of gun they claim killed Nolan and Petrucci?" I said.

"Right on," Hayes said. "So Lou went looking for Joey to tell him what he'd found. Joey went ballistic. Told Lou he should mind his own fucking business. Lou said he wasn't going to get involved in some murder cover-up. When he pulled out his cell to call the police, Joey started chasing him through the store."

"And the gunshot we heard when we were parked outside?" I said.

"Yeah, well, seems that when Joey couldn't catch Lou, he pulled a pistol out of his desk drawer and took a shot."

"Was Lou hit?"

"Shot didn't even come close. Guess the Mayor's better with a rifle than he is with a pistol."

"I'm glad Lou didn't get hurt," Vanessa said. "And I'm really surprised that it was Joey Tobin who shot Benny and Grady. But now maybe it's all over … there's been too much acrimony around here over the casino. And the killings are so ghastly, totally beyond comprehension."

"Hah!" Hayes barked. "This thing with Joey and the councilmen had absolutely nothing to do with the casino."

"What?" I said. "There must be a tie-in someplace."

"Only in the sense that it's a small town and almost everyone is involved in or knows about everything that happens," Hayes said. "Thing is, when the Chief and Charlie Longtree rushed into the store, Joey was sitting in a corner, crying. Told them Grady and Benny had no business dating Annalee when they knew he was sweet on her."

"Shit!" I said. "Another good reason why I stay away from murder cases."

"I think I'd like to tag along with the deputies when they take Annalee over to San Tomas to the jail," Hayes said. "Mind giving Vanessa a ride back to Appa Bay?"

"No problem." I looked over at Vanessa.

"Works for me," she said. "Although I would like to stop and talk to Chief Chubb about Joey before going back to The Pomo House."

"Wouldn't mind hearing what the Chief has to say about that myself. I'd also like to try and find out for sure what Annalee meant about Crandal cheating her."

* * *

"Well, Rolfe, you don't need to worry anymore about who clobbered you and set you adrift down there by the old fishing dock," Chief Chubb said.

"You're saying it was the mayor, Joey Tobin?"

"That's what Joey told us. Seems he got worried about you snooping around. Wanted to scare you off."

"And he admitted to killing Grady and Benny?" Vanessa said.

"Yeah, the poor bastard." Chubb said. "Told him up front he should get a lawyer, but he shook it off. Said he shot them and there was no sense trying to deny it."

"Guess I'm lucky he didn't shoot me, too," I said.

"I asked him about that. Said it was just Petrucci and Nolan that he was pissed at. Wasn't really interested in bumping off anyone else. Claims he'd like to apologize to you, Rolfe, if he gets the chance."

"Think I'll pass on having any heart-to-heart chats with Mayor Joey Tobin, if you don't mind."

"That's so sad," Vanessa said. "I didn't know Annalee was dating any of them."

"Apparently she didn't know about it, either," Chubb said. "They'd all been courting her, so to speak, but according to Tobin, no one had actually gone out with her. Weird! And as you say, Ms. Jimenez, very sad."

* * *

"I suppose you'll be heading home to Las Vegas tomorrow," Vanessa said when we got back to The Pomo House.

"Like the friendly stranger says, 'looks like my work's done here, ma'am.'"

"Any chance you might stick around a day or so? Seems to me you didn't get a chance to do much sightseeing while you were here."

"If I remember correctly, you tried touting me into doing some of that the day after I checked in. Are you offering up your services as a guide?"

"Of course."

"Let me think on that while I check up on what's happening back home. I haven't looked at my email for quite a spell, and there are a couple of messages on my cell that are overdue for a respoonse."

Vanessa rubbed the palms of her hands up and down her denim-covered thighs, cocked her head to one side, and studied me for a moment. "You're not just gently putting me off, are you?"

"Not my style," I said.

"Didn't think so." She started to turn away, then added, "Hungry?"

"Oh, yes!"

"Me, too. Let me see what I can rustle up in the way of food while you tend to business."

She took off for the kitchen and I took off for my room. I fired up the laptop and, as always, emptied the spam folder without even looking at the contents, then scanned my in-box for anything that was urgent, or looked important. There were two messages from Mike Rollins at the Nevada Gaming Control Board. Both said, "Call me … any hour!"

That certainly seemed urgent. When I picked up my cell, I saw there were four missed calls, all from Rollins. I started composing a mental letter of complaint about how my phone wasn't giving me a ring tone, then I saw I'd somehow put the damn thing on *airplane mode.*

"Sorry for the hour," I said when Rollins picked up the phone. "Rolfe here."

"Yeah, yeah! I know who it is … your number's staring me in the face."

"So what's so urgent? I haven't been into my computer for a while, and the sound got turned off on my cell."

"Ah, the always-on-top-of-everything private investigator."

"Let's skip my shortcomings and get to why you've been leaving messages all over the place for me."

"Felix Crandal and Lurton-Bales have been indicted in Washington for all kinds of bad things in connection with their dealings with several Native American tribes, or more appropriately, double-dealing."

"Not much of surprise there," I said. "But it's not going to make much difference in Crandal's case."

"Why?"

"Dead."

I went on to give Rollins a summary of the Temkut situation in Appa Bay.

"And you're telling me you got involved in a deadly love triangle?"

"Quadrangle, actually."

"Whatever." He laughed. "Anyway, the main information I have for you may be too late, or possible even irrelevant. But I thought you should know that Crandal was promising both the

Temkuts and another tribe exclusive gaming rights for the same general geographic area."

"And collecting fees from both?"

"In the multimillions."

"I just told someone my work here was done, but maybe I can offer some help in finding a way to get some of the money back."

"Good luck, old scout."

There was a knock on my door.

"We'll talk later,' I told Rollins. "And thanks."

When I opened the door, Vanessa was standing there, a smile on her face and an arm held out for me to take. "Supper's ready," she said.

Once we'd sat down to eat her "thrown together" meal of salmon fillets on ciabatta rolls, a side of asparagus spears splashed with a paprika-spiced dressing, and a cold bottle of pinot grigio, I told her about my talk with Mike Rollins.

"Those bastards!" She slammed a fist down on the table, making all the dishes do a little dance. "Does Hayes or Frank Ross know anything about this?"

"Probably not. I'll tell them tomorrow."

"All that money thrown away."

"Maybe not. I'll also call Greer Raebeck in the morning. Since Twin Arrows Investments provided the start-up money, I'm sure they're not about to see their investment go down the tube. Good chance they can help the Rancheria get some or all of the money back that they gave Lurton-Bales.

"I hope so," Vanessa said. "This is going to be such a disappointment for the Temkuts."

We finished eating the meal, washed the dishes, and spent the rest of the night in Vanessa's room. It was a delightful way to end up a very hectic day.

* * *

"We'll get the Temkuts' money back … one way or the other," Greer said the next morning. "Tell them they can count it."

"I had a feeling that would be the case, although I didn't want to make any promises I couldn't keep."

"Want to help?"

"Ah, no, don't think so. Right now, my schedule calls for a little sightseeing."

There was a long pause, long enough for me to think we might have been disconnected. Cell phones can be that way sometimes. "Would I be correct," she finally said, "to assume that you're not going sight-seeing all alone, Mr. Rolfe?"

"Redwood forests can be quite dangerous, I've been told."

"Uh-huh! Only I don't think you're the one who is going to be in danger." There was another long beat. "One last chance to join me in sticking it to the bad guys."

"Always an attractive proposition, but not this time, Greer."

"Well, enjoy the redwoods … and other things."

* * *

"Bastard!" Frank Ross said.

"Been hearing that a lot lately." We were standing on the sidewalk outside Temkut Treasures, waiting for Hayes.

"And Ms. Raebeck thinks she can recoup the money we paid Crandal?"

"So she says." We both watched as Hayes' Explorer pulled up and parked in front of the store.

"What's the latest from the Police Beat?" I said as Hayes stepped up to join us.

"Both Joey and Annalee are locked up in the county jail, awaiting arraignment. And do you know what that dimwit Tobin asked? Wanted to know if they could have adjoining cells. Damn!"

Ross and I laughed.

"Well, Frank," Hayes said, "it's time for us to get back to work on making the Temkut Rancheria Casino and Resort a reality."

"I'll call the council together," Ross said. He started to turn away, stopped, and held out his hand to me. "Thank you, Mr. Rolfe. Your presence has been greatly appreciated. And don't worry about Hayes … the tribe will cover what he agreed to pay you."

I shook his hand but before I could say anything, he'd opened the door and disappeared into his store.

"You told him how much I charge?" I said.

"Nope."

"But he seems to know."

"Yep."

"How?"

"It's an Indian thing."

CHAPTER 35

Northern California — 20??

"It is time for you to become headman of the Temkuts," Frank Ross said, easing into the wicker rocker next to the front door of Temkut Treasures. Slowly, painfully, he raised one foot, then the other onto a matching wicker stool.

Hayes Moreno scowled, shook his head, and sat down on the slatted wood bench on the other side of the store entrance. *"Did you die and forget to tell me?"*

"Is that all they taught you at college, Moreno, to be flippant, disrespectful?"

Moreno crossed his legs at the ankles, looked up and down the street before replying. *"Frank, there's no one in this world that I respect more than you. I think you know that."*

"Then please try to pay attention to what I'm telling you."

Moreno nodded for Ross to continue.

"The problem I face is that I have no son take over as headman."

"Nor a daughter."

"Even if I did, I do not think the Temkuts are quite ready for a woman to lead them even though other tribes are doing that." He started to say something else, clamped his mouth shut and glared at Moreno for a long moment. *"The point is, I have no blood relative to succeed me.*

"Not my fault."

"Hayes, this is serious."

"It doesn't get serious until you're dead."

"Soon!"

"Tradition says the headman continues to be headman until he dies."

"Tradition is good ... unless it's bad. There are many traditions we no longer observe, and the next-in-line thing hasn't always been the best way to run a nation, Indian or otherwise. Any student of history will tell you that, Hayes."

"Then take it to the tribe, let The People decide who should be the next headman."

"Yes, but they will look to me for guidance."

"You have a lot of good men to choose from, Frank ... Charlie Longtree, Lawrence Herrera, Lou Galindo, and—"

"You!"

"No!" Moreno straightened on the bench and leaned toward Ross. "Frank, I don't see me as headman of the Temkuts. Not now, not ever!"

Ross dropped his feet from the wicker stool and leaned forward also. Only a couple of feet of space separated their noses.

"Then why did you come back to us from Las Vegas? Tell me that!"

"I told you why. Several times. I'd been watching how other tribes across the country were doing good things for their people by getting into the casino business. I wanted to help the Temkuts get a piece of the action before it was too late."

"And if I remember correctly, you didn't hesitate one second when you were asked to become vice chairman. In fact, I think you pushed to get the job." Ross lowered his chin and looked at Moreno over the top of his half-frames with questioning eyes.

"That was different," Moreno said. "I needed some authority, a little clout to get done what needed to be done. That was then, this is now. Being chairman would ... would—"

"— cramp your style?"

"Yeah, something like that."

Ross pulled back, sighed, and looked up and down the main street as Moreno had done earlier. "Things are already starting to change," he said. "We fought ... won... put the wheels in motion ... and now nothing's going to be the same." He raised one hand and pointed south.

Moreno nodded, matched Ross's sigh, and looked at what Ross was calling to his attention —a large truck-mounted crane was maneuvering a McDonald's "Golden Arches" sign into place where the Wirok Café formerly stood. Before turning back *to Ross, his gaze shifted to the new Appa Bay Ace Hardware banner that had been put up a week or so earlier to cover the previous* Tobin General Store.

"You planning on going back to Vegas after the casino opens next week?" Ross asked.

"Thought about it." Moreno ran his fingers through the long black hair he'd started wearing loose. "Just not sure. Would like to see everything up and running, see if the public is going to make the resort one of those 'vacation destinations,' as the travel magazines call them."

"The main thing is that we won the war."

"Naw! We only won a skirmish, Frank. I don't think the war will ever be over."

"Tell you this," Ross said, the vaguest hint of a smile showing at the corners of his mouth. "You stick around here much longer, and keep talking like that, you're going to be the tribe's chairman ... like it or not."

"You're a very devious Indian, Frank Ross. I can see why the roundeyes thought they needed to get rid of us."

* * *

Hayes Moreno pulled the San Francisco Chronicle *from the delivery tube at the end of the driveway. As he started back toward the Pomo House, he flipped the paper open to the front page.*

New legal attack
On Indian casinos

WASHINGTON — A lawsuit filed in Federal Court This week seeks to set aside virtually all legislation that has allowed the establishment of Indian casino operations throughout the U.S.

"What the fuck?"
Before he could read more, his cell phone rang.
"What!?"

"Guess I don't need to ask whether or not you've seen the story," Zach Rolfe said.

"If you mean the one about the lawsuit, I'm looking at it right now." He glanced at the headline again and re-read the lead paragraph, half aloud.

"When did this happen?" Hayes asked.

"Sometime late yesterday is my best guess," Rolfe said. "I was up late and didn't see anything on TV before I went to bed."

Hayes continued to read aloud as he walked:

> Attorneys representing the United Coalition of Church Councils (UCCC) claim that federal laws affecting the status of Native Americans, going as far back as 1921, are unconstitutional in that they create "a separate class of privileged residents within the borders of these United States."

He slapped the newspaper against his thigh. "Who in hell are these UCCC people, Zach? And what business is it of theirs?"

"I have no idea, Hayes. Never heard of them before."

"Sounds to me like another group of Pilgrims trying to take our land away from us again."

"As good an explanation as any."

"Any insight as to what motivated this?"

"Nope. And everyone I've talked to here in Nevada this morning is as surprised and confused as you are."

"A fat lot of good that does!"

"Yeah, I know. But listen, if there's anything you think I could do to help, just say so. Okay?"

"Count on it, man!" Hayes inhaled and exhaled sharply. "This is a fucking disaster, Zach! I need to get on it ... like yesterday, if not sooner."

"I'll call back if I hear of anything more."

"Thanks."

Moreno jammed the cell into his pocket, stuffed the Chronicle *under his arm, and hurried on up to the back door of the B&B. When he stomped into the kitchen, Vanessa was seated in front of the highchair, feeding their year-old son.*

"What's got you all fired up?" she said. *"You act like someone's chasing you."*

"Look at this!" He tossed the newspaper down on the counter next to her. *"Did you see anything about this on the Internet this morning?"*

"Haven't been online ... been too busy with the baby." She read the headline and first part of the article half-aloud, then looked up at her husband. *"Are these people serious, or just looking for headlines before the next elections?"*

"Wish I knew," Hayes said. *"I know what I think, but I need you to read it all to me before I get so angry I can't see straight."*

Vanessa stuck a spoonful of cereal into the baby's mouth and began to read, stopping ever so often to keep cereal and applesauce flowing toward a happy and eager open mouth.

"It says here that you spoke to the reporter," she said. *"You never said anything about it to me."*

"Didn't think it was all that important ... didn't think the gal who called was serious. I mean, I thought she was doing one of those speculative, 'what-if' kinds of stories. I was hoping that what I told her would discourage her. I even told her that."

"Obviously, she wasn't discouraged."

"Worse, now *I find out it was about a real suit. Shit!"*

Vanessa gave him an exasperated look and continued to read. He leaned over her shoulder to scan the page with her.

"At least she got in the part about how closing the casinos would result in The People losing jobs, homes, schools, and businesses," Hayes said.

"And the loss of tax revenues to the states that have Indian gaming." Vanessa pointed to one of the paragraphs. *She wiped the baby's mouth and continued to read. "Oh, I like what you said here."*

"'More ominous, though, is an underlying motive that supports my long-held belief that the onerous racist and anti-Native American aspects of Manifest Destiny have never died in this country.'"

"Hope that shakes up a few people."

Vanessa stood and took one of her husband's hands in both of hers. "What now, Hayes?"

"This is one of those times when I wish I were back working for the Las Vegas Sun. *"*

"No you don't, Hayes Moreno. You've been busting your butt as chairman these past two years to make the resort and casino a success ... a big success. Do you want all of that to disappear like a smoke signal of defeat? More important, do you want our son to grow up to think his father was a quitter?"

Hayes sighed and pulled Vanessa closer. "No and no! And I definitely don't want him growing up to face the same shit we've been fighting for centuries." He picked up the tiny spoon and gave his son more cereal.

"So you have to fight, Hayes ... you and me ... we *have to fight ...all of The People have to fight."*

"I know."

"And this time it's not just about funds for the Rancheria or jobs for the Temkuts."

"No, it's one helluva lot bigger than that." He looked down again at his son. "Fortunately, we've learned how of fight the white man using the white man's tactics. We're not going to suffer another rout this time."

"Now you're sounding like the man I fell in love with."

Hayes took Vanessa by the shoulders with both hands, pushed his face forward until their noses were touching.

"Remember that sign in Bill Clinton's presidential campaign headquarters years ago?"

"The one that said, 'It's the economy, stupid.'"

"Yeah, that's the one."

"What about it?"

"Well, we need an even bigger sign, one that says, 'It's the land, stupid!'"

He pulled back, looked down, and placed a hand gently on their son's head.

"It's the land ... it's always been about the land!"

The End

ABOUT THE AUTHOR

J. J. Lamb is a former newspaper reporter-photographer, Associated Press staff writer, trade press correspondent, and freelance journalist. His journalism career was interrupted early on by the U.S. Army, which provided him with a *Top Secret* clearance and a locked room with a table, chair, typewriter, and the time to write short stories. He currently divides his time between fiction writing and freelance editing.

The short stories evolved into an original paperback series featuring Las Vegas-based PI Zachariah Tobias Rolfe III. Then came collaboration with wife Bette Golden Lamb to produce four medical thrillers and a suspense-adventure novel. More recent short stories have appeared in such publications as "Over My Dead Body," "New Mystery," and "Kings River Life."

He's also a proud and skilled jack-of-all-trades, typical of a born-and-raised Hoosier.